Praise for Maggie Stiefvater

WINNER
Best Book to Curl Up With
Glamour

"If you are a fan of *Twilight*, then you will love *Shiver*"
Waterstone's Books Quarterly

"A magnificent and haunting love story"
Youngscot.org

"Literary methadone ... all consuming"
Sunday Telegraph

"A haunting, breathtaking and original supernatural
love story"
Lovereading4kids.co.uk

"Full of deliciously illicit, star-crossed love"
Financial Times

"*Shiver* has a sense of unfolding mystery, a genuine
quest and threats from humans and wolves alike"
Observer

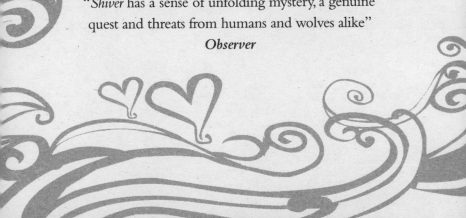

Maggie Stiefvater

The Scorpio Races

■SCHOLASTIC

Scholastic Children's Books
An imprint of Scholastic Ltd
Euston House, 24 Eversholt Street
London, NW1 1DB, UK
Registered office: Westfield Road, Southam, Warwickshire, CV47 0RA
SCHOLASTIC and associated logos are trademarks and/or
registered trademarks of Scholastic Inc.

First published in the US by Scholastic Inc, 2011
This edition published in the UK by Scholastic Ltd, 2011

ISBN 978 1407 12985 3

A CIP catalogue record for this book is available
from the British Library.

Printed and bound by CPI Group (UK) Ltd, Croydon, CR0 4YY
Papers used by Scholastic Children's Books are made from
wood grown in sustainable forests.

1 3 5 7 9 10 8 6 4 2

This is a work of fiction. Names, characters, places, incidents and dialogues are
products of the author's imagination or are used fictitiously. Any resemblance to
actual people, living or dead, events or locales is entirely coincidental.

www.scholastic.co.uk/zone
www.maggiestiefvater.com

To Marian,

who sees horses in her dreams

The Water Horses

capall uisce is pronounced CAPple ISHka

cappaill uisce is pronounced COPple Ooshka

Prologue

Sean

Nine Years Earlier

It is the first day of November and so, today, someone will die.

Even under the brightest sun, the frigid autumn sea is all the colours of the night: dark blue and black and brown. I watch the ever-changing patterns in the sand as it's pummelled by countless hooves.

They run the horses on the beach, a pale road between the black water and the chalk cliffs. It is never *safe*, but it's never so dangerous as today, race day.

This time of year, I live and breathe the beach. My cheeks feel raw with the wind throwing sand against them. My thighs sting from the friction of the saddle. My arms ache from holding up two thousand pounds of horse. I have forgotten what it is like to be warm and what a full night's sleep feels like and what my name sounds like spoken instead of shouted across lengths of sand.

I am so, so alive.

As I head down to the cliffs with my father, one of

the race officials stops me. He says, "Sean Kendrick, you are ten years old. You haven't discovered it yet, but there are more interesting ways to die than on this beach."

My father doubles back and takes the official's upper arm as if the man were a restless horse. They share a brief exchange about age restrictions during the race. My father wins.

"If your son is killed," the official says, "the only fault is yours."

My father doesn't even answer him, just leads his *uisce* stallion away.

On the way down to the water, we're jostled and pushed by men and by horses. I slide beneath one horse as it rears up, its rider jerked at the end of the lead. Unharmed, I find myself facing the sea, surrounded on all sides by the *capaill uisce* – the water horses. They are every colour of the pebbles on the beach: black, red, golden, white, ivory, grey, blue. Men hang the bridles with red tassels and daisies to lessen the danger of the dark November sea, but I wouldn't trust a handful of petals to save my life. Last year a water horse trailing flowers and bells tore a man's arm half from his body.

These are not ordinary horses. Drape them with charms, hide them from the sea, but today, on the beach: do not turn your back.

Some of the horses have lathered. Froth drips down their lips and chests, looking like sea foam, hiding the teeth that will tear into men later.

They are beautiful and deadly, loving us and hating us.

My father sends me off to get his saddlecloth and armband from another set of officials. The colour of the cloth is meant to allow the spectators far up on the cliffs to identify my father, but in his case, they won't need it, not with his stallion's brilliant red coat.

"Ah, Kendrick," the officials say, which is both my father's name and mine. "It'll be a red cloth for him."

As I return to my father, I am hailed by a rider: "Ho, Sean Kendrick." He's diminutive and wiry, his face carved out of rock. "Fine day for it." I am honoured to be greeted like an adult. Like I belong here. We nod to each other before he turns back to his horse to finish saddling up. His small racing saddle is hand-tooled, and as he lifts the flap to give the girth a final tug, I see words burned into the leather: *Our dead drink the sea.*

My heart is jerking in my chest as I hand the cloth to my father. He seems unsettled as well, and I wish I was riding, not him.

Myself I am sure of.

The red *uisce* stallion is restless and snorting, ears pricked, eager. He is very hot today. He will be fast. Fast and difficult to hold.

My father gives me the reins so that he can saddle the water horse with the red cloth. I lick my teeth – they taste like salt – and watch my father tie the matching armband around his upper arm. Every year I have watched him, and every year he has tied it with a steady hand, but not this year. His fingers are clumsy, and I know he is afraid of the red stallion.

I have ridden him, this *capall*. On his back, the wind beating me, the ground jarring me, the sea spraying our legs, we never tire.

I lean close to the stallion's ear and trace a counterclockwise circle above his eye as I whisper into his soft ear.

"Sean!" my father snaps, and the *capall's* head jerks up quickly enough that his skull nearly strikes mine. "What are you doing with your face next to his today? Does he not look hungry to you? Do you think you'd look fine with half a face?"

But I just look at the stallion's square pupil, and he looks back, his head turned slightly away from me. I hope he's remembering what I told him: *Do not eat my father.*

My father makes a noise in his throat and says, "I think you should go up now. Come here and—" He slaps my shoulder before mounting up.

He is small and dark on the back of the red stallion. Already, his hands work ceaselessly on the reins to keep the horse in place. The motion twists the bit in the horse's mouth; I watch his head rocking to and fro. It's not how I would have done it, but I'm not up there.

I want to tell my father to mind how the stallion spooks to the right, how I think he sees better out of his left eye, but instead I say, "See you when it's over." We nod to each other like strangers, the goodbye unpractised and uncomfortable.

I am watching the race from the cliffs when a grey *uisce* horse seizes my father by his arm and then his chest.

For one moment, the waves do not attack the shore and the gulls above us do not flap and the gritty air in my lungs doesn't escape.

Then the grey water horse tears my father from his uneasy place on the back of the red stallion.

The grey cannot keep its ragged grip on my father's chest, and so my father falls to the sand, already ruined before the hooves get to him. He was in second place, so it takes a long minute before the rest of the horses have passed over the top of his body and I can see it again. By then, he is a long, black-and-scarlet smear half-submerged in the frothy tide. The red stallion circles, halfway to a hungry creature of the sea, but he does as I asked: he does not eat the thing that was my father. Instead, the stallion climbs back into the water. Nothing is as red as the sea that day.

I don't think often on my father's body strung out through the reddening surf. Instead, I remember him as he was before the race: afraid.

I won't make the same mistake.

ONE

Puck

People say my brothers would be lost without me, but really, I'd be lost without them.

Usually, if you ask someone on the island where they come from, they say something like *Round about Skarmouth* or *Back side of Thisby, the hard side* or *Stone's throw from Tholla.* But not me. I remember being small, clutching my father's lined hand, and some wind-beaten old farmer who looked like he'd been dug out of the sod asking, "Where you from, girl?" I answered, in a voice too loud for my tiny freckled self, "The Connolly House." He said, "What's that, now?" And I replied back, "Where we Connollys live. Because I'm one." And then — I am still a bit embarrassed about this part of it, as it speaks to a black part of my character — I added, "And you're not."

That's just the way things are. There are the Connollys, and then there's the rest of the world — though the rest of the world, when you live on Thisby, is not very large. Before last fall, it was always this: me, my younger brother, Finn, my older brother, Gabe, and our parents. We were a pretty quiet family altogether. Finn was always putting things together and taking them back apart and saving any spare parts in a box under his bed. Gabe wasn't a huge conversationalist, either. Six years older than me, he saved his energy for growing; he was six feet tall by the age of thirteen. Our dad played the tin whistle, when he was home, and our mother performed the miracle of the loaves and fishes every evening, though I didn't realize what a miracle it was until she wasn't around.

It wasn't that we were unfriendly with the rest of the island. We were just friendlier with ourselves. Being a Connolly came first. That was the only rule. You could hurt all the feelings you liked, so long as you weren't hurting the feelings of a Connolly.

It's midway through October now. Like all autumn days on the island, it begins cold but warms and gains colour as the sun rises. I get a currycomb and a brush and I knock the dust out of Dove's dun hide until my fingers warm up. By the time I saddle her up, she's clean and I'm grubby. She is my mare and my best friend, and I keep waiting for something bad to happen to her, because I love her too much.

As I pull up her girth, Dove pushes her nose into my side, just shy of a nip, and pulls her head back quickly; she loves me, too. I can't ride long; soon I'll have to come back and help Finn make cookies for the local shops. I also paint teapots for the tourists, and since the races are coming up, I have more than enough orders backed up. After the races, there'll be no more visitors from the mainland until spring. The ocean is just too uncertain a thing when it's cold. Gabe will be out all day, working at the Skarmouth Hotel, getting the rooms ready for the race spectators. When you're an orphan on Thisby, it's hard work making ends meet.

I didn't actually realize there wasn't much to the island until a few years ago, when I started reading magazines. It doesn't feel it to me, but Thisby's tiny: four thousand people on a rocky crag jutting from the sea, hours from the mainland. It's all cliffs and horses and sheep and one-track roads winding past treeless fields to Skarmouth, the largest town on the island. The truth is, until you know any different, the island is enough.

Actually, I know different. And it's still enough.

So I am up and riding, my toes cold in my scruffy paddock boots, and Finn is sitting in the Morris in the drive, carefully applying black tape to a rip in the passenger seat. The rip was a gift from Puffin, the barn cat. At least Finn has now learned to never leave the windows rolled down. He's pretending to look annoyed with the repairs, but I can tell that he is actually cheerful to be doing it. It is against Finn's code to reveal too much happiness.

When he sees me riding Dove, Finn gives me a funny look. Once upon a time, before last year, that funny look would've changed into a sly smile and then he would've gunned the engine and we would've raced, me on Dove, him in the car, though he was technically too young to drive. A lot too young. It didn't matter, though. Who was going to stop us? So we would race, me through fields, him on the roads. First to the beach had to make the other's bed for a week.

But we haven't raced for nearly a year. Not since my parents died on the boat.

I turn Dove away, making little circles in the side yard. She's eager and too brisk to concentrate this morning, and I'm too cold to make her soft and round on the bit. She wants to gallop.

I hear the Morris's engine rev. I turn in time to see the car go tearing down the lane, accompanied by a puff of ill-advised exhaust. I hear Finn's whoop a moment later. He pokes his head out of the window, face pale under his dusty hair, smiling a grin that shows every tooth he has.

"Are you waiting for an invitation?" he calls. Then he retreats back into the cab and the engine revs high as he shifts gears.

"Oh, you're on," I tell him, though he is far, far out of earshot. Dove's ears swivel back towards me and then prick towards the road, quivering. It is a wild, cool morning, and she barely needs to be asked. I press my calves into her sides and cluck my tongue.

Dove leaps into action, hooves digging up half-circles of dirt behind her, and we tear after Finn.

Finn's path is no mystery; he has to follow the roads, and there's only the main one, heading into Skarmouth past our house. It's not the straightest way, though. It winds around patchwork fields protected by stone walls and hedges. There's no sense following his serpentine progress, marked by a trail of dust. Instead, Dove and I tear across the fields. Dove is not large – none of the natural island horses are, as the grass isn't great – but she's scopey and brave. So she and I throw ourselves over hedgerows at will, so long as the footing's good.

We shave off the first corner, spooking several sheep. "Sorry," I say to them over my shoulder. The next hedgerow comes up while I'm minding the sheep, and Dove has to twist herself in a hurry to launch herself over. I throw out reins in the world's worst release but at least keep from jerking on her mouth, and she tucks her legs up tight beneath her and saves us both. As she canters away from the hedge, I gather up the reins again and pat her shoulder to show that I noticed her rescuing us, and she tips her ear back to show she appreciates that I cared.

Then it's sailing across a field that used to hold sheep but now holds scrubby heather waiting to be burned off. The Morris is still a little ahead of us, a dark shape in front of a tower of dust. I'm not worried about his lead; to get a car down to the beach, he'll have to either take the road through town, with its sharp right angles and crossing pedestrians, or make a detour around the town, losing several minutes and giving us a good chance to catch up.

I hear the Morris hesitate at the roundabout and then zoom towards town. I can take the road around Skarmouth and avoid any more jumping – or I can skirt through the very edge of the town, popping through a few back gardens and risking being seen by Gabe at the hotel.

I can already imagine being the first to charge on to the beach.

I decide to risk Gabe seeing me. It's been long enough since we did this that the stodgy old ladies can't complain too much about a horse passing through their yards, as long as I don't squash anything useful.

"Come on, Dove," I whisper. She charges across the road and through a break in a hedgerow. Here there are houses looking like they grew out of the rock, and cluttered back gardens full of possessions that have spilled out of the houses, and on the other side of them, a stretch of solid stone that no horse should have to canter on. The only way across is to tear through a half-dozen yards and past the hotel on the other side.

I hope that everyone's busily at work at the piers or in their kitchens. We burst through the gardens, half leaping over wheelbarrows in the first, avoiding a crop of herbs in the second, and getting barked at by an evil terrier in the third. Then, inexplicably, over an old, empty bathtub in the final yard, and we're off down the road to the hotel.

Of course, there is Gabe, and he sees me instantly.

He's sweeping the walk in front of the hotel with a mighty push broom. The hotel is a forbidding, ivy-covered building behind him, the leaves cut in neat squares to let the sun into the windows with their bright blue sills. The height of the hotel blocks the morning light and casts a deeper blue shadow on the stone walk he sweeps. Gabe looks tall and grown-up with his brown jacket stretched across his broad shoulders. His ginger-blond hair creeps down the back of his neck, a little long, but he is still handsome. I feel a sudden surge of fierce pride that he is my brother. He stops what he's doing to lean on the end of the broom and watch me canter by on Dove.

"Don't be mad!" I shout at him.

A smile walks over one side of his face but not the other. It almost looks like he's actually happy, if you've never seen one of his real ones. The sad thing is this – I've become used to this fake one. I've become willing to wait for the real one to reappear, without realizing I should've been working hard to find it again.

I canter on, urging Dove into a gallop once we're off the walk and back on to the grass. Here, the ground is soft and sandy, and begins to slope rapidly, the track becoming narrow between the hills and dunes that lead to the beach. I can't tell if Finn is ahead of me or behind me. I have to draw Dove back down to a trot as the ground grows too steep. Finally, she makes the awkward leap that takes us down to sea level. When we round the final bank, I make a noise of irritation: the Morris is already parked where the grass meets the sand. The scent of exhaust hangs in the air, cupped by the rise of the ground around us.

"You're still a good girl," I whisper to Dove. She is out of breath but she blows out her lips. She considers it a good race.

Finn stands half in and half out of the car, the driver-side door standing open, his feet on the running board. One arm rests on the roof and the other on the upper part of the open door. He is looking out towards the sea, but when Dove blows out her breath through her lips again, he looks back to me, shielding his eyes. I can see that his face is worried, so I nudge Dove next to the car. I let out the reins so that she can graze while we stand there, but she doesn't lower her head. Instead, she, too, turns her gaze towards the ocean, a hundred metres ahead of us.

"What?" I ask. I have a sick feeling in my stomach.

I follow the line of his eyes. I can just see a grey head thrusting its way above the surf, so far away and so close to the colour of the tossed ocean that I can almost believe I'm imagining it. But Finn's eyes wouldn't be so large unless he was certain. Sure enough, the head emerges again, and this time I see dark nostrils blow so wide that I glimpse a tinge of red in them, even from here. Then the rest of the head follows, and the neck, crimped mane pasted to its skin by salt water, and then the powerful shoulders, glistening and damp. The water horse surges from the ocean and gives a mighty leap, as if the final steps over the incoming tide are a huge obstacle to overcome.

Finn flinches as the horse gallops down the beach towards us, and I lay a hand on his elbow, though my own heart is thumping in my ears.

"Don't move," I whisper. "Don't-move-don't-move-don't-move."

I cling to what we've been told over and over – that the water horses love a moving target; they love the chase. I make a list of reasons it won't attack us: we're motionless, we're not near the water, we're next to the Morris and the water horses despise iron.

Sure enough, the water horse gallops past us without pause. I can see Finn swallowing, his Adam's apple bobbing in his skinny neck, and it's so true, it's so hard not to flinch until it's leaped back into the ocean once more.

They're here again.

This is what happens every fall. My parents didn't follow the races, but I know the shape of the story nonetheless. The closer it gets to November, the more horses the sea spits out. Those islanders who mean to race in future Scorpio Races will often go out in great hunting parties to capture the fresh *capaill uisce*, which is always dangerous, since the horses are hungry and still sea-mad. And once the new horses emerge, it's a signal to those who are racing in the current year's races to begin training the horses they caught the years before – horses that have been comparatively docile until the smell of the fall sea begins to call to the magic inside them.

During the month of October, until the first of November, the island becomes a map of safe areas and unsafe areas, because unless you're one of the riders, you don't want to be around when a *capall uisce* goes crazy. Our parents tried hard to shield us from the realities of the *uisce* horses, but it was impossible to avoid it. Friends would miss school because an *uisce* horse had killed their dog overnight. Dad would have to drive around a ruined carcass on the way to Skarmouth, evidence of where a water horse and a land horse had got into a fight. The bells at St Columba's would ring midday for the funeral of a fisherman caught unawares on the shore.

Finn and I don't need to be told how dangerous the horses are. We know. We know it every day.

"Come on," I say to him. Staring out to sea, his thin arms bracing him upright, he looks very young, just then, my little brother, though he's really caught in that strange no-man's-land between child and man. I feel the sudden urge to protect him from the grief that October is going to bring. But it isn't really the grief of this

October I have to worry about; it's that of an October already long gone.

Finn doesn't answer, just ducks back down into the Morris and shuts the door without looking at me. It's already a bad day. And that's before Gabe gets home.

TWO

Sean

Beech Gratton, the butcher's son, has just slaughtered a cow and is draining the blood into a bucket for me when I hear the news. We are standing in the yard behind the butcher's, the sound of our lack of conversation amplified by the echo of our footsteps on the stone around us. The day is beautiful and cool, and I'm restless, shifting from foot to foot. The stones beneath me are uneven, pushed up by roots from trees no longer in evidence, and stained, too, brown and black, in dots and splatters and rivulets.

"Beech, did you hear yet? The horses are out," Thomas Gratton addresses his son, emerging from the open door of his shop. He had started into the courtyard but pauses mid-stride when he sees me. "Sean Kendrick. I didn't realize you were here."

I don't say anything, and Beech grunts, "Came by when he heard I was slaughtering." He gestures to the cow's corpse, which now hangs, decapitated and legless, from a tripod of wood. The ground's awash with blood from where Beech was slow to place the bucket beneath the cow. The cow's head lies off to the edge of the yard, tumbled on to its side. Thomas Gratton's mouth works as if he'd like to say something to Beech about the scene, but he doesn't. Thisby is an island well populated by sons disappointing their fathers.

"Did you hear, then, Kendrick?" Thomas Gratton asks. "Is that why you're here and not on a horse?"

I am here because the new men that Malvern has hired to feed the horses are afraid at best and incompetent at worst, and the hay has been poor and the cuts of meat even worse. There's been no blood to speak of for the *capaill uisce*, as if by treating them as regular horses the grooms hope to make them so. So I am here because I have to do things myself if I want them done properly. But I just say, "I hadn't heard."

Beech slaps the dead cow affably on the neck and tips the bucket this way and that. He doesn't look at his father. "Who did you hear from?"

I don't really care about the answer to his question; it doesn't matter who heard or who saw what, only that the *capaill uisce* are climbing out of the sea. I can feel in my bones that it's true. So this is why I feel restless. This is why Corr paces before his stall door and why I can't sleep.

"The Connolly kids saw one," Thomas Gratton says.

Beech makes a noise and slaps the cow again,

more for emphasis than for any practical purpose. The Connollys' story is one of the more pitiful ones Thisby has on offer: three children of a fisherman, orphaned twice over by the *capaill uisce*. There are plenty of single mothers to be had on the island, their men gone missing in the night, stolen away by either a savage water horse or by the temptation of the mainland. Plenty of single fathers, too, wives snatched from the shore by suddenly present teeth or seized by tourists with large wallets. But to lose both parents in one blow – that's unusual. My story – father cold in the ground, mother lost to the mainland – is common enough to have been forgotten long ago, which is fine by me. There are better things to be known for.

Thomas Gratton watches soundlessly as Beech hands off the bucket to me and begins to indelicately butcher the corpse. It doesn't seem like there should be an artful way to butcher a cow, but there is, and this is not it. For several long moments, I watch Beech carve jagged lines, grunting to himself all the while – I think he may be trying to hum. I am mesmerized by the utter unawareness of the entire process, the childlike pleasure Beech takes in a job ill done. Thomas Gratton and I catch each other's eye.

"He learned his butchering from his mother, not me," Thomas Gratton tells me. I don't quite smile, but he seems gratified by my response anyway.

"If you don't like how I do it," Beech says, not

looking up from his work, "I'd rather be at the pub, and this knife fits in your hand, too."

Thomas Gratton makes a mighty sound that comes from somewhere between his nostrils and the top of his mouth; it is a sound that, to me, effectively proves the etymology of Beech's grunts. He turns away from Beech and looks at the red-tiled roof of one of the buildings flanking the courtyard. "So I expect you'll be riding in the race this year," he says.

Beech doesn't respond, because of course his father is speaking to me. I reply, "I expect so."

Thomas Gratton doesn't answer right away, just continues gazing at the evening sun lighting the roof tiles to brilliant orange-red. Eventually, he says, "Yes, I expect that's what Malvern asks of you, then."

I have worked in the Malvern Yard since I was ten, and some people say that I got the job out of pity, but those people are wrong. The Malverns' livelihood and their name are under the roof of their stable – they export sport horses to the mainland – and they won't have anything compromising that, far less something as humanitarian as pity. I've been with the Malverns long enough to know that the Grattons do not care for them, and I know that Thomas Gratton wants me to say something that will allow him to better despise Benjamin Malvern. So I allow a long pause to diffuse the weight of his question, and then I say, with a rattle of the bucket handle, "If it's all right, I'll settle the account for this later this week."

Thomas Gratton laughs softly. "You are the oldest nineteen I've ever met, Sean Kendrick."

I don't reply, because he is probably right. He tells me to settle the account this Friday as usual, and Beech gives me a parting grunt as I leave the courtyard with the blood.

I need to be thinking about bringing the ponies in from the pasture and adjusting the thoroughbreds' feed and how I will keep my little flat above the stable warm tonight, but I am thinking of the news Thomas Gratton brought. I am here on firm ground, but part of me is already down on the beach, and my own blood is singing *I'm so, so alive.*

THREE

Puck

That night, Gabe breaks the only rule we have.

I am unambitious with dinner, because we don't have anything other than dried beans, and I'm sick of beans. I make an apple cake and feel rather virtuous about it. Finn is annoying me by spending the afternoon in the yard tinkering with an ancient, broken chainsaw that he claims someone gave him but that he probably pulled out of someone's rubbish because it had gears. I'm cross because I'm inside by myself, which makes me feel like I ought to be tidying, and I don't want to tidy. I slam around a lot of drawers and cupboards while sort of messing over the eternally full sink, but Finn doesn't hear me or pretends not to.

Finally, before the sun completely vanishes over the high ground in the west, I throw open the side door and stand there looking at Finn meaningfully, waiting for him to look up and say something to me. He is all buckled over the top of the chainsaw, which lies dismembered in front of him, pieces spread tidily over the packed dirt of the yard. He wears one of Gabe's sweaters that, while several years old, is still too large for him. He has the sleeves doubled back into fat, perfectly even cuffs, and his dark hair is mussed into an oily rooster tail. He looks like an orphan, and that makes me cross, too.

"Are you going to come in and eat the cake while it still remembers being warm?" I sound a little bratty, but I don't care.

Finn says, without looking up, "In a minute." He doesn't mean a minute and I know it.

"I'm going to eat it all myself," I say. He doesn't reply; he's lost in the mystery of the chainsaw. I think, just for that moment, that I hate brothers, because they never realize when something is important to you and they only care about their own things.

I'm about to say something that I might be embarrassed about later when I see Gabe walking his bicycle through the dusk towards us. Neither of us says hi to him as he opens the yard gate, pushes his bicycle through, and closes it again, Finn because he is self-involved, and me because I am annoyed at Finn.

Gabe puts his bicycle away in the little lean-to by the back of the house and then comes to stand behind Finn. Gabe takes off his skullcap and holds it in his armpit, his arms crossed, wordlessly watching what Finn's doing. I'm not sure Gabe can actually tell what it is that Finn has eviscerated in the barely there blue light of evening, but Finn rocks the body of the chainsaw slightly to give Gabe a better view. This apparently tells Gabe everything he needs to know, because as Finn looks up, tilting his chin towards our older brother, Gabe just gives a little nod.

Their unspoken language both entrances and infuriates me. "There's apple cake," I say. "It's still warm."

Gabe removes his skullcap from his armpit and turns to me. "What's dinner?"

"Apple cake," Finn comments from the ground.

"And chainsaw," I reply. "Finn made a lovely chainsaw to go with it."

"Apple cake's fine," Gabe says, but he sounds tired. "Puck, don't leave the door open. It's cold out here." I step back so that he can walk into the house, and as he does, I notice that he stinks of fish. I hate it when the Beringers have him cleaning fish. He makes the whole house smell.

Gabe pauses in the door. I stare at him then, at the way he stands, his hand on the door frame, his face turned towards his hand as if he is studying his fingers or the chipped red paint beneath them. The way his face looks seems far away, like a stranger's, and I suddenly want to hug him like I used to when I was small. "Finn," he says, his voice low, "when you get that together, I need to talk to you and Kate."

Finn looks up, his face startled, but Gabe is already gone, disappeared past me into the room he still shares with Finn despite our parents' room being empty. Either

Gabe's request or his use of my real name has got Finn's attention in a way that my apple cake couldn't, and he begins to assemble the parts rapidly, dumping them into a battered cardboard box.

I feel unsettled while I wait for Gabe to emerge from his room. The kitchen has turned into the small, yellow place that it becomes at night when the darkness outside presses it smaller. I hurriedly wash off three plates that match and cut a fat piece of apple cake for each of us, the biggest one for Gabe. Setting them out on the table, three lonely plates where once there would've been five, depresses me, so I busy myself making some mint tea to go with them. As I arrange and rearrange the teacups by our plates, it occurs to me, too late, that mint tea and apple cake might not go together.

By then Finn has begun the process of washing his hands, which can take centuries. Patiently and silently he lathers his hands with the bar of milk soap, working between each finger and rubbing each line in his palm. He keeps doing it when Gabe emerges in fresh clothing but still smelling of fish.

"This is nice," Gabe tells me as he pulls out his chair, and I'm relieved, because nothing is wrong, everything will be fine. "Mint smells good after today."

I try to think of what Mum or Dad would've said to him then; for some reason, our age difference feels like a massive void just now. "I thought they had you getting the hotel ready today?"

"They were short-handed at the pier," Gabe says. "And Beringer knows I'm quicker than Joseph."

Joseph is Beringer's son, too lazy to be quick at anything. Gabe told me once that we should be grateful for Joseph's inability to think of anything but himself, because it is why Gabe has a job. I'm not grateful at the moment, though, because Gabe smells like fish since Joseph is a feck.

Gabe holds his tea but doesn't drink it. Finn is still washing. I sit down at my place. Gabe waits a few more beats and then says, "Finn, *enough*, OK?"

Finn still takes another minute to rinse, but then he shuts off the tap and comes and sits across from me. "Do we still say grace if it's only apple cake?"

"And a chainsaw," I say.

"God, thank you for this cake and Finn's chainsaw," Gabe says. "Are you happy?"

"God, or me?" I ask.

"God's always happy," Finn says. "You're the one who needs pleasing."

This strikes me as incredibly untrue, but I refuse to rise to the bait. I look at Gabe, who's looking at his plate. I ask him, "So, what?"

Outside, I hear Dove whickering where the pasture meets the yard; she wants her handful of grain. Finn looks at Gabe, who's still looking at his plate, pressing his fingers into the top of the apple cake as if he's checking the texture. I am suddenly aware of how tomorrow, the anniversary of our parents' deaths, has been looming inside me, and how it never occurred to me to think that it might be the same for quiet, solid Gabe.

He doesn't lift his eyes. He simply says, "I'm leaving the island."

Finn keeps his gaze on Gabe. "What?"

I can't speak; it's like he's said it in a different language, and my brain has to translate it before I can understand it.

"I'm leaving the island," Gabe tells us, and this time the statement is firmer, more real, though he still doesn't look at either of us.

Finn manages a whole sentence first. "What will we do with all of our things?"

I add, "What about Dove?"

Gabe says, "*I'm* leaving the island."

Finn looks like Gabe has slapped him. I jut my chin out and try to get Gabe to meet my eyes. "You're going to go without us?" Then, my mind provides an answer, a logical one, one that gives him an excuse, and I give it to him. "So you aren't going long. You're just going for—" I shake my head. I can't think of what he would be going for.

Gabe finally lifts his face. "I'm moving away."

Across from me, Finn is clinging to the edge of the table, his fingertips pressed into the wood so that they're white on the very ends but bright red towards the joints; I don't think he's aware of it.

"When?" I say.

"Two weeks." Puffin is mewling around his feet, rubbing her chin against his leg and chair, but Gabe doesn't look down or acknowledge her. "I promised Beringer I'd stay that long."

"Beringer?" I say. "You promised *Beringer* you'd stay that long? What about *us*? What's going to happen to us?"

He won't look at me. I'm trying to imagine how we can survive with one less earning Connolly and one more empty bed.

"You can't go," I say. "You can't go so soon." My pulse is clubbing inside my chest and I have to press my jaw shut to keep my teeth from chattering.

Gabe's face is utterly unchanged, and I know that I'm going to regret what I say, but it's the only thing I can think of, so I say it.

"I'm riding in the races," I tell him. Just like that.

Now I have both my brothers' full attention, and my cheeks feel like I've been leaning over a hot stove.

"Oh, come on, Kate," Gabe says, but his voice is not as sure as it should be. He half believes me, despite himself. Before I say anything else, I have to think about it and decide if *I* believe me. I think of this morning, my hair tugged in the wind, the feel of Dove stretching out into a gallop. I think of the day after the races, the red-stained sand high up on the beach where the ocean has yet to reach. I think of the last boats leaving for the winter, and Gabe on one of them.

I could do it, if it came to it.

"I am. Didn't you hear in town? The horses are coming out. Training starts tomorrow." I am so, so proud that my words sound firm.

Gabe's mouth works, as if he is saying all sorts of things without parting his lips, and I know that he is going through all the counter-arguments in his head. Part of me wants him to say "you can't" so I can ask "why?" and he would have to realize that he can't answer "because you might leave Finn by himself". And he can't ask "why?" because then he'd have to answer that question as well. I should be feeling very clever and pleased with myself, because it's very hard to render Gabe speechless, but mostly my heart is just going *tip-tip-tip* in my chest, very shallow and fast, and I'm half hoping that he'll say that if I don't ride, he'll stay.

But finally he says, "All right. I'll stay until after the races." He looks cross. "But no longer than that, or the boats will stop running 'til spring. This is a really stupid thing you're doing, Kate."

He's mad at me, but I don't care about that. All I care is that he's staying, for a little while longer.

"Well, sounds like we'll need the money, if I win," I say, trying to sound as adult and blasé as possible, but thinking that maybe if I do win the money, he won't have to leave. And then I get up from the table and put my plate and teacup in the sink, like it was a normal evening. Then I walk into my room, close the door, and put my pillow over my head so no one will hear.

"Selfish bastard," I whisper, the words close under the pillowcase.

Then I burst into tears.

FOUR

Sean

I am dreaming of the sea when they wake me.

Actually, I am dreaming of the night that I caught Corr, but I can hear the sea in my dream. There is an old wives' tale that *capaill uisce* caught at night are faster and stronger, and so it is three in the morning and I am crouching on a boulder at the base of the cliffs, over a hundred metres from the sand beach. Above me, the sea has made an arch in the chalk, the ceiling about thirty metres over my head, and the white walls hug me. It should be dark, hidden from the moon, but the ocean reflects light off the pale rock, and I can see just well enough not to stumble on the coarse, kelp-covered rocks on the floor. The stone beneath my feet has more in common with the seafloor than the shore, and I have to take care not to lose my footing on the slippery surface.

I am listening.

In the dark, in the cold, I am listening for a change in the sound of the ocean. The water is rising, quickly and silently; the tide is coming in, and in an hour, this incomplete cave will be full of seawater higher than my head. I am listening for the sound of a splash, for the rush of a hoof breaking the surface, for any hint that a *capall uisce* is emerging. Because by the time you hear a hoof click on the stones, you are dead.

But there is nothing but the eerie silence of the sea: no seabirds at night, no shouts of boys on the shore, no distant hum of a boat's motor. The wind is ruthless as it finds me in the arch. Unbalanced by its sudden force, I slip and catch my balance again on the wall, my fingers splayed. I hurriedly pull my hand back – the walls of the arch are covered with blood-red jellies that wink and glisten at me by the light of the moon. My father told me they were completely harmless. I don't believe him. Nothing is completely harmless.

Below me, the water creeps between the boulders as the tide comes in. My palm is bleeding.

I hear a sound, like a kitten mewling, or a baby screaming, and I freeze. There are no kittens or babies here on the beach; there is only me and the horses. Brian Carroll has told me that when he is out at sea at night, he can sometimes hear the horses calling to each other under the water, and it sounds like whale song, or a widow wailing, or something chuckling.

I look down to the water in the deepest cleft of the rocks below me; it has risen fast. How long have I been standing here? The boulders in front of me are already nothing but shiny humps of rock barely above the black water. I am empty-handed, but I am also out of time – I need to turn back and pick my way across the seaweed-slimed rocks while I still can.

I look at my hand; a thick trickle of blood has welled in my palm and down between the two bones of my arm. It gathers, swells, drips soundlessly into the water. My palm will hurt later. I look at the water where my blood disappears. I am silent. The cave is silent.

I turn around and there is a horse.

It is close enough to smell the briny odour of it, close enough to feel the warmth off its still-wet skin, close enough to look into its eye and see its dilated square pupil. I smell blood on its breath.

And then they wake me.

It is Brian and Jonathan Carroll, and their faces both spell concern. Brian's face wears the traditional brand: furrowed eyebrows, lips puckered. Jonathan's comes out as an apologetic smile that changes shape every few seconds. Brian is my age and I know him from the piers; we both deal with the water for our living and so we have history together, though we are not friends. Jonathan is his brother, trailing Brian in every way, including brains.

"Kendrick," says Brian. "You up?"

I am now. I lie there in my bunk like I am tied to it and say nothing.

Jonathan adds, "Sorry to wake you, mate."

"You're the man," Brian says. Though I'm feeling no

kinship for him now in the middle of the night, I don't mind Brian. He says what he means. "There's nothing else for it; Mutt's in a world of trouble. He had a mind to wait up for one of the *capaill* to come out of the water and now he's got what he asked for and I don't think he likes it."

"It's going to kill them," Jonathan says. He looks pleased to have been able to state something so obvious before Brian could.

"Them?" I echo. It's cold and I'm wide awake.

"Mutt and a bunch of his mates," Brian says. "They're all in it, and they've got the *capall* sort of caught, but they can't let it go and they can't bring it in."

Now I'm sitting. I don't have any love in the world for Mutt – also known as Matthew Malvern, the bastard son of my boss – or any of the grooms who scurry in submissive friendship behind him, but they can't leave a horse tangled up on the beach in whatever fool trap they've devised.

"You're the one for the horses, Kendrick," Brian says. "I reckon someone's going to get killed unless we fetch you back there."

Back there. Now I understand their expressions; they were part of this and they know that I'll think less of them for it.

I don't say anything else. Just get out of bed, pulling on my old sweater and snatching up my blue-black coat with all my things in its pockets. I jerk my chin towards the door, and they scurry before me like sandpipers, Jonathan wrenching the door open so that Brian can lead the way out of the stable.

Outside, the wind is a live, starving thing. The sky over Skarmouth is a dull brown, lit by the streetlights, but everywhere else is inky. There is a bit of a moon, so it will be brighter by the ocean, but not much. We strike out across the fields, taking the straightest path to the beach. There's nothing out here but rocks and sheep, but it's easy enough to fall over either of them.

"Torch," I say, and Brian flicks on a flashlight and offers it to me. I shake my head. I'll need my hands free. Behind us, Jonathan jogs and trips keeping up with our pace, making a beam of light arc crazily as his flashlight-hand jerks. I'm reminded of my mother pretending to write words on the wall with a flashlight when the storm knocked out our power.

"How far up the beach?" I ask. The tide will be coming in in a few hours, and if they are around the point, a new *capall uisce* will be the least of their problems.

"Not far," pants Brian. He is not unfit, but strenuous activity tends to wind him. If not for their expressions earlier, I would've stopped to let him catch his breath.

I can just see where the hills split and cleft for the path down to the sand — the land is a darker black against the sky — and then I hear a scream. The wind carries it to us, high and thin and ragged, and it is impossible to say whether it is human or animal. The hairs on the back of my neck prickle in a warning I ignore as I break into a run.

Brian does not follow my lead – I don't think he can – and I sense that Jonathan is torn between staying with Brian and accompanying me.

"I need the torch, Jonathan!" I shout back over my shoulder. The wind throws my words behind me and though Jonathan replies, I can't hear him. I pelt out of the dim circle of his flashlight and into the darkness, stumbling and slipping down the steep descent to the beach. For a brief moment I think I can't go forward any more because I cannot see, but then I step a couple of metres on and glimpse a knot of wildly moving flashlights down on the sand. Beyond them, I see the water dimly illuminated by the scant light of the moon.

The wind is sucking the sound away from me, so as I approach the scene, it seems as if the men are voiceless. The struggle is almost artful, until you get up to it. It's four men, and they've snagged a grey water horse around its neck and by the pastern on one of its hind legs, right above the hoof. They tug and they jump back as the horse lunges and retreats, but they are in a bad place and they know it. They have the tiger by its tail and have just realized the tail is long enough for the claws to reach them.

"Kendrick!" shouts someone. I cannot tell who it is. "Where's Brian?"

"Sean Kendrick?" shouts someone else, and this, I know, is Mutt, holding the line that leads to the horse's neck. I can tell by the shape of his silhouette, the broad shoulders and thick neck that is both neck and chin. "Who asked for that bastard to come? Go back to sleep, knacker – I've got this under control!"

He controls the horse like a fishing boat controls the sea. I see now that the other line is held by Padgett, an older man who should know better than to trust Mutt with his life. Next to me, I hear a soft sound in a moment between gusts of wind; I glance over and there is another of Mutt's friends sitting against the rock wall where the cliffs meet the beach. He is curled around his own arms, and one of them he holds gingerly. It looks broken. The sound I heard was his whimper.

"Get out of this, Kendrick!" Mutt calls.

I cross my arms over my chest and wait. The horse has stopped struggling for the moment. Against the light chalk of the cliffs, I can see the trembling dark lines leading to the *capall uisce*. The horse is tiring, but so are the others. Mutt's muscled arms mimic the shaking of the lines. The other men creep around, laying loops of rope on the beach, hoping the horse will step into one. It would be easy, for someone who didn't know the water horses, to think that the *capall uisce*, standing there with its sides heaving, is defeated. But I see its head drawn back, predatory, raptor-like rather than equine, and know that things are about to get ugly.

"Mutt," I say. He doesn't even turn his head, but at least I said it.

The line holding the horse's pastern suddenly stretches taut as the grey *capall* lunges towards Mutt. I am sprayed with sand and small pebbles from its hooves digging into the beach. Shouts punch the air. Padgett reels and tugs on his line, working to off-centre the horse. Mutt is too busy with his own welfare to return the favour. The line around its neck suddenly slack, the horse backs towards Padgett. Its hooves drag circles in the sand. And then the horse is on Padgett, teeth sunk into his shoulder, front legs reared up and embracing him. It seems impossible that Padgett will not fall to the ground under the weight, but the horse's grip on his shoulder holds him upright for a brief moment before it falls to its knees, Padgett tucked beneath its chest.

Now Mutt is hauling the line around the horse's neck, but it is too little, too late, and what is he against one of the *capaill uisce*?

Padgett is beginning to look improbable; something about him is starting to look less like a man and more like meat. I hear, plaintively, from one of the men: "*Kendrick.*" I step forward, and right as I get to the horse, I spit on the fingers of my left hand and grab a handful of its mane at its poll, right behind its ears. Pulling a red ribbon from the pocket of my jacket with my right hand, I press it over the bones of the horse's nose. It jerks, but my hand on its skull and neck is firm.

I whisper in its ear and it staggers back, punching a hoof into Padgett's body as it struggles to find its footing again. Padgett is not my concern. My concern is that I have two thousand pounds of wild animal being held by a string and it has maimed two men already and I need to get it away from the rest of them before I lose my tenuous grip.

"Don't you dare let that horse go," Mutt tells me. "Not after all this. You bring it back to the stable. Don't let this be a waste."

I want to tell him that this is a water horse, not a dog, and that leading it inland, away from the nearly November salt water, is a trick I don't feel like performing at the moment. But I don't want to shout out loud and give the horse any more cause to remember that I am right next to it.

"Do what you need to do, Kendrick!" yells Brian, who has finally made it down.

"Don't you dare let that horse go," Mutt shouts back.

Just to get them all out alive would be a feat. Just to get the horse down to the shore and release it far enough into the ocean that we could get away safe would be impressive. But I can do more than just get them away safe, and they all know it, Mutt Malvern most of all.

But I whisper like the sea in the horse's ear and take a step back from the roving flashlights. One step away from all of them, one step towards the ocean. My sock wicks the tide into my boot. The grey horse is trembling under my hands.

I turn to look at Mutt, and then I let the horse go.

FIVE
Puck

I don't think that I sleep, but I do, because in the morning my eyes are sticky and my blankets look like a mole has tunnelled through them. The sky outside the window is the blue of almost-daylight, and I decide that no matter what time it is, I'm awake. I spend too long standing shivering in my sleeping top – the one with the straps of lace that are just a little itchy, but that I wear anyway because Mum made it – staring at the contents of my dresser, trying to decide what to wear to the beach. I don't know if it will be cold after I've been riding for a while and I don't know if I want to go down there dressed like a girl when Joseph Beringer is probably going to be there looking at me like *hur, hur, hur.*

Mostly I'm trying not to think grandiose things like: *You will remember this day for the rest of your life.*

In the end, I just wear what I always wear – my brown trousers that won't chafe and my chunky dark green sweater that Mum's mother knitted for her. I like to think of Mum wearing it; it gives the sweater history. I look into my spotted mirror and make a fierce face under my freckles, my eyebrows straight across over my blue eyes. I look messy and cross. I pull some of my hair out of my ponytail, across my forehead, trying to look like someone other than the girl I grew up being. Someone people won't laugh at when they see me arrive on the beach. It doesn't work. I have too many freckles. I draw my hair back into the ponytail again.

In the kitchen, Finn is already up, and he is standing at the sink. He is wearing the same sweater as yesterday, and he looks like a man who has shrunk in the night while his clothing pooled around him. Something smells sort of brittle and carbon-like, almost good, like steak or toast, until I realize that it's actually a bad smell, like burned paper and hair.

"Gabe awake?" I ask. I peer uncertainly into the cupboard, to avoid having to look at Finn. I'm not sure I want to talk. Looking in the cupboard, I'm not sure I want to eat, either.

"He's already gone to the hotel," Finn says. "I . . . here." And with this, he sets a mug with a spoon standing in it down on the table. It's got stains of whatever's in it on the sides in such a way that I just know it's going to leave a ring on the table, but it's steaming and I suspect that it's hot chocolate.

"You made this?"

Finn looks at me. "No, Saint Anthony brought it to

43

me in the night. He was very put out I didn't give it to you right then." He turns back around.

I am shocked, both by the reappearance of Finn's humour and the gift of the hot chocolate. I see now that the counter is an absolute mess of pots that Finn used to distil a single cup of cocoa, and I'm certain now that the odour hanging on the air is the smell of milk spilled on the hot burner, but it doesn't matter in the face of his intention. It sort of makes my lower lip not quite sure of itself, but I clamp my teeth on it for a moment until everything's steady. By the time Finn sits down on the other side of the table with a mug of his own, I'm normal again.

"Thanks," I say, and Finn looks uncomfortable. Mum used to say he was like a faerie; he didn't like to be thanked. I add, "Sorry."

"I put salt in it," Finn tells me, as if this eliminates the need to be grateful.

I try it. It's good. If there's salt in it, I can't taste it around the floating islands of partially stirred cocoa. They dissolve in my mouth in not-unpleasant lumps of powder. I can't remember if Finn has ever made cocoa before; I think he only ever watched me. "I can't tell there's salt in it."

"Salt," Finn says, "makes cocoa sweeter."

I think this is a pretty stupid thing to say, because how could something not sweet make something sweeter, but I let it pass. I stir my cocoa and mash a few of the lumps of cocoa against the side of the mug with the back of the spoon.

Finn knows I don't believe him, though, and says, "Go and ask at Palsson's, then. I watched them make the chocolate muffins. With salt."

"I didn't say I didn't believe you! I didn't say anything at all."

He mashes a spoon in his own cup. "I know you didn't."

He doesn't ask me how long I'll be gone today, or how I'm going to get a horse to ride, or anything about Gabe. I can't decide if I'm glad not to talk about it or if it's driving me crazy that he's not. We just slurp down the rest of our drinks, and when I get up to put my mug in the sink, I finally say, "I guess I'll be gone most of the day."

Finn gets up and puts his mug next to mine. He looks very serious, his neck skinny and turtle-like poking out of the oversize sweater. He points to the counter behind me. Among the wreck of pots and dishes is a cut-up apple, with a bit of crumbs from the counter stuck to one of the cut edges. "That's for Dove. I want to come with you today."

"You can't come with me," I say, without even stopping to think about how his words make me feel.

"Not every day," Finn says. "Just today. Just the first day."

I battle momentarily with the image of myself

emerging on the beach proud and lonesome, versus the reality of arriving with one of my brothers to watch from the sidelines and see how it's done. "OK. That would be good."

Finn gets his hat. I get my hat. I knitted both of them myself, and mine is patterned in white and two different shades of brown. Finn's is red and white. They're lumpy, but they fit.

In our hats, we stand among the wreckage of the kitchen. For a moment, I see the room like anyone else might see it. It looks like everything around Finn has crawled out of the mouth of the kitchen sink drain. It's a mess, and we're a mess, and no wonder Gabe wants to leave.

"Let's go," I say.

SIX

Sean

That first day, Gorry has me come down to the beach before anyone else to try a piebald mare he has dredged from the ocean some indeterminate time before. He is so certain that I will want her for Malvern that he's priced her high enough for two horses. Under the dark blue early morning sky, the tide just starting to pull back from the sand, my fingers frozen where they poke from my fingerless gloves, I watch him trot her back and forth for me. Her hoofprints are the first on the beach; the tide has wiped the sand clean, removing all traces of Mutt's botched efforts the night before.

She's striking. Water horses come in every colour that normal land horses do, but, like land horses, most are bay or chestnut. Less often dun or palomino or black or grey. It's very rare to find a piebald water horse, equally black and white, sharp white clouds across a black field. But flashy colour doesn't win races.

The piebald mare doesn't move terribly. She has a good shoulder. Lots of *capaill uisce* have good shoulders.

47

Unimpressed, I watch black cormorants spin through the sky above us, their silhouettes like small dragons.

Gorry brings the mare to me. I hitch myself on to her back and look down at Gorry. "She's the fastest *capall uisce* you'll ever sit on," he says in his grainy voice.

Corr is the fastest *capall uisce* I've ever sat on.

Beneath me, the piebald mare smells like copper and rotting seaweed. Her eye, turned towards me, weeps seawater. I don't like the feel of her – sinuous and hard to hold – but then, I am used to Corr.

"Take her out," Gorry says. "Tell me you can find anything faster."

I let her trot; she minces through the packed sand towards the water, ears pinned to her mane. I thumb my iron pieces out from my sleeves and track them counterclockwise on her withers, right on a heart-shaped spot of white. She shudders and twists her body away from my touch. I don't like the unhorse like tilt to her head or the way that she never unpins her ears. None of the horses are to be trusted. But I trust her less than most.

Gorry urges me to gallop her. Feel her speed for myself. I doubt that there is anything she can do at a gallop to convince me that what she is like at a trot is worth it. But I let out her reins and nudge her sides.

She is down the beach like an osprey diving for a fish. Breathlessly fast. And always, always conscious of the water, angling towards the sea. And again, that sinuous, slippery movement. She seems far less horse than sea creature to me, even now, even in the deep of October, even on dry land. Even with me whispering in her ear.

But she is fast. Her strides eat the sand, and we pass by the cove that marks the end of the good surface in only seconds. The rush of speed bursts through me, like bubbles popping on the surface of water. I don't want to think of her as faster than Corr, but she must be close. Anyway, how can I know, without him there?

It's beginning to get rocky. When I move to slow her, the piebald courses upward in a rear, her teeth snapping, predatory.

All of a sudden she smells overwhelmingly of the sea. Not of the beach, which is what most people think is the odour of the sea. Not of seaweed, or of salt, but of your head beneath the surface, breathing water, lungs full of the ocean. The iron has no effect as we pelt towards the water.

My fingers work through her mane, tying knots in threes and sevens. I sing in her ear, and all the while my inside hand turns her in smaller and smaller circles, each one away from the water. Nothing is sure.

As we charge across the sand, the magic in her calls to me, insidious. Precious little of my bare skin touches her − a wrist against her neck, perhaps, though my leg is guarded inside my boots. But still, her pulse hums through me. Lulling me to trust. Compelling me to join her in the sea. It's only a decade of riding dozens of the water horses that allows me to remember myself.

And only barely.

Everything in me says to abandon the struggle. Fly with her into the water.

Threes. Sevens. Iron across my palm.

I whisper: "*You will not be the one to drown me.*"

It feels like minutes to slow her, to bring her back towards Gorry, but it's probably only seconds. And all the while her neck still feels snaky to me and her teeth are still bared in a way that no land horse would present them. She's trembling beneath me.

It's hard to forget how swift she was.

"Didn't I tell you she was the fastest thing you'd ever ride?" Gorry asks.

I slide off her and hand him the reins. He takes them with a puzzled expression on his already puzzling face.

I say, "This mare is going to kill someone."

"Hey now," Gorry objects. Then: "They've all killed someone."

"I want no part of her," I say, even though part of me does.

"Someone else will buy her," Gorry says. "And then you will be sorry."

"That someone else will be dead," I reply. "Throw her back."

I turn away.

Behind me, I hear Gorry say, "She's faster than your red stallion."

"Throw her back," I repeat, not turning around.

I know he won't.

SEVEN

Puck

I didn't reckon that it would be awful.

But the whole island is crammed on to the beach, it feels like. Finn convinced us to take the Morris, which promptly broke down, so we arrived after just about everybody else. In front of us, there are two seas: one far-off ocean of deep blue and one seething mass of horses and men. All of them are men, not a girl among them unless you count Tommy Falk because his lips are so pretty. The men are a thousand times louder than the ocean. I don't see how they can train or move or breathe. They're all shouting at the horses and at each other. It's like a big argument, but I can't tell who's mad at who.

Finn and I both hesitate on the long sloped path down to the beach. The ground beneath our feet is uneven with divots from horses that have been led down already. Finn frowns as he looks at the collection of people and animals. But my eye is caught instead by a horse galloping at the faraway edge of the sucked-out tide. It is bright red, like fresh blood, with a small, dark figure crouched low on its back. Every few strides, the horse's hooves hit the very edge of the surf and water sprays up.

The sight of the horse galloping, stretched out, breathlessly fast, is so beautiful that my eyes prickle.

"That one looks like two horses stuck together," Finn says.

His observation pulls my gaze away from the red horse and closer to the cliffs.

"That's a piebald," I tell him. The mare he's gesturing to is snowy white splashed with big patches of black. Near her withers she has a small black spot that looks like a bleeding heart. A tiny little gnome of a man in a bowler hat is leading her away from the others.

"'*That's a piebald*,'" mimics Finn. I smack him and look back to where the red horse and rider were, but they're gone.

I feel strangely put out. "I guess we should go down," I say.

"Is everybody down there today?" Finn asks.

"Sure looks like it."

"How are you going to get a horse?"

Because I don't exactly have an answer, the question annoys me. I'm annoyed even more when I notice we're both standing in exactly the same position, so either I was standing like my brother or he was standing like me. I take my hands out of my pockets and snap, "Is this riddle day? Are you going to ask me questions all day?"

Finn makes his mouth and his eyebrows into parallel lines. He's very good at this face, although I don't know exactly what it means. When he was little, Mum called him a frog because of this face. Now that he sometimes has to shave, it doesn't look so much like an amphibian.

Anyway, he makes the frog face and sidles off into the commotion. For a moment, I think about going after him, but I'm suddenly pasted to the ground by a shrill wail.

It's the piebald mare. She's separated from the others, looking back either towards them or towards the sea. Her head's thrown back, but she's not whinnying. She's screaming.

The keening cuts through the wind, the sound of the surf, the bustle of activity. It's the wail of an ancient predator. It's one thousand miles away from any sound that a natural horse would make.

And it's horrible.

All I can think is: *Is this the last thing my parents heard?*

I am going to lose my nerve if I don't get on to the beach right now. I know it. I can feel it. My limbs feel like seaweed. I'm so wobbly that I almost turn my ankle on one of the divots left by the hooves. I'm relieved when the piebald mare stops her crying, but I still can't ignore that the *capaill uisce* don't even smell like proper horses as I get closer to them. Dove smells soft, all hay and grass and molasses. The *capaill uisce* smell like salt and meat and waste and fish.

I try to breathe through my mouth and not think about it. There are dogs careening around my legs and nobody is looking where he's going. Horses are clawing at the air and men are hawking insurance and protection to the riders. They're more riled up than terriers in a butcher shop. I'm glad that Finn's stormed off because the idea of him seeing me totally bewildered seems unbearable.

The truth is, I have a very rough idea of how to go about securing a horse for the race without money up front, but it's mostly based on things that we used to talk about in school, when the boys would all boast that they were going to ride in the races when they grew up. They never really did; mostly they just moved away to the mainland or became farmers, but their big plans were a good source of information. Especially since my family was one of the few that didn't follow the races.

"Girl!" snarls a man holding a roan horse that is pawing and charging, galloping without moving an inch. "Mind your damned feet!"

I stare down at my feet, and it takes me a second too long to realize that there was a circle drawn in the sand, and my boots have scuffed a line through it. I jump out of the circle.

"Don't bother," shouts the man as I try to retrace the line of the circle. The roan tugs towards the break in the

line. I back up and get shouted at again for my trouble –
two men are carrying an older boy away between them.
He's bleeding from his head and he swears at me. I whirl
away and almost trip over a scruffy dog with sand in its
fur.

"Curse you!" I snap at the dog, just because it won't
say anything back.

"Puck Connolly!" It's Tommy Falk with his pretty
lips. "What are you doing down here?" At least, that's
what I think he says. It's so loud that other people's
conversations drown out most of his words and the
wind robs the rest.

"I'm looking for bowler hats," I say. Black bowler
hats are supposed to mean dealers – on the rest of the
island, someone wearing one is called a monger, after
the horsemongers, and it's not the nicest of names.
Sometimes the boys wear them if they want to be seen
as rebels. Mostly it just means they're pissers.

Tommy shouts, "I didn't hear you right."

But I know he did. He just doesn't believe what he
heard. Dad once said people's brains are hard of hearing.
It doesn't matter if Tommy's stone-cold deaf on a plate,
though, because I catch a glimpse of a bowler hat, on
the head of the little gnome-man who had the piebald
mare earlier.

"Thanks," I tell Tommy, though he hasn't really
helped. I leave him behind and wind through the crowd
towards the gnome. Up close, the man does not look

quite so short, but he does look like his face has been hit solidly a few times with a brick, twice to really squish it and once more for good measure.

He is arguing with someone.

"Sean Kendrick," spits the monger, which is a name that sounds familiar for some reason, especially said in that disdainful note. The bowler-hatted gnome doesn't have a gnome-like voice at all. His voice is lined with cigarette smoke and he puts gritty *h*'s at the beginning of his words. "Heh. His head's half full of salt water. What's he saying about my horses, now?"

"I don't like to repeat it," replies the other figure politely. It's Dr Halsal, with his shiny black hair parted neatly on the side. I like Dr Halsal. He's very level-headed and he's a very compact, tidy sort of person, who reminds me of a drawing of a person instead of an actual person. I wanted to marry him when I was six.

"He's crazy as the ocean," says the bowler-hatted monger. "Come now, if you back her, you'll want her."

"All the same," Dr Halsal says, "I'm afraid I'm going to have to pass."

"She's fast as the devil," the gnome says, but the doctor is already retreating, and his back doesn't listen.

"Excuse me," I say, and my voice sounds very high to me. The gnome turns. His mismatched face is fearsome when matched with an irritable expression. I try to organize my thoughts into a respectable-sounding question. "Do you do fifths?"

Fifths is another thing I learned about from the daydreaming boys. It's gambling, more or less. Sometimes a monger will let you have a horse for nothing on the condition that whatever you win in the race, they get four-fifths of it. That's not really anything, unless you come in first. Then you could buy the whole island, if you wanted. Well, at least most of Skarmouth, except for what Benjamin Malvern owns.

The gnome looks at me.

"No," he says. But I can tell what he really means is *Not for you.*

I feel a little shaky inside, because it hadn't occurred to me that they would say no — were there that many people who would ride *capaill uisce* that the mongers could be choosy? I hear myself say, "OK. Could you point me towards someone else who might?" I add, hurriedly, "Sir," because Dad once said that saying "sir" makes gentlemen out of ruffians.

The gnome says, "Bowler hats. Ask 'em."

Some ruffians stay ruffians. When I was younger, I would have spat on his shoes, but Mum had broken me of the habit with the help of a small blue stool and a lot of soap.

So I just leave without saying thanks — he was even less help than pretty Tommy Falk — and I wind my way through the crowd looking for the next bowler hat, only to get the same results. All of them say no to the ginger-haired girl. They don't even consider it.

One frowns and one laughs and one doesn't even let me finish my sentence.

By now it's lunch time and my stomach is snarling at me. There are people hawking food to the riders, but it's expensive and everything smells like blood and bad fish. There's no sign of Finn. The tide is starting to creep in and some of the less brave souls have already left the beach. I retreat a bit and press my back against the chalk cliff, my hands spread out on the cold surface. A couple of metres above my head, the chalk is lighter, marking where the water will rise in a few hours. I imagine standing here until it does, salt water slowly swallowing me.

Tears of frustration burn behind my eyes. The worst of it is that I'm sort of glad they all said no. These terrifying monsters are not at all like Dove, and I can't even start to imagine myself trying one out, much less taking it home and training it to eat expensive, bloody meat instead of me. In the summer, children sometimes catch dragonflies and tie strings round them, just behind their eyes, and lead them like they are pets. Those dragonflies are what these grown men look like with the *capaill uisce*. The horses drag them around like they have no weight whatsoever. What would they do to me?

I look out across the sea. Close to the shore, the water is turquoise in places where white rocks have fallen from the cliffs into the water, and black where dark brown kelp covers the boulders. Somewhere across all these buckets of water are the cities we'll lose Gabe to. I know we'll never see him again. It won't matter that he's still alive somewhere; it will be just as bad as Mum and Dad.

Mum liked to say that some things happen for a reason, that sometimes obstacles were there to stop you from doing something stupid. She said this to me a lot. But when she said it to Gabe, Dad told him that sometimes it just means you need to try harder.

I take a deep breath and head back towards the only bowler hat who doesn't avoid my eye. The gnome. He has only one horse in his hands now: the piebald mare that screamed earlier.

"Heh, you!" He says this as if I'm about to pass him by.

"I think we need to talk," I tell him. I feel unfriendly and messy. Any charm I had when I started this is back at home with the makings of a sandwich.

"I was thinkin' the same thing. I'm about to be off. I'd rather not be back tomorrow and you'd rather have a *capall*. What will you give me for her?"

My first reaction is to think, *Well, how much do I have?* and then I come to my senses and remember his unhelpfulness from earlier. "Nothing up front," I say. I have to be firm on this. If Gabe really does leave us to fend for ourselves, we'll have nothing at the end, either. "I'm just looking for a fifth."

"This mare is amazing," the gnome says. "Fastest

thing on land at the moment." He stands back so I can see her, restless on the end of the lead, a chain wrapped over her nose and fed through her halter. She is drop-dead gorgeous and absolutely giant. I feel I could stack Dove on top of Dove and only then be able to look the piebald in her wild eye. She stinks like a corpse washed up after a storm. She eyes one of the loose dogs that darts around the beach. Something about her gaze is deeply unsettling.

"Then you wouldn't mind taking a gamble on her," I say. I feel petulant but I try to sound businesslike. It's not the easiest thing in the world trying to be treated like an adult during a negotiation when the idea of driving a successful bargain is making you a little sick to your stomach.

"I'm not in the mood to come back and collect," the monger says.

I cross my arms. I pretend I'm Gabe. He has a way of looking both unimpressed and uninterested when he's really both of these things. I sound as bored as possible. "Either she's everything you say, or she isn't. If she's the fastest thing on four legs, don't you trust her to win more than you could sell her for?"

The gnome eyes me. "It's not her I don't trust."

I glower at him. "I was just thinking the same thing."

He grins suddenly.

"Get up on her, then," the monger says. "Let's see

what you got." He jerks his head towards his saddle, tipped up on its pommel on the sand.

I take a deep breath and try not to remember her scream from earlier. I try not to think about how my parents died. I need to think about Gabe and his face when he said that he was leaving. I feel like my hands are fluttering, but they're quite still at my sides.

I can do this.

EIGHT

Puck

The monger leads the mare up to one of the kelp-covered boulders for me to use as a mounting block. She fidgets around and around, never quite close enough to it. She won't stop looking at the dog that's hovering around interested in someone's rejected breakfast near her hooves. The wind is cold on my neck and my toes are numb little stones in my boots.

"She's not getting any stiller than this," the monger says. "Are you on or off?"

My hands are balled into fists to keep them from betraying me. All I can think of is those massive teeth pulling my parents down into the ocean. It's not even fear that's stopping me right now. It's imagining them watching me from wherever they might be – Can they see this beach from heaven? Maybe the cliffs block the view – and thinking about what they would say. They'd always scoffed at the races and the horses had killed them in their boat and now here I was going to get on one of them to ride in the races. I can just imagine Dad's face and the way a small semicircle wrinkle appeared on his upper lip when he got disgusted or disappointed.

The mare jerks her head up; the gnome is nearly lifted from his feet.

There has to be another way. There has to be *something* I can do that will keep me off this horse. But how can I ride in the races without her?

I realize then that Finn has appeared from nowhere to stand beside the boulder I'm balanced on. He doesn't say anything. His fingers are pinching his upper arms over and over again as he looks up at me, but he doesn't seem to notice them.

"Stop that," I tell him, and he stops. I think I've made up my mind.

"Girlie," the monger says. "Come on now." The mare's muscles shudder beneath her skin.

This isn't who I am.

I say, "I'm sorry. I've changed my mind."

I just have time to see him roll his eyes when everything becomes a blur of motion. There is a surge of black and white, and a shove pushes me from the boulder. My breath gasps out in two massive puffs as my back slams the ground. Part of my face goes warm and wet. As the mare rears above me, I realize that there is something screaming at the same time I realize that the wetness on my face is blood, coming from above, not from me. Draining from the thing in the piebald mare's jaws.

I roll out of the way of the hooves, scrubbing sand from my eyes, trying to straighten. Trying to get my breath back. Trying to see. The mare crouches, shaking her dark quarry. She's ripping it, holding part down with a hoof. The sand pools blood.

I scream Finn's name.

Now the mare tosses part of her victim at me, ears flattened back. I half gasp, half sob, jumping back from the bloody joint. There's something stringy coming out of it, like jellyfish tentacles. I want to just kneel down and stop thinking.

The piece in front of me is covered with short, dark hair, matted with sand and blood. It's a ruin, almost unrecognizable. I am in danger of throwing up.

It's the dog.

People are shouting, "*Sean Kendrick!*" but I'm shouting, "*Finn!*" and there he is. He is a copy of the weird carvings on the church doorway in Skarmouth, little old men with big round eyeballs.

He says, "I thought—"

I know, because it's what I was thinking, too.

"Please don't ride her," Finn says, fervent. I can't quite remember the last time he's asked me something and sounded like he really meant it. "Don't ride one of them."

"I'm not," I say. "I'm riding Dove."

NINE

Sean

That evening, long after everyone is driven inland by the high tide, I bring Corr down to the beach. Our shadows are giants before us; this time of year, it gets dark at five and the sand is already cooling. I leave my saddle and boots at the top of the boat ramp, where grass still grows through the soft sand. Corr's eyes are on the ocean as it slowly slides back towards low tide.

We leave fresh prints in the hard-packed sand the tide's left behind; it is frigid against my bare feet, especially when cold seawater presses out of the ground around my skin. My blistered feet welcome it.

End of the first day, the endless first day. The beach has had its share of casualties. One boy fell off and bloodied his forehead on a boulder. Another man got bitten, an impressive-looking wound, but nothing a pint and a few hours of sleep won't fix. And then there was the dog. I couldn't be surprised that its maiming was the piebald mare's handiwork.

All in all, there've been worse starts to the training.

This evening, the registration will start at Gratton's.

I'll put my name and Corr's there, though at this point it feels like a formality. Then there will be a frantic week of uncertain islanders and tourists trying out horses to see if they have the nerve to truly race, and if they do, if they have the nerve to race on the horse they have beneath them. Horses will be bought, sold, bartered. Men become owners, fifths, riders. It's a frustrating time for me. Too much negotiation and not enough training. It's always a relief when the festival ends the first week and forces riders to officially declare their mounts.

That's really when life begins.

Corr lifts his head, ears pricked, neck curved, as if he's courting the Scorpio sea. I whisper to him and tug his lead. It's me I want him paying attention to, not the song of this powerful water. I watch his eye, his ears, the line of his body, to see whose voice will be more potent tonight, mine or the ocean's.

He jerks his head towards me so fast that I have an iron rod out of my pocket before he's finished his turn. But he wasn't attacking, merely moving to study me with his good eye.

I trust Corr more than any of them.

I should not trust him at all.

His neck is soft, though the skin around his eyes is tight, so into the surf we go. I let my breath out in a rush as the cold water creeps up my ankles. And then we stand there, and I watch him again, seeing what effect the magic eddying around his ankles has. He shivers but doesn't tense; we have done this before and the month is young. I cup a handful of salt water and tip it on to his shoulder, my lips pressed against his skin, whispering. Still he stands. So I stand with him and let the gritty surf work on my tired feet.

Corr, red as the sunset, looks out to the ocean. The shore faces east and so he looks out to night, deep blue and then black, the sky and the water mirror images. Our shadows fall into the ocean, too, changing colours with the breakers and foam beneath them. When I look at Corr's shadow, I see an elegant giant. When I look to mine, for the first time, I see my father's shadow. Not quite my father's. My shoulders don't have his slight hunch, as if against perpetual cold. And his hair was longer. But it is there in the rigid posture, the chin always lifted, a horseman even on the ground.

I am caught off guard, so when Corr moves up and away, I do nothing. He is in a half-rear before I realize it, but then he brings both his hooves down in the exact same place they left, making a mighty wall of water spray my face. I stand there, salt in my mouth, and I see that his ears are pricked at me, neck arched.

For the first time in days, I laugh. In response to the sound, Corr shakes his head and neck like a dog shedding water. I back up a few steps in the water and he follows me, and then I come after him and kick a splash at his body. He winces, looking deeply wounded, and then paws to splash me in return. Back and forth we go – I never have my back to him – as he follows me and I him. He pretends to drink the water and tosses his head in mock disgust. I pretend to drink a handful and throw it at him.

Finally, I am out of breath and my feet are sore from the pebbles and the water is nearly too cold to bear. I go to Corr and he lowers his head, pressing his face against my chest; he is warm through my soaked shirt. I trace a letter on the skin behind his ears, to still him, and I rub my fingers through his mane, to still me.

Not too far away, I hear a distant splash. It could be a fish, although it would have to be sizable for me to hear it over the breakers. I look out over the sea as it turns to black.

I don't think it is a fish, and neither does Corr, who is again looking out towards the horizon. Now he trembles, and when I back out of the surf, it takes a long minute to convince him to follow. He takes one slow step, then another, until the water is no longer touching him, and then he stops, rigid-legged. He looks back to the sea, lifts his head, and curls back his lip.

I snap the lead sharply and press the iron into Corr's chest, before he can call. While he's in my hands he won't sing their song.

As I walk back up the gradual slope to the boat slip, I see silhouettes at the top of the road to Skarmouth. They are standing at the ridge where it meets the sky, black against purple. Though they're distant, one of them

is the unmistakably graceless form of Mutt Malvern.
Their posture is undeniably interested in my progress,
so I'm wary as I make my way.

It doesn't take me long to discover that Mutt Malvern
has pissed in my boots.

They're laughing now on the ridge. I won't give
Mutt the satisfaction of my disgust, so I tip the boots
out – this beach is too good for his urine – and tie their
laces together. I let them hang on either side of the
saddle on Corr's back and start up the slope. Though it's
nearly dark, there's still a lot to get done; I have to be to
Gratton's before ten. The day stretches out in front of
me, invisible in the darkness.

We climb inland.

My boots smell of piss.

TEN

Puck

It's been a long time since I've been in Skarmouth after dark, and it reminds me of the time that Dad cut his hair. For the first seven years of my life, Dad had dark curly hair that was like me – in that he told it first thing in the morning what he wanted it to do and then it went and did pretty much whatever it wanted to do. Anyway, when I was seven, Dad came back from the docks with his hair close shaven and when I saw him walk in the door and kiss my mother on the mouth, I started to cry because I thought he was a stranger.

And that's what Skarmouth has done, after dark: it's turned into an entirely different Skarmouth from the one I've known my whole life, and I don't feel like letting it kiss me on the mouth anytime soon. Night has painted the entire town dark blue. All of the buildings press against each other and, clinging to the rocks, peer down into the endless black quay beneath them. Streetlights make brilliant halos; paper lights crawl along wires tied to telephone poles. They look like Christmas lights or fireflies, spiralling up towards the faint dark outline of St Columba's above the town. There is a legion of bicycles leaned against walls, and more cars than I knew existed on the entire island are parked along the streets, streetlights caught in their windshields. The cars have disgorged unfamiliar men and the bicycles have bucked off half-familiar boys. I've only ever seen this many people in the streets on fair days.

It's magical and terrifying. I feel lost, and I'm only in Skarmouth. I can't imagine Gabe making his way on the mainland.

"Puck Connolly," shouts a voice that I know belongs to Joseph Beringer. "Isn't it past your bedtime?"

I park Finn's bicycle as close to the butcher's as I can get it and lean it against the metal rail that is meant to keep you from falling into the quay unless you absolutely mean to. The water smells weird and fishy tonight and I peer down to see if there are any fishermen's boats down there to account for the smell. There's nothing but black water and reflections, making it look like there is another Skarmouth submerged under the salt water.

Joseph crows something else that I don't pay any mind to. In a way, I'm grateful that Joseph's here being an oaf, because he's such a fixture of life here that he makes everything else seem more familiar.

My head jerks as Joseph pulls my ponytail. I whirl around to face him, hands on my hips. He gives me his too-big smile. He is pimply under his blond hair. His mouth goes *whoo* like he's impressed that I'm looking at him.

I try to think of something catchy to say, but there's nothing but irritation that something that was funny to an eleven-year-old boy is still funny to a seventeen-year-old one. So I just say ferociously, "I don't have time for you tonight, Joseph Beringer!"

This is true always, but truer tonight. I'm supposed to sign up as a race participant today, I think. Because of my hurry, Finn graciously offered to feed Dove for me. When I left, he was looking at a bucket as if it was the most complicated invention he had ever seen.

Beside me, Joseph is going on about my bedtime again – he likes to just take a topic and worry it to death, never a danger of missing anything subtle with him – and I simply ignore him as I hurry down the walk to Gratton's, the butcher shop. As I look at all the people, some of them tourists already, I think about how Mum used to say that we needed the races, that this would be a dead island without them.

Well, the island's alive tonight.

Gratton's is a riot of sound, with people spilling out on to the walk. I have to push my way through the door. I wouldn't say people in Skarmouth are rude as a rule, but beer makes people deaf. Inside, the place is abuzz with noise and a crooked line leads around the walls. The ceiling feels low and crowded with its exposed timbers close overhead. I've never seen so many people in here before. In a terrible way, though, it makes sense that the butcher's should be the unofficial centre for the races, on account of this is where all the riders get their meat from.

Except me.

I see Thomas Gratton straightaway, shouting directly into someone's ear by the opposite wall. His wife, Peg, is behind the counter, smiling and chatting, a piece of chalk in her hand. Thomas may own the place, but Dad said that Peg ruled it. Every man in Skarmouth is in love with Peg. Dad said this was because they knew that Peg could cut their heart out neat and they loved her for it. Certainly isn't for her looks. I heard Gabe say once that Mutt Malvern had bigger tits than Peg. Which I suppose is probably true but I remember being very shocked at my brother saying something so crass and unfair, because what say does a girl have in how big her chest gets?

I edge into the single line of people that leads to where Peg writes names up on the chalkboard. I am standing behind a man in a dull blue jacket and a hat, and his back is so high he blocks my view of everything. I feel like I've become a toddler in a room that dangles with meat hooks. Thomas Gratton roars to the crowd to stop smoking in the shop and men roar laughingly back at him about Thomas not being able to stand any heat near his meat.

I begin to feel uncertain, like I'm not sure I'm even supposed to be standing in the line. I think people are looking at me. I hear people at the counter placing bets. Maybe I'm wrong and this has nothing to do with signing up for the races. Maybe they won't even let me sign up with Dove. The only positive thing is that I've lost Joseph Beringer in the process.

I step to the side of the giant in front of me to read the chalkboard again. At the top it says JOCKEYS and then, to its right, CAPAILL. Someone has written *meat* in small letters next to JOCKEYS. And then, beneath all of that, there is a gap, and then the names begin. There are more names under JOCKEYS than there are under CAPAILL. I feel like asking the mountain of a man in front of me why that is. I wonder if Joseph knows. I also wonder if Gabe has got home. And I wonder, too, if Finn has managed to work out how a bucket works yet. Mostly I can't think about any one thing for too long.

And then I see him. A dark-haired boy who is made of all corners. He is standing next in line by the counter, silent and still in his blue-black jacket, his arms folded across his chest. He looks out of place and wild in here: expression sharp, collar turned up against the back of his neck, hair still windblown from the beach. He is not looking at anyone or away from anyone; he's just standing there looking at the ground, his mind obviously far, far away from the butcher's. Everyone else is being crowded and jostled, but no one crowds or jostles him, though they don't seem to avoid him, either. It's like he's just not in the same place as the rest of us.

"Oh, Puck Connolly," says a voice behind me. I turn and see an old man, not in line, just watching those of us who are. I think his name is Reilly, or Thurber, or something. I recognize him as an old friend of my father's, one of those who's old enough that he had a name but I never needed to know it. He's a dry, crinkly thing, with wrinkles in his face deep enough for gulls to nest in. "What are you doing here on this night?"

"Meddling," I answer, because it's an answer that is difficult to argue with. I look back at the boy at the counter. He turns then, so he's in profile, and suddenly, I think I know him from on the beach: the rider on the red stallion. Something about his expression and his wind-torn hair makes my heart go *thump thump stop.*

"Puck Connolly," says the old man. "Don't be looking at *him* like that."

Such a statement is too tantalizing to ignore. "Who is he?"

"Lord, that's Sean Kendrick," the old man says, and I lift my eyebrows as I half remember hearing the name. Like a bit of history you've been told a few times in school but don't quite need to recall. "No one better than him for knowing the horses. He rides every year and I reckon he's the one to beat. Always is. But he's got one foot on the land and one foot in the sea. You steer clear of him."

"Of course I will," I say, though I don't know at the moment where I intend to steer. I look back to him, attaching the name. Sean Kendrick.

He steps up to the counter then, and Peg smiles at him very brightly — too brightly, I think, like she's proving a point. I can't hear what she says, but I can't stop watching as he leans slightly towards her, uncrossing his arms to make some sort of small gesture with his fingers as he speaks. He has two fingers held up and he presses them against the surface of the counter, tapping them twice like he's counting. I can tell that he, for one, is not in love with Peg Gratton. I wonder if it's because he doesn't know that she could cut his heart out neat or if he does know and is just unimpressed with the knowing.

Peg turns around with the chalk and stretches all the way up and I see now that the space just underneath Jockeys was left there intentionally, because she doesn't hesitate as she writes *Sean Kendrick* at the very top of the list above everyone else. There are a few whoops from the crowd around me as she finishes writing his name. Sean Kendrick doesn't smile, but I see him nod to her.

One of the other men pulls him aside to talk and the line moves up. I'm one step closer to signing up. My guts do a small little dance inside me. Another step up. I'm wondering if it's nerves or the pressing heat of all these bodies that's making me light-headed. Another step up.

My stomach is an ocean of trouble as the man in front of me places a bet. And then it is me.

Peg smiles at me, like she smiles at everyone. She doesn't look scary at all. She looks plain and friendly. "Hi, love, what do you need? You've picked quite a night to come out."

I realize that she thinks I'm here for meat. I feel my cheeks warm and try to sound firm. "I'm here to sign up, actually."

Peg's smile remains in place, but it's like a picture of a smile someone has hung on her face instead. It is utterly motionless and her eyes don't match it. "Your brother told me not to let you sign up. He wanted me to find a rule against it."

She means Gabe, of course. My stomach surges in a whole new way. I try not to sound frantic as I lean across the bloodstained counter. And right after that I realize that she knew all along what I was here for and still asked me the first question. Which I think means I need to change how I'm thinking of her, but I can't, because she still looks just plain and friendly. "There's no rule, is there? There isn't any reason I can't."

"There's no rule, and I told him that for sure. But—" Her smile is gone and suddenly I *can* imagine her cutting out my heart, in a hard, blank way that means she wouldn't even notice the blood. "What would your parents think? Have you thought this through? People die, love. I'm all for women, but this isn't a woman's game."

For some reason, this irritates me more than anything

else I've heard all day. It's not even *relevant*. I give her the fierce look I practised in the mirror. "I've thought it through. I want to add my name. Please."

She looks at me a beat longer, and I don't let my face change. Then she sighs, picks up the chalk, and turns to the board. She starts to write a *P* and then rubs it out with the pad of her hand. She glances back at me. "I can't remember your real first name, love."

"Kate," I say, and I feel like everyone in Skarmouth is suddenly staring at my back. "Kate Connolly."

There are moments that you'll remember for the rest of your life and there are moments that you *think* you'll remember for the rest of your life, and it's not often they turn out to be the same moments. But when Peg Gratton turns around and chalks my name on the list, white on black, I know, without a doubt, that it's an image I'll never forget.

When she turns back around, one of her eyebrows is raised. "And your horse's name?"

"Dove," I say. The word comes out too quiet. I have to repeat it.

She writes it down, no questions asked, but of course — why would she doubt that Dove is a *capall uisce*?

I chew my lip. Peg is waiting.

"It's fifty, Puck," she says. "To enter."

I feel a little ill as I dig the coins out of my pocket. For a sickening moment I don't think I have enough, but then I find the money I'd been carrying to buy flour. I hold it out, not releasing it into her waiting hand.

"Wait," I say. I lean across the counter, voice low. "Are there, um, any rules about the horses?" If I get disqualified *and* lose the fifty, I really will be sick. "About them . . . uh. . .?"

Peg says, "You want a rule sheet?"

She has to look for it. I feel like everyone is staring at my name on the board while she does. When she offers it to me, a rumpled piece of paper, I scan the front and back. There are only two lines about the horses: *Jockeys must declare their mount by the end of the first week at the Scorpio Festival riders' parade. Swapping of mounts after that date is not permitted.*

I scan for anything at all, but there's nothing. Nothing to say that I can't enter Dove.

I finally let Peg have the coins. "Thank you," I say.

"Do you want to keep that?" Peg asks, gesturing to the rule sheet. I don't really care, but I nod. "OK," she says. "You're official."

I'm official.

As I push outside into the dark, I take big breaths of the cold air. The briny smell of earlier has been mostly replaced by the faint scent of exhaust lingering in the air, but in comparison to the sweat and raw meat smell of the butcher, it's heavenly. My head feels all spinny and elated and terrified, and I feel like I can see every single little bump on the street in front of me, every bit of rust on the rail before the quay, every ripple in the water. Everything is black – the depthless sky and the inky water – and butter yellow – the streetlamps and light pouring out from the shop windows.

I realize that there is a discussion going on, a few metres away, and I recognize Sean Kendrick's jacket. Mutt Malvern faces him, looking massive and sweaty in comparison to Sean. It's clear from the way that a few people have paused nearby that what's being said is not pleasant.

It's like birds worrying a crow. I've seen them in the fields, when the crow has got too close to their nest or otherwise insulted them. The other birds dive-bomb and scream and the crow merely stands there, looking dark and still and unimpressed.

So it's just this: Sean and Mutt, heir to the island's fortune, and Mutt's spit glistening on Sean's boots.

"Nice boots," Mutt says. He's looking down at them, but Sean Kendrick isn't. He watches Mutt's face with the same looking-but-not-looking expression he had in the butcher's. I'm kind of horrified and fascinated by what I see on Mutt's face. It's not anger, but something like it.

After a long moment, Sean turns as if to go.

"Hey," Mutt says. He has a smile on his face, but it means the opposite of a smile. "Are you in such a hurry to get back to the stables? It's only been a few hours since you've had your fix." He pumps his hips enthusiastically.

I would have felt bad for Mutt's goading if I hadn't seen Sean's smile then. It's barely a wisp of a smile, only there for a second – not even really making his mouth move, just flattening his eyes a bit – and it's canny and condescending and then it's gone. And I realize that what's on both their faces, in two entirely different shapes, is hatred.

"Say something, horse-stroker," Mutt says. "Did you like my present to you?"

But his fists are clenched, and I don't think it's speaking he wants out of Sean Kendrick.

And still Sean says nothing. He looks weary, if anything, and as Mutt shifts his feet to circle him, Sean simply begins to walk away.

"Don't walk away from me," Mutt snarls. He overtakes Sean in three uneven strides, and when he catches Sean's upper arm with his big hand, he spins Sean around as easily as a child. "You work for me. You don't walk away from me."

Sean puts his hands in the pockets of his jacket. "Indeed, Mr Malvern," he says, and his tone is so deadly calm that Dr Halsal, who'd been watching, frowns and ducks back inside the butcher shop. "And what can I do for you this evening?"

This momentarily stumps Mutt Malvern, and I think that he might just hit Sean Kendrick now and rustle up a good reply later. But then, it comes to him, and he says, "I'm having my father let you go. For theft. Don't say it's not so. I had that horse, Kendrick, and you let him go. I'll have your job for that."

Money's not something many people have on this island. Talk of axing someone's job is not a thing to toss around lightly. It's not even my employment, and I already feel the pinch in my stomach, the same one I get when I open up the pantry door and see the shrinking contents.

"Will you now?" Sean says softly. There's a long pause, full of the sound of muffled voices in the butcher's. "I saw you signed up for the races. But there's no horse there beside your name. Why is that, Mutt?"

Mutt's face purples.

"I think," Sean says, and as before, his voice is so quiet that all of us are holding our breath to hear him, "it's because, like every year, your father is waiting for me to pick a horse for you."

"That's a lie," Mutt says. "You're no better than I am. My father lets you put me on the wasters. He lets you put me on the nags and the leftovers and you take the best for yourself. I have no say in the matter or I'd be on that red stallion. I'm not going to have you put me on a loser this year."

The door opens and now Dr Halsal has returned with Thomas Gratton. They stand in the doorway and Thomas Gratton wipes his hands on his butcher's apron as he surveys the situation. Sean Kendrick's low voice has somehow made the argument both quieter and more impressive – a silent night ocean full of restrained power. The space between Sean Kendrick and Mutt Malvern seems charged.

"Boys," Thomas Gratton says, and though he sounds jovial, I can see that he's cautious. "I think it's time you push off."

As if Thomas Gratton hasn't spoken, Sean leans into Mutt, and he says, "Five years I've kept you alive on that beach. That's what your father asks of me, and that's what I'll keep doing. You'll ride what I tell him you'll ride."

He turns to Gratton and nods sharply, suddenly old, before striding inland. Mutt makes an obscene gesture to his back. When Mutt sees Gratton looking at him, he takes his time lowering his hand and putting it in his pocket.

"Matthew," Gratton says. "It's late."

Dr Halsal glances in my direction. His eyes narrow, as if he's convincing himself of what he sees, and I hurry to retrieve Finn's bike before he can say anything. I should be off anyway. Like Thomas Gratton said, it's late. And I have to be up early tomorrow.

Sean Kendrick is no one to me that his worries should be mine. He's just another rider on the beach.

ELEVEN

Puck

That night, I dream about Mum teaching me to ride. I'm nestled in front of her like we are one creature, her arms around me. Her fingers are stubby like mine, and it's easy to compare them — my hands are fisted on the pony's mane, and hers are light on the reins. It is neither raining nor sunny, but somewhere in between, as it often is on Thisby. My hands are wet with the sky's sweat.

"Don't be nervous," she tells me. The wind beats her hair against my face and my hair against hers. It's the same colour as the ruddy fall cliff grass that bows down to the ground and back up again. "The Thisby ponies love to run. But it's easier to get a barnacle off a rock than a Keown woman off a horse." I believe her, because she feels like a centaur, like she's part of the pony. It's impossible for either of us to fall.

I wake from my dream. I have a memory of the door to the house closing and I think this is what woke me. I lie there, looking at nothing because the room is too dark to see, waiting for my eyes to adjust or waiting for sleep to return. I wipe some of the tears off my cheeks. After a few minutes, I start to doubt that I actually heard the door close.

But then there's the smell of salt water, momentarily terrifying, and Gabe, standing at the door to my bedroom, peering in. I can see the line of his neck as he looks. Inside my head, I say *please come in*, over and over again. I want so much for him to sit on the end of my bed like he used to, before our parents died, and ask me what my day was like. I want him to tell me he's changed his mind and I don't have to ride after all. I want him to say where he's been out so late.

But most of all, I just want him to come in and sit.

He doesn't. He silently knocks his fist against the door jamb as if I've said something to disappoint him. Then he turns away, and eventually, I fall back asleep. But I don't dream of our mother again.

· Sean ·

The Malvern stables are a haunted place at night.

Though I have already been awake for seventeen hours and need to be up in another five if I'm to have the beach to myself in the morning, I don't go straight up to my flat. Instead, I take my time in the chilly stable, walking up and down the dimly lit aisles, making sure that the grooms have fed and watered the thoroughbreds and draughts as they were supposed to. They've mucked out most of the stalls but now that it's nearly November, they're too cowardly to enter the few stalls occupied by the *capaill uisce*, even when I had the water horses down at the beach. Part of that is the water horses' reputation, I think, and part of it is the stable's. Regardless, it leaves me with three stalls I don't want the *capaill uisce* to stand in all night. As head trainer, my time's supposed to be too valuable to be bothering with mucking out, but I'd rather do it myself than have Malvern's two new frightened mice do it badly.

So while the horses make their soft, slow night noises, and the dark, knowing walls of this place hold me close, I clean out the three stalls. I wipe down the surfaces in the feed room. I give the water horses their meat, though I think they're too wound up to eat it. And all the while, I imagine that this massive stable is mine, that these horses I care for are in my name, that the buyers who try them will nod approvingly at me instead of at Benjamin Malvern.

The Malvern stables are not truly the Malvern stables, after all, but a complex of stone barns that housed horses on Thisby long before the Malvern name existed on the island. The only thing that can match these buildings in stature, especially the main stable, is St Columba's in Skarmouth. The barns were constructed with the same spiritual fervour. The ceiling is held up with carved columns that depict wide-eyed men whose hands support the feet of men whose hands support the feet of other men in turn and again in turn, and at the top of all of them are men with the heads of horses. Like the church in Skarmouth, the sloped ceiling of the main barn is supported with ribs of stone, and in between, the surfaces are painted with complicated animals whose limbs knot around each other. The walls, too, are painted, with small, twisted figures jotted into the oddest places: a corner of a stall, in the centre of the floor, along the left side of windows. Men with hooves for hands, and women coughing up horses, and stallions with tentacles for manes and tails.

And the most impressive painting of all covers the wall at the end of the main stable. In it, there is the sea, and a man – a forgotten ocean god, perhaps – dragging a horse down into it. The water is the colour of blood and the horse is red as the sea.

It's an old animal, this stable, the oldest on the island.

Everywhere in it are clues to the stable's previous life. The stalls are so large that in all but three, Malvern has put up dividers so that he can accommodate more of the sport horses that he sells on the mainland. The door frames are iron, the door handles will turn only counterclockwise, and there is something written in red runes above one of the thresholds. The floor of the *teind* stall, the stall closest to the cliffs, is stained with blood, the walls arced with a spattered spray like sea foam. Malvern has repainted it many times, but when the morning light comes in full and strong, the stains are still visible. One of them is the print of a human hand, fingers splayed near the door handle.

It was not always stylish sport horses that were housed in this barn.

I finish with the stalls and the feed room and every other chore that I can think of performing, and then I shut down the lights so it's just me in the dark, ancient stomach of the stables. One of the *capaill uisce* makes a clucking sound and another one replies. Even though I know the horses, the sound instinctively makes the hairs on my arms rise. Every other horse in the stable has gone silent and watchful at the noise.

The thing is, I don't actually want the Malvern stables, not in either of its forms. I don't want Malvern's rich buyers, coming each October to watch the races and buy his thoroughbreds. I don't want his money and his reputation and his ability to come and go as he pleases from Thisby. I don't need forty head of horses to feel complete.

What I want is this: a roof over my head that is my own, accounts at Gratton's and Hammond's in my name, and, most of all, I want Corr.

For the first time in nine years, I lock the door to my flat, thinking of Mutt Malvern's purple face and fisted hands. I lie awake for a long time, listening to the ocean violent against the rocks of the north-western shore of the island, and thinking about the piebald mare.

Finally, I sleep, and when I do, I dream of a day when I can turn my back on Mutt Malvern and keep walking.

Twelve

Puck

The morning is raw and pink as I make my way out to Dove's pasture. Cold as a witch's tit, my father used to say, and my mother would say *is that the sort of language you're teaching your boys?* and apparently it was, because Gabe said it just the other day. It's not cold enough to freeze the mud, however – only a few years does it ever get cold enough for that – so I slide and stomp and shiver my way across the muddy yard. I'm trying not to notice that I'm nervous. It's nearly working.

I call Dove's name and bash the coffee can of feed against the fence post. It's not a lot – I'll feed her more after we've worked – but it's enough to tantalize her. I can see her muddy rump poking out from the lean-to. Her tail doesn't even move as I jostle the can again.

I jump as Finn says, right at my elbow, "She knows you're cranky, that's why she won't come over."

I glower at him. Somewhere, someone in Skarmouth is making meat pies, because I can smell them on the wind and my stomach grumbles as it rolls to point in the direction of the scent. "I am not cranky. Aren't you supposed to be cleaning the kitchen or something?"

Finn shrugs and stands on the lowest rung of the fence. He seems unperturbed by the cold. "Dove!" he calls gaily. I am gratified to see that Dove doesn't move an inch for him, either.

"Well," he says, "she's a useless mule. What are you doing today?"

"Taking her down to the beach," I say. I touch my nose with the back of my hand; it's that sort of cold that makes me feel like it's going to run, even though it's not.

"The *beach*?" Finn echoes. "Why?"

The idea of answering him irritates me as much as the answer does, so I pull the rule sheet out of my woolly jacket pocket and hand it to him. I rattle the can while he unfolds the sheet, and try not to feel sorry for myself as he reads. It takes him awhile to get to the rule that answers his question. I can tell exactly when he gets to it, because his mouth gets thin. I had thought, when I first decided to ride Dove in the races, that I would be able to exercise her far away from the beach and go down there only for the race. But the rule sheet that Peg Gratton gave me tells me I can't. All entries must train within one hundred and fifty metres of the shoreline. Penalty: disqualification with no refund of the entry fee. It feels specifically designed to thwart me, even though I know there's a good reason for it. No one wants water horses running amok over the island as it gets close to November.

"Maybe you can ask them to make an exception," Finn says.

"I don't want them to notice me at all," I say. If I went to the officials and made a kerfuffle over Dove, they might disqualify me anyway. My plan seems frightfully thin at the moment. All for a brother who left before either of us got up.

Finn and I both start at the sound of a car coming up the road to the house. Cars are never a good sign. Not many people on the island have them, and fewer still have a reason to come out here. Usually the only people who come this way are men who don't take off their hats as they hand over unpaid invoices.

Finn, valiant soul that he is, vanishes, leaving me to it. The same amount of money has to be handed over regardless, but it stings less if you aren't the one who has to count it out for them.

But it's not a bill collector. It's a long, elegant car the size of our kitchen, with a tall, elegant grille the size of a dustbin. It has round, friendly-looking eyeballs with chrome eyebrows; its tailpipe breathes white puffs that creep around the tyres. And it is red — not the red of the horse I saw on the beach yesterday, but red like only humans can imagine. Red like candy. Red like you'd like to taste or possibly paint your lips with.

Red, Father Mooneyham often remarks sadly, like sin.

I know the car. It belongs to St Columba's, officially, donated to Father Mooneyham for his home visits by a well-meaning parishioner who'd come from the mainland and had some sort of spiritual conversion in the waters near Skarmouth. And it is true that Father Mooneyham travels all over the island in the car, visiting the islanders and giving last rites and first rites and in-between rites. But he never budges from the passenger seat. If he can't find anyone willing to drive, he uses his bicycle as he did before, never mind that he's old as sod.

I feel a little bad that Finn has hidden himself in the house, because he would've appreciated the grand red car of the priest. I tell myself it serves him right for being a coward.

Before I can properly wonder why Father Mooneyham has come out here, the driver's side door opens and out steps Peg Gratton. Her feet are armoured in dark green rubber boots that are unimpressed by our mud. I see Father Mooneyham fretting over something in the passenger seat, but he remains in the car. It's Peg who has business with me, and that is a worrying thought.

"Puck," she says. Her short hair is curled and red – not the same colour red as either the car or the horse from the beach – and frazzled appealingly in a way that gives me hope for mine. "Good morning. You have a moment?"

It's clever the way she says it, not as a question. I would have to contradict her in order to have my moment back. I make a note to use the method in the future.

"Yes," I say, and then, though it pains me to add it, because the kitchen looks like faeries have been using it for black magic all night, "Would you like some tea?"

"I can't keep the Father," Peg says briskly. "He was kind enough to bring me out here."

This of course is not true, as it was the other way around. I narrow my eyes at her. Seeing the red car reminds me both that I haven't been to confession in a very long time and that I've done a great many things that I ought to confess. It's not a comfortable feeling.

Now Peg hesitates. She looks around the yard. It is a bit pathetic looking. Every so often I pull the biggest of the weeds out from the edges of the fence and the house, but there are still dark, leafy intruders everyplace things join up. There is not much in the way of proper grass in the stretches in between, just mud. I should tell Finn to fix the wheelbarrow that has passed out in the corner of the yard. But it's not the mess that Peg's eyes rest on, it's the saddle I have set over the fence, next to my brushes. And the coffee can of grain in my hand.

"My husband and I were talking about you last night, right before we went to sleep," she says, and for some reason, this makes me feel odd, to think of her and ruddy Thomas Gratton in bed together, and to think of them talking about me, of all things. I wonder what they talk about when they aren't talking about me. The weather, perhaps, or the price of marrow, or the way that tourists always seem to wear white shoes in the rain. I think if I had a butcher husband, that's what I would talk to him about. Peg continues, "And he seemed to think that you weren't riding one of the *capaill uisce*. I said no, that's not possible. It's a bad enough decision to ride in the races, without making it complicated."

"And what did he say?"

"He said he seemed to remember," Peg says, looking at Dove's muddy tail, "that the Connollys had a little dun mare by the name of Dove, which I said I thought was what you had me write down on the board last night."

I hold the coffee can of grain very still. "That's true," I say. "Both of those things are true."

"That's what I thought. So I told him I was coming down here to talk you out of it." She looks less than pleased with this idea. I thought it was probably one of those ideas that sounded better when you were lying in bed with your ruddy husband rather than standing in the misty cold morning staring at the reality of me.

"I'm sorry that you came all this way," I say, although I'm not, and it's unusual for me to lie before a proper breakfast. "Because I can't be talked out of it."

She puts one of her hands on her hip and the other on the back of her head, crushing her curly hair flat. It's such a fierce posture of frustration that I feel a little bad that I'm the one causing it. "Is it the money?" she asks, finally.

I'm not sure if I'm insulted or not. I mean, clearly, yes, we need the money, but I would've had to be the island's best fool if I thought that I stood a chance of winning against those massive horses.

A part of me prickles at that, and I realize, guiltily, that a tiny, tiny part of me, small enough to dissolve in a teacup or work a blister in the heel of a shoe, must've been daydreaming of that possibility. Beating the horses that had killed my parents on a pony that I'd grown up on. I must be the island's best fool, after all.

"It's for personal reasons," I say stiffly. Which is what my mother had always told me to say about things that had to do with fighting with your brothers, getting any sort of illness that had intestinal ramifications, starting your period, and money. And this decision covered two out of the four, so I thought the statement was well earned.

Peg looks at me and I can tell she's trying to read between the lines. Finally, she says, "I don't think you know what you're getting into. It's a war down there."

I shrug, which makes me feel like Finn, which makes me wish I hadn't done it.

"You could die."

I can see now that she's trying to shock me. This is the least shocking thing she could say, though.

"I have to do it," I tell her.

Dove chooses that moment to emerge, and she is mud-stained and small and faintly damning. She comes over to the fence and tries to nibble the saddle. I give her a foul look. She's muscled and in good shape, but in comparison to the *capaill uisce* I saw yesterday, she's like a toy.

Peg sighs and gives a nod, but it's not for me. It's a *well, at least I tried* nod. She clomps back through the mud and knocks her boots on the edge of the car door to keep from getting so much filth inside the beautiful red car. I rub Dove's nose and feel bad about disappointing fierce Peg Gratton.

After a moment, I hear my name and see that Father Mooneyham is calling me. I can't believe that Peg would have convinced Father that me on the beach is a spiritual matter, and my path to the passenger-side window is a dutiful rather than happy one.

"Kate Connolly," Father Mooneyham says. He's a very long man all over, with knobs for a chin bone and his cheekbones and the end of his nose. Each knob is slightly reddened. There is a knob for his Adam's apple, too, which I saw once when he had been knocked off his bicycle and his collar had gone askew. It was not reddened.

"Father," I say.

He looks at me and puts his thumb in a little cross on my forehead like he used to when I was small and still spat when I was in church. "Come to confession. It's been a long time."

Peg and I both wait for him to say something else. But he just rolls his window back up and motions for Peg to reverse out of the yard. As they do, I see Finn's face smashed up against the bedroom window, getting a glimpse of the splendid car as it pulls away.

Thirteen

Sean

I stand in a round pen in the Malvern Yard with an American at my elbow, both of us watching Corr trot around us. It's a pale blue morning that needs time to become pleasant. I was intending to spend it on the beach before everyone else got there, but Malvern caught me and pressed the buyer on to me before I could get clear. I didn't think taking a stranger to the beach was a good idea, so I headed to the round pen to school until my visitor got bored. The rule requiring the *capaill* to train on the shore only counts if they're under saddle, something I always take advantage of. There's not much that can be done in a round pen that will prepare you for life on the beaches.

Already Corr has been going in circles at the end of the lunge line for twenty minutes. The American is enthusiastic but reverent, more awed by me, I think, than by Corr. Our accents make us cautious with each other.

"Quite a remarkable structure. This was built just for the *capaill uisce*?" he asks. He's very careful with the last words, but his pronunciation is good. *Copple ooshka.*

I nod. On the other side of the stables is the round pen that I exercise the sport horses in, fifteen metres across with high fence-like walls built of light metal tubing. Corr wouldn't tolerate the metal for very long, and even if he did, everyone is too afraid to put a *capall uisce* in something that looks like it would blow away. So instead we're in this fearfully wondrous pen that Malvern devised sometime before I arrived, dug two metres into the side of a hill so that the earth makes a solid wall around it. The only entrance is a high-dirt-walled path ending at an oak door that serves as part of the pen's wall. I like it well enough, except for when it floods.

"*Capaill uisce? Capall uisce?*" The American frowns now, doubting his usage.

"*Capaill* is plural. *Capall* is singular."

"Roger. It's never sure if it's raining or not here, is it?" asks the American. He's very handsome, in his late thirties, wearing a navy flat cap, a white V-neck sweater, and slacks that won't stay that pressed for long in this humidity. The sky spits at us, but it's not really rain. It'll be gone before I head down to the beach with the others. "How long will you trot him out?"

Corr is already annoyed with the gait. My father once said that no water horse was meant to trot. Any horse has four natural gaits — walk, trot, canter, gallop — and there's no reason for one to be preferable over another. But Corr would sooner gallop until he's lathered like the surf than trot for half the time. My mother once said that I hadn't been built to trot, either, and that's true, too. It's too slow to be exciting, too jolting to be comfortable. I'm perfectly content to let Corr do it on his own right now, without me on his back.

At the moment, he can tell that he's being watched by a stranger, however, so he picks his feet up and tosses his mane just a little more than usual. I allow him his show. There are worse flaws than vanity in a horse.

The American's still looking at me, so I reply, "Just taking the edge off. The beach will be crowded again today, and I don't want to bring three fresh horses down there."

"Well, he's a beauty," the American says. It's meant to flatter me, and it does. He adds, "I see by your smile you already know."

I didn't think I was smiling, but I did already know.

"I'm George Holly, by the way," the American says. "I'd shake your hand if it wasn't occupied."

"Sean Kendrick."

"I know. You're why I came. They said it wasn't a race unless you were in it."

My mouth quirks. "Malvern said you had your eye on some yearlings."

"Well, I came for them, too." Holly wipes the mist from his eyebrows. "But I could've sent my agent for them. How many times have you won?"

"Four."

"Four! You're the man to beat. A national treasure. Regional treasure, perhaps. Does Thisby have home rule? Why don't you race on the mainland? Or maybe you do and I've missed it. We get your news slowly, you know."

George Holly didn't know it, but I had been to the mainland once with my father, for one of the races there. It was waistcoats and flat caps and bowlers and canes, horses in snaffle bits and jockeys in silks and a track contained by a white rail, and wives who looked like dolls. The benevolent hills stretched gently on either side of the stands. The sun had shone, the bets had been cast, the favourite won by two lengths. We came home and I'd never gone back.

"I'm no jockey," I say. Corr starts to come in towards us, and I push him back out to the wall with a flick of my stick.

The stick isn't long enough to touch him, but it's got a length of red leather fixed to the end, and it snaps to remind him of his place.

"Me neither," Holly announces broadly, putting his hands in his pockets like a boy. He rotates on his heel as I turn, watching Corr circle around us. "Just a horse lover."

Now that he's said his name, I know exactly who he is. I've not met him before, but I know his agent, who comes over each year to import a yearling or three. Holly's the American equivalent of Malvern, the owner of a massive breeding farm known for show jumpers and hunters, wealthy and eccentric enough to come all the way to Thisby for a chance to improve his stock. "Horse lover" is a stark understatement, albeit one that makes me like him better.

And Malvern has me babysitting him. I should be flattered. But still, I'm wondering how difficult it will be to hand him off in order to get down to the beaches.

"Do you think Benjamin Malvern would part with this beast?" Holly asks. He's watching Corr's tireless stride and imagining it, I think, on his home soil.

My breath's uncertain. For the first time, I'm relieved by the answer to that question, though it's caused me sleepless nights before. "Malvern won't sell his water horses to anyone."

Also, it's illegal to transport the *capaill uisce* from the island, but that doesn't seem like something that would stop someone like Holly. If he were a horse, I think I'd have to trot him around this round pen for a long time to take the edge off.

"Perhaps he hasn't been offered the right price."

My fingers tighten on the lunge line enough that Corr feels the tension and flicks an ear towards me, always sensitive to my mood. "He's had good offers."

At least one very good offer. Everything I had saved over the years, everything from my share of the winnings. I could buy ten of Malvern's yearlings, ten of any of his other horses. Just not the one I want.

"I expect you would be the one to know," Holly says. "Sometimes it's not money they're looking for." He doesn't sound upset; a man so used to both buying horses and being refused them that neither scenario surprises him. "I sure do like the look of him. Malvern horses! Sh-*ite*."

He's so clearly delighted by it all that it's hard to fault him.

I ask, "How long are you here?"

"I'm on the ferry the day after the race, with whatever Benjamin Malvern has convinced me I can't live without. Want to join me? I could use a boy like you. Not a jockey, but a whatever you call yourself."

I allow him a thin smile that reveals the impossibility of this.

"I see how it is," Holly replies. He gestures his chin towards Corr. "Can I hold him for a moment? Will he let me?"

He is so polite about it that I hand him the lunge line and my stick. Holly takes them delicately, his feet automatically moving apart to give him a better base of support. The stick rests lightly in his right hand, an extension of his arm. The man must have lunged hundreds of horses.

Still, Corr immediately tests him. He tosses his head up and moves in, and Holly has to flick the stick at once. Corr keeps pushing inward.

"Snap," I say. I'm ready to take him back if I must. "It has to snap."

Holly flicks the stick again, this time hard enough to audibly snap the leather, and Corr twists his head, more conciliatory than ill-tempered, before trotting back out to the wall. Holly's smile is broad and pleased. "How long has it taken you to get him like this?"

"Six years."

"Could you do this with the other two mares I saw?"

I had tried the lunge line, in fact, with the pure bay mare, and though it hadn't been a disaster, it hadn't been pretty, either. Surely I wouldn't have wanted Holly or anyone else with me in the round pen that day. I'm not entirely certain that six years with either of the mares would end up the same way that six years with Corr has. I'm not sure, after all this time, if it's because he understands me better than they do, or merely because I understand him better than them.

"Who taught you this? Surely not Malvern." Holly glances at me.

In that brief moment of distraction, the bare second it takes for Holly to look towards me, Corr surges away from the wall towards us. Swift and soundless.

I don't wait for Holly to react. I snatch the stick from his hand and jump to meet Corr, pressing the tip of the stick into his shoulder. Corr rises up, away from the pressure of it, but I follow him. As he rears, I lay the red leather against his cheek, daring him to test me as he tested Holly.

We've played this game before and we both know the outcome.

Corr drops to the ground.

Holly lifts his eyebrows. He hands me the lunge line and wipes his palms on his slacks. "First time behind the wheel. At least I didn't wrap her around a tree."

He's not at all fazed.

"Welcome to Thisby," I say.

FOURTEEN

Puck

After Peg Gratton leaves, Finn and I pack up to go into Skarmouth. I find this pretty disagreeable, being once again denied the proud, lonely entrance on Dove, but we need to bring all of the teapots into town and the Morris won't start. So in the most discouraging turn of events so far, I have to hitch Dove up to our little cart. My future embarrassment makes me cross and I make a lot of noise while loading up the pottery.

I have a sudden thought. "How are you going to get the cart back home?" I ask Finn, who is working on carefully aligning the boxes in the cart so the corners match perfectly. His side of the packing looks like he is laying bricks, but it's taking him a long time. I don't care if the largest boxes go on the bottom or the top so long as they aren't going to crash around. "I'm taking Dove down to the beach and the cart is *not* going down there."

"I'll bring it back myself," Finn says pleasantly. He feathers two of his fingers on the edge of a box in order to move it the distance of a butterfly's breath.

"*Yourself?*"

"Sure," Finn says. "It'll be *empty* then."

I get a momentary image of my brother trudging out of Skarmouth with a pony cart behind him, an emaciated troll in a giant sweater, and I wish that I, too, could disappear to the mainland where no one knew my name. But it's that or get to the beach after the tide has come up. The mist is still clinging to us, but it's starting to brighten, reminding me of time passing.

"Maybe Dory will let us leave it behind the shop," I say. "I'll pick it back up with Dove when I'm done."

Finn scratches Dove's rump with one finger, which makes her stamp her back hoof like he's a fly. He says, "Dove says she doesn't want to pull a cart after you make her run away from sea monsters."

"Dove says you'll look like an idiot pulling a pony cart."

He smiles vaguely at his stack of pottery boxes. "I don't mind."

"Obviously!" I snap.

We haven't come to an agreement by the time we load up, but there's no more time, so off we go, me leading Dove and Finn trailing behind. Puffin the cat follows us for a while, with Finn shooing at her, which only makes her longing to join us more intense.

Partway into town, I smell something like rotten meat on the wind, and Finn and I exchange glances. The island is no stranger to terrible smells — storms throw up great fish on to the beaches to rot, fishermen's spoils go bad on warm days, a cross-eyed wind brings the smell of brine and wet things in the evening – but this is not a sea smell. Something's died that shouldn't have and has been left where it shouldn't have been left. I don't want to stop, but it could be a person, so I make Finn stand by Dove's head as I climb up over the stone wall in the direction of the scent.

The wind is coming straight towards me – the wind manages to cut through the mist instead of pushing it out of the way – and I crumple over myself to stay warm as I step around sheep poo. All the while I am wishing that I could have sent Finn to investigate the smell, but he's queasy and useless with blood. So I am the lucky one to discover the source, which is a pile of parts that used to be a sheep. There's not much left but hooves, a bob of its short tail, a lump of its innards, which is what smells, and its furry skull, which is mangled and crushed around the eye socket. What's left of the wool at the back of the neck is spray-painted blue, to mark it as one of Hammond's flock. There isn't much back of the neck left to be painted, though. My skin prickles with an automatic tickle of fear, though I doubt that the *capall uisce* responsible is anywhere near. Still – this is far inland for one of the horses to come.

I return to Finn and Dove. They're playing a game that seems to involve him tapping Dove on the upper lip and Dove looking peevish. Finn looks up and I say, "Sheep."

He says, "I knew it was a sheep."

I reply, "Next time you can cast your seeing eye into the pasture before I walk through the mud."

"You didn't ask."

And we start on again towards Skarmouth.

We're headed to Dory Maud's shop, which is called Fathom & Sons for no reason that I can imagine, as Dory has no sons and no husband for that matter. She lives with her two sisters, neither of whom are named Fathom or have sons, and she collects things year-round to sell to tourists during October and November. As a child, the chief thing I noticed about Dory was that she was always wearing a different pair of shoes, a strange and extravagant thing on the island. Now mostly what I notice about her is that she and her sisters have no last name, a strange and extravagant thing just about anywhere.

Fathom & Sons is down one of the little side streets in Skarmouth, a stone-lined track barely wide enough for Dove and her pony cart. Neither the mist nor the sun can reach inside this alley, and we shiver as Dove's hoofsteps clatter and echo up the sides of the buildings.

Standing in the blue-morning shadows a few doors down is Jonathan Carroll, throwing pieces of biscuit at a collie. Both Carroll brothers have dark, curly hair, but one of them has a lump of uncooked dough for a brain and the other has a lump of uncooked dough for his lungs. Once, when I came into town with Mum, we ran across Brian, the one with dough for lungs, crouched by the quay, shaking and starving for air. Mum had told him to breathe all of the bad air out before he tried to get more in and then she'd left me watching him while she went to buy him a black coffee. I'd been very annoyed, because she'd promised me one of Palsson's cinnamon twists, which sold out very quickly. I'm a bit ashamed to recall that I told Brian that if he died and kept me from my cinnamon twist, I'd spit on his grave. I don't know if he remembers it at all, since he'd seemed very focused on breathing through a cup made of his hands. I hope he doesn't, because my character's improved a lot since then. Nowadays I would've only *thought* the spitting part instead of saying it to his face.

But, regardless, it's not Brian but Jonathan who's throwing biscuits. He looks at me and Dove and Finn and says merely, "Hi, pony," which only confirms that he's the one with dough for brains.

"Wait here," I tell Finn. "Start unloading. I'll see about the cart."

Fathom & Sons is a narrow, dark corridor of a shop, stuffed like a Cornish hen, with odds and ends labelled with little price tags that glow like white teeth in the dim light. It always smells a little like butter browning in a pan – so, like heaven. I'm not sure how many customers actually come into the shop itself to buy things; I think most of the business is done under a tent on weekends and during the rush for the races. So both the price tags and the delicious butter smell are probably unnecessary for most of the year.

Today is no exception; I take a deep, slightly hungry breath as I open the door. Inside the shop, the sisters are fighting, as usual. I have no sooner got inside the doorway and into the dim clutter than Dory Maud thrusts a catalogue into my hands.

"There," she says. "That. You'd buy from that, wouldn't you, Puck?" The sisters call me Puck instead of Kate because all three of the sisters agree that you should be called what you want to be called instead of simply falling into what you were given at birth. I don't remember ever telling them I wanted to be called Puck instead of Kate – both of them are my names – but still, I don't mind it.

"She's got no money at all," Elizabeth says dismissively from the stairs at the back of the shop. The stairs lead up to the first storey, which the sisters share. I've never been up there and I harbour a secret wish to. I think it must be all shoes and beds. And butter.

Elizabeth continues, "Of course it's going to look good to her."

I glance at what Dory Maud has thrust into my hand. To my surprise, it's a neatly printed catalogue for Fathom & Sons. When I tip my hands, it falls open to a random page with stylish black-and-white illustrations of a woman in a knitted sweater and a pair of hands wearing crocheted gloves and a disembodied neck bearing one of the rock cross necklaces that tourists love. The tidy letters describe each in uncompromising detail while a banner declares SEIZE YOUR HERITAGE! STRETCH YOUR PENNY WITH FASHION THAT LASTS! It looks like a real catalogue that the post boat brings, only it has all the things from the store in it. My bad mood melts away.

"This is amazing!" I say. I move slightly so the dusty antique fertility statue by the door will stop poking my shoulder with her stone fingers. She's been for sale for a long time. "How did you do it? Look at the letters! They're so perfect."

"Mr Davidge the printer did that," Dory Maud replies, pleased, looking over my other shoulder.

"Because Dory Maud did Mr Davidge," Elizabeth says from the stairs. She's still wearing her nightgown and her invented curls are two days old.

"Oh, go on back to bed," Dory replies, without heat. I don't want to think much on this. Dory is what Mum used to call a "strong-looking woman", which meant that, from the back, she looked like a man, and, from the front, you preferred the back. Elizabeth is the pretty sister, with long straw-coloured hair and a nose turned up by lineage and habit. No one notices what the third sister, Annie, looks like, because she's blind.

I page through the catalogue. I know that I'm being

stalled but I discover that I'm rather happy to be stalled. "Are our teapots in here? Who will see this?"

"Oh, the three people who read the adverts at the very end of the *Post*," Elizabeth says. She's gone up two more stairs but is far from back in bed. "And who are willing to wait a few years for shipping."

"The *Post*? On the mainland!" I exclaim. I've found our teapots — there is a very precise line drawing of one of the stout pots with my utilitarian thistles on the side of it, and now I can see that the illustrations are in the same hand that draws the adverts in the back of our own little Skarmouth newspaper that comes out each Wednesday. The printing says that the teapot pictured is a "representative design" and that "supplies are limited". It also says that they are signed and numbered, which my teapots are not. It is strange to think of something of mine heading over the ocean without me. I point to the signed bit and ask, "What's this?"

Dory Maud reads the description. "That makes them more valuable. It won't take you but a moment to sign and number them. Come in and have tea. Elizabeth will stop grousing. Where is your brother?"

"I can't stay," I say regretfully. "I need to take — Dove — tothebeach. Do you think Finn can leave the cart behind the shop when he's done unloading?" I run all the words together to avoid being asked about it, but the sisters aren't paying any attention, so I needn't have bothered. Dory Maud has opened the door and found

Finn standing there holding Puffin, who has followed us all the way to Skarmouth after all.

"I hope you enjoy the taste of poverty in your bowl," Elizabeth is saying. "The price of that advert was dear enough, but have you thought of what it will cost to ship those catalogues out to mainland wives?"

Dory Maud says, "They pay for the catalogue. It says that right in the advertisement that I showed to you not an hour ago. If you didn't have shingles for eyes, you might have seen it. Finn Connolly, come in here. Why do you have that cat? Is she for sale as well? Has it come to that?"

Finn says, "No, ma'am," as he enters the shop, where he gets poked directly in the chest by the fertility goddess. I move a step backwards so he can get away because the last thing I need is for Finn to suddenly decide to become fertile.

"I really have to go," I say. I don't want to seem rude.

"Where are you going again?" Dory Maud asks me.

"Perhaps I should ring Mr Davidge, too," Elizabeth says from the stairs. "Then I might not mind the bills, either. How is it done, sister? 'Mr Davidge, will you set my type?'"

Dory Maud turns to her and thunders pleasantly, "Shut up, you cow."

Finn wears his wide-eyed expression. So does Puffin.

Dory Maud seizes his arm with great enthusiasm and begins to propel him towards the back of the shop, where the teapot waits.

"Bye," I whisper to him. I feel a little bad about abandoning him to their clutches, but at least he'll get tea out of it.

I let the door close behind me.

Dove, patiently waiting by the door, looks up as I step out. Finn has unfastened the cart but she still wears her harness. She doesn't look much like a racehorse.

I pull my hair back into a new ponytail; two or three dozen strands had already begun to escape.

I probably don't look much like a jockey, either.

FIFTEEN

Sean

There's a girl on the beach.

The wind's torn the mist to shreds here by the ocean, so unlike on the rest of the island, the horses and their riders appear in sharp relief down on the sand. I can see the buckle on every bridle, the tassel on every rein, the tremor in every hand. It is the second day of training, and it's the first day that it isn't a game. This first week of training is an elaborate, bloody dance where the dance partners determine how strong the other ones are. It's when riders learn if charms will work on their mounts, how close to the sea is too close, how they can begin to convince their water horses to gallop in a straight line. How long they have between falling from their horses and being attacked. This tense courtship looks nothing like racing.

At first I see nothing out of the ordinary. There is the surviving Privett brother beating his grey *capall* with a switch and Hale selling charms that will not save you, and there is Tommy Falk flapping at the end of the lead as his black mare strains for the salt water.

And there is the girl. When I first see her and her dun mare from my vantage point on the cliff road, I am struck first not by the fact that she is a girl, but by the fact that she's in the ocean. It's the dreaded second day, the day when people start to die, and no one will get close to the surf. But there she is, trotting up to the knee in the water. Fearless.

I make my slow way down the cliff road to the sand. Any wicked thoughts Corr might have had this morning have been jolted out by his trot earlier. But the two mares are neither as tired nor as tame as Corr. Their hooves jangle every time they dance sideways; I've tied bells around their pasterns, reminding me every moment that I cannot let down my guard. The worse of the two mares wears a black netted cloth over her haunches. The cloth, passed down from my father, is made of thread and hundreds of narrow iron eyelets: part mourning cloth, part chain mail. I hope it weighs her to the ground. It's the sort of thing I'd never use on Corr – it would only make him irritable and uncertain, and in any case, we know each other better than that.

Now, closer to the surf, I see why the girl's so brave. Her horse is just an island pony, with a coat the colour of the sand, legs black as soaked kelp. I see from her belly that the poor Thisby grass has stuffed her but not fed her.

I want to know why she's on my beach. And I want to know why no one's confronting her. All of the horses are aware of her, though. Ears pricked, necks arched, lips curled up in her direction. And of course there's the piebald mare among them, wailing her hunger and desire. I should have known Gorry wouldn't let her go.

At the sound of the piebald *capall*, the dun island mare lays her ears back to her neck with fear. She knows that she's a meal here, that the sound the piebald makes is a plea for her death. The girl leans and pats the dun's neck, soothing her.

Reluctantly, I turn to go about my business. My mouth tastes of salt, and the wind finds me wherever I lead the horses. Today's one of those days where no one will get warm. I find a crevasse in the cliffs, a giant's axe mark, and lead the mares and Corr into it. The wind makes a muted scream at the apex of the crevasse, like someone dying out of sight. I draw a circle in the sand and spit into it.

Corr watches me. The mares watch the ocean. I watch the girl.

My thoughts turn the mystery of her presence over and over as I flip open my leather bag and remove the wax-paper bundle I put in there earlier. I toss the bits of meat into the circle, but the mares don't touch them. They're watching the pony and the girl in the ocean, a more interesting meal.

With the bag over my shoulder, I return to the mouth of the crevasse and cross my arms, waiting for a gap in the murder of horses and men to open so I can see the mare and girl again. There's nothing special about the mare, nothing at all. A fine enough head, good enough bone. As a pony, she is a beauty. As a *capall uisce*, she is nothing.

The girl, too, is nothing special – slight, with a ginger ponytail. She looks less afraid than her mare, but she's in more danger.

I hear one of my mares scream, and I turn long enough to flip open my bag and throw a handful of salt in her direction. She jerks her head up as some of it sprinkles her face; she's offended but not hurt. I look her in the eye long enough that she knows there's more where that came from. She's a bay, no white markings on her anywhere, which is supposed to speak to her speed, but I've yet to get her going in a straight enough line to find out.

I turn back to the ocean, and the wind throws sand in my face, hard enough to offend but not to hurt. I smile a thin smile at the irony and turn up my collar. The girl circles her pony through the water again. I have to appreciate that she's chosen the only place she can be sure that no one will approach her today. Of course, it's not just the *capaill uisce* on the beach the girl has to worry about, but I can tell that she's already considered that. She glances towards the curve of the incoming surf every so often. I can't imagine that she'd be able to see a hunting *capall uisce* – when they swim parallel to the breakers, fast and dark beneath the surface, they're almost impossible to see — but I also can't imagine not looking.

Somewhere close by, a man is moaning; he's been trampled or thrown or bitten. He sounds resentful or surprised. Did no one tell him that pain lives in this sand, dug in and watered with our blood?

I watch the girl's hands on the reins, the certainty of her seat. She can ride, but so can everyone on Thisby.

"I'll bet you haven't seen that before," says Gorry's gritty voice. "Their clothes don't come off with your eyes, Sean Kendrick."

I glance at him just long enough to see that he still has the piebald mare, and then a second longer so that he sees that I am looking at how he still has the piebald mare, and then I look back to the ocean. There is a knot of fighting horses in front of us, growling and pawing like tomcats. Bells ring sharply. Every water horse on this beach is hungry for the sea, hungry for the chase.

I glance at the piebald mare again. Gorry's knotted her halter with copper wire, which does nothing but look impressive.

"She's entered in the races," Gorry says. He's smoking, and he gestures towards the girl in the surf with his cigarette. "On that pony. That's what they're saying."

The smell of his cigarette stings worse than the wind. She means to race on that pony? She'll be dead in a week.

The piebald mare paws at the sand; I see her digging

out of the corner of my eye and hear her grinding her teeth. That bridle's her curse, this island her prison. She still smells of rot.

"I can't sell this mare – thanks for that," Gorry says. "Your expert opinion, heh." I don't know what to tell him. When you traffic in monsters, that's the risk you run, that you'll find one too monstrous to stomach.

Bells jangle again, and I look away from the beach, trying to find the sound with my eyes. It is not my mares; it's not the piebald. It's just one horse in a throng of horses, but there's a sharp urgency to the sound that calls to me. Danger sings on the breeze, throws echoes off the sheer white cliffs. There are too many people on horseback today trying to prove themselves, trying to prepare, trying to get faster. They haven't discovered yet that it's not the fastest who make it to race day.

You only have to be the fastest of those who are left.

Suddenly, there's a shout and a terrible screaming whinny, and I turn in time to see Jimmy Blackwell throwing himself from his white-grey stallion as it leaps into the pounding waves. Blackwell rolls narrowly out of the way of another pair of spooking *uisce* mares. He's older, defter. He's survived a half-dozen Scorpio Races.

"And you thought this mare would be trouble," Gorry says. He laughs.

I'm listening, but I'm watching, too. Blackwell is still pulling himself clear of the rioting mares. It's just a petty disagreement between two savage horses, but they're all teeth and hooves. One of the men tries to tear them apart, but he's too cavalier. There's a snap of blunt teeth and just like that, his fingers are gone. Someone shouts "Hey!" but nothing else, moved by the need to speak but having nothing else to say.

My eyes flick beyond all of them to the water to where Blackwell's stallion half leaps, half swims, the water frothing white beneath him. His eyes are on that dun island pony and the girl on her back.

I hear a wail, and at first I think it is a scream, but then I hear my name. "*Where's Kendrick?*"

Someone is about to die.

I set my bag down by the cliffs, out of the way, and I begin to run, heels digging deep into the sand. I can only be in one place at a time, and the fight on the beach is out of my control. In the surf, the dun pony is chest deep in the water and the white stallion rears before her, hooves slicing down towards the girl. The girl jerks the dun mare off balance, sparing them both from the hooves but delivering the girl into the freezing water.

And that was what the *capall uisce*, a fearful dull Pegasus with disintegrating wings of sea foam, wanted. His teeth flash, the colour of dead coral, and his great head smashes against the girl as her head comes up above water. Teeth clamp on to her hooded sweater; legs kick in preparation for his dive. I am already in the water, my fingers numb with the cold, and I swim to him through this perilous water, my progress agonizingly slow. The girl keeps going below water and clawing her way back up.

I drag myself closer with the floating hairs of his tail. I straddle his back and grab a handful of mane as I make my way up his neck. There is no time to trace the outlines of his veins with iron or push him widdershins. He is beyond anything I could whisper in his ear. There is only time for me to grip a handful of death-red holly berries from my coat pocket and to press them into his flared nostrils.

His massive legs slash convulsively through the water, and I see one of his knees glance off the girl's head. I can't see if she stays above water, though, because now the stallion is snorting, seaweed and jelly and bits of coral all spewing from his nostrils around the red berries, and in his drowning and his death throes, it's taking all my energy to keep from going underwater with him.

The stallion's jaw swings towards me, wide open, and I see, in a suddenly frozen moment of time, the coarseness of the hairs on his jaw and the way that salt water has beaded along them.

My vision explodes into one thousand colours, not one of them the sky.

And then, in a rush of sound, my sight returns, and with it, sensation: the girl's hand pulling my head above water and the sting of ocean in my nostrils. The white *capall* is nothing but his mane floating in the water, the surf kicking his corpse towards the beach. The dun pony stands on the sand and whinnies to the girl, a high, anxious sound. There's blood in the water and blood there on the sand, too, where the man lost his fingers. They are still calling my name on the beach, though I can't tell if it's to solicit my help or to solicit help for me. The girl coughs but no water comes up. She's shivering, though her eyes are fierce.

I've killed one of the beautiful, deadly *capaill uisce* that I love, and I've nearly died, and a fever is racing through my veins, but all I can find to say to the girl is "Keep your pony off this beach."

Sixteen

Puck

I'm still shaking and coughing by the time I get into the yard. Dove spooks at every shadow, her every movement as jerky as a puppet's. Even the sound of the gate closing behind her sends her dashing further into the paddock, her haunches tucked underneath her. I'm lucky she's not lame.

I close my eyes. I'm lucky she's not *dead*.

It only took moments for the stallion to overpower us, and in another moment, I would've been under the water for good.

I lean on the gate, waiting for Dove to calm down enough to pick at her hay – she doesn't – until I'm too cold in my wet clothing. Inside, I peel off my layers and replace them with new ones, but I'm still freezing.

She could've died.

In the kitchen, I eat an entire orange and a piece of bread slathered with quite a bit of our precious butter. The price of an orange is so dear that normally I would have borrowed one of Mum's techniques for making each fruit go as far as possible. With a few oranges, Mum would make an orange cake, flavour butter or icing for a treat, and simmer some marmalade with the rest. If we did eat an orange just as an orange, we'd share the sections among us.

But I eat the entire thing, and by the time I get to the end of it, I've stopped shivering. My head still thuds dully from where the *capall uisce*'s knee hit it.

I suck on my index finger to get the last of the orange flavour, but all I taste is salt from the ocean, which makes me even more irritable. My first day on the beach with Dove and all I have to show for it is sand in every crevice of my skin and a kick in the head.

I couldn't even make it one day without being rescued.

I keep trying to put Sean Kendrick out of my head, but my mind keeps conjuring up images of his sharp face and the sound of his voice made hoarse by swallowing the sea. And every time I relive the moment, my face flushes hot with embarrassment again.

I run a hand over my forehead, which is gritty with salt, and sigh a long, shuddering breath.

Keep your pony off this beach.

I want to give up. I'm doing all this to win just a few bare weeks with Gabriel on the island. And for what purpose? I haven't seen a hair on his head since I announced I was racing. My plan seems suddenly foolish. So I'm going to make an idiot of myself in front of the entire island and possibly get myself and Dove killed for a brother who can't be bothered to come home anyway.

The idea of throwing in the towel is simultaneously relieving and discomfiting. I can't bear the idea of going back to the beach. But I can't even imagine telling Gabe that I changed my mind. It's hard to think that I have enough pride left to damage, but there it is.

There's a knock on the door. I don't have any time to make my hair look better – actually, I don't think there is a way to make it better; it has that greasy, thick feeling of hair bathed in salt water. My heart feels leaden inside me. I can't think of anyone positive who knocks on the door.

The door opens and it's Benjamin Malvern. I know it's Benjamin Malvern because there's a signed photo of him on the wall behind the bar at the Black-Eyed Girl. I once asked Dad why it was there, and he said that was because Benjamin Malvern had given a lot of money to the pub so it could open. But I still didn't see why that was a good reason to have someone's signature on your wall.

"Gabriel Connolly here?" Malvern asks as he comes into the kitchen. I'm left holding the door open. The richest man on Thisby stands in our house with his arms crossed, his gaze shifting from the cluttered kitchen counter to the collapsed pile of wood and peat by the sitting room fireplace to the saddle I've perched on the back of Dad's armchair. He wears a V-necked wool sweater and a tie. He's got grey hair and is not good-looking. He smells nice, which I resent.

I don't close the door. It seems like closing the door would be like saying that I invited him in, and I didn't.

"Not at present," I say.

"Ah," says Malvern. He's still looking around. "And you're the sister."

"Kate Connolly," I clarify, with as many bristles as I can manage.

"Yes. I think we should have some tea."

He sits at our table.

"Mr Malvern," I start, sternly.

"Good, you know who I am. That saves us some trouble. Now, I wouldn't presume to tell you your business, but it's cold out there and an open door makes a very poor windbreak."

I shut it. I shut my mouth as well. I start to make some tea. I'm equal parts offended and curious.

"What brings you this way?" I ask. I'm unhappy about how polite I sound.

His eyes were on my saddle but he shifts them to me when I speak. I'm intimidated by them, a little. The rest of him looks like a moneyed old man, but his eyes are clever.

"Unpleasant business." But he says it pleasantly.

"I would have thought that you have people to do

your unpleasant business for you," I say, and feel cheeky. "Sugar or milk?"

"Butter, milk, and salt, please."

I turn to Malvern, sure I'll see humour on his face. But there isn't any. I'm not sure, now that I think of it, that it's a face I could imagine humour on. It's more like a face I can imagine on a pound note. I hand him his cup of tea, a salt shaker, and our little butter bowl. Sitting down with the milk jug opposite, I watch him slice a small piece of butter into his tea, add a healthy dose of salt, and top it all up with milk before stirring it thoroughly. The liquid has a froth on it. It looks like something I saw come out from under a cow once. I don't think that he'll drink it, but he does.

Malvern braces his fingers on the edge of his teacup. "Is that your pony outside?"

"Horse," I say. "She's fifteen two hands."

"You'd get better performance out of her with better food," Malvern tells me. "Switch her from that poor hay and she'd have more energy. Less of a hay belly."

Of course she'd have more energy on better hay and grain.

I'd have more energy if I were eating something besides beans and apple cake, too, but we're both going without better for the same reason.

We drink our tea. I think about Finn coming home right now and finding Malvern at our kitchen table. I sweep some crumbs into a pyramid behind the butter bowl.

"So your parents are dead," Benjamin Malvern says.

I set my teacup down.

"Mr Malvern."

"I know the story already," he interrupts me. "I don't want to talk about that. I want to know what comes after the story. What are you three – it is three, isn't it? – doing with yourselves?"

I try to imagine how my parents would handle this situation. They were unfailingly polite and private. I am good at one of those things. Uncomfortably, I say, "We're getting along. Gabe works at the hotel. Finn and I do odd jobs. Paint things for tourists."

"Making enough for tea," Malvern says, but his eyes are on the pantry door. I know he saw its lack of contents when I took out the butter bowl.

"We're getting along," I repeat.

Malvern swallows the last of his tea – how he's managed to drink that concoction so fast and without holding his nose is beyond me – and rests his crossed arms on the table. He leans towards me so I smell his cologne.

"I am here to evict you."

For a moment, it doesn't mean anything, and then I scramble to my feet. My head pounds like the surf where the water horse struck it. I keep replaying that sentence.

He continues, "No one has made payments on this house for a year, and I wanted to see who lived here. I wanted to see your faces when I told you."

I think, just then, that in an island populated by monsters, he's more monstrous than any. My tongue takes a long time to unstick. "I thought the house was paid for. I didn't know."

"Gabriel Connolly knew better, and has for quite a while," Malvern says. His voice is calm. He's watching my reaction carefully. I cannot believe that I've served him tea.

I look at him and smash my lips together. I want to be sure I don't say something I will regret. I am struck, more than anything, by the sense of betrayal: that Gabe knew that we were living in a ticking time bomb and didn't tell us. Finally, I manage, "And what is it that you see in my face right now? Is it what you came to see?"

It comes out like a challenge, but Malvern seems unflustered. He just nods a little. "Yes. Yes, I think so. Now tell me this: what are you and your brothers willing to do to save this house?"

There was a problem with dogfighting on the island a few years back. Bored, drunk fishermen raised island dogs to tear each other's faces off. I feel like one of those dogs now. Malvern has thrown me into the pit and is now peering over the side to see what I will do. He wants to see if I will retreat or if there's fight in me.

I won't give him the satisfaction of seeing me give up. My future crystallizes suddenly.

"Give me three weeks," I say.

Malvern doesn't dance around the point. "After the races."

I wonder if he's thinking that it's crazy that a girl like me is riding in the races and that there's no point waiting until the end of the month because there will be no money because I will be dead last or just plain dead.

Keep your pony off this beach.

I just nod.

"You don't stand a chance," Malvern says, but without malice. "On that pony. Why her?"

Horse, I think. "The *capaill uisce* killed my parents. I'm not going to dishonour them by riding one of the water horses."

Malvern doesn't smile, but his eyebrows lighten like he's considering it. "That's noble. It's not because no one would give you a chance on one of the *capaill*?"

"I had a chance to be a fifth," I shoot back. "I chose not to."

Malvern considers all this. "There's only real money if you win."

"I know," I say.

"And you really expect me to put this off on the idea that you and that island pony will cross that line before everyone else?"

I look at his silly teacup with his silly tea in it. Wasn't regular tea interesting enough? Who drank their tea with butter and salt? Nobody but bored old men who ran their islands like a chess game. I say, "I think you're interested to see what will happen. And you've already waited twelve months."

Malvern pushes his chair back and stands up. From his pocket, he takes out a piece of paper, unfolds it, and lays it on the table. It's an official document. I recognize his signature at the bottom. My father's, too. He says, "I'm not a generous person, Kate Connolly."

I don't answer. We regard each other.

He pushes the document across the table with two fingers. "Show that to your older brother. I'll be back to collect it when you're dead."

SEVENTEEN

Sean

They're all afraid.

I sit in a boat, half-turned, watching my charge. The boat has the words *Black as the Sea* painted in white on its black hull. Behind it swims Fundamental, a bay colt full of promise and promises, a sport-horse colt poised to sell for hundreds on the mainland. One of the colts I'm sure Malvern means to tempt George Holly with. Fundamental's coat is turned dark by the water. He snorts out water and breath every few strokes, but shows no sign of tiring. Boat and horse make their slow way across the sheltered cove. The cliffs here are slanted, like a child shoved them over, and they block most of the wind and all of the waves. The sound of the boat's motor slaps back at me.

Normally, I would find this ordinary training a bitter drink during race month. But after the strange morning, I'm relieved to have a few moments to sit and let my mind work over events. I still cannot imagine what that girl was thinking.

I glance up to the mouth of the cove. One of the

new men, Daly, stands watch. With the clatter of the boat's motor and the ripple of Fundamental's breaths, I'm unable to keep an eye out for hunting *capaill uisce*. This cove is easy to protect, however; its narrow mouth means that one can keep watch while the other trains. Swimming is such a low-impact way to build strength that it's worth the risk. Daly has a shotgun, which won't do much, but he also has a set of lungs, which should give me enough time to get Fundamental out of the water.

Daly is from the mainland, and he's young and nervous. I prefer nervous to cocky. He needs to be my eyes, and my eyes would be fixed on that narrow passage into the cove.

Fundamental keeps swimming. I was there when he was born, just a collection of knobby joints and massive eyes. He doesn't look at me as he swims. Behind the boat, swimming is his sole purpose. He has enough *capall uisce* blood in him to lend him a single-mindedness. I have to watch him as closely as Daly guards the entrance to the cove. Fundamental would swim until he sank.

Tomorrow, Malvern will want me to assign Mutt a horse. Every year on the third day, he asks me to decide, and every year I'm afraid he will ask me to put Mutt on Corr.

I cannot bear the thought of it.

Fundamental shakes his head, as if to unstick his wet mane from his neck. I lean to make certain that he's not tiring. Exercising in the water is lower impact than on land, but I don't want him exhausted; I was told buyers are coming to look at him tomorrow.

I feel disquieted. I'm not certain why. If it's because of the girl, interrupting the routine I've followed for years. Or if it's because of Mutt's piss in my boots. Or if it's because, as we make our way back across the cove, the water level against the cliffs appears slightly wrong to me. Too high, perhaps. The sky is bright and populated with fluffy clouds; if there's to be a storm, it's days away.

But I cannot settle.

"Kendrick! Kendrick!"

My name, a shout made thin by the boat motor.

I have seconds to see it:

Daly is standing on the small crescent beach by the boat slip, far from the cove's entrance. I don't have time to think about why he's moved. The shout is his.

There's a silhouette at the point of the cove where Daly had been. Mutt Malvern. Just watching me. No — watching a point in the water just before me.

A slight drop in the water only ten metres from us.

I know that dip, that unnatural crevice into the sea. It looks like nothing, but it's what happens to the salt water when there's a massive body travelling very fast just under the surface.

There's no time to make it to shore.

Fundamental kicks his hind legs, his head thrown back.

Then he goes under.

Mutt Malvern stands motionless at the point of the cove.

I dive into the water.

EIGHTEEN

Sean

I'm not swimming through water. I'm swimming through blood. It billows around me in great underwater thunderheads as one of my hands finds Fundamental's spine. In my other hand I have a fistful of the holly berries. I've gone years without using them to kill one of the water horses, and now I have them in my palm twice in one day.

Fundamental's spine writhes. I feel a strange sucking sensation beneath me as one of his legs cuts through the water under my feet, the current dragging at me. I feel forward along his mane. My lungs feel pressed small in my chest.

I can't see, and then I can.

Fundamental's eye is wide open, white all around it, but he can't see me. A slick, dark *capall uisce* holds Fundamental's throatlatch in its jaws. Blood floats from a ragged tear like steam. The *uisce* horse's legs slice through the salt water, smooth and purposeful. It spares no attention for me. The *capall uisce* has the colt in a steel grasp and I, a small, vulnerable stranger in this world, am no threat.

I need a breath. I need more than a breath. I need a long gasp and another one and another one. But in front of me I see the *capall*'s nostrils, long and thin. The berries are hard and deadly in my hand. I could watch it drown.

But next to their two heads, I see the edge of Fundamental's wound. The colt's great, brave heart pumps his life out in time with my hammering pulse.

There's no saving him from this.

I watched him being born. Fundamental, rare colt, so close to the water horses that he loves the ocean like I do.

Colours without any name flicker at the corner of my vision.

I have to leave him behind.

NINETEEN

Finn and I both wait up for Gabe that night. I boil beans — infernal beans, it feels like that's all we eat — and simmer inside my skin, planning what I will say to him when he gets here. Finn messes over the windows while I cook, and when I ask him what he's doing, he says something about a storm. Outside the window, the night-darkening sky is clear except for some high, wispy clouds thin enough to see through, far out at the horizon. There's no sign of foul weather. Who knows why Finn does any of the things he does? I don't even try to talk him out of his fiddling.

We wait and wait for Gabe, my sense of betrayal simmering and then boiling and then simmering again. It's impossible to be angry for so long. I wish I could talk to Finn about what's eating me, but I can't tell him about Malvern. It'll just make him start picking at his arms and obsessing over his morning rituals even longer than usual.

"What do you think," I ask casually, turning the little butter bowl around and around again, so that the

141

owl painted on the side looks at me and then Finn and then me again, "about selling the Morris – why are you laughing?"

He rattles at one of the windowpanes experimentally. "It's not even running."

"If it *was* running?"

"I might fix it tomorrow," Finn says vaguely. I think, now, that he is using the windows as an excuse to stare outside for signs of Gabe. "I don't want it to be out there when the storm gets bad."

"Rain, yes, sure," I say. "Selling it. What do you think?"

"Well, I guess that depends on why we're selling it."

"To get Dove better food during training."

There is an agonizingly long pause before Finn responds. During the pause, he taps his finger all along the edge of a pane of glass before leaning in to peer at the join between glass and wood from a couple of centimetres away. He seems quite content to finish experimenting with his weatherproofing before continuing the conversation.

Finally, he says, "Is better food that expensive?"

"Do you see alfalfa growing on this island?"

"It depends," Finn says. "I don't know what alfalfa looks like."

"Like the inside of your dusty head. Yes, it's expensive. It comes from the mainland." I feel slightly bad about snapping at him. It's not his fault that I'm cross — it's Gabe's. I can't believe that I might not get to confront him tonight about Malvern's appearance at the house. I can't stay up for him. I have to be up early tomorrow if I'm going back to the beach again.

Finn looks mournful. I feel terrible. Maybe there's something else we can sell, like the useless chickens that spend most of their time dying before we can kill them for dinner. The whole lot of them would buy one bale of hay and not a bite of good grain.

"Will it make her faster?" Finn asks.

"Racehorses should eat racehorse food."

Finn casts a glance towards our dinner, beans with a lump of bacon donated by Dory Maud. "If that's what it takes."

He sounds like I've asked him to saw off his left leg. But I know how he feels. He loves the Morris like I love Dove, and what will he have left if he doesn't have the car to putter over? Just the windows, and we only have five of them in the house.

"If I win," I tell him, "we'll have enough money to buy it back." He still looks glum, so I go on. "We'll have enough to buy two of them. A car to pull the other car when the engine stops on the first one."

Now he has the ghost of a smile. We sit down and eat our beans with the lump of bacon. Without saying anything about it, we eat the rest of the apple cake, not leaving any for Gabe. Two people at a table meant for five. I don't see how I'll be able to sleep with this knot of anger inside me. Where is he?

I think about that decapitated sheep that Finn and I found on the way to Skarmouth. How are we supposed to know if Gabe's working late or if he's dead by the side of the road? How is he supposed to know if we're home safely or dead by the side of the road, for that matter?

Finn is the one who says it finally. "It's like he's already gone."

TWENTY

Sean

That night, instead of dreaming, I lie in my bed and stare at the small square of black sky that I can see out of the window of my flat. Though I'm dry now, I feel cold to my bones, as if I've swallowed the sea and it lives inside me. My arms ache. I'm holding up the cliffs.

I think of Fundamental swimming so purposefully behind the boat. No, that's not what I think of. I think of Fundamental's head thrown back, the whites of his eyes, the vanishing beneath the water churned to mist around me.

Again and again I dive into the water. Again and again it is too dark, too cold, too fast, too late.

Again and again I see Mutt Malvern standing on the point of the cove, watching.

I haven't heard from Benjamin Malvern yet, but I will. It's just a matter of time.

Kendrick! Daly's voice, warning me, too late.

I can't stay in bed any longer. I roll to my feet. My jacket is still wet and gritty where I hung it over the iron curl of the radiator. Without turning on the light,

I find my trousers and my wool sweater and make my way down the narrow stairs to the stables.

The three light bulbs that have been installed in the main aisle illuminate circles just below them. Everything else is in shadow; the way the sound of my breath disappears makes the darkness feel vast. As the thoroughbreds and the draught horses hear my footsteps down the aisle, they nicker hopefully. After what happened this afternoon, I can't look at them. I watched them all being born, just as I watched Fundamental being born.

I can't block out their sounds as I pass, though. They slowly chew hay and stomp their hooves as an itch tickles their legs. Straw whispers against straw. Comfortable horse sounds.

I walk past all of them to the stall at the end of the aisle, and there is Corr. Just out of the reach of the light, he is the colour of old, dried blood. I lean on the edge of the stall, looking in. Unlike the land horses, Corr doesn't loiter over hay all night or sigh through his lips. Instead, he stands in the centre of his stall, utterly still, his ears pricked. There is something in his eyes that the thoroughbreds will never have: something intense and predatory.

He looks at me with his left eye and then looks past me, listening. There is no way for him to relax; with the sound of this rising sea, with the smell of horse blood on my hands, with me restless before him.

I don't know why Mutt Malvern was in Daly's place,

and I don't know how he thinks it will escape his canny father that Mutt was on the point when the *capall uisce* entered the cove. I think of Fundamental again, of his wide, rolling eyes. Mutt was willing to sacrifice him for the possibility that it would hurt me. For the possibility of getting what he wanted.

What am I willing to risk for the possibility of getting what I want?

"Corr," I whisper.

Instantly the red stallion's ears turn to me. His eyes are black and mysterious, pieces of the ocean. He is more dangerous every day. We are more dangerous every day.

I can't bear the idea that Mutt Malvern would ride him if I left.

Mutt thinks Benjamin Malvern will have my job for what happened today. I could just quit, instead. I think of the satisfaction of that possibility, of taking the money I've saved and leaving the Malverns and everything they own behind.

Corr makes a night noise — a barely audible, descending wail. It's the sound of a scream underwater. But from Corr, it's a homing beacon. A confirmation that waits for an answer.

I cluck my tongue, once, and he immediately falls quiet. Neither of us moves towards the other, but we both ease our weight off one foot at the same time. I sigh, and he sighs as well.

I can't go without Corr.

TWENTY-ONE

Puck

Based upon my experience on the beach the day before, I form a new plan. Brave high tide, with its possibility of water horses swimming up from the ocean, instead of riding later, at low tide, with its certainty of water horses menacing me on the beach. So I set my alarm clock for five o'clock and saddle Dove before she's properly awake.

Gabe is already gone. I'm not even sure if he came home. I'm a little glad for the treacherous dark slope, because it doesn't let my thoughts linger on what his absence means for us.

Once we've reached the base of the cliffs, I have to move slowly, trying not to lead Dove into any of the boulders that scatter above the high waterline. What little light there is reflects off Dove's breath, turning it white and solid. It's so dark that I can hear the sea better than I can see it. *Shhhhh, shhhhhh*, it says, like I'm a fretful child and it's my mother, though if the sea were my mother, I'd rather have been an orphan.

Dove is alert, her eyes pricked to the tide, which

is still a bit too high for proper training. When dawn finally arrives good and proper, the sea will grudgingly give up several dozen metres of packed sand for the riders to train on, giving them more room to get away from the ocean. But now, the surf is still wild and close, cramping me to the cliff walls.

I don't feel brave.

High tide, full dark, under a nearly November sky – the ocean near Thisby holds so many *capaill uisce* right now. I know that Dove and I are vulnerable on this dark beach. There could be a water horse in the surf right now.

My heart's a low throb in my ears. *Shhhhhh, shhhhhh,* says the sea, but I don't believe her. I adjust my stirrups. Dove doesn't take her ears from the surf. I don't mount up. I strain my ears for any sounds of life. There's just the ocean. The sea glints suddenly, like a crafty smile. That could be a reflection off a *capall uisce*'s sinuous spine.

Dove would know. I have to trust her. Her ears are still pricked. She's watchful but not wary. I kiss her dusty shoulder for luck and mount up. I steer her as far away from the tide as I can. Too far up and the sand gives way to pebbles and rocks, impossible to ride on. Too far down and *shhhhhhhh, shhhhhh.*

I warm Dove up in easy, trotted circles. I keep waiting for my body to relax, to forget where I am, but I can't. Every reflection on the water makes me jerk. My body is screaming at me about the threat of that black ocean. I remember the story we're all told as soon as we become teens, of the two teen lovers who met illicitly on the beach, only to be dragged into the waves by a waiting water horse. It was considered a good cautionary tale to all the youth of Skarmouth: that would teach us to kiss.

But that story never seemed real, told in a classroom or related over a counter. Here on the beach, it feels like a promise. But it's no use to think about that. I need to use my time wisely. I try to pretend I'm up in the muddy pasture. For endless minutes Dove and I exercise like this, trotting one way and then the other, then cantering one way, and then the other. I stop between them to listen. To scan the darkness for anything more dark. Dove is calming down, but I can't stop shivering. Both because it's cold and because I'm still wound so tight.

There's just barely a bit of dawn, far away on the horizon. The others will be here soon.

I stop Dove and listen. Nothing but *shhhhhh, shhhhhh.*

I wait for a long, long moment. Only the ocean.

And then I push her into a gallop.

Joyfully she springs forward, tail snapping in her thrill. The waves become one long dark blur beside us and the cliffs transform into a wall of formless grey. Now I can't hear the ocean's shushing, only the pounding of Dove's hooves and the huffing of her breath.

My hair escapes from its ponytail and beats my face, tiny lashes from tiny whips. Dove bucks once, twice, from the sheer excitement of running, and I laugh at her. We pull up short and race back the way we came.

I think I see someone standing up at the top of the cliffs, watching us, but when I look again, there's no one.

I consider the morning's work. Dove is out of breath, and I'm out of breath, and the sea is retreating. The other riders have yet to come down to the beach, and we're already done for the day.

This might work.

I don't know how fast we were, but right now it doesn't matter. One victory at a time.

TWENTY-TWO

Sean

There's no one on the second floor of the tearoom at this time of day. It is only me and a herd of small, cloth-covered tables, each bearing a purple thistle flower in a vase. The room is long and narrow and low-ceilinged; it feels like a pleasant coffin or a suffocating church. Everything glows in slightly rose hues because of the pink lacy curtains in front of the small windows behind me. I am the darkest thing in the room.

Evelyn Carrick, the young daughter of the owner, stands by the table I sit at and asks what I'd like. She doesn't look at me, which is all right, because I don't look at her, either. I look at the little printed card on the tablecloth in front of me.

There are some French words on the menu. The items in English are long and descriptive. Even if I wanted to order tea, I'm not sure I would recognize it.

"I'll wait," I say.

She hesitates. Her eyes flicker to me and away again, like a horse uncertain about an unfamiliar object. "May I take your coat?"

"I'll keep it." Having dried on my radiator overnight, my jacket is crisp with salt water and stained with mud and blood. Every day that I've been on the beach is written on it. I can't imagine her touching it with her small white hands.

Evelyn does something complicated and useful-looking with the napkin and saucer on the other side of the table, and then slips back down the narrow stairs. I listen to the creak of her footsteps; every single step pops and groans. The tall, narrow teahouse is one of the oldest buildings in Skarmouth, pressed right against the grocer and post office. I wonder what it was before it sold *petit pain*.

Malvern is late for the appointment he has set, an appointment whose timing I was expecting, if not the location. I turn to look out of the rose-curtained window at the street below. Already there are a few long-necked tourists down there, here in advance of the festival, and I can hear the drummers practising a few streets away. In a few days, I think the tables on this level of the teahouse will be full, as will the streets. At the end of the festival, the other riders and I will be paraded among the crowd. If I still have my job.

I pull up the cuff of my sleeve a little to look at my wrist; the stiff jacket has rubbed my skin raw during the morning's training. There was a fight this morning among the horses and I had to intervene. I wish Gorry would give up trying to sell the piebald mare; she's a bad influence on the others.

The stairs pop and growl as someone heavier than Evelyn climbs them. Benjamin Malvern strides across the room and then stands by the table until I rise to greet him. Malvern, who has been moneyed for his whole life, has that air about him of well-cared-for ugliness, like an expensive racehorse with a coarse head. The glossy coat, the bright eye, the bulbous nose over too-fleshy lips.

"Sean Kendrick," he says. "How are you?"

"Tolerable," I reply.

"How is the sea?" This is where he makes a joke to show empathy with me, and where I pretend it is funny to show I appreciate my salary.

I smile thinly. "Well as always."

"Shall we sit?"

I let him sit first, and then follow him. He picks up the menu card but doesn't read it. "So you are ready for the festival this weekend?"

The stairs creak again and it's Evelyn. She sets a cup full of frothy liquid in front of Malvern.

"What'll you have?" she asks me again.

"I'm fine."

"He'll not abuse your hospitality, dear," Malvern tells her. "Bring him a cup of tea."

I nod to Evelyn. Malvern doesn't seem to notice her going.

"No sense going without, when there's unpleasant business making it unpleasant enough," Malvern says. He drinks his strange, frothy tea.

I am still and silent.

"You're a man of no words, Sean Kendrick," he says. Outside the window, the practising Scorpio drummers beat a tripping, ascending rhythm firmly at odds with the soft pink world we're in. He leans forward, elbows on the table. "I don't think I've told you the story of how I got into horses, have I?"

I meet his eyes.

He goes on. "I was young, poor, an islander, but not on this island. I had nothing to my name but my shoes and the bruises on my skin. There was a man who sold horses down the road from us. Royal horses and nags, jumping horses and eating horses. Every month there would be an auction and people would come from further than you've been in your life to see it."

He pauses, only to see if I am sad that my legs have grown into this island already. When he doesn't find what he's looking for, Malvern goes on, "He got this one stallion in, golden like Midas touched him. Seventeen, eighteen hands tall, mane and tail like a lion's. To see him in the yard was to know what a horse should look like, but there was a problem: no one could back him. He'd thrown four men and killed another and he was eating four or eight bales of hay a day and no one would touch an unbackable man-killer at that auction. So I told the man that I would break him, and if I did, he'd give me a job and I'd never be poor again. The horsemonger told me he couldn't promise me that I'd never be poor again, but he'd give me a job as long as he was alive. So I took that golden stallion and I bridled him. I cut a blindfold from a virgin's dress and covered his eyes and I backed him. We galloped all over the countryside, him blind and me a king, and when I brought him back, he was tame, and I had a job. What do you think of that?"

I look at Malvern. He tips his foreign tea against his lips. I can smell the butter in it from here.

"I don't believe you," I say. When Malvern raises an eyebrow, I add, "You were never young."

"And here I was thinking you had no sense of humour, Mr Kendrick." He pauses as Evelyn sets my cup of tea before me. She offers milk and sugar and I shake my head. Malvern waits until she has gone back down the stairs before he speaks again.

Malvern puts a napkin over the top of his teacup, as if it's a corpse instead of an empty cup. "My son says you killed one of my horses."

Anger touches the top of my mouth, my chest, with a hot hand.

"You look unsurprised," Malvern adds.

"I'm not surprised," I say.

Outside, the Scorpio drummers beat closer, louder, and there is laughter among them. One of the laughs in particular is a low, derisive chuckle, the sort that elicits a frown from those not in on the joke. Malvern's eyebrows draw down over his eyes, and his head is cocked as if he can imagine the scene outside more clearly than my face. The drums now sound quite intentionally like hoofbeats, and I wonder if he is seeing again the golden stallion the size of a barn galloping over the countryside of some alien island.

"Quinn Daly told me what he saw," Malvern says. "He told me how you were exercising Fundamental in the cove. He said that you seemed distracted. He said your mind was far from your job and you would have never seen a threat in the water."

Of course I had been distracted. That ginger-haired girl and her island pony and the smears of blood on the sand from the savage mares. I cannot imagine that Malvern will fire me for this, cannot imagine that he would fire me for anything, but then again, I can. I stand on a knife blade.

I meet Malvern's gaze. "What else did Quinn Daly tell you?"

"That Matthew told Daly he would relieve him at his post and watch the cove. That the next thing Daly saw was Fundamental going under and you diving after him." Malvern folds his hands together on the table before him. "But that is not the account my son gave. It's their words against each other. What do you have to say?"

I set my teeth. This is an unwinnable game. I drag the words out. "I cannot speak out against your son."

"You don't have to," Malvern answers. "Your jacket tells me which story is the true one."

We're both silent.

Finally, Malvern says, "I would know your mind. What is it you want out of this life?"

The question catches me off guard. There may have been a person who I would turn the pockets of my heart out for them to see, but there was never a time when Benjamin Malvern was that person. I can't imagine confessing my wants to Malvern any more than I can imagine him confessing his to me.

With his gaze on me, I say, "A roof over my head and reins in my hand and the sand beneath me." A slender and abridged truth.

"Ah, so you have what you want already, then."

I cannot sit here drinking this tea and tell him that what I want is to be free of him.

"It has been a long time since I broke that first stallion," Malvern says. "I don't know what it looked like from the outside, this path I took to get to this ruin of an island in the middle of the ocean. I can't compare Matthew's path to see where he might be going."

There are many paths that Mutt Malvern might be on, but I think we both know that none of them ends as the mogul of an internationally famous breeding yard.

"Ah, well. Have you been at this long enough to know how the horses will go?" Malvern means which of his water horses is the fastest.

"I knew that the first day."

Malvern smiles. It is not a pleasant smile, but its unpleasantness is not directed towards me. "Which, then, is the slowest of them?"

"The bay mare without white," I say, without pause. I haven't named her because she has yet to earn a name. She's flighty and sea-wild; she is not fast because she takes no pleasure in what the rider wants.

Malvern asks, "And which is the fastest?"

I pause before answering. I know what I say dictates who he puts Mutt on this November. I don't want to answer truthfully, but there is no point lying, as he'll find out eventually. "Corr. The red stallion."

Malvern says, "And which is the safest?"

"Edana. The bay with the white blaze."

Malvern looks at me then. Really looks at me, for the first time. He frowns, as if he is seeing me anew, the boy who has spent years growing up above his stable, raising his horses. I look at my teacup. He asks, "Why did you jump into the sea after Fundamental?"

"He was my charge."

"Your charge, but a Malvern horse. My son owned that horse." Benjamin Malvern pushes his chair back and stands. "Matthew will ride Edana. Turn the other bay loose, unless you think she'll shape up next year."

He looks at me for verification. I shake my head.

"Turn her loose, then. And you'll" – he tucks some coins beneath the edge of his teacup – "you'll ride Corr."

Every year I wait and wait for him to say it. Every year when he makes his decision, it eases my heart.

But this year, I feel like I'm still waiting.

TWENTY-THREE

Puck

By lunch time the next day, I'm in poor spirits. When I find Gabe already missing by the time I get up, I decide to take matters into my own hands and go to the Skarmouth Hotel to find him. At the hotel they tell me he's at the piers and at the piers they tell me he's gone out on a boat, and when I ask which boat, they laugh at me and say maybe one that had a drink in the bottom of the glass.

Sometimes, I hate all men.

When I get back, I rant to Finn about how we never talk to Gabe any more. "I talked to him this morning," Finn tells me. "Before he left. About the fish." I manage to contain my fury, but only barely. "Next time you see him, I need to talk to him," I tell Finn. "What fish?"

"What?" Finn answers. He is smiling at a porcelain dog head in a faraway fashion.

"Never mind," I say.

Then I take Dove to the beach for the afternoon high tide and she's irritable and sluggish, in no mood to work. She's had plenty of days like that in the past, of course, but they've never mattered. Not that it matters today, either, but if she's like this on the day of the race, I might as well not get out of bed.

When I get her back to the house, I turn her loose in her paddock and toss a flake of hay over the fence. It's cruddy island-grass hay, I know, though I've never cared much until now. I glower at Dove's hay belly and open the door to the house.

"Finn?"

He's not here. I hope he's out fixing the stupid Morris. Something on this island ought to work.

"Finn?" I ask again. No reply. Feeling guilty, I go to the biscuit tin on the counter and rattle the coins that we've stashed inside. I count them, then put them back in the biscuit tin. I imagine what Dove might do with better feed. I pull them back out again. I think that this will only buy her a week's worth of better feed, and use up all of our money. I put the coins back in.

We're going to lose the house anyway, unless I do something.

I fist my hands and stare at the tin.

I'll get Dory Maud to advance me on the teapots.

Leaving a few of the coins in the tin, I stuff the rest in my pocket. Without Finn or the probably still dead Morris here, there's no chance of me getting a ride to Colborne & Hammond, the farmer's supply, so it's out to the lean-to, shoving Dove out of the way to reach Mum's bicycle. I check the tyre pressure and teeter off down the road, avoiding potholes. I'm glad that Finn's storm prediction has yet to pass, because Colborne & Hammond's is in Hastoway, all the way past Skarmouth. My shins will be sighing enough from the ride without soaking them in rainwater as well.

I pedal off the gravel road and on to the asphalt, glancing behind me to make certain no cars are coming. They rarely are, but since Father Mooneyham got knocked into the ditch by Martin Bird's truck, I'm careful to look.

The wind is coming straight across the hills as I pedal. I have to lean against it to keep the bicycle from tipping. Ahead of me, the road winds to avoid the more formidable outcroppings. Dad said that when they first paved the road, it looked like a scar or a zipper, black against the muted browns and green hills around it. But now the asphalt and the painted lines on it have faded so that the road seems like just another part of the crooked, angular landscape. There's patches on the road, too, where craters have opened up in it and been sealed with darker tar. It's like camouflage. At night, it's almost impossible to stay true to it.

Behind me, I hear the sound of an engine separate itself from the sound of the wind, and I pull over to the side to let them pass. But instead of passing by, the vehicle stops. It's Thomas Gratton in his big sheep truck, a Bedford whose headlights and grille make it look like Finn when he's making his frog face.

"Puck Connolly," Thomas Gratton, ruddy-faced

as always, says through the open window. He's already opening his door. "Where are you headed on that?"

"Hastoway."

I can't quite figure how I make it off the bicycle, but the next thing I know, Gratton is lifting it over the side of the truck bed for me and saying, "I'm headed down there myself."

I know good fortune when I see it, so I climb in the passenger seat, moving a tin, a newspaper and a Border collie out of my way before I settle.

"Also," Thomas Gratton says, pulling himself into the truck with a groan, as if it takes a bit of doing, "have some biscuits. So I don't eat them all myself."

As we drive off down the road, I eat one and I give one to his dog. I cast a sly look to Thomas Gratton to see if he's noticed – and if he's noticed, if he minds – but he's humming and gripping the steering wheel as if it might get away. I think about him and Peg talking about me and wonder if I've made a mistake trapping myself here in the cab with him.

For a moment we ride in comparative silence – the truck rattles as if the engine is climbing out of the compartment, so *quiet* is not exactly the word for it. I'm pleased to see that the cab is cluttered with cough drop wrappers and empty milk bottles and bits of mud-smeared newspapers made brittle by age. Neatness makes me feel like I have to be on my best behaviour. Clutter is my natural habitat.

"How's that brother of yours?" Gratton asks me.

"Which one?"

"The heroic one with the cart."

I sigh so deeply that the collie licks my face to cure me. "Oh, Finn."

"He's a dedicated one. Do you think he's up for an apprenticeship?"

An apprenticeship with the butcher would be a very wonderful thing indeed. It pains me to say, "He can't stand the sight of blood."

Thomas Gratton laughs. "He's picked the wrong island."

I think, not fondly, about the dead sheep I investigated earlier. And also about Finn haunting Palsson's bakery. If he could apprentice anywhere, I'm certain it would be there. Where he could put salt in his hot cocoa. They'd have to apprentice someone else to tidy up the kitchen after him, though.

"Oh, what have we here?" Thomas Gratton says. It takes me a moment to spot what he does, which is a lone dark figure picking its way parallel to the road. Gratton stops the truck and rolls down his window.

"Sean Kendrick!" Gratton calls, and I start at that. And it *is* Sean Kendrick, his shoulders hunched against the cold, dark collar turned up to the wind. "What are you doing without a horse beneath you?"

Sean doesn't answer right away. His expression doesn't change, but something about his face does, like he's shifting to a different gear. "Just clearing my thoughts."

Gratton says, "Where are you clearing them to?"

"I don't know. Hastoway."

"Well, you can clear your thoughts in the truck. We're headed the same way."

For a moment I am completely struck by the injustice of this, that I've been offered a ride and now I have to share it with Sean "Keep Your Pony Off This Beach" Kendrick of all people. And then I see that Kendrick, too, has seen me, and is uncertain about getting into the truck, and that pleases me. I would like to be terrifying. I glower at him.

But Gratton's expression must counteract mine, because Sean Kendrick glances back the way he's come and then starts around to the other side of the truck. My side. Gratton opens his door and tells the dog to get in the back, which she does, shooting us all a filthy look. I move into the seat she'd been occupying – now that I'm sitting right next to Gratton, he smells like the lemon throat lozenges whose wrappers are scattered on the floor. All the while, I'm madly trying to come up with something catchy to say when Sean opens the passenger-side door, something that will at once indicate that I remember what he said to me on the beach and also carry that I am not impressed or intimidated, and possibly convey the message that I'm more clever than he thinks, as well.

Sean Kendrick opens the door.

He looks at me.

I look at him.

This close, he's almost too severe to be handsome: sharp-edged cheekbones and razor-edge nose and dark eyebrows. His hands are bruised and torn from his time with the *capaill uisce*. Like the fishermen on the island, his eyes are permanently narrowed against the sun and the sea. He looks like a wild animal. Not a friendly one.

I don't say anything.

He gets into the truck.

When he shuts the door, I am squeezed between Thomas Gratton's great leg, which I imagine is as ruddy as the rest of him, and Sean Kendrick's rigid one. We are shoulder to shoulder due to the size of the cab, and if Gratton is made of flour and potatoes, Sean is made of stone and driftwood and possibly those prickly anemones that sometimes wash up on shore.

I lean away from him. He looks out of the window.

Gratton hums to himself.

From the back of the truck, the Border collie whines. The vibration of the truck makes it a broken, intermittent whistle.

"I hear that Mutt – Matthew – is having a bit of an upset over the horse you've picked for him," Gratton says pleasantly.

Sean Kendrick looks at him sharply. "And who's saying such things?"

I'm surprised by his voice, for some reason, the way it sounds when he's speaking instead of shouting over the wind. It makes him seem softer. I notice that he smells of hay and horses and that makes me like him a bit better.

"Oh, he is," Gratton says. "Threw a tantrum right in the shop earlier. Says you want him to lose and you can't stand competition."

"Oh, that," Sean replies dismissively. He looks back out of the window. We're passing by one of the pastures that Malvern owns, and there is a splendid spread of broodmares grazing among the green.

Gratton taps his fingers on the steering wheel. "And then of course Peg went off on him."

Sean looks back again. He doesn't say anything, but just waits. I see how it pulls the words out of Gratton and gives Sean a subtle upper hand, and I vow to learn how to use this technique.

"Well, he was saying that if he was on that red stallion of yours, he'd be a four-time winner, too. So Peg told him he didn't know a thing about horses if he thought all there was to the race was the horse under you. She had a short fuse this morning, because it was a day that ended with y, you see."

I laugh, which reminds Gratton that I'm there, because he says, "And of course, you don't need Mutt Malvern for competition. You've got your hands full with Puck right here."

I vow to poison Thomas Gratton slowly, later. I want to sink into the seat and disappear. But instead I glare at Sean, daring him to say something.

But he doesn't. He just looks at my face, frowning a little, as if somehow my reasons for disrupting his training will reveal themselves. Then he glances back out of the window.

I can't decide if I'm insulted or not. To not say anything at all seems worse than saying something awful. I turn to Thomas Gratton, ignoring Sean Kendrick. "You said you were looking for an apprentice?"

"That's the truth."

"What about Beech?"

Gratton says, "Beech is going to the mainland after the races."

I open my mouth but no sound comes out.

"He and Tommy Falk and your brother Gabriel are all going at the same time. I should thank you, Puck, for giving us a few more weeks with him. I hear that your brother's staying until after the race because of you being in it, and that held them all up."

I feel, sometimes, like the rest of Thisby knows more about my business than I do.

"That's the truth," I say, repeating what he said. I feel darker, for some reason, now that I know that Gabe's not going alone. "Tommy's racing, though, isn't he?"

"Yeah, he decided to, since he's going to be here for it."

"Are you upset about Beech?" After I say it, I realize it might not be the most sensitive thing to ask, but I can't un-ask it.

"Ah, that's the way of this island. Not everyone can stay, or we'd fall off the edges, wouldn't we?" Thomas Gratton's voice doesn't match his light words, though. "And not everyone belongs to this island. I can tell you do, don't you?"

"I'd never leave," I say fervently. "It – it's like my heart, or something."

I feel silly for being so sentimental. Outside the window, across the water, I can see one of the tiny rocky islands near us, a little blue silhouette too small to be inhabited. It's beautiful in the sort of way that you never get used to.

We're all quiet, very quiet, and then Sean Kendrick says, "I have another horse, Kate Connolly, if you want to ride one of the *capaill uisce*."

Twenty-Four

Finn eyes me as he slowly uses his fingers to rend a biscuit into a pile of crumbs.

"So Sean Kendrick's going to sell you one of the water horses?"

We're sitting in the back room of Fathom & Sons. It's a claustrophobic room lined with shelves of brown boxes, the floor barely big enough for the scratched table that stands on it. It smells less like the butter scent of the rest of the building and more of musty cardboard and old cheese. When we were small, Mum would park us here with some biscuits while she chatted with Dory Maud out front. Finn and I would take turns guessing what was in the brown boxes. Hardware. Crackers. Rabbit paws. The private parts of Dory Maud's invisible lovers.

"Not necessarily," I say, not looking up from my work. I'm signing and numbering teapots while nursing a cup of tea that's gone regretfully cold. "I'm just looking. He didn't say 'selling', really."

Finn looks at me.

"I didn't say 'buying', either," I shoot back at him.

"I thought you were riding Dove."

I sign my name on the bottom of a pot. *Kate Connolly*. It looks like I'm signing a school paper. What I need is more flourish. I add a curl to the bottom of the *y*.

"I probably still am," I say. "I'm just looking!"

I'm blushing, and I don't know why, which infuriates me. I hope that the little bit of light from the bulb above us and the narrow windows over the shelves doesn't reveal it. I add, "I only have two more days to change my horse. I might as well make sure."

"Are you going to be in the parade of riders?" Finn asks. He's not looking at me now. Having completely taken apart the biscuit, he's begun to squish the crumbs back together into something lumpier and smaller.

Every year the Scorpio Festival is held a week after the horses emerge. I've only been once, and even then, we didn't stay long enough for the parade of riders, which is the culminating event of the night, when the riders declare their official mounts and betting goes crazy.

I get a little pit of nerves in my stomach thinking about it.

"Yes, are you?" Dory Maud's voice carries into the room. She stands in the doorway, one of her eyebrows arched. She's wearing a dress that looks like she stole it. It has lace sleeves and Dory Maud does not have lace sleeve arms.

I frown at her with bad temper. "You aren't going to try to talk me out of it, are you?"

"The parade, or the race?" Dory Maud pulls out the third chair at the table and sits down. "What I don't understand," she says, "is why such a clever and useful girl as yourself, Puck, would waste so much time looking like an idiot or being dead?"

Finn smiles at his biscuit.

"I have my reasons," I snap. "And don't tell me that my parents would be so sad about it, either. I've already heard it. I've heard it *all*."

"Has she been this short all week?" Dory Maud asks Finn, who nods. To me, she adds, "Your father would be displeased, but your mother — she wouldn't have much room to talk. She was a hellion and the only thing she didn't do on this island was ride in the races."

"Really?" I ask, hopeful for more information.

"Probably," Dory Maud replies. "Finn, why are you eating that? It looks like cat food."

"Brought it from home." Finn sighs heavily. "At Palsson's, they were setting out cinnamon twists."

"Oh yes." Dory Maud begins scratching something on a piece of paper. Her handwriting is so utterly illegible that I have to believe she works at it. "Even the angels could smell them."

Finn's expression is wistful.

I feel guilty about the load of hay and grain I

just bought. I'm not sure it's a better investment than cinnamon twists would've been.

"Could I get an advance on some teapots, Dory Maud?" I ask. I push a signed and numbered one towards her so she is convinced of my dutifulness. "Horse food's expensive."

"I'm not a bank. If you help me set up the festival booth Friday afternoon, I'll do it."

"Thanks," I say, without feeling much gratitude.

After a moment, Finn says, "I don't know why you aren't just riding Dove."

"Finn."

"Well, that's what you *said*."

"I'd like to have a chance of winning money," I say. "I thought it might actually help to ride, you know, a water horse in a race for, you know, water horses."

"Mmm," remarks Dory Maud.

"Exactly," Finn says. "How do you know they're faster?"

"Oh, *please*."

"Well, you are the one who told me that they don't always go in straight lines. I just don't see why you're changing your mind now just because some expert told you."

I feel my cheeks warm again. "He's not some expert. And he didn't tell me anything. I'm just looking."

Finn presses his thumb into his pile of crumbs, hard, so that the tip turns white. "You said that you weren't riding one of them on principle. Because of Mum and Dad."

His voice is even because Dory Maud is there and because he's Finn, but I can tell he's agitated.

I say, "Well, principle won't pay the bills."

"It's not much of a principle when you can just change it like – like that. Overnight. Like—" But he must not be able to think of what else it's like, because he stands up and storms past Dory Maud's chair and out of the room.

I blink after him. "What? *What?*"

I think brothers are the most inexplicable species on the planet.

Dory Maud brushes invisible crumbs from her paper and studies what she's written. "Boys," she says, "just aren't very good at being afraid."

TWENTY-FIVE

Sean

That evening, I saddle up a filly named Malvern Small Miracle, so called because she was so motionless and quiet when she was born that everyone thought she was stillborn.

I'm worn and tired. Something's wrong with my right arm where one of the horses jammed it earlier today, and I want nothing more than to crawl into my bed to consider whether or not my meeting tomorrow with Kate Connolly is a poor idea. But there are two buyers here, just off the boat, and word's come that I need to show two of the three-year-olds to them while there's still light. Why it won't hold until tomorrow, I don't know.

When I walk out into the golden evening yard to meet the buyers, I'm surprised to find that the other filly, a grey named Sweeter, is already out there, someone on her back. It only takes me half a moment to recognize the silhouette as Mutt Malvern's, and something in my gut snarls and turns. Three men stand at her shoulder, their attention on Mutt. He turns his head towards me, face in shadow, and I know he means for me to see that it's him. That he thinks that it's any of his business to be showing Sweeter offends me badly enough, but when I hear him tell one of the buyers how much he loves this filly, all I can think of is him standing at the point of the cove, waiting for Fundamental to be pulled under.

Miracle's hot. She skitters sideways and then shoots across the yard to where Mutt stands, bold enough that Sweeter moves out of her way. Our blue shadows stand beneath us.

"Sean Kendrick," says George Holly gladly. At my name, the other two buyers turn to observe me. I don't recognize either of them. Fresh blood, perhaps.

"Sean will be riding the other filly out," Mutt tells them, his expression paternal. He smiles. "Since I can't ride two at the same time."

I'm not sure he can ride one at the same time. I can't remember the last time I've seen him at the gallops.

One of the buyers mutters my name to the other and Mutt leans towards them to ask, "What's that?"

"Kendrick. The name sounds familiar."

Mutt looks at me.

"I just ride the horses," I say.

George Holly's smile is light in the darkness.

"Are you riding in the race, too?" asks a buyer. I nod.

"On the red stallion," Holly tells him. "The one you saw earlier."

They mumble their appreciation and ask Mutt who he's riding in the races.

Mutt sets his jaw. I don't think he even remembers Edana's name. He has yet to ride her.

I know this is where I, in the employ of the Malverns, am meant to step in and be helpful and humble, to save Mutt's face. It's what I've done for most of my life, and I can feel on my lips the words that will make Mutt look good. The words that will remind the clients of my relative hierarchy in the Malvern Yard.

But instead, I say, "I've chosen the bay mare with the white blaze, Edana, for him. I think they'll be a good match."

The yard is silent. There's something coiled and repugnant in Mutt's posture as he fixes his gaze on me. The buyers exchange glances as Holly rocks on his heels.

I can see my words burrow under Mutt's skin. I feel untethered and dangerous.

Miracle shies at nothing in particular, dancing in place. Her hooves clatter and echo across the stones. I turn to Mutt. I imagine him going beneath the water instead of Fundamental. In Corr's grasp. Beneath hooves in my father's place. "Light's failing. Shall we take your fillies out, then?"

Mutt turns Sweeter without a word.

The gallop is seven furlongs, nearly a mile, and straight as an arrow. The horses are spirited as they step on to it, knowing what is coming next. I feel Mutt's gaze on me, and when I meet it, his mouth twists. This was not meant to be a race between Miracle and Sweeter, but I see now that there's no way that it won't be.

Sweeter leaps out. Miracle is only a moment behind as I give her some rein. We streak along the pale gallop, its surface striped with blue shadows. The air screams by my ears, cold and painful. The shadows are so heavy that both fillies mistake them for real things and lift their knees, jumping invisible hurdles.

Mutt glances over at me to see how far I am, but he needn't bother. We're right on him. Shoulder to shoulder, the fillies surge down the track. Speedwise, I know the fillies are evenly matched, but I also know that only half of racing is how fast your horse is. I've been on this gallop hundreds of times on hundreds of horses, and I know where the incline starts, I know where the ground is soft by the rail, and I know where the horses slow and stare at the tractor parked near the road. I know everything there is to know about Miracle, too, how she likes to run herself out if you don't keep her in check, how much I'll need to push her to keep her strong up the incline, how to wave my crop just a bit to keep her attention on the task at hand and not the tractor.

All Mutt knows is how to beat the hell out of his mount as he's losing.

I know I should hold Miracle back. I know I should let Mutt and Sweeter finish first.

I feel the buyers' eyes on me.

I lean forward and whisper to Miracle. Her ear tips back at me, and I release the reins.

It's not even a contest.

Miracle pulls away from Sweeter by one length, two lengths, three lengths, four, not even breathing that hard. Mutt is bogged down somewhere in the wet ground near the rail, Sweeter slow and inattentive.

I turn around, standing in my stirrups, and salute Mutt Malvern with my crop.

I know it's a deadly game I'm playing.

"Not a jockey?" Holly says to me as I walk Miracle back into the yard.

"Just a horse lover," I reply.

TWENTY-SIX

Puck

Sean Kendrick told me to meet him at the point of the cliffs over Fell Cove, but there's no sign of him when I get there.

The cliffs here aren't as high as the ones that border the racing beach, and they're not as pure white. The shore by the cove is a weird, awkward place to get to, and once Dove and I manage to creep down the narrow, uneven path to the beach, I find that it's no good for riding on. The beach here is rocky and uneven, and the sea hugs it closely. It's low tide, but still, there's only five metres of rocks before the unruly sea smashes itself against them. It's the sort of place we were always warned against, because a horse could be up out of that ocean and back down with us before one wave had gone out and another taken its place.

I wonder, suddenly, if Sean Kendrick sent me here as a prank.

Before I have time to consider if he seemed like that sort of person and think something truly foul about him, I hear hoofbeats. I can't tell at once where they're coming from, and then I realize that they're coming from above me. I crane my head up to look.

I see a lone horse, stretched out to its fullest, galloping along the edge of the cliff, bits of turf ploughed up beneath its hooves. I recognize the horse a moment before I recognize the rider – Sean Kendrick, folded up tightly along the stallion's back, moving as one with the horse. As the bloody red *capall uisce* pounds past me overhead, I see that Sean rides bareback, the most dangerous way of all. Skin to skin, pulse to pulse, nothing to protect you should the horse's magic seize you.

I don't want to admire them, to admit that the two of them together are something altogether different than I've ever seen, but I can't help it. The red stallion is so fast that it steals my breath and speeds my heart with the thrill of it. I thought the horses I saw on the first day of training were fast, but I've never seen a horse move like this before. And Sean Kendrick on him, bareback. He is a pisser, for sure, but the old man I met in the butcher's is right: there is something about him. He knows his horses, but there is something else about him, too.

I think about the way his face felt in my hand when I pulled it above the water.

I think, too, about what it would be like to ride a horse like that. A bit of guilt stabs just inside my ribs as I remember Finn and his principles, or rather, my principles, the ones that started to slip when the house was at stake. I wish the idea of this sat more easily with me.

Back we go to the top of the cliff, Dove prancing a bit. Even going uphill, even after being ridden well for days now, she's still excited about running. I hear Finn's voice whispering in my ear as she flicks her tail.

By the time I get to the top of the cliff road, I know what I'm going to ask Sean.

· *Sean* ·

There's no sign of Kate Connolly when I arrive at the point of the cliff, though I wait for several long moments — moments I can't spare. I tie the bay mare down, draw a circle around her and spit in it, and take Corr out for a run. If Kate doesn't show up, I'll at least have stretched him out. He's eager and forward today, glad as me for the gallop.

Galloping up at the top of this cliff requires a gull's heart and a shark's nerve. It's not as high as the cliffs over the racing beach, sure, but a fall over these would kill you just the same. And to a *capall uisce*, the call of the sea is nearly as powerful thirty metres above it as it is thirty metres across a beach from it. More than one man has ridden that sinking ship over the edge and on to the rocks, just shy of the ocean.

But these low cliffs are the first place that my father ever set me on one of the *capaill uisce*. Not the beach where he had been taught. Because always, always, my father feared the sea more than he feared the heights.

I think they're both deadly, which isn't the same as being afraid.

When I double back, Corr stepping high over the long cliff grass, I see Kate Connolly standing beside her little dun pony. Kate's hair is the colour of the cliff grass turned red by autumn, and she has a spatter of freckles across her face that at first glance makes her look far younger. It's a strange magic: at once she's a cross child and also something older and wild, something grown from this coarse island soil. She's looking at my things – my saddle tipped up on its pommel, my rucksack, my thermos, my bells – where I've left them, and for some reason, that makes me feel odd, like skin rubbed raw by sand in the wind.

When Kate notices me, she frowns, or at least narrows her eyes. I don't know her to be able to tell the difference. I feel that same disquieted feeling I had in the cove. Again Fundamental goes under the water, and me with him. But I'm not drowning now; I let out my breath.

Corr's inspired by the appearance of the mare; instead of slowing to a walk, he trots nearly in place, shivering with his excitement. I don't dare get as close to her as politeness demands, so from five metres away, Corr dancing beneath me, I say, my voice louder to be heard over the wind, "What do I call you?"

"What?"

I ask, "Is your name Kate or not?"

"Come again?"

"It says 'Kate' on the board at Gratton's, but that's not what Thomas Gratton called you."

"Puck," she says, her voice soaked in lemon juice. "It's a nickname. Some people call me that." She doesn't invite me to be one of them. The wind gasps, long and low, around our feet, flattening the grass and tangling through the horses' manes. Up here, for some reason, it always smells more strongly of fish. After a moment, she adds, "I thought the rules say that you have to train on the beach."

I don't understand her for a moment, then I clarify, "Within one hundred and fifty metres of the shore."

Something dawns over her face, and for a moment, I needn't be there – it is merely her and her epiphany. I look at my watch.

"Where's the other horse?" she asks. Her mare tries to nibble her hair, and Kate slaps at her, absently. The pony tosses her head up with mock displeasure. It's a game bred of familiarity, one that warms me to both of them.

"Just a bit inland."

Kate regards us. "Does he always do that?"

Corr hasn't stopped moving. His neck is arched, too. I'm sure he looks ridiculous as he preens for them. *Uisce* stallions generally prefer to view land horses as meals, not mates, but sometimes a particular mare will take a stallion's fancy and he'll make an idiot of himself. "The bay mare's worse," I say.

Kate makes a face that I think might be humour. "Tell me about her."

"She's moody and she's slippery and she's in love with the ocean," I reply. I'd caught her in a rainstorm, salt water making all of my leather straps too slick to hold, clouds turning the sky into sea and vice versa, the cold making my fingers imprecise. She came up in a net behind the boat as I dredged the breakers just off the shore. Local lore had it that a *capall uisce* caught in the rain wanted to stay wet, but I wouldn't believe it until I'd tried it for myself.

"That sounds bad," Kate says.

"It is."

"Then why am I here?"

I study her. It's a question that's been plaguing me since I first saw her on the beach. "Because she'd be a *capall uisce* in a race made for *capaill uisce*."

She looks past me at the cliff's edge then, her eyebrows drawn close together, her mouth set. There's something uncompromising about her, a fury that I associate with youth.

"I don't want to consider this unless I'm sure she's going to be a better bet than Dove," she says. It's not until she's been quiet for a long moment that I realize that she's looking at me, waiting for me to agree or disagree.

I'm not certain what she expects me to say. She must know all this, but still I say, "There is nothing faster than a *capall uisce*. Period. I don't care what sort of training regimen you're doing, circles in the surf, or whatever. They have strength on your mare, they have height on her, and your mare runs on grass. The *capaill uisce* run on blood, Kate Connolly. You don't stand a chance."

This seems to solidify her opinions, because she nods, once, sharply. "OK. So, you'll race me, then, won't you?"

It's a curious way that she phrases it. The "won't you?" means that I'll have to disagree with her just to keep things as normal.

"Race? Me on the mare, you on Dove?"

Kate nods.

The wind buffets us again, finally stilling Corr as he stops to scent it. I can smell rain on it, far away. "I don't understand the purpose."

She just stares at me.

Back at the yard, I have two lots of horses to take out to the gallops yet. I have George Holly and at least two other buyers poking around the barns, looking for the horse that will make their mainland yards famous, or at least famous for the year. I have too much to do in too few hours before the October night comes early. I don't have time for a fool's race, a *capall uisce* against a pony that couldn't begin to look Corr in the eye.

"It's no more time than it would take for me to try

her," Kate says. "So if you say no, it's just because the idea insults you."

Which is how we end up racing.

I retrieve the bay mare, leaving Corr in her place with a lump of beef heart from my satchel, and find Kate adjusting her stirrups from the back of her pony, one leg crossed over the saddle as she does. It's something you can't do on a horse you don't trust, something I don't know that I'd ever do on one of the *capaill uisce*.

Beneath me, the bay mare is twisting and anxious. She's as hard to hold as the piebald, but less malevolent. She would sooner drown you than eat you.

"Are you ready?" Kate asks me, though I think it's a question I should've been asking instead. I don't think there's even a ghost of a chance she wants this horse I'm on. "To the big outcropping over there?"

I nod.

I reason with myself: this doesn't have to be an entirely wasted exercise. If I can get this bay mare running straight and true for these five minutes, then I'll reconsider what I told Malvern. I hate releasing a horse after I've invested time in it, and she's had plenty of time sunk into her. Maybe I was wrong and she will shape up for next year. Corr took years to settle.

"Are we waiting for a sign?" Kate says, springing off across the field. The bay mare's after her like a shot, all predator, and I let her have her head until we've caught up. Kate has a big handful of Dove's mane, which I think is for grip until I realize it's to keep the strands from slapping the girl's hands and face with their length. I don't have to worry about that with the bay mare; she's rubbed most of hers off on the door frame of her stall, longing for the sea.

The two horses gallop through the cliff grass, both of them nimble over the uneven surface.

The bay mare's not even really trying. I nudge her to get a bit more speed out of her, to pull away from Dove and end this. But the mare curves her body around my leg instead of away from it. She tugs towards the cliff edge, moving more to the side than forward.

And of course that island pony tracks straight and true ahead of us.

It takes me several long seconds to sort my bay mare out again, but when she decides to run, she catches up easily. Kate's dun pony gallops along – joyfully. Her ears are pricked with the glee of the run, her tail cracking every so often as she bucks playfully with excitement. If my mare is not focused, neither is she.

Kate glances at me, and I urge the bay mare on. I whisper to her for speed and she surges forward, listening. The dun mare doesn't stand a chance.

I hear a crack over the sound of the wind in my ears and turn just in time to see that Kate has reached behind her and, with her open palm, slapped her mare on the haunches, hard. It's got her pony's attention and Dove charges forward, giving it everything.

It's no good, though. My *capall uisce* has more speed than any island pony has dreamt of, and we're pulling away, fast. We'll have thirty lengths between us by the time we make it to the outcropping.

The bay mare stumbles but doesn't lose her footing. My arms are sprayed with bits of mud. I steal a glance under my arm to see where Kate is. She and her pony are far, far behind. There's no thrill to this race. No pleasure in such an easy victory. Above all, no joy in a win that the horse has no interest in.

And that's when the wind throws the scent of the sea at us. The bay mare flags and then twists, throwing her head up, her nostrils flared. I whisper to her and trace letters on her shoulder, but she won't settle.

She wants that cliff edge. The ocean is thick in the wind and she cannot think for it. I shuffle my iron out of my pocket, trace it along her veins, but – nothing. She rears, clawing at the air, and when that doesn't unseat me, she decides to take me with her. Her skin's hot and charged where my leg touches her. Nothing I do to her will turn her head.

Before us, I see cliff grass, and more cliff grass, and then, beyond it, nothing but sky. I pop one rein up, a dangerous way to stop a normal horse as you could pull it on to yourself, but it makes no difference to the bay mare. She has the bit solidly in her teeth and the sea in her lungs.

Five metres to the edge.

I have half a heartbeat to make a decision.

I throw myself off her, slamming my shoulder hard into the ground and rolling to diffuse the blow. I see chestnut-coloured grass, then blue sky, then chestnut-coloured grass again. Pushing myself up on my elbow, I catch sight of the mare just in time to watch her bunch her muscles and leap.

I scramble as close to the cliff's edge as I dare. I'm not sure if I can stand to see her dash herself on the rocks below, but I can't not look, either.

The bay mare looks fearless as she sails through the air, as if it's no more than a casual leap over a hurdle. Already she looks less horselike, her body streamlined.

I can't look.

I hear a terrific crash. She has disappeared into the surf, her tail the last thing I see.

I sigh and put my hands in my pockets. I can't tell if she's survived the dive or not. My saddle's gone, either way. I'm glad it wasn't my father's, back at the barn, though it was still dear; I'd had it made for me two years ago, a rare indulgence. I don't swear, but I consider the shape of the word in my mouth.

Hot breath whuffs out on my shoulder. It's Dove, and Kate standing on the other side of her, her ginger hair all pulled out of its ponytail. Dove is out of breath, but not as much as I'd expect.

Kate looks over the cliff and frowns for a moment, and then she points.

I follow her gaze to a glistening dark back swimming out to sea. My mouth quirks. "It looks like you won, Kate Connolly."

She pats Dove's shoulder and says, "Call me Puck."

TWENTY-SEVEN

Sean

I get back to the yard and find it in disarray. Half the horses didn't make it out for their exercise on time. Mettle is up in the paddock by the stable, chewing and sucking steadily on the top board of the fence. Edana hasn't been taken out at all, and there's no sign of Mutt. If he's thinking that he means to challenge me and Corr at the races this year, he's going about it the wrong way.

I keep feeling I've forgotten to do something, until I realize that I'm disconcerted by leaving with two horses and returning with one. I've no horse to untack, no saddle to put away.

George Holly finds me just as I'm walking back into the yard, a blood-streaked bucket in my hand from feeding the *capaill uisce*. He's found a brilliant red flat cap to hold his hair down and a smile to hold his face on. "Hullo, Mr Kendrick," he greets me brightly, falling into step with me across the cobbles of the yard. "You look in fine spirits."

"Do I?"

"Well, your face looks like it remembers a smile," Holly says. He looks down at my clothing; I'm wearing the island all over my left side.

I kick on the hose pump with my knee and begin to rinse the bucket over the top of the drain. "I lost a horse today."

"That sounds careless. What happened?"

"She jumped off a cliff."

"A cliff! Is that normal?"

In the barn, Edana lets out a keening, impatient wail, hungry for the sea. This time last year, Mutt was already pounding the hell out of his chosen mount on the beach. Right now, the yard seems quiet without him: the blue sky before a storm. I think about the Scorpio Festival tomorrow, how the riders' parade this year will be me and Mutt and insane Kate Connolly.

I shut off the water pump and regard him. "Mr Holly, nothing about this month is turning out to be normal."

TWENTY-EIGHT

So tonight is the night of the great Scorpio Festival.

I've only been to the Scorpio Festival once; Mum took us one year while Dad was out on the boat. Dad didn't approve of the festival or the races in general. He said that one bred hooligans and that the other gave those hooligans two more legs than they could steer. We'd always thought Mum didn't approve, either. But still, that year, when it became clear that Dad wasn't going to be back that evening, Mum told us to fetch our hats and coats and told Gabe to kick the Morris into life (it was dodgy, even back then). With illicit fervour, we piled in: Gabe took the coveted passenger seat while Finn and I fought and slapped each other in the back seat. Mum shouted at us and tore along the little road to Skarmouth, bent over the steering wheel like it was a troublesome horse.

And then, Skarmouth! Everywhere there were costumes and the Scorpio drummers and the wail of the singers. Mum bought us bells and ribbons and November cakes, which made my hands sticky for days. Everywhere, noise, noise, noise, until Finn, who was just a little urchin then, had started to cry from it. Dory Maud whirled over from nowhere with one of the terrifying curse masks and put it on Finn. Hidden behind the flat-toothed monster mask, he became as fierce as my mother.

Over the years that I knew Mum, I more often saw her mucking out Dove's lean-to or cleaning pots or painting pottery or leaning up against the roof to smack a shingle back on with a hammer. But for some reason, now, when I call up thoughts of Mum, I remember that night at the festival, her dancing wildly in a circle with us, a mouth full of glinting teeth, face strange in the firelight, singing the November songs.

And now it's years later, and it's the day of the festival, and we can go if we want to because there's no one alive to tell us otherwise. It's a strange and hollow feeling.

"I got the Morris running," Finn says now, coming into the house. He regards my dish-washing with more interest than dish-washing warrants. "It took awhile." I believe him. He's grubby and black.

"You look like home-made sin," I tell him. "What are you doing?"

Instead of heading to the bathroom to clean up, he's fetching his coat, which has fallen on to the floor behind Dad's sitting chair by the fire.

Finn rubs his forehead, leaving a black smear. "I'm afraid to turn the Morris off or it might not start again."

"You can't let it run all night."

My brother puts on his lumpy hat. "I can't believe Mum called you the clever one."

"She didn't. She called Gabe that," I say. As he puts his hand on the door, I realize where he thinks he's going. "Wait – you think you're going to the festival?"

Finn just turns and gives me a look.

"Gabe's not even here. Why do you think we're going? I have to be up early."

"Because you have to go finalize your registration," Finn says. "That's what *your* rule sheet says."

Of course he's right. I feel foolish for not remembering it, and then I feel my stomach drop to my feet. Before, I had a few metres of seawater between me and everyone who might say something about me being in the races. Now the only thing between me and everyone else will be a few pints of beer.

But there's no way around it. And maybe, just maybe, Gabe will be there. The rest of the island will be.

Unreluctantly, I abandon the dish-washing, and reluctantly, I find my ratty green coat and get my hat as Finn flings open the door. Now that I know to look for it, I can see that he's crawling out of his skin with excitement. Finn never looks more excited – he just gets faster. Finns are generally slow-moving creatures.

The Morris looks ominous under the darkening pink sky, the widening black hands of clouds stretching across the sunset, but Finn's face is a shining beacon in the driver's seat as he waits for me. I think of him behind Dory Maud's fearsome curse mask and imagine him that happy again, his fingers sticky for days.

"Wait—" I say, and run back inside to pull a few slender coins from the increasingly shallow collection in the biscuit tin on the counter. I will find a way to earn it back. Even if we eat nothing but November cakes for this week. I run back out into the car and sit. Finn's repair of the seat digs into my thigh. "Is this thing going to stop on us? I don't want to be stuck in the middle of some field after dark with a horse looking in."

"Just don't turn on the heater," Finn says.

I don't want to know how he got it started. Last time it required two men pushing it at a run while Finn steered. As we bump along the roads, he adds, "I'll bet that's where Gabe is. I'll bet he's at the festival."

And at that, I get an even more severe prickle of nerves, because the idea of confronting Gabe over Malvern's eviction threat is one that has been dogging me. If he's at the festival, he won't be able to avoid me.

"Ho!"

At first I think it's Finn who's said it, even though it's not his voice and I don't think Finn has ever said "Ho!" in his life. Then I see that it's the Carroll brothers. They're both stumping along like black guillemots in the twilight, and Jonathan's shouted to get our attention.

Finn lets the Morris sway to a halt. I slide the window open.

"Give us a ride into town?" Jonathan asks.

In response, Finn drags up the parking brake. I'm shocked, somewhat, by his boldness. I would've let the Carrolls ride with us, of course, but in my head, Finn is more shy than that. He keeps getting older while I'm not paying attention.

I have to get out to let the two boys in. Jonathan climbs in first and kicks the back of Finn's seat, and Finn looks affably in the rear-view mirror. Brian says thanks to me. Whether for the ride or for getting out to let him in, I don't know. The car feels full of people, like we've increased our number by five instead of two.

As we pull off again, Jonathan leans forward and clutches the shoulders of the driver's seat to ask, "When's the bonfire go up, do you know?"

"I dunno," Finn replies.

I twitch as a hand grips the back of my seat. A fishy smell accompanies it. I hear, "Evening, Kate."

I glance back at the hand; it's a nice, square hand, even if it smells like fish. "Evening."

Jonathan shakes Finn's seat. "I think I'm legit to bet this year. Do you know if it's sixteen or seventeen? The age to bet?"

"I dunno," Finn replies.

"Well," Jonathan says cheerfully, "you're useless as tits on a boar. Saw you setting up Dory Maud's booth yesterday morning, Puck. What's she selling these days? Stuff."

I don't know why he asked the question if he was just going to answer it for himself anyway.

Brian leans towards the window and me and his voice gets a little closer. It's nice and square, like his hand, one of those old island accents that sounds good talking about the weather or how many gannets there were on the rocks the other day. When I was younger, I used to stand in the bath where it was echoey and try to mimic it. It's something about the *r*s that's quite different from how my parents spoke. "I hear you're going to ride. Is that true?"

Finn flicks on the headlights as Jonathan keeps chattering at him. Night's coming fast under the thin gauze of clouds. Something smells of burning. I hope it's not the Morris.

I say, "It's true."

He doesn't say anything, just makes this sort of low, tuneless whistle to indicate surprise or awe, and then leans back in his seat. Meanwhile, Jonathan Carroll keeps up a running commentary with himself. He only needs to see Finn's head incline slightly to encourage him to start up again. I'm not sure Finn's even nodding his head; I think it's just the pits in the road. As we come along the high part of the road, though, even Jonathan falls silent. From here, you can see the ocean for just a few moments. It's grey and vast under an equally vast sky and even from this distance, I can see how the waves tear each other apart. We get plenty of rain, and storms often enough, but our weather is not given to extremes. Still, something about the white churning against the rocks is not comforting.

"Ho!" Jonathan says again. "Look! Look there! A head!"

And despite ourselves, we all look. The water shifts, black then grey-blue then black again, the froth a white ruffled collar, and then, out of the froth, we all see it. A dark horse's head surges above the water, jaw wide open. And then, before the sea swallows the first, we see a chestnut mane break the surface, along with a brief glimpse of a brown spine curving in the water alongside it. Then they're all gone beneath the water and I have goosebumps creeping up my arms.

"Good night to be on land," Brian Carroll says. Not lightly, like his brother would have said it. I think of the smell of fish he brought with him and think of the plain way that he asked me if I was riding. Riding in the races might not seem so impossibly brave to someone who fishes the November sea for a living.

"If I were catching one, I'd catch that chestnut," Jonathan says. "The red ones always win."

Brian says, "You mean Sean Kendrick always wins."

Jonathan shuffles in his seat. "I reckon chestnuts look faster."

"I reckon," Brian says, "Sean Kendrick makes them look that way. Have you met him, Kate?"

Finn looks amused at the "Kate", probably because

207

when Brian says it, it sounds like I'm more responsible than I really am.

"Yes," I mutter. I've seen him twice since we raced, but nothing about him suggested that he wanted to speak to me. In fact, sort of the opposite. He's not the kind to say "Ho!" either.

"Queer sort," Jonathan says.

"Only a water horse knows the *capaill uisce* better than him." Brian Carroll's voice is admiring. "You could make worse friends than him, Kate, right now. Though I 'spect you know that already."

All I know is that Sean Kendrick rode that bay mare and waited until he was nearly over the cliff edge before saving himself, and that the dead speak more than he does.

"I'd bet on you," Jonathan says generously, "if I wasn't betting on him."

"Jonathan." This is Brian, warningly. As if I care who his dim brother is betting on.

"Or Ian Privett," Jonathan concedes. "He's got that wicked fast grey from last year." He slaps a Scorpio drumbeat on the back of Finn's seat and then leans forward to speak to me. "Betting's crazy on you down at the pub. On whether you'll show up tonight for the parade. Gerry Old says that you haven't been on the beach for days and you've given up. Whatshisface says that you're dead, but obviously that's not true. So what do you think, Kate, are you a good bet?"

Brian sighs noisily.

I say, "If it was my horse against your mouth, not a chance."

Brian and Finn laugh. Jonathan tells me I'm made of piss. I think it's a compliment.

I look out of the window. The sky's turning black quickly under the stripes of clouds. There's a red glow in the distance where Skarmouth crouches, but the rest of the island is black and mysterious. In the dark, there's no difference between the sea and land. I remember riding Dove on the cliff top this morning. The way the air bit my cheeks and the smell of the sea set my heart pounding. I know I should be terrified of tonight and of tomorrow and of the next day, and I am, but I can feel something else, too: excitement.

TWENTY-NINE

Puck

"The riders' parade will be at eleven," Brian Carroll says. "I suppose you know that already."

I didn't, but now I do. Eleven seems like a long way away, hours filled with the noise of the festival. "I need to find my brother," I tell Brian. "My other brother."

In reality, what I need to find is my footing. I'm standing in this festival of Mum's, but I don't have Mum. Finn and Jonathan Carroll have vanished off into the crowds, leaving me with Brian, whose lungs I know better than the rest of him, and a pit of snaky nerves in my stomach.

I thought my statement was a goodbye, but Brian says, "All right. Where do you think he'll be?"

If I knew the answer to that, I would've spoken to him three days ago. The truth is I don't know anything about my older brother these days. Brian cranes his neck to look over the crowd, scanning faces for Gabe. We're standing at the head of the main street of Skarmouth, and I can see clear down to the pier. There's people filling every centimetre. The only bare bit is where the

Scorpio drummers make their way through, far down near the water. Something smells delicious, and my stomach growls.

I say, "Someplace I won't think to look, probably. Do you have any other brothers?"

"Sisters," Brian says. "Three of them."

"Where are they tonight?"

"The mainland."

He says it without force, and I wonder if it's stopped stinging or if it never stung at all. "OK, if they were here tonight, where would they be?"

"Well," Brian says, thoughtful and slow, hard to hear above the shouted conversation around us, "the quay or the pub. Shall we look?"

Suddenly, I feel strange having this conversation with Brian Carroll. He's standing close enough to be heard, looking at me, and he seems enormous and square and grown-up with his curls and his fisherman's muscles, and the steady way he looks at me is not like I'm used to. Part of me thinks he's just humouring me, me a kid, him most of the way to man, but then part of me sees my hands in front of me. They're Mum's hands, not a little girl's hands, and I know I'm wearing Mum's face, too. I wonder how long it will take for me to feel as adult inside as I look outside.

"OK," I agree.

We strike off down the street. Brian's broad shoulders plough a way through the people. Tourists, a lot of them, wearing unfamiliar faces. There is something subtly *different* about them, like they're a different species. Their noses are a little straighter, their eyes a little closer together, their mouths narrower. They're related to us like Dove is related to the water horses.

There's no sign of Gabe. But how would we find him among all these people anyway? Brian keeps pressing on, though, downward in the direction of the pier.

There's noise, noise, noise. Drums and shouts, laughing and singing, motorbikes and fiddles.

We push our way down to the quay, which is a little quieter, flanked by ocean on one side instead of people. The water moves restlessly against the wall, closer than usual, reaching up towards us. It's quiet enough that I hear commotion from the cliffs above the town.

"What's going on up there?" I ask. "The bonfire?"

Brian squints up as if he can see anything but the buildings glued to the side of the incline. "That, and the sea wishes."

The only thing I know of the sea wishes is that Father Mooneyham told us not to do them. I'd been unable to get more information out of Mum. "Have you made a sea wish before?"

Brian looks stricken. "No, indeed."

"What are they?"

"It's a bit of paper you write on with charcoal from the bonfire. You write something on it and toss it over the cliffs."

"That doesn't sound bad."

"A curse, Kate. They're curses. You write them backwards and throw them to the sea."

I'm thrilled and horrified. Immediately I try to imagine if there is any curse that I can see myself throwing over the cliff. I pose a striking figure in my mind, silhouetted by the bonfire, hurling something foul into the ocean.

"You're wild, Kate Connolly," Brian says. "I can see it in your face."

I'm not sure about that, but when I look up at him, he's studying me intently. Suddenly and terrifyingly, I get the idea that he's going to kiss me, and I shy backwards a metre or so before I realize that he hasn't moved a centimetre. He laughs at me, a kind, safe laugh. Maybe I am wild after all.

"Come on," Brian says. "Let's see if he's here."

We continue down the quay. Here there are food vendors beneath canvas, and this is clearly where Brian thought that Gabe might be. The vendors are doing brisk trade, and we have to thread through the lines. Brian is craning his neck again to look for my brother, and again, I feel strange, performing this personal quest with someone outside my family. What business is it of his, spending his festival finding Gabe instead of having a good time?

"You shouldn't be spending your evening doing this," I say. "You should be having fun. I'll keep looking."

Brian looks down at me. I think he's been getting taller throughout the evening. By the time we find Gabe, he'll be as tall as St Columba's on the hill and I'll have to have a stepladder to hold a conversation with him. "I am having fun. Do you want me to go?"

I don't believe him. I've seen fun, and it involves hooting and tearing in circles and possibly getting a skinned knee. This is interesting, not fun. "I just feel guilty for keeping you."

Brian swallows and looks off over the crowd as if he's still searching for Gabriel. "The last of my sisters went to the mainland last year. Normally I would have been here with her."

"Gabe says he's going."

It's out before I even think of it, and immediately, I can't imagine why I said it. Why did I mention this to Brian Carroll when I haven't even really discussed it with Finn? The most detailed conversation I've had with Brian Carroll in my life involved spitting on his yet-to-be-dug grave and now I'm turning my pockets inside out on family secrets.

"So he says," Brian replies.

I want to shout, *He didn't tell us until he had to*, but that really would be a family secret, so I just seal my mouth shut. I wish I hadn't come. I wish I were at home. I wish Brian Carroll weren't looking at me from his ever-increasing height. I cross my arms and stuff them into my armpits. When I find Gabe, I'm going to punch him right in his eye.

Brian Carroll seems oblivious to my distress. He adds, "I think he said he was going over with Tommy Falk and Beech Gratton."

I let a small noise of rage escape from me. "Of course! Everyone knows! Everyone's going. Are *you* going to the mainland, too?"

"No," Brian says seriously. "My great-great-grandfather helped build this pier, and I'm not leaving it."

He sounds like he's married to it, and that suddenly makes me feel tired and cross.

"Hey now," Brian says, as if he has now finally discovered my annoyance. "Let's go look in the pub. That's where I was headed. He might be there – that's where the locals hide, sometimes. If nothing else, we can get out of the cold for a moment."

We make our way back through the people to the Black-Eyed Girl, a green-fronted building with the doors propped open. It always struck me as too distinguished to be a pub, all polished wood and dimpled leather and brass fittings. It's impeccably clean and, for most of the day, incredibly empty. Then, at night, when the sailors get tired of being sober, the pub fills up and becomes the sort of noisy that spills out into the street and vomits into the quay.

I've never been inside that second version of the

pub until tonight. It's a completely different kind of full from the street. A dense, smoky, too-hot claustrophobia, full of shouting and laughter and, disconcertingly, my name in conversations.

"Hey now, is that our Kate Connolly?" says a man standing by the door. The mention of my name turns a few other heads our way. It feels like they all have more than one set of eyes each.

"Kate Connolly!" shouts another man, gladly, by the bar. He pushes off a barstool to come closer. Barrel-chested and ginger-haired, he smells like garlic and beer. "The hen among the cocks!"

Brian takes my arm, not gently, and gestures with his other hand to the back of the pub. Then he turns to the man and says, "It sure is. So, now, John. What do you think of this tide coming in? Due for a storm?"

I know a rescue effort when I see one, so I push further into the pub away from them. I search the back of the pub and there, in the corner booth, is Gabe. He's leaned forward, a pint in front of him, long fingers spread like a spider on the table as he makes some point. When he laughs, even without hearing him, his expression looks looser and coarser than I remember. Anger snakes through me.

Brian's still covering for me, so I surge through the smoke and stand beside Gabe's chair at his shoulder. I wait for him to notice me; Tommy Falk – damnable co-conspirator — across the table has already seen me and smiled prettily. But Gabe keeps gesturing.

"Gabe," I say. I feel, annoyingly, like a child standing at the arm of Dad's chair, interrupting him from reading the paper.

He turns. I can't tell if his expression is guilty. Now that I look, I don't think it is at all. He says, just this, "Oh, Puck."

"Yes, oh, Puck."

"I can't believe you're riding in the races," Tommy breaks in. He has two empty glasses in front of him and so all of the words become one effortless word, no real pauses, just *s* sounds between them. "Saw you there that first day. First girl ever. Here's to us."

"Don't encourage her," Gabe says, but he's jovial. His breath smells like alcohol.

"You're *drunk*," I say.

Gabe glances at Tommy, then back to me. "Don't be stupid, Kate. It's one drink."

"Dad didn't want you to drink. You told him you wouldn't!"

"You're being hysterical."

But I don't feel hysterical. "I need to talk to you."

"OK." Gabe doesn't move. The way he's sitting, I can tell that he's very aware of Tommy watching, and he's working the conversation to make himself look clever.

I lean over to say, "*Privately*."

The thing that is hurting me the most is the look on his face. One eyebrow raised, as if he still thinks that I am overreacting.

He lifts one palm towards the ceiling. "There isn't really a place to be private here. Can't it hold?"

I put my hand on his arm and grip his shirt. "No. Not any more. I need to talk now."

"I guess I'm going, Tommy. I'll be back."

"You show him, Puck!" Tommy says, with a fist punch into the air. Right at that moment, I despise Tommy and every bit of prettiness about him. I don't even look at him. Instead, I lead Gabe towards the door at the very back of the pub. It's a tiny toilet that smells a little like recent vomit. I shove the door shut behind him. I wish I had a moment to collect my thoughts, to remember exactly how I wanted to confront him, but I seem to have shut everything I wanted to say outside of the room.

"This is cosy," Gabe says. A mirror the size of a book is hung above the sink, and I'm glad I can't see myself in it.

"Where have you been?"

Gabe eyes me as if the question is a ridiculous one. "Working."

"Working? All the time? All night?"

Gabriel shifts his weight, stares at the ceiling. "I haven't been gone all night. Is that all this is about?"

It wasn't all it was about, but I can't remember what exactly it was that I was going to shout at him. My thoughts are scattered and gritty underneath my feet. I can only remember clearly my desire to hit him in the eye, and then all of a sudden, the most important thing comes back to me. "Benjamin Malvern came to the house this week."

"Hmm."

"Hmm! He said he's going to take the house!"

"Ah."

"Ah! Why didn't you tell us?" I ask. I hate that I am still clutching his arm. But how do I know that he won't leave without my fingers on him?

"How could I?" Gabe replies. He's dismissive. "Finn would go crazy and fret himself to death and you would become hysterical."

"I would not," I snap. I'm not sure if I'm hysterical right now. Everything I've said seems logical to me, but my voice feels a little out of control.

"Clearly."

"We deserved to be told, Gabriel!"

"What good would it do? You two weren't going to make any more money. What do you think I've been doing all these nights? I'm doing my best."

"And then you're leaving."

My brother looks at me and his smile has vanished. What replaces it isn't unhappiness. Just no expression at all, eyes narrowed against a wind I don't feel. I can't appeal to the feelings of this Gabe, because I can't tell if he has any. "A person can only try so hard. I did my best."

"That's not good enough," I say.

He removes his sleeve from my fingers and opens the door. The sound and smell of the pub swell into the airless room.

"That's too bad. It's all I've got." Gabe shuts the door behind himself. I swallow my sadness as hard as I can. It only makes it halfway down my throat.

It's all up to me. That's what it comes down to.

I spend a long few minutes in the bathroom after he's gone, my forehead resting against the door frame. I can't go out right away, because then Tommy Falk will grin at me and make some stupid joke and I'll burst into tears in public and I'm just not going to do that. I know that Brian Carroll is probably still waiting at the front of the pub for me, and I'm sorry about that, but not sorry enough to come out.

After a bit, I take a deep breath. I guess I thought, before, that somehow I could convince Gabe to stay. That somehow, through all this, he would change his mind. But it feels undeniable now. It feels like he's already stepped on to the boat.

I slip out of the bathroom and find there's a back door a couple of metres away from it. Two great decisions battle inside me for a moment – go up front, past Gabe and Tommy Falk and the staring men to where Brian Carroll maybe still waits. Or slide out the back door into the alley to lick my wounds and bide my time until the riders' parade. Really, I just want to go home and crawl into my bed and put my pillow over my head until December or March.

I could eat my shame for dinner, it's so thick, but I take the back door and leave Brian Carroll behind.

The wind tears down the narrow, stone-walled alley behind the pub, and as I head back to the street, I think crossly of hot chocolate and home that doesn't feel like home any more. I can see that there's an even denser sea of people on the street now, and I'm feeling not at all motivated to swim in it at the moment.

Then I hear "Puck!" and it's Finn's voice.

He grabs my elbow, unsteady, and for a brief, uncertain moment, I think *Finn is drunk* because I can believe anything of my brothers now, but then I see that he was just shoved from behind by the seething crowd. Finn finds my left hand, opens my fingers, and puts a November cake in my palm. It oozes honey and butter, rivulets of the creamy frosting joining the honey in the pit of my hand. It begs to be licked. Someone nearby screams like a water horse. My heart goes like a rabbit's.

I let the cake drip and meet Finn's eyes. He's a stranger, a black demon with a ghastly white grin. It takes me a moment to properly recognize him beneath the charcoal and chalk striped across his cheeks. Only his lips are pink, where the frosting from his own November cake has rubbed him clean. He wears one of the false spears made of driftwood on his back, secured with a leather thong.

"How did you get that?" I have to shout to be heard over the mob.

Finn grabs my other hand and stuffs something into it. When I go to open my fist to see what it is, he pushes my arm closer to my body, shielding it from general view. My eyes blink at the wad of money in my palm.

Finn leans towards me. His breath is sweet as nectar; he's had more than one cake. "I sold the Morris."

I hurriedly shove the money out of sight. "Who gave you that much for it?"

"A silly tourist woman who thought it was cute."

He smiles at me, teeth crooked and bright in his coal-black face, his hair crazy, and I feel my face soften into a grin. "Thought *you* were cute, probably."

Finn's smile disappears. One of the lines in Finn's code is that you're not to say anything about Finn being attractive to the opposite sex. I'm not sure which exact statute governs this, but it's closely related to the one that won't let you thank him. Something about compliments and Finn don't work.

"Never mind," I say. "Good job."

"Only thing," Finn says, licking his hand, "is I'm not sure how we're getting home now."

"If I make it through the riders' parade," I reply, "I'll fly us home."

THIRTY

The Scorpio drums pound a ragged heartbeat as I wind my way through the crowds that fill the streets of Skarmouth. The cold air smarts as I breathe it in; the wind carries all sorts of foreign scents. Food that's only made during the race season. Perfume only women from the mainland wear. Hot pitch, burning rubbish, beer spilled on the stones. This Skarmouth is raw and hungry, striving and unknowable. Everything the races make me feel on the inside is bleeding up through the seams in the street tonight.

In front of me, people shoulder their way through the tourists, who are slow with drink and loud with excitement. If you hold yourself a certain way, though, even the drunk will part for you. I slide through the crowd towards the butcher's, my eyes wide open. I'm watching for Mutt Malvern. It's better to see than be seen, until I know what he is up to tonight.

Sean Kendrick. I hear my name, whispered, then called, but I keep walking. There are many who'll recognize my face tonight.

As I walk, I look past the people at the town that stands beneath them. The stones are gold and red in the streetlights, the shadows black and brown and deep death blue, all the colours of the November ocean. Bicycles lie up against the walls as if a wave has washed them there and then retreated. Girls push by me, their strides ringing from the bells tied around their ankles. Firelight flickers from one of the side streets, flames licking from a barrel, boys gathered around it. I look at Skarmouth and it looks back at me, its eyes wild.

On one of the walls, there's an advertisement for the Malvern Yard. FOUR-TIME WINNER OF THE SCORPIO RACES, it says. OWN A PIECE OF THE RACES — YOUNGSTOCK AUCTION ON THURSDAY AT 7 A.M.

Everything in that advertisement is my business, but my name is nowhere on it.

I have to stop for the drummers as they crash up from a side street that leads to the water. They're fourteen strong, driven by enthusiasm rather than talent. They all wear black. The Scorpio drums are wide as the span of my arms, the heads made of blood-spattered leather and rope. The drums throb, replacing my pulse with theirs. Behind the drummers is a woman who wears a horse's head and a blood-red tunic. A tail curls behind her, and it's hard to tell if it is rope or hide or a real tail. Her feet are bare by tradition. It is impossible to tell who she is.

The drums thump by and we press against the walls to allow them to pass. Some of the tourists clap. The locals stomp. The mare goddess scans the crowd slowly, the stuffed horse head dwarfing her body. I see someone make the sign of a cross over the front of them and then again, backwards this time. In the centre of the street, the horse-headed woman holds out her hand and one thousand tiny pebbles rain out across the street. By tradition, she'll drop a single shell in the course of the night, and whoever gets the mare goddess's shell will have a wish.

There is nothing but sand in her hand this time.

One night, many years ago, as I stood beside my father, she looked at me and dropped her handful of sand and pebbles, and the single shell spun across the ground in front of me. I had darted away from my father's side to catch the shell where it stopped. I had my wish formed before my fingers curled around it.

I turn my face to the side, waiting for the woman to pass, waiting for the memory to pass.

I hear an exhalation, at once human and equine, and I turn my head. The mare goddess stands directly in front of me, centimetres away. The great old grey head is turned so that the left eye regards me, like Corr would have with his one poor eye. Only this horse's eye has been replaced with a shiny bit of slate, polished so that it winks and weeps like the piebald's. This close, I can see the streaks of darker red in the woman's tunic where the fabric wrinkled and caught more blood in the folds. The costume is fearfully made: even close, it's hard to tell how the woman ends and the false head begins, and it's impossible to determine how she can see. I imagine I feel hot breath on my face, huffing from the nostrils. My heart speeds.

I'm once again a boy and I'm watching her hand open, releasing pebbles and sand. The island, the beach, life stretches before me.

The mare goddess seizes my chin with her hand. The shale eye stares at me. The hair around it is matted with age, too long since death.

"Sean Kendrick," she says, and the voice is throaty, barely human. I hear the sea in it. "Did you get your wish?"

I cannot look away. "Yes. Many times over."

The shale glints and blinks.

The voice again takes me by surprise. "Has it brought you happiness?"

The question is not one that I would normally consider. I'm not unhappy. Happiness isn't something this island yields easily; the ground is too rocky and the sun too sparse for it to flourish. "Well enough."

Her fingers are tight, tight, tight on my jaw. I smell blood and I see, now, that fresh blood, soaked into the shirt, has dripped on to her hands.

"The ocean knows your name, Sean Kendrick," she says. "Make another wish."

She reaches up and smears the back of her hand across both of my cheekbones.

Then the mare goddess turns away to follow the

drummers, just a woman in a dead horse's head. But there is something hollow inside me, and for the first time, winning doesn't feel like enough.

I can't get the mare goddess out of my head: the timbre of her voice, the imagined feel of her breath on my skin. My throat burns as if I've swallowed seawater. I swim now through the crowd, from my encounter with the mare goddess and back into the real world. I pin myself to the ground with the memory of my ordinary errand at Gratton's. I need to settle up the account, and I need to place another order for the water horses. But my mind keeps turning over the woman in the horse head, trying to decide whose hands they could've been. If I can place her, I can fill the void inside me. It becomes only a parlour game again, then, if I know whose voice it was, made gritty inside the dead skull. I think it may have been Peg Gratton, no stranger to blood on her hands, and no taller than me, even with the horse head on.

I push into the butcher's. As always, it's the cleanest place in Skarmouth, and it's lit to a bright, daylight white inside. Two birds have somehow got into the building, and as I press my way in, the lights seem to flicker and dim as their wings flash in front of the bulbs.

I don't see Peg Gratton behind the counter, so it could have been her in the horse costume. I feel lighter. Less *called*.

I stand at the counter and Beech Gratton sullenly

takes my order. It's not me he resents, but the job, keeping him in when he wants out to the festival.

"Your face is a ruin." Beech grunts with admiration, and I remember the woman smearing my face with blood. "You look like the devil."

I don't reply.

"I'll be out of here in twenty minutes," he tells me, though I didn't ask.

"Thirty!" calls Peg Gratton from the back.

I taste blood in my mouth. An eye made of shale blinks at me.

Beech jots down my order, and as he does, I look up at the board behind the counter. There is my name, and Corr's, and beside us are our current odds: 1–5. Below us are also the names of a score of new entrants from the mainland who have found mounts in the first few days of training. They'll crowd the beach bad as the first day of training, inept and over-brave. I scan down the list to find Kate Connolly; I see her pony's name first, and then her name. Her odds are 45–1. I wonder how much of that is because of her pony and how much is because of her gender.

I let my eyes trail down the words to find Mutt's name on the list. There it is, and his horse's beside it. By all rights, the name written beside his should have been Edana, the horse that he has not touched for two days, the bay with white markings. The horse that I told his father to put him on.

But it doesn't say Edana.

The word printed beside Mutt's is *Skata*. A good name for a horse, hard and short. *Skata* is a local name for the magpie. A bird known for its cleverness, for its affection for shiny things, for its black-and-white colouration. There's only one thing on that beach that's black-and-white.

Skata is the piebald mare.

THIRTY-ONE

Sean

I find him by one of the bonfires.

The flames strive high into the black sky, tangled with the night. I can taste the smoke on my tongue.

"Matthew Malvern," I say, and it comes out a snarl, a call to battle, no more friendly than one of Corr's screams across the sand. Mutt is a giant, a mythical creature outlined in black before the bonfire, charcoal in one hand and a scrap of paper in the other: a sea wish. If he has a face, I cannot see it. I shout, "Is it a death wish you have written on that?"

Mutt twists the paper just long enough for me to see my name on it, written backwards. Then he lets it fly over the edge of the cliff. It disappears into the black.

"That horse will kill you."

Mutt swaggers up to me. His breath is dark, the underside of the sea. "And when, Sean Kendrick, have you ever cared for my safety?"

He stands closer, and closer, until our shadow is the same. I don't flinch. If he means to fight tonight, I mean to fight him back. The storm's inside me already and I can see Fundamental go under again, fresh as the minute it happened.

"It might not be you she kills," I say. "And no one deserves to die because of you."

The fire is hot on my skin.

"I know why you don't want me on her." Mutt laughs. "You know she's faster than him."

For so many years I have taken every precaution to keep Mutt alive for his father: put him on the safest horse I can manage, trained the hell out of that horse to make it impervious to the ocean, watched him in training to make sure that no one else interfered with him. I have two healed ribs that should be his.

Now he's put himself so far outside my ability to protect him that it's almost a relief. On the piebald, I can do nothing for him.

I put my hands up. "Do what you want. I'm done."

I see figures at the corner of my eye; they're here to bring us over for the riders' parade. The night's nearly over, and then the training really begins. It's hard to imagine, right now, a day after this night, which seems like it could go on for ever.

"Yes," Mutt says, "you are."

Thirty-Two

Puck

The riders' parade is not really a parade at all.

There's a man calling over the crowd, "Riders? Riders! To the rock!" He clearly means for us to follow him. I keep waiting for it to sort itself out into something more organized, but it never does. The only time it looks anything like a parade, kind of, is when I spy a few of the riders all heading in the same direction, up to the cliff top. The crowd parts for them, and I hurry after them, Finn trailing as best he can. No one moves for me, however, so I get a mouthful of wayward shoulders and a ribcage full of elbows.

By now it's blacker than black, and the only light comes from two bonfires, one burning high and furious, and the other smaller and spitting. I'm not certain where I should be.

"Kate Connolly," someone says, not in a nice way. When I turn my head, I see nothing but eyes glancing away and eyebrows pulled together. It's a strange thing, to be talked about instead of talked to.

A hand grabs my arm, and I turn, hissing and spitting,

until I see that it's Elizabeth, Dory Maud's sister. Her hair is fair, even in this dim light, and she's wearing a red frock the colour of Father Mooneyham's car. She makes a sour face. Her lips match Father Mooneyham's car, too. I'm sort of surprised to see her here; I've never seen her outside of the booth or Fathom & Sons, and I thought, possibly, that she would melt or disintegrate if she crossed into the real world. Each of the sisters has her realm: Dory Maud's is the widest, including the whole island, and then Elizabeth's is the building and booth, and then Annie's is the smallest of all, only the first floor of Fathom & Sons.

"You *are* lost, aren't you? Dory Maud said you wouldn't lose your way but I knew you would." Elizabeth's expression is pure disdain.

"Lost means I know where I'm going," I snap. "I've never been to the parade before."

"Don't bite me," Elizabeth says. "It's this way. Finn, boy, are you catching midges? Close your mouth and come on."

Her fingers are claws in my upper arm as she guides me up, up, up to the cliff above the racing beach. Finn trots after us, as twitchy as a puppy.

"Where is Dory?" I shout.

"Gambling," snarls Elizabeth. "Of course. While I do the work."

I'm not certain how guiding me to the top of the cliff counts as work, but I'm grateful for it. I'm also not certain I can imagine Dory Maud betting on the horses. Certainly not in any way that justified Elizabeth's snarled *of course*. I do my best to imagine Dory Maud in the butcher's, placing a bet, but the best I can imagine is her in the Black-Eyed Girl. In my imaginings, she manages it better than I do, swaggering up to the bar like a man.

Elizabeth snaps at me to wake up and propels me with great confidence through the crowd at the cliff top. Only after several long minutes does she stop to catch her bearings. But I can see now that we're in the right place. Because I spot a point of stillness in the seething crowd: Sean Kendrick. His clothing is dark, his expression darker, and he looks off into the black night in the direction of the sea. He is unmistakably waiting.

"There," I say.

"No," says Elizabeth, following my gaze. "That is *not* where you're headed. I think the race is dangerous enough without that, don't you? This way."

Sean turns his head just as Elizabeth jerks me in the opposite direction, and our eyes meet. There's something sharp and unprotected in his expression, and then I have to look down to keep Elizabeth from hauling me off my feet.

Finn scoots up beside me, hands shoved in his pockets against the cold. He casts a doleful look towards Elizabeth.

I turn my head and whisper to him, "You'd think *this* is the race by the speed she's going."

Finn doesn't smile, but his eyes do. Then Elizabeth comes to a halt. "Here," she says.

We've come around to a third bonfire, and before it is a great, flat rock, splattered and streaked with brown. It takes me a moment to understand what I'm seeing. It's old, old blood, stained all over the rock. Finn's face is pinched. There's a huge crowd of people circling the rock, waiting as Sean was waiting, and already I recognize a few of the riders a short distance away: Dr Halsal, Tommy Falk, Mutt Malvern. Ian Privett. Some of them are talking and laughing with each other – they've done this before, and there's a sense of familiarity. I feel suddenly ill.

"What's the blood from?" I whisper to Elizabeth.

"Puppies," Elizabeth says. She's caught Ian Privett looking at her and she bares her teeth at him in something that I don't think is supposed to be a smile. Taking me by both my upper arms, she holds me in front of her like a shield. "It's the riders'. You'll go up and put a drop of your blood on there to show you're riding."

I stare at the rock. That's a lot of blood for just a drop from each rider over the years.

Now a man's climbed on to the rock. I recognize him as Frank Eaton, a farmer my father knew. He's wearing one of the weird traditional scarf-things that the tourists like to buy – it wraps over his shoulder and pins at his hip and looks utterly ridiculous with his corduroy trousers. I have a very strong association of sweat-smell with the traditional costume and he doesn't look like he will change that impression. Holding a small bowl in his hands, Eaton shouts to the crowd, which is a little quieter now, "It falls to me to speak for the man who will not ride."

Eaton tips the bowl and blood splashes down over the rock at his feet. He doesn't stand back, and so drops of it mist his trousers. I don't think he minds.

"Rider without a name," he says. "Horse without a name. By his blood."

"Sheep's," Elizabeth says. "Or maybe horse. I don't remember."

"That's barbaric!" I'm aghast. Finn looks like he may throw up.

Elizabeth shrugs just one shoulder. Ian Privett watches her do it. "Fifty years ago, it was a man they killed up there, just like every year before. The man who will not ride."

"*Why?*" I demand.

Her voice is bored; there's a real answer, possibly, but she's not interested in knowing it. "Because men like to kill things. Good thing they stopped. We'd run out of men."

"Because," cuts in a voice that I recognize instantly, "if you feed the island blood before the race, maybe she won't take as much during it."

Elizabeth turns to Peg Gratton with a sour look. I blink at Peg — she's barely recognizable under her elaborate headdress. It looks a little like one of the scary tufted puffins that you can sometimes find on the island: it has a great pointed visor that forms the beak, and ropy yellow tassels that come off over each ear like long horns. I search for signs of Peg's curly hair, but it's hidden securely under the fabric lining of the headdress.

"Don't expect them to be friendly to you, Puck," Peg Gratton tells me, as if Elizabeth's not there. "A lot of them consider a girl on the beach bad luck. They won't be happy to see you."

I press my lips together. "I don't need them to be friendly. Just need them to let me go about my business."

"That would be a kindness," Peg says. She turns her head, and it's a strange, jerky motion with the bird head on top of hers. If I wasn't unsettled by anything that I saw tonight, that motion would've done it. She says, "I have to go."

On the rock, a woman wearing a real horse head stands over the place where the man poured the blood. Her tunic is soaked in blood; her hands run with it. She faces the crowd, but with that massive head, it doesn't seem like she's looking at us but at some point in the sky. I feel swimmy and feverish from the heat of the bonfire, from the sight of the blood. I'm dreaming, but I'm not.

There's murmuring from the people assembled. I can't pick out individual words, but Elizabeth says, "They're saying no one got the shell. She didn't drop a shell this year."

"The shell?"

"For the wish," Elizabeth says in her impatient way. "She drops a shell and you get a wish. Probably she dropped it down in Skarmouth and they were too dull to find it."

"Who is it?" Finn asks Elizabeth, the first thing he's said in a long while. "In the horse head?"

"The mother of all horses. Epona. Soul of Thisby and those cliffs."

Finn, patient, clarifies, "I meant, who is the woman?"

"Someone with more up front to look at than you," Elizabeth replies. Finn's eyes instantly go to the horse-woman's breasts, and Elizabeth laughs, high and wild. I scowl in defence of Finn's virtue, and she gives me a healthy shove. "They're calling for the riders."

They are. The woman with the horse head has gone, though I didn't see her going, and Peg Gratton has climbed the rock and stands in her place. A dozen or so men are gathered around one end of the rock, waiting to go up, and still more are moving restlessly towards the group. I am a small, motionless animal.

Elizabeth clucks her tongue. "You can wait if you like. They go up one at a time."

My hands aren't very steady, so I fist them. I watch

closely to see what's expected of me. The first rider walks up the natural steps at the end of the rock. It's Ian Privett, who looks older than he is because of his hair, gone grey when he was a boy. He storms across the rock towards Peg Gratton.

"I will ride," he tells her formally, loud enough for us to hear clearly. Then he thrusts out his hand towards her, and she slices his finger with a tiny blade, the motion too fast for me to see it properly. Privett holds his hand out over the rock and blood must fall, though I'm too far away to see it.

He doesn't seem to be in pain. He says, "Ian Privett. Penda. By my blood."

Peg answers in a low voice not hers. "Thank you."

Then Ian is off the rock and the next rider is mounting the steps. It's Mutt Malvern, who repeats the process, holding his hand out to let it drip after she's cut it. When he says, "Matthew Malvern. Skata. By my blood," he looks out from the rock to find someone in the audience, and his mouth makes a sort of not-smile that I'm glad I'm not the recipient of.

Again and again, riders step up on to the rock, holding out their hands, giving their names and their horse's names, and again and again, Peg Gratton thanks them before they go. So many of them! There must be forty. I've seen the race reports in the paper before, and there's never been anywhere near forty in the final race. What happens to all of them?

I imagine I can smell the blood on the rock from here.

And still the riders come up to the top of the rock, to have their fingers sliced and to announce their intention to ride.

As it gets closer to when I must go up, I'm shivering and nervous as can be, but I'm also aware that I'm waiting for Sean Kendrick to step on to the rock. I don't know if it's because he raced me or because I watched him lose that mare or because he told me to stay off the beach when no one else would speak to me at all, or merely because his red stallion is the most beautiful horse I've ever seen, but I'm curious about him in a way that puzzles even me.

Most of the group has come and gone by the time Sean comes up on to the rock. I barely recognize him. He has blood smeared across both of his sharp cheekbones, and the way he looks is at once striking and disturbing, harsh and godless, wary and predatory. Like someone who would climb this rock back when it was a real man whose blood they spilled on it, not just a bowl of sheep's blood.

I wonder suddenly what Father Mooneyham is doing on this night – if he's sequestered in St Columba's, praying that the members of his congregation keep their wits about them until tomorrow and that they won't forget themselves to pagan mare goddesses. But I wonder what sort of goddess our island goddess could possibly be, anyway, even if she had existed, that she is satisfied by a bowl of animal blood in place of a man. I've seen sheep's blood and I've seen a dead person, and I know the difference.

Sean Kendrick holds out his hand. "I will ride," he says, and when he says it, I feel heavy, like my feet are being pulled into the rock below me.

Peg Gratton slashes his finger. She really doesn't look like Peg Gratton at all, not when she's up there in the light of the bonfire, the shadow of the beak hiding her face.

His voice is barely audible. "Sean Kendrick. Corr. By my blood."

There's a great roar from the crowd, including from Elizabeth, who I thought was too dignified for such things, but Sean doesn't look up or acknowledge their cheers. I think I see his lips move again, but it's such a slight movement that I'm not sure. Then he's off the rock.

"This is you," Elizabeth says. "Up with you. Don't forget your name."

As cold as I was a moment before, I'm now blazing hot. I throw my chin up and walk around the rock to where I can step up on to it like the others. It seems wide as the ocean as I walk across it to Peg Gratton. Though the rock must be quite solid, the surface seems to tip and roll as I make my way across it. I can see three different colours of blood under my feet. I keep thinking in my head, *I will ride. By my blood.* I don't want to forget them in my nerves.

Now I see Peg Gratton's eyes, bright and piercing beneath the beaked headdress. She looks fierce and powerful.

I feel the attention of everybody in Skarmouth, everyone on Thisby, and all the tourists that the mainland's released. I stand as straight as I can. I will be as fierce as Peg Gratton, even if I don't have her great bird headdress to hide under. I have my name, and that's always been good enough.

I stretch out my hand. I wonder how much her little knife will hurt. My voice sounds louder than I expected. "I will ride."

Peg lifts her blade. I brace myself. No one has flinched and I refuse to be the first.

"Wait!" says a voice. Not Peg Gratton's.

We both turn our heads. There's Eaton in his sweaty traditional garb, standing at the base of the rock, his head craned back so he can see us. A group of men stands around him, hands in pockets and tucked in waistcoats. Some of them are riders who still hold their hands gingerly so they won't bleed more. Some of them wear traditional scarves like Eaton does. They're frowning.

I said it wrong. I came up out of turn. I did something wrong. I can't think of what it would be, but I feel uncertainty chewing on my guts.

Eaton says, "She can't ride."

My heart falls out of me. Dove! It must be Dove. I should've got the piebald mare when I had the chance.

"No woman's ridden in the races since they began," he says. "And this isn't going to be the year when that changes."

I stare at Eaton and the men around him. Something about the way they stand together is familiar, comradely. Like a herd of ponies bunched up against the wind. Or sheep, staring warily out at the collie that means to move them. I'm the outsider. The woman.

Of all the things that could stand between me and the races, I can't believe that this will be it.

My face flushes. I'm aware that hundreds of people are watching me stand on this rock. But I find my voice anyway. "It didn't say anything about that in the rules. I read them. Every single one."

Eaton looks to the man next to him, who licks his lips before saying, "There are rules on paper and rules too big for paper."

It takes me a moment to realize what this means, which is that there really is no rule against it, but they're not going to let me ride anyway. This is like when Gabe and I would play games when we were younger – as soon as I got close to winning, he would change the rules on me.

And just like back then, the unfairness of it makes my chest burn.

I say, "Then why have rules on paper at all?"

"Some things are too obvious to have to write down," says the man next to Eaton, who is wearing a very tidy three-piece suit with a scarf in place of the jacket. I can see the neat triangle of the waistcoat, dark grey against white, more clearly than his face.

"Come down now," Eaton says.

There is a third man at the base of the rock where I just climbed up, and he holds his hand up in my direction, as if I am going to just take it and go back down.

I don't move. "It's not obvious to me."

Eaton frowns for half a moment, and then he explains, slowly putting the words together as the explanation comes to him, "The women are the island, and the island keeps us. That's important. But the men are what drive the island into the seabed and keep it from floating out to sea. You can't have a woman on the beach. It reverses the natural order."

"So you want to disqualify me because of superstition," I say. "You think ships will run aground because I ride in the races?"

"Ah, that's putting too fine a point on it."

"So it's just me. You think it's wrong to have me in the races."

Eaton's face reminds me of Gabe's, down at the pub, as he looks to the crowd with an incredulous expression, certain they, too, see how difficult I'm being. The longer I look at him, the more I find to dislike. Does his wife not find his larger lower lip horrifying? Can he not part his hair so it doesn't reveal such a lot of scalp? Does he have to work his chin like that between words? He tells me, "Don't take it personally, now. It's not like that."

"It's personal to me."

Now they're annoyed. They thought I would just come down at the first whisper of the word *no*, and now that I haven't, I'm less of a story for later and more of a fight for now. Eaton says, "There are other things you could do in the month of October that will please more people than just you, Kate Connolly. You don't have to ride in the races."

I think about Benjamin Malvern sitting at our kitchen table, asking what we're willing to do to save the house. I think about how if I step off this rock right now, Gabe will have no reason to stay, at all, and no matter how angry I am with him, I can't have that conversation be our last. I think about how it felt to race Sean Kendrick on his unpredictable *capall uisce*.

"I have my own reasons for riding," I snap. "Just like every man who climbed on to this rock. Just because I'm a girl doesn't make those reasons any less."

Ian Privett, from a few steps away, says, "Kate Connolly, who do you see standing beside you? A woman takes our blood. A woman grants our wishes. But the blood on that rock is men's blood, blood of generations. It's not a question of if you want to be up there or not. You don't belong up there. Now stop this. Come down and stop being a child."

Who is Ian Privett to tell me anything? This, too, reminds me of Gabe, telling me to stop being hysterical when I didn't think I was being hysterical at all. I think of Mum on the back of a horse, teaching me to ride, so much a part of the horse herself. They can't tell me I don't belong up here. They might force me off no matter what I say, but they can't tell me I don't belong.

"I'll follow the rules I was given," I say. "I'm not following something unwritten."

"Kate Connolly," says the man in the waistcoat. "There has never been a woman on that beach and you're wanting us to make this the first year for it? Who are you to ask for that?"

By some unspoken signal, the man who'd held out his hand for me to come down starts up the stairs; they will take me down if I won't come.

It's over.

I can't really believe that it's over.

"I'll speak for her."

Every face turns to where Sean Kendrick stands a little apart from the crowd, his arms crossed.

"This island runs on courage, not blood," he says. His face is turned towards me, but his eyes are on Eaton and his group. In the hush after he speaks, I can hear my heart thudding in my ears.

I can see they're considering his words. Their faces

are clear: they want to be able to ignore him, but they're trying to decide how much weight you give the words of someone who has cheated death in the races so many times.

As before, in Thomas Gratton's truck, Sean Kendrick says nothing more. Instead, his silence draws them out, forces them to meet him.

"And you say to let her ride," Eaton says finally. "Despite everything."

"There's no everything," Sean replies. "Let the sea decide what's right and what's wrong."

There is an agonizingly long pause.

"Then she rides," Eaton says. Around him, there's head-shaking, but no one speaks out. Sean's word holds. "Give your blood, girl."

Peg Gratton doesn't wait for me to stretch my hand out any further. She snakes forward and slices my finger, and instead of pain, there's a searing heat that runs all the way up to my shoulder. The blood wells and drips freely on to the rock.

I have that feeling again like I did before, when Sean Kendrick was up here; my feet are rooted to the rock, part of the island, and I'm grown up out of it. The wind rips at my hair, pulling it out of my hair band and whipping the strands across my face. The air smells like the ocean breaking up across the shore.

I lift my chin again and say, "Kate Connolly. Dove. By my blood."

I find Sean Kendrick in the crowd again. He's turned as if he's going, but he looks over his shoulder at me. I hold his gaze. I feel like everyone in the crowd is watching this moment, like to hold Sean Kendrick's eye is to promise something or to get into something I'm unsure of, but I don't look away.

"By their blood, let the races begin," Peg Gratton says to the night and to the crowd, but they aren't watching her. "We have our riders, let the races begin."

Sean Kendrick holds my gaze a second longer, and then he strides away from the crowd.

Two weeks until the races. Everything starts tonight. I can feel it in my heart.

THIRTY-THREE

Sean

The next morning finds the island ghostly quiet. Though the frenzy of last night seemed to suggest that training would begin in earnest today, the stables are still, the roads silent. I'm happy for it; I have a lot to get done in the next twenty-four hours. I cast a glance towards the sky; a dimpled quilt of cloud hides the sun, and below it, smaller clouds race by, in a hurry to get on their way. I'll know better how long I have until the storm gets here once I see the ocean.

In the eerie quiet of the morning, I turn out the youngest of the thoroughbreds for a bit of exercise and grass before the weather gets poor, and then I gather my supplies to take down to the shore. Two buckets and my pockets sunk full of weak magic.

As I'm about to head out, I hear a voice. "So you're not a churchgoer, then."

"Good morning, Mr Holly," I reply.

He's in what I think they must consider Sunday finery in America: a white V-necked sweater and light jacket over creased khaki trousers. He looks like he might be ready to pose for one of the mainland paper's society pages.

"Good morning," Holly returns. He peers inside my buckets and rears back with a wince. They're full of Corr's rank manure and even I have a hard time getting used to the odour. "Sweet Mary and Coca-Cola, that's hard to bear." Seeing that I'm struggling to open the gate without setting down my buckets, he opens it for me and closes it behind me, following amiably. "So you're not a believer?"

"I believe in the same thing they believe in," I say, with a jerk of my chin towards town and St Columba's. "I just don't believe you can find it in a building."

The ground is soft and scented lightly with horse manure as I start down the roads towards the shoreline that borders most of Malvern's pastures. It's on the opposite side of the island from the racing beach, and while there are still cliffs, they're lower and more uneven, with uncertain beaches and more places for the ocean and the creatures who live in it to crawl on to shore.

Holly trots to catch up with me and slides one of the bucket handles out of my hand and into his. He grunts at the weight but says nothing else.

"What are you doing?" I ask.

"Looking for God," Holly says, matching my stride. "If you say he's out here, I'll take a gander."

I'm not certain he'll find his sort of God sharing this work with me, but I don't protest. It's a bit of a walk to the cliffs and having company might not be terrible. As we get further away from the protection of the stable yard buildings, the wind becomes more insistent, gusting across the fields unchecked. The only signs of civilization are the stone walls that mark Malvern's pastures. They long predate Malvern's herds; this is a Thisby many have forgotten.

Holly, to his credit, walks in silence for several long minutes before he asks, "What is it we're doing, exactly?"

"Storm's coming," I answer. "Already it'll be worse out at sea, and that will drive the horses in."

"By horses, you mean" – again he pauses carefully before attempting a pronunciation – "the *capaill uisce*."

I nod.

"And drives them in where, exactly? Whoa and hey!"

This last exclamation is because we've just got to a high point where we can see the ocean and the area around us. The land is all perilous, low cliffs, cracked and cut deeply into the green: pasture and then suddenly empty air and then pasture again. Below us and beyond us, the sea is whitecaps and foam and black rocks like teeth. A busy sea. Tomorrow will be hell, I think. I give Holly a long moment to drink in the sight before I answer his question.

"Drives them inland. If they're in the shallow water around the island, they'd sooner be on land than facing those rocks and current. And *capaill uisce* newly on land isn't something you'd like to see."

"Because they're hungry?"

I tip my bucket to allow a bit of the foul cargo to spill out on to the path, then continue picking my way along. "Because they're hungry, yes. But they're also uncertain, and that makes them worse."

"So you're dumping crap—"

"To mark territory. If they come onshore here, I want them to think they'll meet Corr."

"And not Benjamin Malvern's broodmares?" finishes Holly. We work in silence then, marking the places of easy access along the high ground first, and then working our way down. Finally, there's only the rocky beach to attend to.

"Perhaps you'd like to stay up for this," I suggest. I can't guarantee his safety next to the water. The sea is already tumultuous and dangerous, and there's nothing to say that there won't already be *capaill uisce* down there. Malvern would be displeased if I lost one of his buyers two days after losing a horse the same way.

Holly nods as if he understands me, but when I start down the path, he comes with me. This is a small bravery and I respect him for it. I trade my empty bucket for the one he holds and he massages his palm where the bucket handle pressed into it.

Here at the base of the path, the best of the shoreline is made of rocks the size of my fist, and the rest is boulders and pieces of the cliff that fell short of the water. Before me, the ocean stretches longingly towards my feet. It smells like dead things off at sea.

"If I were trying to catch another horse," I say, "this would be a good time to do it."

The surf has found its way into a shallow pool by our feet and George Holly inexplicably dips his fingers into the water. The pool is full of opportunistic anemones that stretch their tentacles out in the surf and urchins that would cut you if you stood on them and crabs that are too small to make a good meal.

"Warmer than I expected," Holly remarks. "Why aren't you trying to catch another horse, then? Since you lost one the other day?"

The truth is that there's precious little reason to catch another *capall uisce* now that Mutt Malvern has put himself on Skata. There's not much reason to have Edana, either, at this point. "I don't need another horse. I have Corr."

Holly prods one of the urchins with a stone. "How do you know there isn't a faster horse than Corr out there? Waiting to be caught?"

I think of the piebald and her tremendous speed.

"Maybe there is. I don't need to know. I'm not tempted," I say. Of course, it's not just the winning. I don't know how to explain that I know his heart better than anyone's, and he mine. "I don't need another horse. I just—"

I close my mouth and pick my way to the other access point on this otherwise inaccessible beach. Drawing a handful of salt out of my pocket, I spit on it before throwing it across the mouth of the other path. I tip some of Corr's manure out. Then I head back up the path without another word.

Holly follows me, and though I don't turn around, I hear his voice clearly.

"It's just that he's not yours."

I'm not certain I want to have this conversation. "It's not that he's not mine. It's that he's Benjamin Malvern's."

"That doesn't make any sense."

"It makes all the sense in the world, on this island." Thisby is defined by things that are Malvern's and things that aren't. "It matters, like this: I belong to Malvern. You don't."

"So, freedom."

I stop what I'm doing and regard him. Holly stands there below me on the path, gazing up, looking incredibly well kept and domesticated in his clean sweater and his pressed slacks. But his expression is anything but vapid. I still don't think that freewheeling George Holly, American investor, has ever been anything but freewheeling George Holly, American investor, but for the first time, that doesn't matter. I think he understands me regardless.

"So why don't you buy Corr from him?"

I smile thinly.

Holly reads my expression. "Is it the money? Ah, he's not willing. Do you have no leverage? Surely he needs more from you than to win the races. I'm sorry. I've overstepped. It's not my business. Let's go. Pretend I didn't say anything."

But he did say something, and it can't be unsaid. The truth is this: for eleven months of the year I make myself valuable to Malvern, and then for one month, I make myself invaluable. Would he be willing to give up that one month to keep the other eleven? Am I willing to risk it?

We stand back on the high ground; Holly is white against the green and I am black. I knock out the bucket, glad to leave the contents behind, and Holly wordlessly watches me scoop up a handful of clean dirt and whisper to it before scattering it back over the ground again.

"Magic," says Holly.

"Is a snaffle bit magic?" I ask him.

"All I know is that when I whisper to dirt, my conversations are less than meaningful."

He watches me treat the other two paths up from the cliffs. He doesn't ask how I do it, and I don't tell him, and then, after we've started back and the quiet seems long for him, I tell him, "You can say what you're thinking."

"No, I can't," George Holly says immediately, glad to be invited to speak. "Because it's more of not my business. And seeing as I've poked a stick in my eye once already, I don't want to do it again."

I raise my eyebrow.

Holly scuffs off his hands as if he's been handling something dirtier than water from the tide pool. "All right, then. So what's going on between you and that girl? Kate Connolly, right?"

I let out a breath, stack my buckets, and head back down the road towards the yard.

Holly says, "If you think by not answering that you'll convince me there's nothing, it won't work."

"That's not why I'm not answering," I say, as he catches up to me again. "I won't say there's nothing. I just don't know what it is."

I can see her clearly, standing on the rock beside Peg Gratton, unflinching before Eaton and the rest of the race committee. I can't remember when I've been that brave, and it shames me. The truth is, I feel myself being fascinated and repelled by her: she's both a mirror of myself and a door to part of this island that I'm not. It is like when the mare goddess looked into my eye; I felt that there was a part of myself that I didn't know.

"I'll tell you what it is in American," George Holly says, "but you might not want to hear it."

I cast him a withering glance and he laughs with good humour.

"This is worth every day away from home," he says. "Should I gamble on her, then?"

"You should save your money for hay," I mutter. "It'll be a long winter."

"Not," says Holly, "in California." And he laughs, and from the distance of his laugh I realize he's stopped walking. I turn.

"I think you're right, Mr Kendrick," George Holly says, eyes closed. His face is to the wind, leaning forward slightly so that it doesn't tip him. His slacks are no longer pristine; he's tracked bits of mud and manure up the front of them. His ridiculous red hat has blown off behind him, but he doesn't seem to notice. The wind has its fingers in his fair hair and the ocean sings to him. This island will take you, if you let it.

I ask, "What am I right about?"

"I can feel God out here."

I brush my hands off on my trousers. "Tell me that again," I say, "two weeks from now when you've seen the dead bodies on the beach."

Holly doesn't open his eyes. "Let no one say that Sean Kendrick isn't an optimist." After a pause, he adds, "I feel you smiling, so don't deny it."

He's right, so I don't.

"You going to try Benjamin Malvern for that horse, or what?" he asks.

I think of Kate Connolly standing before Eaton, her face brave, looking like a sacrifice on that old killing rock. I feel the mare goddess's breath on my face, and it carries the scent of thunder in it.

"Yes," I say.

THIRTY-FOUR

Puck

I don't bother tacking up Dove on Sunday after church. Everyone and their grandpa will be tacking up their *capaill uisce* after they get out of Mass, and I think it might be a good opportunity to learn something about my competition. I'll bring Dove up to the cliffs this evening, maybe, after she's had the day to eat expensive hay and get used to the idea of being fast.

I leave Finn and Gabe alone back at the house – Gabe came to service with us, though he looked at his watch and left halfway through, which made Father Mooneyham stare first at him and then at us. Father Mooneyham's homilies are not generally painful, but you're meant to suffer through them nonetheless. If your leg falls asleep, you don't move. If the tea you drank before Mass has you dreaming of toilets on the way to Damascus instead of epiphanies, you pinch and burn and bear it. If you are Brian Carroll and you have been night fishing, you tip your head back so that holding your eyes open is not such an impossible task.

You don't get up and leave. But Gabe did. And then

Beech Gratton did as well. If Tommy Falk hadn't been too pretty to come to church in the first place, I'm sure he would've left, too.

And now I definitely need to go to confession because I've not only thought dark things about my brother, I've thought them while in Mass. It is slightly uncomfortable to know that if I die in the next few hours, I'll go to hell, but I have to get outside before the tide comes in and all the riders disappear.

Anyway, all of that seems far away when I'm out on the cliffs above the racing beach. Because though I don't want to ride on the windy cliffs, I don't mind sitting on them. I trudge out with a pack on my back made of a wool blanket gathered into a pouch, and when I get there I release its contents on the ground and find myself a secure perch close to the edge where I can see the training down below. I wrap the blanket around my shoulders, take a sip of tea from my thermos, and start on one of the November cakes. I heated three of them in the oven this morning along with some stones, and now the stones have kept them nice and hot. I'm feeling quite virtuous and useful as I take out my paper and pencil and the stopwatch that Finn found for me. If I sit here long enough, surely the horses will give up their secrets. I want to know how fast they cover the ground, and then I plan to take Dove over the same stretch and time her as well. If I know what my handicap is, maybe I can prepare better.

I've been sitting for about ten minutes when I catch movement out of the corner of my eye. Someone sits down a few steps away from me, one knee drawn up, an arm resting on top of it.

"So you've discovered the secret to winning, have you, Kate Connolly?"

I recognize the voice without turning my head and my pulse goes *bump bump bu—* and thinks about starting again, but doesn't quite manage it. "I said you could call me Puck."

Sean Kendrick doesn't say anything else, but he doesn't get up, either. I wonder what he's thinking as we sit here, watching the horses down below. They look so different from above: the training looks orderly, quiet, on purpose, not like the chaos it felt like when I was down there. Even when I see two horses rear up to fight, their handlers working to tear them apart, the sound is muffled by distance and wind and this somehow lessens it. Toy soldiers.

I watch Ian Privett on his grey — Penda — as they gallop parallel to the water. I click my stopwatch and make a note.

"He'll go faster than that," Sean Kendrick says. "Later. He's not pressing him now."

I'm not sure if he's being condescending that I'm bothering to write down this meaningless time, or if he's awarding me with knowledge I wouldn't otherwise have had. So I just trace my pencil over the numbers again, imprinting them into the paper. I want to ask him why he spoke up for me last night, but Mum told me that it was rude to dig for compliments, and this feels like it would be digging for compliments. So I don't ask, though I want to, badly.

Which means we sit in silence some more, the storm wind cutting through my blanket and my hat and ruffling the pages of my notes. I reach into my pack and take one of the precious November cakes – still warm – and offer it to Sean.

He takes the cake without saying thank you. But the thank-you is somehow implied. I'm not sure how he does it, because I wasn't looking at him to see his face when he took it.

After a moment, he says, "Do you see the black mare? Falk's? She's excited to chase. If she were mine, I'd keep her just behind the lead so she'd stay motivated. Make my move late."

I frown down at the beach, trying to see what he sees. The beach is a mess of fake races and aborted gallops. I find Tommy and his black mare and watch them for a moment. She's a fine-legged thing for a *capall uisce*, and when she steps, her head bobs just a bit when her left rear hoof touches the ground. "Also," I say, because I have to say something, "she is a bit lame in the left rear."

"The right, I think," Sean Kendrick says, but then he corrects himself. "No, left, you're right."

And I feel pleased, although he is only agreeing with what I already knew.

Now I feel brave enough to ask him, "Why aren't you riding?" I look at him, too, when I ask, studying his sharp profile. His eyes jerk back and forth, following the movements down below, though the rest of him stays motionless.

"Racing is about more than riding."

"What are you watching for?"

There is, again, a tremendously long pause between my question and his answer, and I think that he'll just not reply, and then I think that maybe I only thought the question and didn't actually say it, and then I consider that possibly it had been somehow insulting though by now I can't remember exactly what it was that I said to double-check my words to be sure.

And that's when Sean says, "I want to know who's afraid of the water. I want to know who can track straight. I want to know who will tear Corr apart as soon as overtake him. I want to know who can't hold their horses. I want to know how they like to run. I want to know who's lame in the left rear. I want to know how the beach has worn this year. I want to know what the race will look like before it's run."

Down below, the piebald mare screams, loud enough that we both hear it, even up here on the cliff. I can't believe that last night I was regretting not taking her on when I had the chance. I follow Sean's gaze.

"And," I say, "you think the piebald mare is something to be watched out for."

"By you and me both."

Just then, the piebald mare surges forward, exploding along the line of the aggressive surf. She angles sharply towards the sea and jerks back towards the cliff again as quickly. She is so fast that she's got to the end of usable beach before I've thought to look at my stopwatch.

"Your brother is going to the mainland," Sean says.

I hold my breath in my mouth for a long moment, and finally say, "Right after the races." There's no point in treating it as a secret; everyone knows. He already heard me talking about it with Gratton in the truck.

"And you're not going with him."

I'm about to answer *he didn't ask* but I realize before I do that that's not the reason, anyway. I'm not following him because this is home, and everywhere else isn't. "No."

"Why aren't you going?"

The question infuriates me. I demand, "Why is it that going away is the standard? Does anyone ask you why *you* stay, Sean Kendrick?"

"They do."

"And why do you?"

"The sky and the sand and the sea and Corr."

It's a lovely answer and takes me entirely by surprise. I hadn't realized we were having a serious conversation, or I think I would've given a better reply when he asked me. I'm surprised, too, by him including his stallion in his list. I wonder if, when I talk about Dove, people can hear how I love her the way that I can hear his fondness for Corr in his voice. It's hard for me to imagine loving a monster, though, no matter how beautiful he is. I remember what the old man said in the butcher's, about Sean Kendrick having one foot on land and one foot in the sea.

Maybe you need a foot in the sea to be able to see beyond your horse's bloodlust.

"It's about wanting," I say eventually, after some considering. "The tourists always seem to want something. On Thisby, it's less about wanting, and more about being." I wonder after I say it if he'll think I sound like I have no drive or ambition. I suppose in comparison to him it must seem that way. I seem at once cursed to say precisely what I'm thinking to him and unable to tell what he thinks about it.

He says nothing at all. We watch the horses mill and surge below us. Finally, he says, not looking at me, "They'll still try to keep you off the beach. It won't have ended last night."

"I don't understand *why*."

"When the races are about proving something about yourself to others, the people you beat are as important as the horse you ride." His eyes don't leave the piebald.

"But that's not what they're about for you."

Sean pushes up to his feet and stands there. I look

at his dirty boots. *Now I've offended him*, I think. He says, "Other people have never been important to me, Kate Connolly. Puck Connolly."

I tip my face up to look at him, finally. The blanket falls off my shoulders, and my hat, too, loosened by the wind. I can't read his expression – his narrow eyes make it difficult. I say, "And now?"

Kendrick reaches to turn up the collar on his jacket. He doesn't smile, but he's not as close to frowning as usual. "Thanks for the cake."

Then he strides off across through the grass, leaving me with my pencil touching my paper. I feel like I've learned something important about the race to come, but I've no idea how to write it down.

THIRTY-FIVE

Sean

The first thing I do when I get back to the yard is search for Benjamin Malvern. I feel the same slanting, groundless sensation that I felt while training Fundamental, after encountering Puck for the first time. That I felt after the mare goddess told me to make another wish. I'd never realized how changeless this changeable island was until it turned into something different than I'd ever known.

I find Malvern at the gallops with two men at his elbow. He's got his head jutted forward like he does when he's with buyers, as if he can bully them into buying. The other two men are standing huddled; they look cold and damp, cats left out in the wet.

The first thing I notice when I draw closer is the filly they're looking at: Malvern Mettle, a filly with promising speed and heart. She's generally willing to do more than she's able, which is always better than the opposite.

The next thing I notice is that one of the buyers is George Holly. When he sees me, realization dawns on his expression. He says something to the other buyer and then to Malvern. Malvern nods his head, smiling but looking like he's unhappy about it. He points them back towards the house, and George Holly shepherds the other buyer in that direction.

As we pass, Holly juts his hand out in my direction and says, "Sean Kendrick, right? Happy morning."

I allow him to shake my hand as if we are strangers and I raise an eyebrow at his guile. Then he and the other buyer are gone, leaving me to Malvern.

I join Malvern by the rail of the gallop. He frowns in the direction of Mettle. One of the grooms is riding her, and she's playing and lazy. Mettle's got a peculiarly ugly face – ugliness and coarseness are traits that for some reason seem to accompany the fastest of the thoroughbreds – and right now she is flipping up her mule-like upper lip as she gallops. The groom's not taking her to task, either; I'm not sure if he just doesn't know what she's normally capable of doing or if he's uninterested. But either way, Mettle is taking him for a walk in the park.

Malvern speaks, finally. "Mr Kendrick. Is this filly always like this?"

I consider how to answer. "She's out of Malvern Penny and Pound and by Rostraver." Penny and Pound is one of Malvern's favourite broodmares and the rumour is that Rostraver's won so much over hurdles on the mainland that no one will race against him.

"The blood doesn't always come through," Malvern says. He spits and looks back to her.

"It came through."

"And she's out for a lark in front of the buyers, is it?"

All I can think about is what I'm about to ask him, but it's not the right moment. Instead of answering, I grip the rail and slide beneath it, walking across the track to where the groom — another one of Malvern's new ones; no one tolerates the grooms' quarters and the pay for long — leads Mettle around in a circle, cooling her down. I walk up to Mettle and take hold of her bridle.

"Ho," the groom says to me, surprised. He's young as I am. I think his name is Barnes but I can't be sure. Maybe Barnes was the last one. "Sean Kendrick!"

With my free hand, I reach up and snatch the crop out of his hands. I haven't even touched Mettle with it and she dances in a circle, pivoting around where I hold her. "Malvern is watching you. You're going to take her out again and you're going to make her work. She's having you on."

"I was pressing her," Barnes insists.

I lightly touch the crop to Mettle's hamstrings and she crow-hops forward as if I've slapped her. She knows my voice and she feels my certainty where I hold her bridle. "Maybe you were. But she didn't believe you, and neither did I. Take this back."

Barnes takes the crop and gathers the reins back up again. Mettle is trembling and eager now, held only by my touch on her bridle. Barnes looks at me, and I can see that he's scared of the potential, scared of speed. I think he'd better learn to love it soon.

I release her bridle and lift my other hand as if I've still got the crop in it, and Mettle explodes off the mark, down the gallop. I watch her for a moment to see how Barnes handles himself – he's not half-bad, despite his terror – and to see if Mettle stays on it. I could've done better, but still, at least she's working now.

I walk back to the rail and duck under. Malvern's eyes follow Mettle as he scratches his chin; I can hear his fingernails on his skin.

I put my hands in my pockets. I don't need a stopwatch to know that Mettle has bettered her time. For a moment, I'm silent, reaching for something that will give some weight to what I'm about to say. But there's nothing for it but to just say it. "I would buy Corr from you."

Benjamin Malvern casts me a look that is cross if it is anything, and looks back to the gallop. He produces a stopwatch, which I see now he's had nestled in his hand all this time, and clicks it as Mettle reaches the end of the gallop.

"Mr Malvern," I say.

"I don't like having the same conversation twice. I told you years ago, and I can hear that I'm repeating myself, he's not for sale to anyone. Don't take it personally."

I know, of course, his reasoning for not selling Corr. To sell him is to lose a strong contender for the Scorpio Races. To sell him is to lose one of the biggest pieces of advertising he has.

"I understand why you don't want to sell him," I say. "But maybe you've forgotten what it was to ride for someone else and not have a horse to call your own."

Malvern frowns at his stopwatch; not because Mettle was slow, but because she was the opposite.

"And I told you before, I'll sell you any of the thoroughbreds."

"I didn't make any of those thoroughbreds. I didn't make them what they are."

Malvern says, "You made all of them what they are."

I don't look at him. "None of them made me who I am."

It feels like an incredible confession. I've turned my heart out for Malvern to examine the contents. I've grown up alongside Corr. My father rode him and my father lost him, and then I found him again. He's the only family I have.

Benjamin Malvern rubs his great coarse thumb over his chin, and for a moment I think that he's actually considering it. But then he says, "Choose another horse."

"I'll train the others. That's the only thing that will change."

"Choose another horse, Mr Kendrick."

"I don't want another horse," I say. "I want Corr."

He still doesn't look at me. If he looks at me, I think, I have him. My blood sings in my ears.

Malvern says, "I'm not having this conversation again. He's not for sale."

As Malvern watches the next horse stepping on to the track, I fist my hands in my pockets, remembering how Kate Connolly didn't back down at the riders' parade. I remember Holly saying that there must be something that Malvern wanted more than Corr. I remember the mare goddess's strange voice: *Make another wish.* I even think of Mutt Malvern, risking everything for fame on that piebald mare. I had always thought that I'd spent my entire life gambling, risking my life each year on the beach, but I now know that I've never risked the one thing that I truly was afraid to lose.

I don't want to do this.

I say, very quietly, "Then, Mr Malvern, I quit."

He turns his head and one of his eyebrows is raised. "What's that?"

"I quit. Today. Find another trainer. Find someone else to ride in the races."

The faintest hint of a smile moves his lips. I recognize it: disdain. "Are you trying to blackmail me?"

"Call it what you like," I say. "Sell me Corr, and I'll race for you one last year, and I'll keep on training your horses."

On the gallop, a dark bay gelding lopes along,

breathing hard. He's not in racing condition yet. Malvern rubs his hand over his lips again, an action that somehow reminds me of Mettle.

"You overestimate your importance to this yard, Mr Kendrick."

I don't flinch. I'm standing in the ocean, feeling it press against my legs, but I won't let it move me.

"Do you think I can't find someone else to ride your stallion?" Malvern asks me. He waits for me to answer, and when I don't, he says, "There are twenty boys I can think of dying to get on the back of that horse."

The image splinters in my heart, and I'm sure he means it to.

When I still don't speak, he says, "Well, that's that. Have your things out by the end of the week."

I've never had to be this steady. Never had to make myself so still and fearless. I can't breathe, but I make myself hold out my hand.

"Don't play that game," Malvern says, without looking at me. "I invented it."

The meeting's over.

I might never ride Corr again.

I don't know who I am without him.

THIRTY-SIX

Most of the time, I trust Dove more than just about anybody, but she does have her moments. She doesn't like to be in water above the knee, which on Thisby is probably wisdom instead of cowardice. As a filly, she had an altercation with a sheep truck and she has yet to make her peace with them. And she's generally daunted by anything that could be described as *weather*. I can forgive her these, though, because it's not often I need to plough through a river or race a sheep truck or trot to Skarmouth in a gale.

But by the time I return to the cliff tops that afternoon, there is definitely weather. The wind cuts straight and low across turf made deep, dark green by the clouds pressing overhead. When the gusts blast across Dove's face, strong enough to check her speed, she spooks and shivers. The air stinks of the *capaill uisce*. Neither of us wants to be here in this night-dark afternoon.

But I know we ought to stay. If there is wind or rain on the day of the race, I need Dove to be solid. Not the slippery, jerky animal that she is right now.

"Easy," I tell her, but her ears are swivelling to catch everything but my voice.

A howl of wind sends her skittering dangerously close to the cliff edge. For a moment I see the hump of the cliff grass where it falls over the edge of the rock, towards the froth of the surging ocean far below. I feel the timeless, swimming sensation of possibility. Then I jerk one of the reins and kick her forward.

Dove shoots inland, still out of control, twisting and impossible to sit on.

I use everything my mother ever told me about riding. I imagine a string attached to my head pulling down through my spine, tying me to the saddle. I imagine I'm made of sand. I imagine my feet are stones hanging on either side of Dove's belly, too weighty to be shifted.

I keep my balance and slow her down, but my heart's hammering.

I don't like being afraid of her.

This is when Ian Privett arrives. Under this iron sky, he looks dark as a funeral-goer. He rides up on his sleek grey, Penda, who's not so much dappled as streaked with white like the storm-crazed ocean down below. A few lengths away from him is Ake Palsson, the baker's son, on a chestnut *uisce* mare, and with him is a bay *capall uisce* ridden by Gerald Finney, who's a second cousin or something of Ian Privett's. There's an attending group of men on foot, noisy and wind-tossed.

I can't imagine why they'd be coming up here, full of purpose, until Tommy Falk trots up behind them on his black mare. When his gaze finds me, there's a warning in it.

Ake Palsson leads the way towards me. He looks like his father the baker, which should be bad, since giant Nils Palsson has wild tufts of white hair, deep crevices for eyes, and a paunch that looks as if he's smuggling a bag of flour under his shirt. But Ake's squinted eyes only make the blue shock of them more impressive, and his white-blond hair is carefree instead of startling. He's intimidatingly tall, and if there are sacks of flour in his future, his hard frame has no hint of it now. My father always liked Ake. He said, *Ake gets things done*, which is a compliment because on this island, so many people don't.

Curled on the back of his chestnut, Ake calls, jolly, "And how is the third Connolly brother doing today?"

This earns him a laugh. It's not until the laugh's over that I realize he means me.

Finney's bay snaps at Ake as they trot closer. Just a squabble, but the sound of those teeth snapping makes Dove flinch.

"It's a shame what passes for humour these days," I reply. I try to hide how much work it's taking for me to hold Dove steady. The wind was bad enough, and now *capaill uisce*.

"It's got a bit of currency," Ake says. I can't see the

important parts of his expression in this light, so I can't tell if his smile is a funny one or not. "Down on the beach, they've started calling you Kevin."

Before I can stop them, my fingers dart self-consciously up to the edge of my hat to feel if any of my hair curls out. Gabe once joked, years ago, that Finn and I looked alike if you looked at just our faces. I'm a bit ashamed at how much the idea that I might be mistaken for a boy distresses me.

"That's hilarious," I say. "I'm riding in the race, so I must be a boy." As Ake and Finney come closer, I let Dove trot around in a small circle to hide the fact that I can't hold her in a full stop.

Ake shrugs, like he could've thought of better. Behind him, Finney's bay crow-hops, crashing into the chestnut, who nearly stumbles into Dove. Dove's fear shivers through the reins.

Ake laughs as Finney hurriedly gathers up his bay.

"Pisser," Finney says, pulling his bowler hat down to restore his ego. He jerks his chin in my direction. "Come on, Kevin, let's see what you got."

"Don't call me that," I reply. He and Ake circle me; their horses dwarf Dove. They must know that it's driving her to a frenzy. "And I was just finishing up."

Finney says, "Come now, be a sport. They said you were a whip."

"I'm not racing you right now," I say. I grid my teeth into a smile. "But I'll watch you boys."

Ake laughs. It's not a mean laugh, but it's not a thoughtful one, either. He says, "Tommy says you'd race us."

I find Tommy beyond them. He shakes his head.

"Then Tommy doesn't know what he's talking about," I reply.

Finney asks, "Where are your balls?"

I need to get away. In the back of my head, I'm thinking that this is going to be a problem, that Dove's going to have to deal with a lot more than this on the day of the race. But that's a faraway concern. The more immediate one is that Dove is shaking and ready to break.

"You're the one who said I have them, not me." I glance behind me, looking to see if there's room to back Dove away from them. A few drops of rain spatter across my face. The worst of it is that there's nothing mean about Finney and Ake; they're being just like Joseph Beringer. Only Joseph Beringer never teases me from the back of a massive *capall uisce*.

"The bookies are here," Finney says, elbowing back towards the onlookers. "Don't you want to show them something better than your forty-five to one?"

Finney lets his bay jostle into Ake's mare again, and the chestnut shoves against Dove, hard. I hear teeth snapping and Dove squeals, the wind ripping through her mane. I cling to her as she rears. Behind her left ear, I see a shallow scrape where the *capall*'s teeth grazed her. The blood wells up in a dozen small drops.

"Give me some room!" I shout.

I'm simultaneously terrified and humiliated as I hear myself. It's the voice of a scared little girl.

Ake and Finney hear it, too, because their faces change. Ake hauls on his chestnut's reins so hard that she nearly rears. Finney kicks his bay away from Dove.

They're both looking at me, Ake especially, with apologies in their expressions.

Dove lifts her head to the wind and whinnies, shrill and terrified. Ake keeps backing his horse away. I'm relieved to have distance between her and the *capaill uisce*, but at the same time, I'm ashamed down to my bones by this space suddenly surrounding me.

From their vantage point nearby, the bookies wipe moisture from their hats and murmur to each other before they walk away without a glance back for me. Ian Privett, still watching from Penda, nods to Ake before he turns as well.

"Later, Kate," Ake says, not quite meeting my eyes, suddenly demure. He lays his reins against his chestnut mare's neck and she pivots back towards Skarmouth. Finney touches his hat and is gone as well.

The cliff top seems quiet now, just the wind and the sound of intermittent drops sinking into the grass around me. I cannot stop hearing the sound of my own voice, and every time I do, I feel a little smaller.

Tommy's face is pensive. For a moment it looks like he's starting towards me, but at the movement of his *uisce* mare, Dove squeals and lays her ears back again. So he merely waves at me with just one hand close to his reins, and follows the others.

I'm left alone, the gusts beating the breath out of me. I'm furious with Dove for being so fearful, but I'm more furious with myself. Because it doesn't matter how brave I've been or how brave I will be. It only took a casual handful of minutes to convince everyone here that I don't belong on the beach.

THIRTY-SEVEN

That night Finn and I make a picnic in Dove's one-sided lean-to. Dove is still strung out and fretful, and I don't think she'll touch her hay unless I'm out there with her. And Finn says that the storm's going to keep us inside for a few days anyway, so we might as well be outside while we can. Also, Mum used to tell us to picnic outside when we were being horrid and loud in the house, so it has a sort of comfortable nostalgia to it.

Of course, it's getting dark, and it's drizzling fitfully, but still, under the lean-to it's dry, and an electric lantern provides enough light to see our soup by. I break open one of the cheap bales of hay to use as a blanket over our legs and we lean back against the wall of the lean-to. Finn, sensing my black mood, clinks the edge of his bowl against mine as a cheers. Dove stands half in and half out of the lean-to and picks at her hay. I have a clear view of the scratch on her neck from here, and again, I hear the sound of my cry on the cliff top. I can't stop wondering what would've happened if I'd just galloped with them when they'd first asked. I can't stop seeing their faces as they pulled their horses back from Dove.

For a few minutes, we're all silent, slurping potatoes and broth, listening to Dove's teeth grinding up the expensive hay and the sound of the light rain whispering across the metal roof of the lean-to. Finn piles more hay across his legs for insulation. Outside, the sky is going blue-brown and black at the edges.

"She looks faster already," Finn says. He slurps the bottom of his soup to annoy me, and then smacks his lips to make sure he's succeeded.

I set my own empty bowl on the hay bale behind me and take a piece of bread. My stomach still feels empty. "Can you come at me again with that sound? I don't think I heard you."

"You're in a black mood," Finn says.

I think of three things I could reply to that and in the end just shake my head. If I say it out loud, it will only make it harder to forget.

Finn is enough of a private creature that he doesn't try to make me speak. He spreads the hay thin and then thick again over his legs, trying to make it even. After a long pause, he says, "What do you think will happen?"

"Happen when?"

"With the race. And with Gabe. What do you think will happen to us?"

Crossly, I throw a stick of hay towards Dove. "Dove will eat her expensive food and the *capaill uisce* will eat beef liver and the bets will all be against us, but on the day of the race it'll be warm and windy and Dove will go straight while the others go right, and we'll be the richest people on the island. You'll drive three cars at the same time and Gabe will decide to stay and we'll never have to eat beans again."

"Not that one," Finn says, like he'd asked for a story and I'd picked the wrong one. "What will really happen."

"I'm not a fortune-teller."

"What about if you don't win? I'm not saying anything bad about Dove. But what if she doesn't make any money?"

I glance at him to see if he's picking at his arms yet, but he's just mutilating a piece of hay. "We lose the house. Benjamin Malvern kicks us out."

Finn nods at his hands, like he'd guessed this before. Gabe had underestimated both of us.

"And then I guess..." I try to imagine what it will look like if I fail. "I guess I will have to sell Dove. And we'd have to find someplace to live. If we got a job, the living could come with it, if it was something like ... cleaning. Or at the mill. There's mill housing."

No one wants a life at the mill.

I try to think of something else truthful but not so dire. "Gratton said he was eyeing you as an apprentice. I know you couldn't, but maybe he'd consider me instead..."

Finn says, "I'd do it."

"You couldn't bear it."

He's demolished the hay in his hands; it's just dust. "You couldn't bear to ride in the race, either, but you are. I reckon I could learn to bear it, if I had to."

I don't want him to learn to bear it, though. I want to keep my sweet, innocent brother the way he is, and I want to keep my best friend Dove here beside me and I don't want to trade the house I grew up in for a tiny flat and a mill job.

"But it won't happen that way," I say. "The first way is how it's going to happen."

Finn shreds another piece of hay. So does Dove.

And, just then, there's an odd creak.

The lean-to's metal roof is old, so there's plenty to creak there, and its one wall forms part of the fence, so where the boards meet the posts of the lean-to, there's yet another chance of creaking. And the fence itself is not the youngest thing on the island, so, really, it could creak anywhere there's a joint.

But this isn't that sort of creak.

It's more like a creak plus a knock. Not quite a knock. Softer. A pat. I can't think of how I even heard it, really, once I think about it, until I see Finn looking at me, completely still, and realize I didn't just hear it – I felt it.

Finn and I both turn our heads towards the lean-to wall that we lean against.

I want to say, *Maybe it was Puffin*. But Dove has

stopped chewing and has pricked her ears towards the sound, though of course there's nothing to see. I don't think she'd prick them for a cat.

Finn and I sit motionless. The drizzle goes *sssss* on the roof. We're trying not to look at each other, because looking would make it harder to hear. There's nothing. Nothing at all. Just the rain on the roof. Dove's still listening, but there's nothing to hear. It was just the lean-to settling. Our little electric lantern makes a circle of yellow up on the ceiling. The world is quiet.

Then:

Whuff

And the unmistakable sounds of slow steps on the other side of the wall.

It's not the sound of feet.

It's the sound of hooves.

We stare at each other.

There is the *creak-pat* again, and this time, we both know what it is. I feel the experimental push on the other side of the wall and I bite my lip, hard. With a questioning expression, Finn puts a finger on the switch to the electric light. I shake my head furiously. The only thing I can think of that's worse than facing a *capall uisce* in this drizzly night is to do it without light.

Instead, I start to burrow down into the hay blanket I've made; slowly, to keep the pieces from making noise. Finn immediately follows my lead. Dove's ears swivel to follow an invisible signal on the other side of the wall. If

I strain my ears, I can hear the sound of a hoof hitting the ground, then another. Another exhale of breath, no louder than the rain on the roof.

I don't know what the *capall uisce* is doing. Maybe it'll lose interest. Maybe it'll be discouraged by the fence between it and us. In my head, I trace the steps we'd have to take to get back to the house: around the other side of the lean-to, down two sections of fence, over the metal-tube gate, then five metres to the door.

Maybe one of us would get over the gate in time. That's not enough.

The night is dark and silent. I strain my ears for another hoofstep. Dove's attention remains fixed on the last point where the sound came from. Finn, mostly covered in hay, meets my gaze. His jaw's clenched.

The mist hisses over the roof. Water drips down off the edge of the metal, one drop, two drops at a time, making a soft, barely audible sound when it lands on the ground. Somewhere far away, I hear what sounds like a car engine, maybe. The wind teases the hay. There's nothing from the other side of the wall.

Dove jerks to attention.

Looking in the side of the lean-to is a long black face.

It is the devil.

It takes everything in me not to whimper. The creature is black as peat at midnight, and its lips are pulled back into a fearsome grin. The ears are long and wickedly pointed towards each other, less like a horse and more like a demon. They remind me of shark egg pouches. The nostrils are long and thin to keep the sea out. Eyes black and slick: a fish's eyes.

It still stinks like the ocean. Like low tide and things caught on rocks. It's barely a horse.

It's hungry.

The *capall uisce* has hooked its head around the side of the lean-to, over the fence. All that stands between us and its strangely light grin is three boards that I nailed up myself while Mum watched. Three nails, not two, into each, because ponies, she said, will test everything.

And now this night-black horse presses its chest against them. Not hard. Only as hard as it had pushed against the lean-to wall.

The nails creak.

I can hear my heart or Finn's heart or maybe the both of them, and it's going so fast and loud that I can't breathe. My hands are fisted over the hay, the nails biting into my palms.

We're hidden, you can't see us, go away.

Dove is utterly still.

The *capall uisce* looks at her and opens its jaw, and then it makes a sound that turns my blood into ice. It's a hissed exhalation with low clucks behind it, clicking from somewhere deep in its throat: *kaaaaaaaaaaaaaaaaaw.*

Dove flattens her ears back to her head but doesn't

move. How many times had we been told that the *capaill uisce* want a moving target? That to move is to die?

Dove is a statue.

The *capall uisce* pushes again. The boards creak again.

I hear Finn sigh. It's so quiet that I know no one but me could've heard it, and only me because I've spent my whole life listening to every sound that my brothers could possibly make. It's a soft, scared little noise that I haven't heard him make in a long time.

Then I hear a wail.

It's coming from out in the pasture. Both Dove and the *capall uisce* flick an ear towards it.

It comes again, and my stomach is an endless pit. It's another one, I think, that's pushed down the fence on the other side, that's in the pasture with us, not even three nails a board to keep us alive.

The black monster swivels its strange long ears again.

The wail, again. It sounds a little like a baby crying, and then I see Finn's mouth moving. It's about all I can see of him.

He mouths at me with exaggerated syllables: *Puffin*.

The sound, again, and this time, I recognize it immediately. Puffin the barn cat, always in search of Finn, back from her travels and drawn by our light. She wails again, her baby-cry meow that she uses to call him. When he's feeling indulgent, he'll repeat it back to her and she'll use the sound as a homing beacon.

Now she cries again, closer, and the *capall uisce* shifts its weight away from the fence.

In the grey light of the mist that the rain drives up from the ground, I see Puffin's form, trotting towards us, her tail a question mark. *Wow?* she asks.

The *capall uisce*'s grin closes.

Puffin sees the *capall uisce* only when it moves. The fence tears like paper, the boards exploding off with a sound like the world being destroyed.

She bolts and the *capall uisce* charges after her, made hungrier by the chase. They both vanish into the mist, and the last thing I hear is hooves scrabbling, frenzied, and then Puffin wailing.

Finn covers his face, the hay falling from his hands, and I see his shoulders shake.

I can't think about that, though. I think about this: the *capall uisce* coming back and killing my brother.

I grab his shoulder. "Come on."

I don't have a plan yet, but I know we can't stay.

From behind me, I hear a sound, and I jerk so hard my muscles hurt. It takes a full second for me to realize it's a voice, saying my name.

"Puck!"

It's Gabe, stepping through the ruined bit of fence the horse has just plunged through. His voice is a hiss as he takes my arm. "Hurry up. It'll come back."

I'm so shocked to see him – now, now of all times – that at first I can't get the words out. "Dove. What about Dove?"

282

"Bring her," snaps Gabriel, just audible. "Finn. Wake up. Come on."

I snatch up Dove's halter; she tosses her head in the air and jerks my arm at the shoulder. She's trembling like she was on the cliff top. "Puffin," I tell Gabe.

"She's a cat. I'm sorry, but come on." Gabe pulls at Finn. "There's two others. They're coming."

Gabe leads the way back through the ruined fence. When I get Dove to the fence, she pulls back, held by the memory of it being a barrier, and for a brief, terrible moment, I think I'll have to leave her behind. I cluck, softly, and she finally steps over the broken boards. In front of the house, I see headlights, and now there's Tommy Falk with half his face illuminated. He jerks open the car door and gestures hurriedly for Finn to get in.

Gabe appears beside me with a lead rope. "Hold it out the window."

"But—"

"*Now.*"

And just as he says that, I hear the same cluck that I heard earlier, only now it comes from somewhere in the paddock where we just were. Distantly, I hear it echo back through the mist, an answering sound. I clip the lead on to Dove's halter and scramble into the car. Tommy Falk's already behind the wheel, and Gabe slams the door after himself.

Then we're off down the narrow road, the headlights

reflected in the mist and rain as they jump back up from the ground. Beside us, Dove trots and then canters. I roll up the window to leave just enough room for the lead to fit through. Tommy Falk is utterly focused on his driving – checking the mirrors constantly, making sure that we're not being followed, taking care to make it easy for Dove to keep up with us – and the intensity of it makes me remember, suddenly, that I saw him on the beach just earlier today.

The car is silent and hot; the heater was turned up all the way and no one's thought to turn it down. The entire car smells, not unpleasantly, of the inside of a new shoe. Beside me, in the back seat, Finn is insensible because of Puffin.

The only thing that's said is when Gabe turns his face to Tommy and asks, "Your place?"

Tommy says, "Not with the pony. Has to be Beech's."

Then Finn pinches me and points out of the front window. Just illuminated by the headlights is a dead sheep. It's mutilated and strung out all the way from the ditch to the middle of the road.

I can't stop seeing its torn body, even after we have left it far behind. That could have been us. Tommy and Gabe don't comment on it, however. They don't comment on anything, actually. They sit in grim, familiar silence, Gabe looking out of windows and communicating to Tommy that it's all clear without saying a word.

Tommy doesn't take the road to Skarmouth as

I expected, but rather the one towards Hastoway. He slows at the crossroads but doesn't stop, and both he and Gabe peer anxiously out in all directions until we get going once more. I press my face to the glass, to make certain that Dove is not having a hard time keeping up.

"I could ride her and follow you," I say.

Gabe's voice leaves no room for negotiation. "You're not getting out of this car until we're well clear."

And then there's silence again, nothing but night and stone walls and the rain.

"Finn," Gabe says, finally, his voice raised to be heard over the sound of the engine. "This storm that's coming – how long will it last?"

Finn's eyes are bright in the back seat, and he's so incredibly pleased to have been asked that it hurts me. "Just tonight and tomorrow."

Gabe looks at Tommy. "One day. That's not long."

"Long enough," says Tommy.

THIRTY-EIGHT

Tommy Falk takes us to the Grattons' house, which is near Hastoway, though how near I can't be sure, because everything looks the same in the spitting rain and narrow yellow of the headlights. Beech meets us, his shoulders hunched against the wind, and shows me where I can leave Dove. He swings his torch around to reveal a little four-stall stable with a low ceiling and no electric lights. One of the stalls is occupied by damp goats, another by chickens, and one by a grey cob gelding who stretches his head over the unbarred stall door when Dove comes in. Dove flattens her ears back by way of an ungrateful hello, but I put her in the stall next to him anyway. I want to spend more time with her, but it feels rude to linger while Beech stands there illuminating the stall with the light. So I just pat her neck and tell Beech thank you. He grunts and points back towards the house with his flashlight.

Back in the house, Gabe and Peg Gratton are talking easily while Tommy Falk peers under the lid of a pot on the stove. I don't see Finn.

The kitchen itself reminds me of the butcher shop, if the butcher shop was made into a house. Despite the dark outside, the kitchen is all bright whitewashed walls and pots and knives hung up on them. The image of clean whiteness isn't at all diminished by the fact that the floor is filthy with footprints. There are knick-knacks on a half-dozen shelves, but they're entirely different from our sort of knick-knacks: crude wooden statues that could be either horses or deer, a broom of grass with a red ribbon tied around it, a piece of limestone with the name *PEG* written on it. None of the painted glass figurines or charming landscapes dotted with sheep and cheerful women that Mum liked. Stuff but not clutter. The room smells piercingly and wonderfully of whatever is cooking on the stove.

"They'll have your room," Peg says to Beech as soon as he comes in. In the light, I can see that Beech has grown into a great, ruddy creature who clearly takes after his father. He looks a little like he's made of wood, and because wood is fairly inflexible, it takes him awhile to change his expression. When he does, it's not pleased.

"They never will," Beech replies.

"And where, then, would you like them to stay?" Peg Gratton asks. It's strange to see her in this context, not in the butcher's as someone who will cut your heart out, not in our yard telling me not to race, not in a headdress cutting my finger with a knife. She is smaller, somehow, neater, though her ginger curls are still unruly as ever. I'm bewildered at how easily she and Beech and Gabe go around and around about where we will sleep, and I realize that some of the time that Gabe was gone must have been spent here. Maybe a lot of it. It makes me realize we've come here because this is where Gabe feels safe. It makes me feel strange and sad, like we've been replaced with another family.

"Where's Finn?" I break in.

"Washing his hands, of course," Gabe says. "It may be decades."

I feel weird about that, too, the rather free admission of Finn's foibles, though I've always thought it was something private, something only Connollys knew about. Gabe didn't say it like he was making fun of Finn, but it feels like it.

"Where is the toilet?"

Tommy, not Peg or Beech, gestures towards the stairs on the other side of the kitchen. It's like it's everyone's house, not just the Grattons'. Feeling sulky, I head out of the room. There's a tiny, dark hallway with three doors off it up at the top of the stairs, but only one of them has light coming from underneath it. I knock. There's no response until I say Finn's name and then, after a pause, the door opens. It's a tiny room, just big enough for a tub and a toilet and a washbasin if they're very good friends and don't mind rubbing shoulders, and Finn sits on the toilet with the lid down. There are big manly footprints on the small tiles of the floor.

I shut the door behind me and check to make certain that the tub is dry before stepping into it and sitting down.

"He comes here all the time," Finn says to me.

"I know," I reply. "I can tell."

"This is where he's been."

The betrayal sits thick between us. I want to say something to make this better for Finn, who idolizes Gabe, who would do anything for him, but I can't think of anything.

"Do you think Puffin's dead?" Finn asks.

"No, she got away," I say.

He studies his hands. They're a little chapped on the knuckles from all the washing he's been up to. "Yes, I thought so, too."

I look away, to the shiny handles of the bathtub, so shiny that they remind me of the grille of Father Mooneyham's car. "So," I say, "one day?"

Finn nods solemnly. "One day. The worst will be early tomorrow morning, I think."

"Sure, of course. How do you know?"

He looks impatient. "Everything. If people used their eyeballs, everybody would know."

The door swings open then, without a knock, and Gabe stands in the doorway. He looks in better humour than I've seen him for a long time. "Is it a party you're having in here?"

"Yes," I say. "It's started in the tub and then it

295

spread to the loo. All that's left is the sink if you want it."

"Well, everyone's wondering where you are. There's lamb stew in the works, but only if you come out of the toilet."

Finn and I exchange a glance. I wonder if he's thinking what I'm thinking: that Gabe can't just pretend that there's no bad feeling, that he hasn't been gone, that things will just go back the way they were. I thought, before, that a word from him would be enough, but now I know that I want him to court my good graces. If I can't have a grovelling apology, I don't want anything at all.

As we head down the stairs, Gabe says, "You have the couch, I'm afraid, Finn, because you're the shortest."

"Under whose measure!" I say.

Gabe shrugs. "Well, you're the shortest, technically, but Peg thinks you should be in a room with a door. So we're in Beech's room."

"Where is Beech, then?"

"He and Tommy are on a mattress in the living room. Peg says it'll work this way."

Back in the kitchen, the boys are loud and talking over each other. Beech and Tommy have ahold of something and are trying to keep it out of each other's reach, and a sheepdog's appeared from nowhere and is trying to get it as well. Peg holds a spoon in one hand and a cat by its scruff in the other. She's swearing at both of them.

"Put that out," she says to Gabe, and he takes the cat from her and puts it on the other side of the door. She scowls at me. "I don't cook. Cats make it worse."

Before I have a chance to answer, Gabe asks, "Where's Tom?"

It takes me a moment to realize that he means Thomas Gratton. I'd never considered that Thomas Gratton became Tom under his own roof.

"He went out to see if the Mackies were doing all right. Beech, get out. All of you, out. Go into the living room while I get this done. *Out.*"

Beech and Tommy obey and take their noise with them, and Finn files after them, interested because of the appearance of the dog.

I turn to go, but in the doorway, I hesitate and look back over my shoulder. Peg Gratton has turned back to the great black range to stir the pot, and Gabe stands just behind her, saying something into her ear. I just catch him saying "strong enough" and—

"Puck, catch it!" Tommy shouts.

I turn my face towards the living room in time to catch a sock full of beans in the mouth.

Beech guffaws but Tommy looks aggrieved and apologizes. The collie is now frolicking around my feet with great friendliness, very eager to have the sock, and I realize that this is what Beech and Tommy were fooling around with earlier.

"You should be sorry," I say sternly to Tommy, who

still looks beaten, standing on the other side of the worn green couch that will be Finn's bed. And then I hurl the sock back to him.

Pleased to be so easily forgiven, he grins and whips it without pause to Beech, who loses it to the dog. Tommy has no qualms about making a fool of himself, scrabbling after the collie as she leads him on a merry chase, and even Finn's laughing. I find myself wondering what drives Tommy to leave the island; he doesn't have the brooding of Gabe or the sulkiness of Beech. I've never seen him when he doesn't seem perfectly content, perfectly a part of island life. On the floor, Tommy snags the sock, finally, and around and around it goes to all of us, even the dog again, until Finn says, "Where's Gabe?" and we realize that he hasn't come out of the kitchen.

I start towards the kitchen, but Tommy takes my arm. "I'll go."

He peers around the door frame and I can't hear what he says. Then he turns back to us, and he has a smile pinned on for us. "Good news. Food's done." Gabe appears in the doorway beside him and they exchange a look that infuriates me, because it's yet more of the secret language of men.

Finally, Peg appears and addresses all of us. "If you want it, you have to serve yourself. And if you don't like it, blame Tom. He did it."

There's not much conversation as we eat – maybe, like me, they're all reimagining the events of the evening.

But it's a quiet without demands. The storm's not loud enough to make itself known and it's easy to pretend that we're just over for a social visit. The only time Peg Gratton addresses me is to tell me that I'm welcome to give Dove more hay if she needs it before the end of the night, before the storm gets bad.

And she's right about the storm. By the time we go to bed, the wind has become fitful and furious, shaking the windowpanes. The sheets on the bed are clean but the room still smells like Beech, who smells like salt ham. Before we turn off the lights, I see that there are no personal effects in the room, nothing to say that it is Beech's. Just this bed and an austere desk with an empty vase and some coins on it, and a narrow dresser with well-worn corners. I wonder if there used to be more of Beech here, but he packed it all away to take with him to the mainland.

I consider this as I try to sleep. I lie on one side of the bed and Gabe lies on the other, but it's a twin bed, so the two sides are really one side, and his elbow is kind of in my ribs and his shoulder is mashed against mine. It's warmer here, too, than at our house, and having Gabe here makes it warmer still, so I'm not sure how I'll sleep. Gabe's breathing doesn't sound like he's sleeping, either.

For a long moment we lie there in the dark, listening to the rain on the roof, and I think about the broken fence back home and the last sound I heard out of

Puffin and that long, long black face looking into the lean-to.

Because I'm tired, I say exactly what I'm thinking, without a lick of tact to make it go down easier.

"Why did you come back for us?" Even though I'm whispering, my voice is loud in the little bedroom.

Gabe's reply from the other side of the bed is withering. "Honestly, Puck, why do you think?"

"What does it matter to you?"

Now he's indignant. "What kind of a question is that?"

"Why are you answering all of my questions with other questions?"

Gabe tries to shift to put space between us, but there's no more mattress for him to move to. The bed groans and creaks like a ship at sea, only the sea is the bare floor of Beech's ham-scented room. "I don't understand what you want me to say."

I don't want to be accused of being hysterical, so I measure my words out, careful and slow. "I want to know why you care about us now, when next year you'll be gone and we could both be eaten in October and you'll be off on the mainland and never know."

In the dark, I hear Gabe sigh heavily. "It's not like I want to leave you two behind."

I hate myself for the little flutter of hope that I feel when he says it. But it's true that I imagine him with his arms flung wide, announcing that he's changed his mind as he embraces Finn and Dove and me at once. I say, "Then don't. Just stay."

"I can't."

"Why not?"

"I just can't."

It's the most we've spoken in a week and I wonder if I should just let it go at that. I imagine him leaping up, throwing the bedclothes from himself, and bolting from the room to avoid further questioning. Only, if he wanted to escape, he'd have to cross the bodies of Tommy Falk and Beech Gratton on the mattress on the floor and avoid falling over the couch with Finn on it and then sit by himself in the dark kitchen, and I don't think he'll do that.

So I say, "That's not a real reason."

For long moments, Gabe doesn't answer, and I just hear him breathing in and out, in and out. Then he says, in a strange, thin voice, "I can't bear it any more."

I'm so strangely grateful for this honesty that I don't know what to think. I struggle to think of a good question, a question that will keep him talking like this. It's like the truth is a bird that I'm worried of frightening away. "What can't you bear?"

"This island," Gabe says. He breathes a long pause between every word he says. "That house you and Finn are in. People talking. The fish – goddamn fish, I'll smell like them for the rest of my life. The horses. Everything. I can't do it any more."

He sounds miserable, but he didn't look miserable earlier, when we were all in the kitchen, when we were perched all over the sitting room eating. I don't know what to tell him. Everything that he said are things that I love about the island, except for maybe the smell of fish, which I guess might ruin everything else. But I don't know if that's a good enough reason to leave everything behind and start over.

It feels like he's confessed that he's dying of a disease I've never heard of, with symptoms I can't see. The utter wrongness of it, the way it won't fit in my head, keeps coming back to me again and again, as if I've only just learned about it.

The only concept I can truly understand is that this thing, this strange and incomprehensible and invisible thing, is big enough and strong enough to drive my brother from Thisby. As much of a pull Finn and I might have on him, this has more.

"Puck?" Gabe says, and I start, because his voice sounds like Finn's for some reason.

"Yes?"

"I'd like to go to sleep now."

But he doesn't. He turns on to his side and his breathing stays light and watchful. I'm not sure how long he stays awake, but I know that I fall asleep before he does.

THIRTY-NINE

Sean

In the early, black morning, the storm wakes me.

The wind roars overhead, an engine, the surf, the howl of a sea creature. My eyes adjust to the darkness and I see lights moving outside. Rain bursts across the glass in waves, furious and then more furious.

Now I hear the horses. They whinny and call and thump the walls. The storm has whipped them to a frenzy, and outside, something is screaming. It's this scream that's woken me, not the wind.

I sit up to act without considering, and after I do, I hesitate. Those are my horses down there in this beleaguered stable, out there in that fearful night. But at the same time, they are not mine, too, and I've quit, making them even less mine than they were before. I should stay here, doing nothing, letting the night do what it will. Let Malvern survey the havoc in the morning light and decide that I'm invaluable.

I close my eyes, my forehead on my fist, and listen to the wail outside. Even closer, downstairs, I hear a terrified horse kicking its stall wall, smashing either the wall or itself to destruction.

You overestimate your importance to this yard, Mr Kendrick.

But I haven't.

I can't let a single horse die because I am playing games with Malvern.

I shove on my boots and snatch my jacket, and as I reach for the knob of my door, there's a knock on the wood.

It's Daly. His hair is plastered wet over his face and there's blood on his shirtsleeves. He shivers helplessly. "Malvern says to do it without you, but we can't. He doesn't have to know. Please."

I lift my jacket to show him I was already coming, and together we jog down the narrow dark stairs to the stable. Everything smells of rain and the ocean and yet again more rain.

Daly hurries alongside me. "They won't calm down. There's a *capall uisce* somewhere outside and we don't know if he's among the horses or – we don't know who's hurt, because that sound – you can hear it. They're all kicking themselves lame. You get one calm and the others drive it crazy again."

"They won't be calm with that scream going on," I say. Every groom and stable boy and rider that Malvern has is in evidence, trying to calm the most precious of the horses. The bulbs overhead sway in wind that's found its way inside, and the swinging light stripes over me and away, like I am losing consciousness. I pass Mettle in her stall. She keeps rearing and clawing her front hooves against the wall as she comes back down. If she's not unsound now, she'll be soon. I hear Corr clucking and singing, driving the horses near him to madness. Somewhere behind me, another horse is slamming a hoof against a wall, rhythmic and senseless. Outside, the screaming continues.

Daly trails me as I go to Corr's stall. In my pocket, my hand closes around a stone with a hole through it. If Corr were any other water horse, I'd string it on to his halter tonight, to make more noise in his head than the approaching November sea does. But Corr is not any other water horse, and my tricks will only make him more anxious.

I open my hand and leave the stone in my pocket.

"Keep everyone clear," I snap. "Keep them out of my way."

I push open Corr's door and he charges towards the aisle. I press my hand into his chest and then slap it, shoving him back. One of the thoroughbreds whinnies piercingly.

"Keep them clear," I remind Daly.

He bolts ahead of me to pass this along, and then I let Corr plunge out of his stall and tug me down the aisle towards the door to the yard. It's closed against the rain and worse.

"Not out there—" Daly protests from behind me. "Malvern's out there."

That's too bad. So Malvern will know that I'm still among his horses. But I can't stop any of what is going on in here without fixing the problem out there first.

I push through the door, Corr strong and difficult on the other end of my lead line. I'm instantly wet to the skin. There's water in my ears, my eyes. I'm drinking the sky. I have to swipe the water from my forehead and blink to clear my vision. Shingles from the stable are scattered all across the yard. Every light in the yard is on, and there are waterlogged halos around each of them. Three mares stand at the gate, pressing, desperate to get in – they're broodmares from some of Malvern's far-flung pastures on the way to Hastoway. The fact that they're free means that something bad has happened to their fencing and they came seeking the familiar. One of them limps so badly that my heart sinks. The largest of the mares must recognize something in my walk, because she stops struggling and whinnies to me, long and entreating. Trusting me to rescue her from whatever made her come here.

And there's Malvern and David Prince, the head groom. Malvern holds a shotgun; it's an optimistic thought on his part.

Out here, the scream sounds like it's coming from all around us. It vibrates in every raindrop, throbs in the clouds overhead. It's a howl like venom, a paralysing promise. This storm has driven the island mad.

Corr jerks and hauls at my arm. I see his hooves leave the cobbles and return, but I can't hear the sound of them. I can only hear the throbbing scream, loud as if it's in my head. It's meant to travel miles underwater.

I yank Corr's halter to catch his attention, and then I haul his head down next to mine. His lips are pulled back in a ghastly grin; it's not a Corr I like seeing. My pulse races despite every year we've spent together. He's a monster. With one hand, I press those teeth away from me, and with the other, I turn his ear towards me.

Pursing my lips, I keen into his ear. It's lower than the scream that we hear now. The scream that's getting closer.

Corr is distracted. His lips are pulled far, far back from his teeth; he is no horse. I twist his ear hard enough to hurt, and again, I hum into his ear, a low hum that dips to a groan at the end.

Malvern lifts his shotgun, looking at something I can't see in the dark and the mist.

"Corr!" I shout. Rain creeps into my mouth when I do. And I keen again to him.

Malvern fires, but the scream from the approaching *capall uisce* is unbroken. It cannot get any louder.

And then, finally, Corr begins to keen as I prompt him. Low, groaning, so that I feel it in the lead rope I hold. So I feel it in the soles of my shoes. So it bubbles beneath the scream. Corr's keen grows and widens to a groan, a growl, a roar like the wind against the buildings. The sound fills the yard and rolls out through the rain. It's a territorial battle cry, a threat, a statement: *This land is already mine. This is my herd.*

The other scream diminishes in the wake of Corr's howl, which ascends to fill the space that's left behind. The mares at the gate go wild with fear and I know the horses in the stable are worse for it. Corr's pure, high scream is no different from the scream it replaced – except this one I can stop.

I listen and listen to be sure that Corr's cry is the only one. One of my eardrums, the one closest to Corr, merely hisses. But my left ear hears no other contender.

Now I hold Corr's halter in a tight fist and press my fingers against his veins, tracing counterclockwise. Corr's scream falters. I press my lips to his shoulder and whisper to his rain-soaked skin.

The night falls silent. My right ear still hums, a radio tuned to an empty frequency. Malvern and Prince look at me. The broodmares at the gate shiver and huddle together. Inside the stable, the kicking has died down.

The rain streams down; there's not a single dry thing left in the world. Across the yard, Malvern gestures shortly to me.

I lead Corr into the hazy light that Malvern stands in.

Malvern's eyes flick from me to Corr, who's black in the wet and the night.

"Have you changed your mind yet?" Malvern asks me.

"No."

Malvern's tone is dismissive. "I haven't, either. This changes nothing."

I'm not sure I believe him.

FORTY

Puck

As Finn predicted, the storm pounds Thisby for a night and a day, and by the end of that rainy day, we're able to retreat back to our house. I'm relieved because I'd rather run barefoot in the Scorpio Races than try to sleep in Beech's narrow ham-scented bed with Gabe again. Tommy's eager to return home because he left his *capall uisce* in the care of his family across the island and he's not certain how well they're doing. I think that I'd like to meet Tommy's family, if they are the sort who wouldn't mind having a water horse left in their care while Tommy ventures out to save the neighbours. It's not exactly like asking your mother to put out a tin of chopped meat for your cat while you're gone. I know I must've met Tommy's parents at some point – I must've met everyone on Thisby at some point – but I cannot accurately place them in my head. In my imagination Mr and Mrs Falk both have Tommy's brilliant blue eyes and his lovely lips. I also grant him some siblings, while I'm at it. Two brothers and a sister. The sister is homely. The brothers are not.

By evening, we are ready to strike out. The boys are so manly that they have to ride in Tommy's car again, but I make a hasty bridle by looping Dove's lead line back through her halter, creating reins so that I can ride her bareback after them.

The door to the house slams, and a moment later, I realize Peg Gratton has come out to stand by me. Her arms crossed, she watches silently as I curry off Dove's shoulders.

"Thank you again," I say finally, because I need to say something.

She doesn't reply, just lifts her eyebrows, like a nod without the head movement. "There's still a lot of people who don't want you on that beach."

I try not to feel angry at her. "I told you I wasn't going to be talked out of it."

Peg laughs then, a sound like a crow cawing. "I'm not talking about me. I'm talking about men who don't want a girl in their race."

My mouth says "oh" but my voice doesn't.

"You just watch yourself. Don't let anyone tighten your girth for you. Don't let anyone else feed your mare."

I nod, but I'm thinking that it's easy to imagine someone being annoyed by me riding, but harder to imagine someone being willing to do anything nefarious about it.

I ask, "What about Sean Kendrick?"

I look at Peg Gratton, and she is smiling a small, secret smile at me, as masked as she was beneath the bird headdress. "You sure don't like to do anything the easy way, do you?"

"I didn't know," I start truthfully, "that it was the hard way when I started on it."

Peg plucks a piece of straw out of Dove's mane. "It's easy to convince men to love you, Puck. All you have to do is be a mountain they have to climb or a poem they don't understand. Something that makes them feel strong or clever. It's why they love the ocean."

I'm not sure that is why Sean Kendrick loves the ocean.

Peg continues, "When you're too much like them, the mystery's gone. No point seeking the grail if it looks like your teacup."

"I'm not trying to be sought."

She purses her lips. "All I'm saying is that you're asking them to treat you like a man. And I'm not sure either of you want that."

There's something discomfiting about what she says, though I'm not sure if it's because I disagree or agree with it. I think of Ake Palsson backing his horse away from me and the combination of her words and the memory sit uneasily in my chest.

"I just want to be left alone," I say.

"Like I said," Peg replies. "You're asking to be treated like a man."

She makes a step out of her fingers laced together to help me up. Then she pats Dove's rump so that Dove'll move to follow Tommy's car as it leaves. I turn around as we go. Peg's still standing there watching us, but she doesn't wave.

My spirits slowly lift as we put distance between us and the Grattons' white house. After so much time cooped up, the air feels clean and well washed. The island itself looks like our kitchen – too much stuff, not enough tidying. There's bits of wooden fence thrown far away from fence lines, shingles and roof tiles resting in hedgerows, branches from faraway trees abandoned in the middle of fields. Sheep wander freely across the road, which isn't so unusual, but I spot some glossy mares grazing outside of their fence as well. The watery evening light is like a cautious smile through tears.

There's no sign of the *capaill uisce* that came up out of the storm, and I wonder if they've all climbed back into the sea again. For the moment, the island seems so utterly peaceful, unmarked by trouble and horses and weather. I think we'd have entirely different tourists if this were the face Thisby wore all the time.

Only I know this isn't the real Thisby. The real Thisby starts again at sun-up tomorrow. Just a little over a week to go until the races. I don't think I'm ready. It's hard to imagine that our story will end the way I told Finn. Good luck doesn't seem to be something that holds the hands of the Connollys these days.

But when I get home, Finn's face is shining and joyful. Behind him in the kitchen is Puffin the barn cat. Her tail is bitten off and ugly, and she's very indignant and sorry for herself, but she's also very alive.

This island is a cunning and secretive thing. I can't say what it has planned for me.

FORTY-ONE

Sean

That evening, as the last light is fading, I do as my father used to and strike off across the fields to the beach that faces west. As the sun shines low and red across the water, I wade into the ocean. The water is still high and brown and murky with the memory of the storm, so if there's something below it, I won't know it. But that's part of this, the not knowing. The surrender to the possibilities beneath the surface. It wasn't the ocean that killed my father, in the end.

The water is so cold that my feet go numb almost at once. I stretch my arms out to either side of me and close my eyes. I listen to the sound of water hitting water. The raucous cries of the terns and the guillemots in the rocks of the shore, the piercing, hoarse questions of the gulls above me. I smell seaweed and fish and the dusky scent of the nesting birds onshore. Salt coats my lips, crusts my eyelashes. I feel the cold press against my body. The sand shifts and sucks out from under my feet in the tide. I'm perfectly still. The sun is red behind my eyelids. The ocean will not shift me and the cold will not take me. Everything about me is exactly the same as it was five hundred years ago, when Thisby priests would stand in the freezing, dark sea and give themselves over to the island.

I try to make the inside of me as still as the outside. I have no more care than one of the gulls circling above me, thinking only of how to survive this moment and then the next.

I whisper to the sea three times. Once I ask that Corr will be meek and good, so they'll have no reason to use the bells and magic that he so despises.

But twice I whisper for him to be despicable, so that they'll beg for me to come back.

FORTY-TWO

The island's mad.

Because I rode Dove back from Hastoway the evening before, I give her the morning off and tell her to eat some expensive hay. I give her a bit of the grain, too − not too much, because she'll just get ill on it − and leave her behind to go watch the training and take notes. I don't have any more November cakes and we weren't home to bake anything, so I have to settle for a pocketful of stale biscuits.

It doesn't take me long to realize that Thisby has completely changed now that the festival is done and the storm has passed. Aside from the stray shingles and branches, it looks as if the wind brought people and tents. The road from Skarmouth clear on to the cliffs is lined with tents and tables of every sort. Where I'd helped Dory Maud set up her booth is now a city of booths, all populated by locals trying to seduce tourists with their stuff. Some of them are the vendors who Brian Carroll and I saw while making our way through the festival. But some of them are new: the booth selling riders' colours, the hasty and incredibly tacky paintings of the race favourites, the mats to sit on to watch the race from the cliffs without getting your backside wet.

I feel, suddenly and alarmingly, like the races are very close. All at once I realize that it's only days before I will walk Dove down to the beach, and I feel completely unprepared. I don't know anything about this. Nothing at all.

I'm resurrected from my funk by Joseph Beringer, who dances around behind me singing some poorly rhymed and slightly dirty song about my odds and my skirts.

"I don't even wear skirts," I snap at him.

"Especially," he says, "in my daydreams."

I had thought, for some reason, that being one of the riders in the Scorpio Races would get me a bit more respect, but it's ever surprising, the things that don't change.

I ignore him, which helps a little, if only because it feels familiar, and thread through the people towards Dory Maud's booth, avoiding puddles and Joseph as best as I can. I can hear the commotion from the beach already, even among all the people poking in the booths. There's something about the sound that seems unlike the normal noise of the training, and I'm not sure if it's just because everyone is down on the beach at once as the races draw close.

"Puck!" Dory Maud spots me before I spot her. She is festively dressed in a traditional scarf and rubber boots, a combination that is at once ridiculous and, unfortunately, extremely representative of Thisby. "Puck!" she says again, this time shaking a string of November bells at me – an action that attracts the attention of at least two others near me. She carefully lays the bells down on the table in front of her so that the price tag is showing.

"Hi," I say. There's a great shout from the direction of the beach, which I find oddly unsettling.

"Where's your horse?" Dory Maud asks. "Or do you mean to practise out there without her?"

"I rode her back from Hastoway yesterday evening. She's taking a break and I'm going to watch from the cliffs."

Dory Maud eyes me.

"It's strategy," I add crossly. "I'm devising strategy. Not all of racing is riding, you know."

"I know nothing about it," Dory replies. "Except that Ian Privett's horse likes to come on strong from the outside at the very end, if it's anything like the last year he rode him."

I remember what Elizabeth said before about Dory Maud gambling on the horses. Mum once told Dad that vices were only vices when looked at through the frame of society. I see a possible ally in Dory's vice. "What else do you know?"

Dory Maud reaches up to better secure a bit of the

flapping canvas tent, and then she says, "I know that I'll tell you more if you come back after and mind the booth for an hour while I go get lunch."

I regard her darkly. Again, it's not something I thought I'd have to do as a rider in the races. "I'll think about it. What's that commotion anyway, do you know?"

Dory Maud looks enviously down at the road to the beach. "Oh, it's Sean Kendrick."

Interest prickles in me. "What about Sean Kendrick?"

"They're taking his red stallion down there. Mutt Malvern and some of the other boys."

"With Sean?"

Dory Maud looks wistful then that she's trapped in the booth instead of down seeing the action. "I didn't see him. Talk's going around that he won't be in the races. That he and Benjamin Malvern fought over the stallion and he quit. Kendrick, I mean."

"Quit!"

"Are you deaf?" Dory Maud rings the bells right by my ear. She calls out to someone just behind me. "November bells! Best price on the island!" Sometimes she reminds me a lot of her sister Elizabeth, and not in a favourable way. Then she says to me, "It's all talk, isn't it? They say Kendrick wanted to buy the stallion and Malvern said no, so he quit."

I think of Sean folded low over the red stallion, riding bareback at the top of the cliffs. Of the easy way

314

they had with each other when I met him to look at the *uisce* mare. I think, even, of the way Sean looked when he stood on the bloody festival rock and said his name, and then Corr's, like it was just fact, one after the other. Of the way he said "the sky and the sand and the sea and Corr" to me. And I feel a bite of unfairness, because in everything but name, it seems to me that Sean Kendrick already owns Corr.

"So what are they doing with him?"

"How should I know? I just saw them parading past and Mutt Malvern looking like it's his birthday."

Now my sense of injustice is truly ringing. I abruptly change my plans from going to the cliff to watch from above to going down the cliff path to find out what's happening on the beach.

"I'm going down there."

"Don't talk to Malvern's son," Dory Maud warns.

I'm already heading away, but I glance back over my shoulder. "Why not?"

"Because he might talk back!"

I hurry down the cliff path past the rest of the tents; as the path descends steeply, the vendors can no longer get their tables to sit evenly so it grows more quiet. And there, down below, is the red stallion, surrounded by four men. I recognize the square form of Mutt Malvern, and the man holding the lead – David Prince, because he used to work Hammond's farm near us – but none of the others. There's a loose circle of people gathered around them as well, watching and laughing and shouting. Mutt shouts something back to them. Corr lifts his head, jerking the arm of the man who holds him, and calls to the sea, high and pure.

Mutt laughs. "Having some problems holding him, Prince?"

"I'll hold him!" shouts someone from the gathered group, and there's more laughter.

I imagine Dove taken from me in this way, and anger churns in my stomach.

I know that Sean must be here, somewhere. It takes me a moment to spot him, but by now I know how: look for the place with no movement, for the person who's just a little part away from the rest. Sure enough, there he is, standing with his back to the cliff, an arm across his stomach, his other elbow resting on it. His knuckles push tightly against his lips, but his face is expressionless. There's something terrible about the way he stands there, watching. He's not so much still as frozen.

Further down the beach, Corr keens again, and Mutt loops a scarlet ribbon tied with bells around Corr's pastern, just above his hoof. At the sound of them, the red stallion flinches, as if the bells are physically painful, and I find myself unexpectedly blinking away tears.

Sean Kendrick turns his face away.

There's something so wretched in that that I can't just leave him there by himself. I elbow my way through the tourists and the locals who are watching this spectacle.

My heart thuds in my chest. I think of Sean telling me: *Keep your pony off this beach.* It's possible I'm the last person he wants to see.

I stand next to him with my arms crossed. We don't speak. I'm glad that he doesn't look up, because Mutt has put a saddle on Corr and now they're draping a breastplate with nails and bells sewn into it over Corr's withers. The stallion's skin shivers wherever the iron touches him.

After a moment, Sean says in a low voice, still looking at the ground, "Where is your horse?"

"I worked her last night, after the rain stopped. Where's yours?"

He swallows.

"How can they do this?" I demand.

Corr makes a strange, frenzied sound, like half a whinny, a sound cut off before it began. He stands still, but he jerks his head as if trying to rid himself of a fly.

"I reckon," Sean says, in that same low voice, "that it's wise of you to ride your own horse, Puck, even if she's just an island pony. Better that your heart's your own."

Mutt Malvern says, "I thought he'd be bigger."

He's climbed on to Corr, though Prince still holds the lead rope. One of the other men stands between Corr and the sea, his arms held out on either side like a fence. Mutt swings his legs and looks at the ground as if he's a child on a pony.

"This is Mutt Malvern's gift to me," Sean says, and there's enough bitter in his words for me to taste it with him. "This is my fault."

I try to think of what I can say to comfort him. I don't even know if he wants it. I don't know if I'd want to be comforted, if I'm being honest. If I'm being forced to eat soot, I want to know that somewhere else in the world, someone else has to eat soot as well. I want to know that soot tastes terrible. I don't want to be told that soot's good for my digestion. And of course, by soot, I mean beans.

"Probably it is," I reply. "But in twenty minutes or thirty minutes or an hour, Mutt Malvern will get bored of this. And then he will be back on that wretched black-and-white creature that he's put on the butcher's board by his name. And I think the piebald's quite enough of a punishment for anyone."

Sean looks at me then, his eyes bright, in a way that makes me feel out of sorts. I glare back.

"Where did you say your horse was again?"

"Home. Trained yesterday evening. Why did you say you quit again?"

He looks away with a rueful snort. "It was a gamble. Like you and your pony."

"Horse."

"Right." Sean looks back to Corr. "Why did you say you were racing again?"

I hadn't said, of course. It goes against everything

in me to confess the true reasons behind my decision. I can imagine it being chatted all over Skarmouth, as easily as Dory Maud told me how Sean Kendrick had quit over Corr. I haven't told Peg Gratton, even though it seems like she is on my side, nor Dory Maud, and Dory Maud is nearly family. But I hear myself say, "We'll lose my parents' house if I don't win."

I realize then how foolish it is to say it. Not because I think Sean Kendrick will gossip. But because he'll know now that I hope not only to race but to make money at it. And that's a terribly fanciful thing to be saying to Sean Kendrick, four-time winner of the Scorpio Races. He is quiet for a long moment, his eyes on Corr and Mutt on his back.

"That's a good reason to gamble," he says, and I feel incredibly warm towards him for saying that, instead of telling me that I'm a fool.

I exhale. "So was yours."

"Do you think so?"

"He's yours no matter what the law says. I think Benjamin Malvern's jealous of it. And," I add, "I think he likes to play games with people."

Sean looks at me in that sharp way of his. I don't think he realizes how it impales people. "You know a lot about him."

I know that Benjamin Malvern likes to drink his tea with butter and salt in it, and that his nose is big enough to hide acorns in. I know that he wants to be entertained but that few things manage it. But I don't know if that means that I know him.

"Enough," I reply.

"I'm not," he says, "fond of games."

We both look back to Corr, who has, against everything I would've thought, settled down. He stands perfectly still, looking over the crowd, his ears pricked. Every so often, he quivers, but otherwise he doesn't move.

"Should I see how fast he is?" Mutt says. He turns in the saddle to eye Sean, who doesn't flinch. David Prince, still holding the lead, has an odd expression as he glances over to us. A bit guilty, a bit apologetic, a bit thrilled.

"Ho, Sean Kendrick," Prince says, as if either we or he has just appeared on the beach. "Any advice?"

"Don't forget about the sea," Sean says.

Mutt and Prince exchange a laugh at this.

"Look how tame he is," Mutt tells Sean. And surely, Corr's ears are pricked and interested. He sniffs at his saddle and at Mutt's leg as if surprised only that it's not his usual, as if it's a curious turn of events. The bells on his bridle shrill almost inaudibly with the movement. "None of Sean Kendrick's much-touted brand of witchcraft needed. Does it bother you that he's so faithless?"

Sean doesn't reply. Mutt's eyes swipe over me

dismissively. I don't think I've ever seen someone take so much pleasure in making someone else miserable. I remember that first night when I saw them both outside the pub, the hatred that lurked in both their expressions. There's nothing hidden about it now; it's an ugly sore. Mutt addresses the crowd – tourists, most of them. "What do you think? I'm about to take the fastest horse on the island out for a gallop. He's a legend, right? A hero? A national treasure. Who doesn't know his name?"

They clap and hoot. Sean is immobile, a piece of the cliffs.

"I know it!" I shout then, and my voice is so loud that it surprises me. Mutt's gaze finds me next to Sean. I call, "But what's yours, again?"

I give him my most horrible smile, the one that I learned from having two brothers.

As I watch Mutt's face light up with anger and listen to the murmur of amusement from the onlookers, I remember, too late, Dory Maud's advice.

"Where's your pony, then?" Mutt snaps back. "Ploughing fields?"

I'm more embarrassed by the attention than by the insult. Probably because when I'm done down here, I'll be back in Dory Maud's booth selling baubles to tourists. It occurs to me that Mutt Malvern doesn't know me well enough to say something to properly hurt me.

It's not me that Mutt wants to hurt anyway. He calls,

"I have to say I'm pleased for you, Kendrick. Is she a better ride than you're used to?" He pretends to caress Corr's rump. I feel my cheeks go hot. Sean's face doesn't change and I wonder at it — is it practice? Is it that he's heard all these things too many times for them to prick his skin?

Beneath Mutt, Corr moves restlessly. He pushes his nose towards Prince, nuzzling into his chest. Prince scratches his forehead and pushes back.

"Steady, old lad," he says. Prince tilts his head back to face Mutt. "Are you taking him out, then? Before the tide gets up on us?" As he speaks, Corr presses again, more insistently, so that the bells ring again, and Prince pushes back.

"Yeah, indeed," Mutt replies. He wiggles one of the reins to get Corr's attention; Corr still nuzzles and pushes at Prince. I see the shudder of Corr's skin beneath the ironbound breastplate they've put on him.

"OK, now," Prince says. Corr's muzzle is at his collarbone, like Dove does when I scratch her mane and she's feeling fond. Prince lays his hand flat on Corr's cheek as Corr's breath whuffs against Prince's neck.

Sean's feet kick up sand even as he shouts. "*David!*"

Prince looks up.

Quick as a snake, Corr's flat teeth crush into his neck.

Mutt Malvern hauls back on the reins; Corr climbs into a rear. The crowd shouts and scatters. The other two men who were with Mutt leap back, uncertain if they should defend themselves or help Mutt. Sean jerks to a stop, face turned from the spraying sand. On the ground, Prince arches his back, his feet scrabbling. I can't look away.

Corr rears again, and this time, Mutt can't keep his hold. He rolls out of the reach of Corr's hooves and comes up bloody. Prince's blood, not his. The stallion's eyes are white and rolling as he spins. His gaze is on the surf. Everyone else's gaze is on him and on Sean, but none of them is moving.

When Corr circles another time, I dart across the sand to where Prince lies. I can't tell how badly he's hurt; there's too much blood to see his skin. I'm afraid that Corr will trample him, but I don't know if I can move him. The best I can do is stand between him and the hooves and try to press down this horror inside me.

Corr turns and cries out again; this time it's like a choked sob. There's a spiderweb of veins standing out on his shoulder.

"Corr," Sean says.

He doesn't shout it. It doesn't seem loud enough to be heard above the sound of the hoofbeats and the surf or the sound of Prince's gagging, but the red stallion stills. Sean holds his arms out and approaches slowly. There's blood on Corr's lower jaw; his lips quiver. His ears are flat back against his head.

"Hold on," I whisper to Prince. Up close, he's not as

young as I thought; I can see every line carved around his eyes and mouth. I don't know if he can hear me. He holds fistfuls of sand and his eyes on me are a terrible, terrible thing. I don't want to touch him, but I reach down. When he feels my fingers, he clutches my hand so hard that it hurts.

Near Corr, Sean shoulders off his jacket and abandons it on the sand, then tugs his shirt off over his head. Underneath, he's pale and scarred. I've never given much thought to whether broken ribs healed straight before now. Sean speaks to Corr in a low, low voice. Corr shakes, his eyes rolling towards the ocean.

Prince's blood is all over me. I've never seen so much blood before. *This is how my parents died.* I tell myself not to imagine it, but it doesn't matter; I can't picture it. There's just no way to make my mind accept the possibility of it, and I'm sorry that I can't. Because as terrible as imagining that might be, it has to be better than living in this current reality with Prince's shaking hand gripping mine.

Sean slowly approaches Corr, speaking in the same low voice all the way. He's three steps away. Two. One. Corr lifts his head, pulling back, his teeth bared and bloody; he's shaking as much as Prince. Sean balls up his shirt and then presses it to Corr's muzzle. He waits a long moment until Corr smells nothing but Sean Kendrick, and then Sean wipes the blood from Corr's mouth. As the stallion stands, rigid, Sean folds the shirt so that the blood faces the sky, then wraps the fabric over Corr's nostrils and eyes.

"Daly," Sean says. Beside him, Corr's nostrils suck the fabric of his shirt against them, showing the outline of his muzzle through the shirt, and then blow it back out again. One of the men who'd come with Mutt jerks at his name. He looks terrified. Sean's eyes flit away, disappointed by whatever he sees in Daly's face, and then they find me. "Puck."

I don't want to leave Prince as long as he's holding my hand so tightly, but I realize suddenly that somewhere along the way it switched to me holding his hand and not the other way around. Horrified, I drop his fingers with a start and climb to my feet.

Sean gestures to the reins that trail from Corr's bridle. "Hold this. Will you hold this? I need. . ." The red stallion still quivers beneath the mask Sean's made. I can't seem to feel afraid — it's like my fear has fled somewhere deep inside me. Someone needs to hold the horse. I can hold the horse. I wipe my bloody palm on my trousers and step forward. Taking a deep breath, I hold out my hand.

Sean puts the reins and a bunch of fabric in my fist, whether or not I'm ready. This close, I hear a faint metallic humming, and I realize that it's the bells around Corr's bridle and pasterns. The stallion shakes so subtly and constantly that the metal balls inside the bells whirr like metal grasshoppers.

Sean checks my grip and then, swift and certain,

he crouches and slides beneath the red stallion. He produces a knife from his pocket, and runs his palm down Corr's foreleg.

"I'm here," he says, and Corr's ear trembles and turns to catch his voice.

Sean deftly slices off each of the red ribbons, casting them angrily behind him with a tinny jangle. I start as the stallion moves. Now that his hooves are free of the bells, he picks up and puts down his legs, trotting without moving. Sean exhales sharply; he's trying to unfasten the breastplate and Corr's moving too much. I'm not sure how handling a killer *capall uisce* is any different from handling Dove, so I just react the same way. I pop the reins down smartly and the stallion jerks his head up. I think he's trembling less, but it's hard to tell without the bells singing to tell me. I try not to think about how it's Prince's blood still wetting my palm. I try to remember what I've seen Sean doing with the horses.

Shhhh, shhhhh, I say to the stallion, like the ocean, and his ears instantly prick towards me, his tail hanging motionless for the first time. I'm not entirely sure I like his attention, even blindfolded.

Sean looks at me over Corr's withers, his expression odd – approving? – for just a moment. Then he throws the iron breastplate behind him into the sand by the bells.

"I'll take him now."

"What about that man? Prince?" I ask, not releasing

the reins until I'm sure that Sean has them.

"He's dead."

I glance over. Now that Sean and I have calmed Corr, someone from the crowd has pulled Prince to safety. But they've put a jacket over his face. I shudder in the wind. "He died!" I know it's stupid to say it, but I can't not say it.

"He was dead before. He knew it, didn't you see it in his eyes? My jacket."

"Your *jacket*?" I say, with enough force that my shaky voice makes Corr start. "How about 'my jacket, *please*'."

Sean Kendrick looks at me, perplexed, and I can see that he hasn't a clue of why I'm upset with him. Why I'm upset at all. I can't stop shaking, as if I've taken all of Corr's trembling and made it my own.

"That's what I said," he says after a pause.

"No, it's *not*."

"What did I say?"

"You said *my jacket*."

Sean looks a little bewildered now. "That's what I said I said."

I make an angry noise and go to get his jacket. If there was any chance that the tide wouldn't take it before he got back down here, I'd have left it. All I can think about is that that man is dead, the man who was just holding my hand, and the more I think about it, the angrier I get, although I can't think of who to blame except this *capall uisce* that I just agreed to hold. And somehow that makes me feel like I'm complicit, and that makes me angrier still.

His jacket is absolutely filthy, caked with dried sand and blood and stiff with salt water on top of it all. It's like a piece of canvas sail. I was going to just drape it over Sean's bare arm, but without his shirt to soften it, it would chafe.

"I'll bring it to you," I tell him. "I'll wash it with my horse blanket. Where do I bring it?"

"The Malvern Yard," he says. "For now."

I look back to Prince. There he is, stretched out, and someone's gone to get Dr Halsal to declare him well and truly dead. The men chat quietly next to his body, as if lowered voices show their respect. But I can catch snatches of their conversation and they're talking about race odds.

"Thanks," Sean says.

"What?" But I've already realized what he's said, my brain catching up to real time. He sees the realization in my face and nods, shortly. Pulling Corr's head down, Sean whispers to him, and then he puts his hand to the red stallion's side. The stallion starts as if Sean's palm is fiery. But he doesn't lash out, and Sean leads him away from the beach and back towards the cliffs. He stops only once, an arm's length from Mutt. From here, he looks wiry and pale without his shirt on, just a boy with a blood-red horse.

"Mr Malvern," he says, "would you like to take your

horse back to the yard?"

Mutt just stares at him.

As Sean leads Corr away from the beach, I crumple and uncrumple his jacket in my hands. I can't quite make myself believe the truth of it. That ten minutes ago I held a dead man's hand. That days from now I will put myself on a beach with a few dozen *capaill uisce*. That I told Sean Kendrick I'd clean his jacket for him.

"Bit of a bollocks."

I turn. It's Daly.

"Excuse me?" I ask.

"Bollocks," Daly says again, that helpless swearing that comes from needing something better to say but not having it on hand. "The whole island is."

I don't reply. I don't have anything to say. I hold Sean's jacket tightly to still my shaking hands.

"I want to go home," Daly tells me, voice miserable. "No game's worth this."

FORTY-THREE

Benjamin Malvern wants to meet at the hotel in Skarmouth. That's a game itself, somehow, because these days the Skarmouth Hotel will churn with people, every room filled with tourists for the races. While the butcher's is a local hub for betting and news, a place where the riders know to come for talk, the hotel is where the mainlanders compare notes and talk about the day's training, scratch their heads, and wonder if this mare or that stallion will calm down enough to be a contender in the race. For me to stand in the hotel lobby where Malvern arranged for us to meet is for me to be gobbled up.

So I step into the hotel, out of the cold, but I slide through the lobby as quickly as I can and find a stairwell to wait in. It looks like it leads upward to only a few of the guest rooms, so the odds of being bothered are slight. I rub my arms — it's draughty — and peer upward through the stairs. The hotel is the grandest building on the island, everything about it designed to make someone from the mainland feel at home. So the architecture inside is painted columns and civilized wooden arches, cornices and polished wood. A Persian rug cushions my feet. On the wall adjacent to me is a painting of a thoroughbred posing in a bridle, standing before a halcyon landscape. Everything about the hotel says that those who stay here are gentlemen and scholars, cultured and safe.

I steal a glance into the lobby, looking for Malvern. Knots of race tourists stand in twos and threes, smoking and discussing the training. The room is full of their foreign, broad accents. From a room off the lobby, a piano plays. The minutes move sluggishly. It's a strange neverland, right now, between the festival and the races. The most die-hard of race enthusiasts arrive for the Scorpio Festival, but Skarmouth isn't large enough to entertain them long. There's nothing for them to do until the races but watch us live and die down on the sand.

I retreat back into the stairwell and cross my arms against the draught. My thoughts won't be contained, and they run out again to the memories of the image of Mutt Malvern on Corr. Of the sound of Corr's cry. Of the curl of afternoon-red hair on Puck Connolly's cheek.

This feels like dangerous ground.

I hear the stairs above me creak as footsteps descend. I look just in time to see George Holly trotting brightly down the stairs, like a boy. When he catches sight of me, he checks himself sharply and ducks against the wall as if it were his destination all along.

"Hello and hello," Holly says to me. He looks like he hasn't slept, like the storm cast him up on the shore and left him to choose land or sea for himself. It's an odd thought, as I can't think of what George Holly does with himself when he's not watching the horses. Something loud and enthusiastic, no doubt, anything that can be accomplished in a white sweater. It's strange how I've come to feel friendship with someone so different from myself.

I nod.

Holly says, "Right, and always the nod. So you're waiting on Malvern, then."

I'm not surprised that he knows. News of my quitting took only a moment to spread across the island like a cough, and I'm sure that whispers of Corr's violent morning took even less. I nod again.

"And of course he's meeting you in this stairwell."

I glance out into the main room again. I realize that I'm at once impatient for Malvern to come and say his piece, and hoping that he'll be late so I can delay hearing what he has to say. I ball my fists up in my armpits, but this cold inside me is nerves, not temperature.

"What you want is a jacket," Holly says, observing my posture.

"I have a jacket. Blue one."

Holly ruminates on this for a moment. "I remember it now. Thin as a dead child?"

"That's the one." In Puck Connolly's custody. That might be the last I see of that jacket.

"Did you ever wonder..." Holly says, after a pause. "No, perhaps you don't. Perhaps you know. If anyone knows, you do. I've been wondering as I've been here, why it is that Thisby has the *capaill uisce* and no one else does?"

"Because we love them."

"Sean Kendrick, you're an old man. Do you smoke? Me neither. We might as well with the air in here. Have you ever seen so many men doing nothing so busily? Is that your final answer, by the way?"

I shrug and reply, "This island's had horses for as long as it's had men on it. On the other side of Thisby, there's a cliff cave with a red stallion drawn on the wall. Ancient. How long do you have to be in a place before it's your home? This is their home on land."

I'd found the drawing once while looking to catch a *capall*. At low tide, the cave led so far into the island that it felt I'd come out the other side if I pressed much further. Then, all at once, the tide had roared in so fast and sudden that I'd been trapped. I'd spent hours braced on a tiny, dark ledge, each push of the surf soaking me again. Below me, I'd heard the low shrills and clucks of a water horse somewhere in the cave. To keep myself from falling, I'd eventually rolled on to my back on the ledge, and there, high above me where the water couldn't reach: the drawing. A stallion brighter than

Corr, painted in a red that had only faded a little, the pigment out of the reach of the sun. There was a dead man at his feet, too, in the drawing, a dash of black for his hair, a line of red for his chest.

The Scorpio sea has thrown *capaill uisce* on to our shore since long before my father or my father's father was born.

"Were they always revered? Never eaten?"

My expression is withering. "Would you eat a shark?"

"In California we do."

"Well, that's why California doesn't have *capaill uisce*." I pause for him to finish laughing and add, "You have lipstick on your collar."

"It's from the horses," Holly says, but he tries to catch a glimpse. He finds the edge of it and rubs his fingers over the mark. "She's blind. She was aiming for my ear."

It explains his rumpled look, in any case. I lean again to look into the lobby. There are more men than before, piling in as the afternoon gets elderly and the shadows get cold outside. Benjamin Malvern isn't yet among them.

Holly asks, "Do you know what he'll say? You're so calm."

I say, "I'm sick over it."

"You don't look it."

Corr can hold a thousand things in his heart and

reveal only one of them on his face, like he did earlier today. He is so very like me.

I let myself, for one brief moment, consider what Malvern may want to meet about. The thought stings inside me, a cold needle.

"Now you do," says Holly.

Frowning, I look again, and this time I see Benjamin Malvern stepping into the lobby, closing the door behind him. He has his hands in the pockets of his greatcoat, and he strides into the lobby as if he owns it. Perhaps he does. He looks like a prizefighter, the slope of his shoulders in the coat, the forward jut of his neck. I hadn't seen any of Benjamin Malvern in Mutt before, but I finally see the resemblance.

Holly follows my gaze. "I'd better go. He won't be happy to see me."

I can't imagine Benjamin Malvern being displeased to see one of his buyers. Or at least, I cannot imagine him revealing that he was displeased to see one of them.

"We quarrelled," Holly says. "It's a smaller island than I imagined. But don't worry, my dollar bills mean that our friendship will endure."

We part ways, Holly creeping towards the sounds of the piano and me stepping into the lobby. I know the exact moment I am recognized, as everyone looks away so discreetly that it's obvious they were just looking the second before.

It takes me a moment to spot Malvern in the crowd, but then I see him speaking to Colin Calvert, one of the race officials. Calvert's kinder than Eaton, the anachronistic bully who Puck had to knock heads with, but he wouldn't have been at the festival. His wife's the brand of Christian that forbids a gathering that involves young women dancing in the streets but not races where men die. Calvert sees me and nods, and I return it, though my mind is already on the conversation ahead. Malvern approaches me slowly, like I'm not the destination.

"Well, Sean Kendrick," Malvern says.

I want Corr.

I can't say anything.

Malvern thumbs one of his ears and looks at a painting of two tidy thoroughbred racers over the great fireplace. "You're a poor conversationalist and I'm a poor loser, so let's put it at this. If you win, I'll sell him to you. If you don't win, I never want to hear about this again."

And the sun's come out over the ocean.

I realize now that I didn't think that it would.

Four times I've won. I can do it again. We can do it again. I see the beach before me, the horses around me, the surf under Corr's hooves, and at the end of it, there's freedom.

"How much?" I ask.

"Three hundred." His face is sly. My salary is one

hundred and fifty in a year, and he's the one paying it, so he knows it to the penny. Winning years, I get eight per cent of the purse. I've saved what I can.

"Mr Malvern," I say, "do you want me back or do we still play a game?"

"Want and need are two different things," Malvern says. "Two hundred and ninety."

"Mr Holly has offered me a job."

Malvern looks pained, though I'm not certain if it's at the idea of losing me or at the mention of Holly's name. "Two hundred and fifty."

I cross my arms. Two hundred and fifty is unattainable. "Who else will touch him after today?"

"They've all killed someone."

"Not all of them have killed someone with your son on their back."

His expression is cut glass. "Tell me a price."

"Two hundred." This is dear, but doable. Only just. Only if I can count this year's unwon purse as part of my savings.

"This is where I walk away, Mr Kendrick." But he doesn't. I stand and I wait. I realize that the hotel lobby has gone quiet. I realize that this is the reason why we aren't meeting in the tea shop or the stables or his office. Here, it's the best advertising Malvern can get. His name will be on everyone's lips.

Malvern exhales. "Two hundred. Enjoy your races, gentlemen."

He puts his hands in his pockets and walks away. Calvert opens the door for him, letting in a shaft of brilliantly red afternoon light.

I have to win.

FORTY-FOUR

Puck

"Kate, you do realize that you aren't at fault."

Father Mooneyham sounds a little tired, but he always seems to sound that way to me when I go to confession. I smooth my hands over my smock. I felt bad coming to church in my trousers, but I wasn't about to ride Dove in a dress, so I put a smock on over them. I feel it's a fair compromise.

"But I *feel* guilty. I was the last one to hold his hand. And when I let go, he was dead."

"But surely he would have died anyway."

"Maybe not, though. What if I'd stayed and held his hand? I won't ever know now. I'll always wonder."

I stare at the brilliant stained-glass window over the altar. The peculiarity of the confession booth allows me to see the rest of the building from my vantage point. Because St Columba's apparently predates confession or priests or sin, the booth was added much later. The confessional is open to the rest of the church, and the curtain is only between the confessor and the priest. And the curtain is ridiculous not only because Father

Mooneyham can just watch the penitent walk through the pews towards him, but also Father knows everyone's voices on the island, so even blind, he'd know whose sin was whose. The only real benefit of the curtain is to allow you to pick your nose without a holy audience, something I'd seen Joseph Beringer take advantage of before.

Now Father sounds a little cross. "This sounds more like egotism to me, Kate. You are ascribing much power to what was, after all, only your hand."

"You're the one who says that God works through us. Maybe he wanted me to stay there and keep holding it."

There's silence for a moment on the other side of the curtain. Finally, he says, "Not everyone's hands can always be the site of miracles. We would be afraid to touch anything. Did you feel called to stay by his side? No? Then put down your guilt."

He makes it sound like something I can wrap in wax paper and leave by the door for Puffin. I slouch back in the chair and look at the ceiling of the church.

"I'm also very angry with my brother," I add. "Anger's a sin, right?" I remember, however, that God sometimes came over all righteously angry, and that was all right. I feel slightly righteous about my anger over Gabe's decision to leave the island, so perhaps it's not a sin after all.

"Why are you angry at him?"

I wipe a tear off my cheek. It's a very cunning tear, because I didn't even feel it coming. "Because he's leaving us behind, and not even for a good reason. Nothing I can change."

Father Mooneyham says, "Gabriel." Because of course he knows which brother I mean now.

He doesn't say anything for a few minutes, just lets me cry. Orange and blue light from the stained-glass windows finds its way through my hands cupped over my face. It's very quiet in the church. Finally, I wipe the sleeve of my shirt across my cheek.

The curtain shivers slightly and I see Father Mooneyham's hand offering a handkerchief. I use it to dry my face and his hand withdraws.

"I can't tell you anything that he's said in here, Kate. And I don't know if it will make you feel any better to know that he has sat in that same chair where you sit now, and he has cried as well."

I try, without success, to imagine Gabe crying. Even at our parents' burial, he had looked dry-eyed into the hole in the ground, shivering in the wind, letting Finn and me lean against him and weep. Despite that, the image of him in this chair, crying, creeps into my head, and I can feel myself softening towards him. I'm resentful that this hypothetical Gabriel can work such magic on me. I say, "But he doesn't even have to go."

"Mm. I will tell you one thing he said, Kate. He said that you don't need to ride in the races."

"Of *course* I do! We need the money."

"And the races are your answer to that problem. It's how you feel you can solve it. Gabe has a problem, too, and leaving is how he feels he can solve it."

It's a horribly wise way of looking at it, and it annoys me. "Isn't there something holy about taking care of widows and orphans? Isn't he supposed to be taking care of us?" But even as I say it, I remember him saying *I can't bear it*. He had been taking care of us. From that dry-eyed funeral where he let us lean on him in our grief to working late on the docks to trying to spare us from Malvern. I suddenly feel very selfish to begrudge him his escape. I sigh. "Why does it have to be leaving, though? Can't he come up with a different answer? Can't I change his mind?"

Father Mooneyham considers this. "Leaving doesn't mean not coming back. It wouldn't hurt you to meditate on the story of the prodigal son."

This is about as comforting as a cold brick when you're lonely. I stuff Father Mooneyham's handkerchief back under the curtain, and when he takes it, I scowl at the stained-glass window over the altar. There are thirteen red panes in the middle of it, and Mum or someone told me once that they were supposed to represent drops of Columba's blood. He was martyred here. It was back before the natives knew that confession and priests and sin were good for them, so they stabbed Columba and threw him off one of the western cliffs.

Then his body washed up with the *capaill uisce* one October and because it wasn't disgusting, even after being in the ocean for so long, he was sainted. I think his jawbone is still kept there behind the altar.

This reminds me, suddenly, of how Gabe had decided when he was fifteen that he was going to be a priest. He'd been absolutely no fun for about two weeks. It was Gabe who'd told me the story of Columba; I remember sitting in the pew with him then. His hair had been slicked back with water because he'd felt it added to his ethereal appearance. I feel a sudden pang of longing for that foolishly serious Gabe and the trusting and always ill-contented Puck that I'd been then.

"Aren't you going to give me a penance, Father?" I ask.

"Kate, you have yet to confess any sins to me."

I cast my mind back over the past week. "I considered taking the Lord's name on Monday. Well, not 'God'. I thought about saying 'Jesus Christ!' I also ate an entire orange without telling Finn, because I knew he'd be annoyed."

Father Mooneyham says, "Go home, Kate."

"I *have* been horrid. I just can't think of them right now. I don't want you to think otherwise."

"Will it make you feel better to say two Hail Marys and a Columba Creed?"

"Yes, thank you." He absolves me. I feel absolved. As I get up, I see that someone is waiting in the pews on the opposite side of the church, waiting to confess. It's Annie, Dory Maud's youngest sister. Her lipstick is a little smeared, but it seems cruel to tell a blind woman that, so I don't say anything. I almost don't notice Elizabeth, sitting at the end of the same pew with her hair pinned up to her head and her arms pinned across her chest. I can't decide which of them is confessing. Annie looks dreamy, but she always does because she can't see further than a metre away. Elizabeth looks vaguely angry, but she always does because she can see further than a metre away.

"Puck," Elizabeth says.

Annie says hello to me in her soft voice.

"Where are you headed?" Elizabeth asks.

I feel a little lighter. "I have to return a jacket."

FORTY-FIVE

Puck

Even before I get down the twilight-darkened lane to the Malvern Yard, I can see evidence of it — the fields and fields of horses — and I can smell it — good horses making good manure from good hay. I reckon horse manure is a lot like a cat scratch. There's nothing too disagreeable about either of those things so long as there's not too much of it and it's not too fresh. And there's nothing disagreeable about the grass-hay-manure scent of the Malvern Yard. Because it's been a long day and there's no reason to expect that it's not going to get longer, I allow myself the small pleasure of imagining that the sloping fields and glossy mares on either side of the lane are mine, and that I'm strolling pleasantly down to my own yard, filled with the buoyant contentedness that comes from the certainty of one's holdings and the knowledge that dinner will have once been a cow.

On the gallop to my left, there's a scrawny guy on a trotting thoroughbred gelding. He's got his stirrups strapped up short like a jockey, which I guess he is, and when he trots, he looks like he's hovering over his mount instead of riding it. A man leans on the rail watching, and if I were a betting sort like Dory Maud, I'd put money that he isn't from Thisby. He's wearing white shoes, for starters, and I don't think there's a place on Thisby that sells white shoes. Closer to the main building, another groom leads a dusky grey with a soaking coat back towards one of the pastures. The horse looks cleaner than I feel, and considerably better fed. Then, through the open stable doors, I glimpse a chestnut standing in cross ties in the aisle while a boy brushes it down. The evening light pours in around them and makes a purple copy of the horse and groom on the ground behind them. A whinny peals across the yard, and another horse replies from inside the barn.

It's all very much like I expected a famous race yard to look like, and I feel a little funny about it. I'm not an ambitious person, I don't think, and it's not as if I ever spent any time daydreaming of having a farm of my own. And I generally have a pretty dim view of people who waste time sighing and moaning and rending their clothing about things that they don't have and never will, because Dad's religion was all about knowing the difference between need and want. But standing here looking into the heart of the Malvern Yard, I feel a small, fierce pang of sadness that I won't ever have a farm.

I try to decide if it would be worth being Benjamin Malvern if it meant that I could live in a place like this.

"Who are you looking for?"

I scowl at my shadow before locating the voice. It's the groom with the just-bathed grey thoroughbred — imagine a world where the horses get baths; how does a horse ever get dirty in a place like this? — stopped halfway across the yard. The grey shoves at his back, but he ignores him.

"Sean Kendrick."

It feels strange to say it out loud. I hold up his jacket, like it's an invitation. My heart taps lightly against my breastbone.

"Where's Kendrick?" the groom calls to a man who's just come from one of the smaller buildings. They confer. I fidget. I didn't expect to be taken seriously.

"Stable," the groom says. "Probably. Main stable."

They don't ask me what I want with him or tell me to go away, though they have that curious, helpful look about them like they're waiting for me to do something. I just say thanks and let myself into the yard. I'm careful to close the gate as I found it, because I'm aware it's the worst crime on a farm to do otherwise.

I pretend I can't feel the grooms looking after me as I step into the stable. It's hard to think of it as a stable, even with the obvious presence of horses in it, because it's awesome in the way that St Columba's is. It has the same high ceiling, the carved stone, the carried sounds. The only thing that's missing is the afterthought confessional with the inadequate curtain. The stable reminds me, for some reason, of the great rock that all of the riders spilled their blood on.

With effort, I draw my eyes down. I don't want to stare because the boy is still currying the chestnut in the aisle, and I don't want to be seen looking like Finn with his round-eyed, ogling face. Both boy and chestnut look clean and purposeful, and I feel grubby and mismatched in my trousers and smock and hooded sweater. I point to where the cross tie meets the wall, which is the universal way to ask, *Can I duck under this?* and the groom nods. He wears the same sharp, curious expression as the others. I think that the interest is simply because I'm a stranger, until I'm past him and he says, "I think you've got a real head of hair on you to ride that mare of yours in the races."

The way he says it, I think it's a compliment, but I'm not sure.

"Thanks," I say, in case it is. "Do you know where Sean Kendrick is?" Again, I hold up his jacket. It feels very important that everyone know that I have a real purpose for seeking him out. The boy jerks his chin down the aisle past him, past endless beautiful, shining stall doors with stone arches over the doors as if each stall is a shrine and the horses gods within them. I walk past them until I see a stall at the end with pale white bars instead of iron ones, and the unmistakable shape of the red stallion's head behind them.

I step quietly up to the stall, and I think, at first,

that Sean's not here. It's a concept that, for some reason, aggravates me to no end – and then I see him in the dim shadows near the floor of the stall, crouched around Corr's legs, wrapping them below the knee. He's very slow about it – he turns the wrap around Corr's leg once, then spits on his fingers and reaches up to touch Corr's body. Then he winds it once more before spitting again. All the while Corr's neck is arched and he's looking out of the small window of his stall. He has a view of bare rock with just a bit of sod clinging to the edges. It's a dreary view, I think, but he seems to enjoy looking at it well enough. I reckon it's better than the walls.

For a moment I just watch Sean wrap Corr's leg, watching how his shoulders move when they're not hidden by his jacket, how he tilts his head when he's involved in his work. He either hasn't noticed my arrival or he's pretending that he hasn't, and either's fine by me. There's something rewarding about watching a job done well, or at least a job done with everything you've got. I try to put my finger on how it is that Sean Kendrick seems so different to other people, what it is about him that makes him seem so intense and still at the same time, and I think, finally, that it's something about hesitation. Most people hesitate between steps or pause or are somehow uneven about the process. Whether that process is wrapping a leg or eating a sandwich or just living life. But with Sean, there's never a move he's not sure of, even if it means not moving at all.

Corr turns his head to look at me with just his left eye, and the movement makes Sean look up. He doesn't say anything, and I hold his jacket up high enough that he can see it.

"I couldn't get all the blood out."

Sean ducks back down, leaving me standing there with the jacket. I debate whether I'm supposed to leave it in front of the stall or wait for him to say something else, but before I can decide, Sean has finished the wrap and stood up to face me. His fingers press on the side of Corr's neck.

"That's kind of you," he says.

"I know," I reply. Dove's blanket didn't really need washing but it got washed anyway, since I had Sean's jacket to do as well. I worked at it until my fingers became wrinkled and my benevolence became irritation. "What are you doing?"

"Wrapping his legs with seaweed."

I've never heard of wrapping a horse's leg with seaweed, but Sean seems to be approaching it with great confidence, so clearly it must have some good purpose.

I gesture with the jacket. "Do you want me to leave this somewhere?" I only ask it because it's polite. I don't want him to say yes. I don't know what exactly it is I want him to say, only for it to be something that gives me an excuse to stay here watching him for a few more minutes. Admitting this to myself is a sharp blow to my pride, as, with the exception of my six-year-old self's desire to marry Dr Halsal, I'd always thought I was above being fascinated by anyone but myself.

On the other side of the stall door, Sean looks up and down the aisle, as if he's scouting for a place for me to hang the jacket, but then he frowns at me as if that wasn't what he was looking for at all. "I'm nearly done. Can you wait?"

I try not to stare at where his hand rests on the red stallion's neck. It's a warning, the way his fingers lean into his skin, telling Corr to keep his distance, but it's a comfort as well, the way that I would touch Dove to remind her just that I'm there. The difference, though, is that Corr killed a man yesterday morning.

I say, "I suppose I have one minute or two to put together."

Sean does the sweep of his eyes that he does, the one that goes from my head to my toes and back again and makes me feel that he's scanning the depths of my soul and teasing out my motivations and sins. It's worse than confession with Father Mooneyham. At the end of it, he says, "If you help, this will go faster."

There is a little narrowing to his eyes at the end of it that makes me understand that this is a test. Whether or not I'm brave enough to go into the stall with Corr after yesterday morning, after I've had time to think about what happened. The thought of it makes my pulse trip. The question is not if I trust Corr. The question is if I trust Sean.

"What would helping look like?" I answer, and Sean's face clears like a fair day over Skarmouth. He spits on his fingers again and pushes Corr towards the back wall of the stall to give me room to open the door. I stand inside the stall.

He says, "Don't trust him."

I narrow my eyes. "What about you?"

Sean's expression doesn't change. "I won't be the one to harm you. Do you know how to wrap a leg?"

"I was born wrapping legs," I say stiffly, because I'm insulted.

"Must've been a challenging delivery," Sean notes, and points to a bucket against the wall. It's black as pitch inside. "That goes under the wrap. It has to be even."

Keeping a watchful eye on Corr, I pick up the bucket.

"Make sure the seaweed lies flat."

"OK."

"Leave a couple of centimetres below the knee."

"OK."

"It's got to be loose enough to put a finger in the top."

"Sean *Kendrick*." I say it emphatically enough that the stallion's ears prick towards me. I preferred when he didn't notice me. His attention reminds me of the black *capall uisce* that found Finn and me in the lean-to.

Sean doesn't appear to be at all apologetic. "I think you'd better let me do it after all."

"*You're* the one who had me in here in the first place," I say. "Now I think it's you who doesn't trust me."

"It's not just you," he replies.

I glower at him. "Well, I tell you what. I'll hold him and you wrap. That way, when it's done wrong, there's only yourself to slap. And take your jacket. I'm tired of holding it."

Sean's look is appraising, as if he's trying to decide if I really mean it. Or maybe he's just trying to decide if I'm capable.

"All right," he says. He holds a hand in front of Corr's face like a warning. We trade — with his other hand, he takes his jacket and I take the lead. He shrugs the jacket on, suddenly and magically becoming the Sean Kendrick I saw in the butcher shop as he does. He says, "The teeth are what to watch."

My tone comes out unintentionally bitter. "I saw."

"That wasn't Corr," Sean says. "You have to know them. You only use what you need. You can't just hang every bell in Thisby on every horse in the sea. They react differently. They aren't machines."

"So you're saying David Prince would still be alive if you'd been on Corr?" But it's a question that we both already know the answer to, so I ask, "Why?"

Sean ducks by Corr's leg, sliding his hand down it so that the stallion knows he's there. "Don't you know when your mare is anxious?"

Of course I do. I've grown up on her back and by her side. I know when she's unhappy sure as she knows when I am.

I ask, "Did you un-quit?"

I glance up as the lights switch on in the barn, filling the stall with a yellow glow that doesn't quite reach the floor. Sean's much faster with the wrap now. He works steadily without stopping to spit, so that must've been something to keep Corr standing still while he had no one to hold him. Is there no one in this fancy barn who would hold Corr while Sean worked? All this time, Corr's been standing sweet as a sheep, though his eyes are canny as a goat's. Sean doesn't look up when he replies. "Malvern told me I could buy Corr from him if I won."

"Is that un-quitting?"

"Yes."

"What about if you don't win?"

Sean looks up at me. "What if you don't?"

I don't want to answer, so instead I fire back, "What will you do if you win?"

He's done with the wrap, but he stays crouched by Corr's leg. "With my savings and my part of the purse, I'll buy Corr and I'll move back to my father's house out on the western rock and let only the wind change my direction."

Perhaps because I've only just discovered the formidable beauty of the Malvern stables, I'm incredulous. "Wouldn't you miss all this?"

Now he looks up at me, and from this angle, it looks like someone has smeared charcoal beneath the skin under his eyes. "What's there to miss? This was never mine to miss." This makes him heave a deep sigh, which seems like the closest thing to a confession I've heard from him, and then he pushes to his feet. "What about you, Kate Connolly? Puck Connolly?"

The way he says it, I feel certain he misremembered intentionally, because he liked the weight of the words when he said my name twice, and that makes me feel warm and nervous and agreeable.

"What about me?"

He trades me again, the bucket for the lead, and I step back. "What will you do if you win the Scorpio Races?"

I look into the bucket.

"Oh, I'll buy fourteen dresses and build a road and name it after myself and try one of everything at Palsson's."

Though I don't quite look up, I can still feel his gaze on me. It's a heavy thing, this look of his. He says, "What's the real answer?"

But when I try to think of a real answer, it reminds me of Father Mooneyham saying that Gabe had sat in the confessional and cried, and it makes me think of how, no matter what happens in the races, the best option still has Gabe sailing away in a boat. So I snap, "Do you think I just turn my secrets out for everyone?"

He is unfazed. "I didn't know they were secrets," he says. "Or I wouldn't have asked."

It makes me feel ungenerous, since he'd answered so honestly. "I'm sorry," I say. "My mother always said that I was born out of a bottle of vinegar instead of born from a womb and that she and my father bathed me in sugar for three days to wash it off. I try to behave, but I always go back to the vinegar." When Dad was in one of his rare, fanciful moods, he told guests that the pixies left me on the doorstep because I bit their fingers too often. My favourite was always when Mum said that before I was born, it rained for seven days and seven nights solid, and when she went out into the yard to ask the sky what it was weeping for, I dropped out of the clouds at her feet and the sun came out. I always liked the idea of being such a bother that I affected even the weather.

Sean says, "Don't apologize. I was being too free."

And now I feel even worse, because that wasn't what I meant at all.

Beside Sean, Corr abruptly shifts his weight and the motion of his head seems more lupine than equine. Something in his expression makes Sean spit on his fingers and press Corr towards the wall again.

I'm afraid that he's going to ask me to leave the stall now, so I ask hurriedly, "What is the spitting? I saw you do it before." I don't have to fabricate interest. It appeals to a part of me that has been repressed by years of studious effort on the part of the adults in my life.

Sean looks at his fingers as if he means to spit on them to demonstrate, and then he simply opens and closes them. He studies Corr as he thinks, as if Corr will somehow provide a way for him to frame his answer. "It's – spit. Salt. Me. It's a part of me, it's a way for me to be somewhere. When the rest of me can't be."

I remember how Corr stilled for Sean as he would for no one else on the beach. How the scent of Sean on his shirt calmed him when nothing else would.

I reply, "Something tells me my spit wouldn't mean as much to Corr as yours would."

There's a long pause before Sean speaks. He says, "Maybe not yet."

Yet! I don't think I've heard such a fine word before.

I say, "And the whispering. What do you tell him?"

Sean stands at Corr's shoulder, and for the first time he smiles at me. It's the smallest of things, and it's not amusement or humour, so I'm not sure what it means. He's younger when he has it on, easier to look at, which is maybe why he avoids it. He leans his cheek against Corr's withers and says, "What he needs to hear."

One of Corr's ears flicks back to him; the other stays trained on me. I don't want to look away from Sean leaning on Corr. There's something about it – this massive red giant that killed a man and slight, dark Sean Kendrick beside him as if they are friends – that fascinates and terrifies me.

Sean watches me watching him and then says, "Are you afraid of him?"

I don't want to say yes, because I'm not afraid of him right now when he looks more like a horse and less like a fiend, but I don't want to say no, either, because yesterday morning, on the beach, I was horrified and terrified. I would just say no anyway, but I feel certain that Sean Kendrick with his lacerating gaze would see right through me to the vagaries behind that no. So instead I reply, "You said you didn't trust him."

"I don't trust the ocean, either; it would kill me as soon as not. It doesn't mean I'm afraid of it."

I frown at him. I'm thinking again of that image of Sean crouched tightly on top of the red stallion, galloping bareback on the top of the cliffs. Of Sean, unable to watch Mutt Malvern on Corr's back. For once, I don't look away from his narrow gaze. "But you aren't just unafraid. You love them, don't you? You love Corr."

Sean Kendrick flinches as if I've startled him. He is quiet so long that I notice the sounds of the yard outside the stable, the calls and whinnies and water running and doors shutting. Then he says, "And you love the island. Tell me how it's any different."

As soon as he says it, I know that I can't counter his argument. Of course, it's true the island would just as soon see me dead as alive and it's also true that I love it despite that. Possibly because of it.

"I don't think I'd like to argue with you," I say. "I think it would be a very dissatisfying pastime."

He looks out of the window, as if in reply, and he studies that hopeless landscape so intently that I look, too, certain he must have seen something. It's only because I've lived with brothers that I realize, after a moment, that he's not looking outside but rather inside, wrestling with something inside himself. And there's nothing for it but to wait.

Finally, he asks, "Do you want to ride him?"

I don't think I've heard him right. I don't want to say *excuse me?* because if I *did* hear him right, it sounds like I don't want to, and if I've heard him wrong, it sounds like I wasn't paying attention.

He adds, "I'll ride with you."

My mind is a jumble of thoughts. That I watched this horse rip a man's throat out only a day ago. That he's the fastest horse on the island. That I'll dishonour my parents' death. That I'm afraid that I'll love it. That I'm afraid I'll be afraid. That I want Sean Kendrick to think well of me. That I need to be able to live with myself at night when I'm lying in bed and thinking about what I've done that day.

"On the cliffs," I say. The tide is high so it would have to be. I imagine the other *capall uisce* he rode, throwing herself over the edge.

He watches me for a long time. "You can say no."

But he knows I won't.

FORTY-SIX

Sean

When I was eight, the October wind brought a storm that twisted the sea around Thisby. Days before the rain came, the clouds hugged the horizon and the ocean crawled high up on the rocks, hungry for the warmth of our homes. My mother cried and covered her eyes when the shingles of the roof chattered like teeth. I heard her tears against the windows even before the skies clouded. This was before spring came, before the next October came, before the tide took her to the mainland and gave my father Corr instead.

In the dark, my father opened the door and led me out of the cottage and into the briny night. The moon was round and full and brave above us. The beach my father led me to was flat and glasslike, the wet sand reflecting the moon. The ocean stretched out and stretched out and stretched out, and my heart hurt to see it.

My father took me to a cleft in the cliff. We had to climb on ever-larger rocks to reach the end, a hollow in the cliff where a long-ago furious sea had thrown a lovely, dead-white conch shell and a man's leg bone.

Here it was dark and the moon couldn't see us, although we could see the moon. The beach spread down below us.

I don't remember my father telling me to be quiet, but I was. The moon moved across the sky as the tide slowly crept in. The surf was storm-maddened and frothy.

They came in with the tide. The moon illuminated long lines of froth as the waves gathered and gathered and gathered offshore, and when they finally broke on the sand, the *capaill uisce* tumbled on to the shore with them. The horses pulled their heads up with effort, trying to break free from the salt water. As they climbed from the ocean, my father gripped my arm with a pale-knuckled hand. "Be still," he told me.

But I was already still.

The *capaill uisce* plunged down the sand, skirmishing and bucking, shaking the sea foam out of their manes and the Atlantic from their hooves. They screamed back to the others still in the water, high wails that raised the hair on my arms. They were swift and deadly, savage and beautiful. The horses were giants, at once the ocean and the island, and that was when I loved them.

Now Puck and I walk my stallion out to the cliffs under a deep blue sky. Her expression is fierce and uncompromising, full of the intrepid bravery of a small boat in an uncertain sea. Above us is the same full moon that lit the ocean all those nights ago.

I remember my father's white-knuckled hand holding my arm. *Be still.*

She stands beside Corr, looking up at him.

I want her to love him.

FORTY-SEVEN

Out here on the cliffs, the red stallion moves constantly. His nostrils flare to catch the sea wind that lifts my hair from my forehead. When I was younger and I'd ride Dove bareback and bridleless and filthy in her paddock, I'd use the fence or a rock outcropping to scramble on to her back. Today, with Corr, it's no different, only the outcropping we stand by is taller than the ones I'd need for Dove. Sean manoeuvres him into place and says, "That's as still as he's going to get."

My heart is already galloping. I cannot believe that I'm really about to get on to a *capall uisce*. And not just any *capall uisce*, but the one whose name is on the top of the board at the butcher's. The one who has won the Scorpio Races four times. The one who tore out David Prince's throat yesterday morning. I grab a fistful of his mane and struggle to keep from being tugged off the rock as he dances. Finally, I pull myself on his back, clutching his mane with both hands like a little kid.

Sean says, "I'm going to give you the reins now. I'll

need you to hold him while I get on or you'll be on your own. Can I trust you to hold him?"

The way he says it makes me realize just how much he's risking right now, putting me on his horse, giving me the reins.

"Could others hold him?"

His face remains the same. "There are no others. You're the only one."

I swallow. "I can hold him."

Sean drags his foot in a semicircle before Corr and spits in it. Then he quickly loops the reins over Corr's head and hands them to me. If I had never seen or touched Corr, this would be the moment when I realize just how large he is, how unlike Dove. Through the reins, I can somehow feel how powerful he is. They're spiderwebs anchoring a ship. He tries my hold and I try him back. I don't want him to try harder.

Sean settles swiftly behind me, and I'm startled by the sudden closeness of him, my back suddenly warm against his chest, the press of his hips against me.

I turn to ask him a question, and he jerks his face away from the proximity to mine. I say, "Oh. Sorry."

"Are you all right with the reins?" He's all black and white in this light, his eyes hidden in shadow beneath his eyebrows.

I nod. But Corr won't go forward; he only backs, shaking his head. When pushed, he lifts his front feet a little off the ground. Not rearing, but warning me. Sean says something that's lost to the wind.

"What?"

"My circle," Sean says, right into my ear, his breath warm. I shiver, hard, although the wind is no colder than before. "He won't want to cross it. Go around."

As soon as we're free of the circle, Corr is like a bird in a gale. I can't tell if he's walking or trotting, only that we're moving, and that all directions feel possible. When Corr jerks to the side, I press my legs into his sides to straighten him and Sean's arms go around me to grab his mane.

I know that Sean only did it to steady himself, not me, but suddenly, I feel more grounded. I turn my face, and again, he moves his head to give me room. But I don't know what I was going to say.

"What?" His mouth makes the shape of the word although I don't properly hear it. "Is it—?" He starts to withdraw his arms, and I shake my head. My hair whips across my forehead, and he winces as it lashes him, too. He says something again, and once more, the wind steals his voice.

When Sean sees that I didn't hear him, he leans forward to my ear again. I can't think of the last time I was so close to another person. I can feel the rise and fall of his chest when he breathes. His words are warm in my ear: "Are you afraid?"

I don't know what I am right now, but it's not afraid.

I shake my head.

Sean takes my ponytail in his hand, his fingers touching my neck, and then he tucks my hair into my collar, out of the reach of the wind. He avoids my gaze. Then he links his arms back around me and pushes his calf into Corr's side.

Corr springs into the air.

When Dove moves up from a canter to a gallop, sometimes the only way I can tell the difference is because her hooves pound a four-time rhythm instead of a three.

But when Corr moves into a gallop, it's as if it's a gait that's just been invented, something so much faster than all the others that it should be called something else. The wind roars savagely across my ears. There are uneven stones standing watch in the field, but they're nothing to Corr. He barely lifts his knees and they're behind us. Each stride feels like it takes us a mile. We'll run out of island before he runs out of speed.

We're giants, on his back.

Sean says into my ear, "Ask him for more."

And when I squeeze my legs around him, Corr bounds forward again, as if we'd been merely straggling before. I can't believe that any of the horses on the beach are faster than this. I can't believe there's a horse in the world faster than this. And this is with two people on him. With only Sean during the race, how can he lose?

We are flying.

Corr's skin is hot against my legs – clingy, somehow, like when the current pushes your toes deeper into the sand. I feel his pulse in my pulse, his energy in mine, and I know this is the mysterious, terrifying power of the *capaill uisce*. We all know it, how it seizes you and confuses you and then you are in the water before you know it. But Sean leans forward, hard, against me, in order to reach Corr's mane, and ties knots in it. Three. Then seven. Then three again. I try to focus on what he's doing instead of his body pressed against mine, his cheek against my hair.

I lay the rein against Corr's neck and he gallops to the left, away from the line of the cliffs. Sean is still tightly against me, the fingers of one hand pressing into one of Corr's veins while the other grips his mane. The magic becomes a dull hum through me. My body warns me of the danger of this *capall uisce* beneath me, but at the same time it screams that it's alive, alive, alive.

We wheel back the way we came. I keep waiting for Corr to flag, to show some signs of tiring, but there's nothing but the pounding of his hooves across the turf, the snort of his breath around the bit, the wind blowing across my ears.

The island spools out beneath the moonlight. We gallop parallel to the cliff edge, and beyond it I see a flock of white birds keeping pace with us. Gulls, perhaps, soaring and gliding on air currents that send them violently upward as they get close to the rocks.

This is Thisby, I think. *This is the island I love*. I suddenly feel I know everything about the island and everything about me all at the same time, only I know that it will go away as soon as we stop.

We are back to where we began, and reluctantly I slow Corr. My heart is crashing in my ears, galloping even though Corr has stopped.

I slide off and step a metre away, turning to watch Sean dismount as well. He reaches into his pocket and gets a handful of salt or sand from it, then drops it in a circle around Corr and spits in it while I watch. Once this is done, he walks over to me, dark and silent. He's looking at me like he looked at me at the festival, and I know I'm looking back. Something wild and old spins inside me, but I don't have any words.

Sean reaches out between us and takes my wrist. He presses his thumb on my pulse. My heartbeat trips and surges against his skin. I'm pinned by his touch, a sort of fearful magic.

We stand and stand, and I wait for my pulse against his finger to slow, but it doesn't.

Finally, he releases my wrist and says, "I'll see you on the cliffs tomorrow."

FORTY-EIGHT

Puck

When I get home, the house is neat as a pin. It hasn't looked like this since our parents died. I stand in the doorway for a moment, lost in wonder and bemusement, and then Finn bursts out of the hallway. He looks like a man who has been on fire and put himself out; he is frazzled, even more than usual. I swim out of my thoughts to try to puzzle what has happened.

"What's wrong?" I ask.

Finn tries several times to say something, but only his hands are successful at it. Eventually, he manages, "I thought something — how would I know if something had happened to you?"

"Why would something have happened to me?"

"Puck, it's *night*. Where have you been? I thought—!"

Slowly it dawns on me. He'd seen me before I left for confession and must've expected me not long after.

"I'm sorry," I tell him.

Finn storms mightily around the room, and I realize that he's done all this cleaning because he was fretting over me.

"The house looks amazing," I offer.

He snaps, "Of course it does! I cleaned the whole bloody thing! I didn't even know how long it would be, if you died, before I knew. Who'd tell me?"

"I'm sorry, I forgot. Time got away from me."

This makes Finn rage even more. I've never seen him in such a state. He's like my father when he found out that my mother had bought a grey gelding off a farmer. He'd raged about, a furious silent storm contained by the walls, clutching the backs of chairs and staring at the ceiling, until Mum had agreed to sell the gelding.

"*Time got away*," Finn says finally.

"I can say I'm sorry some more, but I don't see what it will do."

"No good at all is what it will do!"

"Then what is it you want from me?" The truth is that I did feel bad before, but now my patience is at a thread. It's not as if I can go back and undo the past.

Finn leans on the back of my father's armchair, his knuckles white around the top of it.

"I can't bear it," he says, and I suddenly see Gabe in him. "I can't bear not knowing what will happen."

I creep around to the armchair and crouch in front of it. I fold my arms on the seat and peer up at his face. I'm not sure why he looks so young, if it's the worry that's taking the age from him or if it's because I've been looking at Sean Kendrick's face. I say, "It's almost over.

We'll be OK. Nothing will happen to me. Even if I don't win, we'll be OK, right?"

Finn's face is bleak and terrible, and I don't think he believes it.

I add, "Puffin came back, didn't she?"

"Missing half her tail. You don't have a tail to spare."

"Dove does. And that expensive food means hers grows back fast."

I'm not sure if he's comforted, but he doesn't protest further. Later, he drags his mattress into my room and pushes it against the opposite wall. It reminds me strikingly of my childhood, when he and I used to share a room with Gabe, before my father built another room on to the side of our house for him and Mum.

After the light is off, we're quiet for several long moments. Then Finn says, "What did Father Mooneyham give you?"

"Two Hail Marys and a Columba."

"Jesus," says Finn in the dark. "You were worse than that."

"I tried to tell him."

"I'll tell him again, when I go tomorrow. Did you already say them?"

"Of course. It was only two Hail Marys and a Columba."

Finn rustles in the darkness.

"Do you still talk in your sleep?" I ask.

"How would I know?"

"I'm going to hit you, if you do."

Finn turns over again, punching his pillow. "This isn't for always. Just until after."

"OK," I say. Out of the window, I can see the shape of the moon, and it reminds me of Sean's finger pressed against my wrist. I hold the thought carefully in my head, because I want to consider it some more once Finn has stopped speaking. But instead, as I wait for sleep, I find myself thinking about what Finn said about me dying. About how he didn't know how long it would be before he knew or who would tell him. I realize then that I can't remember how it is that we found out that our parents were dead. I just remember them going out to the boat together, a very rare occasion indeed, and then I remember knowing they were dead. Not only can I not see the face of who told us, I can't even remember the telling. I lie there with my eyes tightly closed, trying to bring the moment back to focus, but all I can call up is Sean's face and the sensation of the ground rushing by beneath Corr.

I think that's the mercy of this island, actually, that it won't give us our terrible memories for long, but lets us keep the good ones for as long as we want them.

FORTY-NINE

Sean

The morning of the Malvern youngstock auction dawns exceptionally fair, too kind for October. I lost too much sleep after I left Puck behind last night, so I snatch an extra half-hour to steel me for what's to come, and then I dress and head down to the yard. There'll be no riding Corr this morning, none of my usual stable work. The warm weather that would make the beach bearable is lost to the auction.

The yard is buzzing, full of mainland men holding champagne at nine in the morning and ignoring wives wearing absurd furs too warm for the weather. Every so often, the sound of a horse whinny peals out above their voices. These tourists are a tidier sort than those who arrived in time for the Scorpio Races, more kin to the gentlemen I'd seen staying at the hotel than to any local. Every man Malvern employs is out in force today; this auction funds the yard for the rest of the year.

I've only had my feet on solid ground for about a minute when George Holly catches my elbow. "Sean

Kendrick. I thought you'd be out there among the beasts."

"Not today." The truth is that I'd rather be down there with the grooms, leading the horses into the ring for the buyers to look at. Instead I am to stay always within earshot of Benjamin Malvern so that if he catches my eye or tips a champagne glass in my direction, I'm available to sing the praises of whichever horse is about to go on to the auction block. "Today I'm to sell myself, not them. I'm the novelty."

"Oh, hence the sharp apparel. I nearly didn't recognize you in that suit coat."

"I bought it to be buried in."

George Holly claps my shoulders. "Planning on staying trim or dying young, then. Such a wise head on such young shoulders. If your Kate Connolly hasn't seen you in that suit coat, she should."

I doubt very much that Puck would be affected by the sight of me looking as if I am wanting only for a pocket watch. If she preferred this version of me, it would be unfortunate in any case. I lay a hand flat on the waistcoat and smooth the buttons.

"It's such a fine thing to see you uncomfortable, Mr Kendrick," Holly says. "She has got you bothered! Now tell me which horses to buy."

Bothered isn't the word for it. I can't focus. I need to be on Corr instead of simmering in this coat. I say, "Mettle and Finndebar."

"Finn–deh–bahr? I can't even say it much less remember it. Did Malvern show her to me?"

I say, "Probably not; she's a broodmare. Getting a little old, so he's selling her." I look up in time to see Malvern arrive with a posse of potential buyers following him. They look delighted by the island weather and these island racers and their droll owner. Malvern spots me and I see him filing away my location for future reference.

Holly exchanges a look with Malvern that is not entirely cordial. "Oh, I'm not in the market for baby-makers."

"She drops nothing but winners. What is that look there?"

Holly frowns as a groom leads by a yearling. "It's my look for broodmares."

"No, you and Malvern. What did you quarrel about?"

He rubs the back of his neck and refuses the tray of champagne offered him. "While I was wandering in my altogether, I discovered one of his old flames. I didn't know that beforehand. I think he fancies me a playboy now." He looks hurt.

I don't tell Holly that I'd shared that impression. "I would've thought all was well now that you're here at the auction."

"All will be wonderful once I buy something," Holly notes, glancing over his shoulder. "Mettle and the baby-dropper. I don't mean to buy a broodmare, you know.

We have fields of them. Can't you merely cross her to your red stallion and sell me the product of that happy union next year?"

"Getting a *capall uisce* into the line is not as easy as all that," I reply. "Sometimes mares are mares to them and sometimes mares are meals." If there is a rhyme or reason to why an *uisce* stallion would take to a horse mare or why an *uisce* mare would take to a horse stallion, I haven't discovered it yet. There are Malvern horses with *capall uisce* blood in them, but it is dilute and old, showing up in odd ways. Horses who love to swim, like Fundamental; fillies with shrieking whinnies; colts with long, slender ears.

"That," says Holly bitterly, "is precisely the way it works with humans."

I consider whether this means that his blind lover has jilted him or the other way around, but I'm distracted by a glimpse of Mutt Malvern among the buyers. He's talking and gesturing to a filly standing in the ring as if he knows anything about her, and the feathered and leathered mainlanders listen and nod their heads because he is the son of the owner, so of course he knows something. Holly follows my gaze and for a moment we stand there, shoulder to shoulder.

"Why, good morning!" Holly says broadly, and when I see who he addresses, it makes me glad that I hadn't spoken against Mutt. Benjamin Malvern stands just behind us.

"Mr Holly. Mr Kendrick," Malvern replies. "Mr Holly, I trust that you've found something that interests you?"

He eyes me.

Holly's smile is wide and abusively American, rows and rows of white glowing teeth. "Benjamin, so many things about Thisby interest me."

"Anything of the four-legged variety?"

"I'm looking at Mettle and Finndebar," Holly says. Despite his earlier protests, he pronounces *Finndebar* without a stumble.

Malvern says, "Finndebar drops nothing but winners."

My mouth plays at the sound of my own words from someone else's lips.

Holly nods his head towards me. "So I've heard. Why are you selling her, then?"

"Just getting a little long in the tooth."

"Something to be said for age and cunning, though," Holly remarks. "I mean, you should know, ha! Ah, this is a fine country full of fine people. Oh, I see we have all the Malverns here now. And there's Matthew, looking like his father."

This last is because Mutt Malvern has found his way within earshot and stands there, deep in conversation with a man about a filly. I think he's trying to look useful in front of either me or his father. I can hear what he's saying and it sounds ridiculous, but the man is nodding.

Malvern's gaze is on Mutt, his expression difficult to discern but certainly nothing that could be called pride.

"So I'll confess," Holly says, "that I'm quite taken with Sean Kendrick here. You have quite a right hand in him."

Malvern's gaze shifts swiftly to me and then Holly, an eyebrow raised. "I hear that you were making a level effort to export him."

"Ah, but his loyalty was too strong," Holly says. The smile he turns on me is ferocious in its sincerity. "Which is just disappointing. You treat him too well, I suppose."

Nearby, Mutt glances in my direction, his eyes narrowed, and I can see that he has caught wind of the subject at hand.

"Mr Kendrick's been with us for close to a decade," Malvern says. "Since his father died and I took him in."

In just that phrase, he paints a picture of an orphaned boy sitting at his kitchen table, raised side by side with Mutt, revelling in the pleasures of being a Malvern.

"So he's practically a son," Holly says. "That explains the bond. These horses all bear his handprint, don't they? Seems to me he's the logical heir to the Malvern Yard, if you were asking me."

Benjamin Malvern had been looking at his son, who was staring back at him, but when Holly finishes, Malvern's eyes sweep over me in my suit and he purses his lips. "In many ways, Mr Holly, I think that is very true." He looks back up to Mutt and adds, "In most ways."

I can't think that he means it. I can only think that he says it because he's playing a game with Holly. Or because he means for Mutt to hear it, which Mutt clearly does.

Holly exchanges a glance with me, and I can see that he's as startled as I am.

"Unfortunately," Malvern says, turning away from Mutt, "the blood doesn't always come through." He eyes me and suddenly I realize that I have never once known what he's truly thinking behind those clever, deep-set eyes. I know nothing of him aside from his horses and the little cold flat above the stable addition. I know that he owns much of Thisby but not which parts. I know that he rode once but doesn't now, and I know that his son is a bastard but not if the mother still lives on the island. I know that I win the races for him and every year he takes over nine-tenths of the purse, as he would for any man in his employ.

Malvern says, "Mr Kendrick was born on a horse and he'll die on one, and maybe that's not something you can breed for. He's one of those rare men who can make a horse work for him but never asks for more than they have. If he's told you to put your money on Mettle and Finndebar, then you'd be a fool not to. Good day, Mr Holly."

Malvern nods at Holly and then strides away. In his

379

absence, Holly says something to me that I miss, because I am looking at Mutt. Written on his face is furious rejection and disbelief. In just that moment, it doesn't matter that both he and I have done our part to earn Malvern's words. It's only that they were wounding that matters.

I watch his stare become fearsome as he holds my gaze. Something demanding and uncompromising claws inside Mutt Malvern. He pushes his way back towards the house.

"Sean Kendrick," Holly says. "What is it you're thinking?"

"That this doesn't sit easy with me," I reply.

Holly looks at the space Mutt has left behind and advises, "I would bolt your door tonight."

FIFTY

Puck

In the morning, before I head to the cliffs to train and possibly find Sean, Finn and I go to Dory Maud's – him on his bicycle, me on Dove. The truth of it is that Finn means to do some odd jobs for them if he can and I'm hoping against hope that Dory's sold some more teapots, because we've one lump of butter but no bread to stick around it and no flour to make bread.

We trudge into Skarmouth. I lead Dove at the moment to make certain she doesn't turn a leg in a bit of uneven cobble. Finn leads the bicycle to make certain he can stare into Palsson's shop without falling off a moving vehicle.

We both look mournfully in the bakery window as we pass, though I'd sworn to myself that I wouldn't. Nothing says *orphans* like two kids breaking their necks looking at trays of November cakes and platters of shaped cookies and lovely soft loaves of bread still steaming the window they're next to. Finn and I sigh at the same time and continue on our way to Fathom & Sons. I tie Dove out front and Finn tells his bicycle to stay. I'm not sure if the shop will be open or not; Elizabeth and Dory Maud might be at the booth by the cliff path instead.

But the door opens, and when we push inside, I'm surprised to find both Dory Maud and Elizabeth there, as well as a handsome blond man who is exclaiming over a stone grave pillow that Martin Devlin found in his field last year when he was digging for potatoes.

". . .really put the head on this at burial!" he says.

Finn gives me a look. I eye the stranger. He's a foreigner and in his thirties, maybe, but in the best possible way. I think the word for it is *dashing* or *dapper* or something like that. He holds a red flat cap in his hands.

"Ah, Puck," says Dory Maud. "Puck *Connolly*."

Finn and I exchange another look.

"Pleased to meet you," I say to the stranger.

"Oh, but you haven't met," Dory Maud says. "Mr Holly, this is *Puck Connolly*. Puck, this is Mr George Holly."

"*Now* I'm pleased to meet you," I say crossly. "I was just dropping Finn off here and—" Elizabeth sidles up to me and places her claws in my skin.

"Just a moment! I need to steal her," Elizabeth chirps. She whisks me into the back room and shoves closed the door behind us. So it is just us and four chairs and a table bigger than the floor and an audience of boxes filled with Dory Maud's love letters to sailors. We are nose to nose and Elizabeth smells like a shipload of English roses. "Puck Connolly, you be your absolute level best to that man."

"I *was* being nice."

"No, you weren't. I saw your face. I'm no fool! We need to encourage him. That American is richer than the Queen and we think he means to take a piece of Thisby back with him."

I hope he's taking the fertility statue. "What is it you're trying to shove off on him?"

Elizabeth leans against the door to ensure no one interrupts. "Annie."

"Annie!"

"If you're going to repeat everything I say, I'll give your tongue to him as well."

"Does Annie *know* about this?"

"If only you had the brains to match your looks." Elizabeth realizes she's still holding my arm and releases me. "Now you go out there and be charming. As you can."

I scowl and follow her back into the main room. All eyes turn towards me. Finn has somehow ended up holding the stone burial pillow.

"Done, ladies?" Dory Maud asks. I can't think of the last time she's used the word *ladies* to refer to something other than our chickens. "Mr Holly was just expressing interest in you, Puck."

Perhaps my alarm is written upon my face, because Holly adds quickly, "Sean Kendrick's spoken of you."

"You didn't mention that before," Dory Maud says, looking at me. "Puck, do you know what would be a wonderful thing, is if you took Mr Holly and found him some breakfast."

"Oh—" Holly and I protest at the same time.

"I have Dove outside," I say.

Holly glances at me and says meaningfully, "And I was going to go watch the training." I decide that I like him. It helps that he's dapper, but the clever cinches it.

"Then you should take him by Palsson's to get him one of the November cakes. Of course Annie knows how to make them as well, even better than Palsson's," Dory Maud says. "She was just saying that she'd like to make them for you, Mr Holly, but of course there's been no time. If you get them at Palsson's, you can carry your breakfasts with you."

Holly's smile lights the room; Dory Maud and Elizabeth are both blown back fairly by the sheen of it.

"Will you let me buy you one of these things, Miss Connolly?" Holly asks. "And your brother, too?"

I think I may die from the stinging power of the knowing gaze Elizabeth wields. It is a gaze that says, *I told you he was a rich American with money to spend*. I glare at her and Dory Maud. "Certainly. And Dory, if you give me a bit of change, I'll buy some extra . . . for Annie."

We momentarily battle with our eyes, and then Dory Maud relents and gives me a few coins. And so it is two triumphant Connollys who lead George Holly from Fathom & Sons, Finn on one side and me on the other. Holly watches me untie Dove with great interest, and I watch him watching me with even greater interest. The way his eye travels along Dove – hock to stifle placement to topline to shoulder angle – tells me that he's not just a casual tourist. I wonder how well he knows Sean.

"You know," Finn says on the way back to Palsson's, cheerful now that he's getting food, "that Annie is blind, right?"

"Not entirely," Holly corrects him. "Not entirely blind, I mean."

"Is that what they told you!" Finn exclaims. I stare at them. Who is this person who can make Finn so loud so quickly?

"It is," Holly says warmly. He inclines his head towards Finn and asks, "Now, what, exactly, is a November cake?"

He asks it with such genuine curiosity that of course Finn has to speak even more, describing the moist crumb, the nectar that seeps from the base of it, the icing that soaks into the cake before you can lick it off. It is probably the kindest thing I have ever seen in my life, George Holly asking my brother about baked goods. When Holly glances to me, I give him a sharp look, which I realize might not fall under being as charming as possible. But I'm not sure that clever, kind George

Holly could possibly be played as easily as Dory Maud and Elizabeth think.

Together we stroll into Palsson's. I try to maintain an air of dignity but it's difficult to not be overcome by the odour that hangs in the air. It is all cinnamon and honey and yeast. Palsson's is on a corner and made of windows and light. The walls are lined with unstained wooden shelves with open backs, so the sunlight comes unimpeded through the glass panes and makes big squares of gold across the floor. Every shelf towers with bread and cookies, cinnamon twists and November cakes, scones and biscuits. The only wall not so anointed is the back wall behind the counter, which is lined with sacks of flour waiting to become bread. I can smell even the flour, because there's so much of it, and it's sweet and palatable all on its own. Everything is golden and white and honey and nectar in here and I think that possibly I could live in this building and sleep among the flour sacks.

Palsson's is crowded today, as always, with both customers and housewives who hold better conversations near someone else's baking. George Holly gathers stares and whispers as he and Finn move among the shelves and then into the long line. He fits in perfectly, as blond as a November cake himself.

"Your aunt is a strong woman," George Holly says to me.

"Dory Maud?"

"That's the one."

If Dory Maud has told him we're related, I might take up spitting again. "She's not my aunt."

He is graciously apologetic. "Oh, I'm sorry. You seemed so familiar with her. I didn't mean to overstep."

"Everyone on Thisby is familiar," I reply. "Stay here for a month and she'll be your aunt as well."

This makes Finn smile at the floor.

"My," says George Holly. "What a laden promise that is."

We move forward in line. Finn's head is going back and forth like an owl's from tray to tray as he weighs the merits of the different possibilities.

"Mr Kendrick tells me that your pony has quite a set of legs on her," Holly says conversationally. I hear someone behind the counter say *bright red hat*.

"Horse."

"Hmm?"

"She's fifteen-two hands. Horse. He said that?"

"Oh, excuse me, madam," Holly says. This is because Mary Finch has just squeezed between him and a shelf to get to the window, and her hand went somewhere untoward on his person, a most fortunate accident on her part. Holly moves towards the counter and gathers his dignity back up to himself before he turns back to me. "Word on the beach is he said that if your pony — horse — goes straight while the *capaill uisce* go right, you might get somewhere."

I wonder if Sean really believes this. I wonder if I really believe that. I must, or else why am I doing this? "I reckon that's the plan. If we're being familiar, how well is it you know Sean Kendrick?"

Mary Finch squeezes back by George Holly and his eyes go round for a moment as he receives some more Skarmouth hospitality. I try not to laugh.

"Oh," he says. "Oh. Well, I was here to look at Malvern horses and we met. He's a strange old bird, which is to say that I like him quite a bit."

Finn taps on the counter to draw Holly's attention to the cakes they've just set out under the glass. For a brief moment, their faces wear the same boyish, wistful longing, longing that's not tempered by the knowledge that the line until they get to the cakes is only two metres long.

"In the interests of familiarity," Holly says, "how well do *you* know him?"

My cheeks redden, which infuriates me. Curse this ginger hair and everything that comes with it. My father said once that if I didn't have my mother's ginger hair, I wouldn't blush or curse as easily. Which I thought was unfair. I hardly ever curse or blush, even though I've had plenty of days that required both. I'm a quite level person, I think, given the circumstances.

Finn's eyeballing me, too curious about the answer to Holly's question. I say, "A little. We're friendly."

"Like you and your aunt?" Holly asks. When I scowl at him, he suggests, "Like cousins? Like siblings?"

"I don't know him as well as Mary Finch knows you," I tell him. When he looks perplexed, I make a little pinching motion and he winces as if his underparts feel her attentions once more.

"Fair enough," Holly says.

We stand at the counter and Bev Palsson swaps money for cakes. Finn buys an obscene number of cinnamon twists with Dory Maud's money. Once we actually have them in our hands and stand outside the door where Dove is tied, Finn makes George Holly unwrap one of the cakes so that Finn can observe his reaction. Holly takes a bite, honey slipping over his lip, and closes his eyes in pleasure so pronounced that it's hard to tell if it's exaggerated for Finn's benefit.

"I'm told," Holly says, "that food tastes better in your memories. I don't see how I can improve on this in a memory."

Finn is pleased by this. It's as if he made them himself. I see something bittersweet in Holly's expression, though; I think, possibly, that this island has begun to get its hooks into him, and this makes me like him even more. Anyone Thisby chooses to seduce can't be half-bad.

Holly asks, "Finn, would you be so kind as to ask them for another bag so we can separate these into two parcels? And if I give you this, would you fetch me another twist to take back to my room? Get another one for yourself, too, so your other hand doesn't feel empty."

Once Finn is dispatched, Holly says, "Puck, I'm

stepping so badly over the line here that I might never return. But there's quite a few people who don't care to have you on the beach. I'm not sure if you've heard."

I think of Peg Gratton telling me not to let anyone else tighten my girth. I lose my appetite for my sticky breakfast. "I've an inkling."

There's genuine worry on George Holly's face. "You're the first, aren't you? The first woman?"

It's strange to be called a woman, but I nod.

"It just sounds quite bad down there," he says. "I wouldn't say anything if I didn't think it seemed dangerous."

How quickly George Holly's become one of us – that I should be riding in a race against a few dozen *capaill uisce* and he thinks it's the men I should be worried about.

"I know not to trust anyone," I say. "Except. . ."

Holly studies my face. "You do fancy him, don't you? What a strange, wonderful, repressed place this is."

I glare at him, relieved that I seem to be out of blushes, or perhaps I'm still blushing and can't get any redder. "I'm not the one letting myself be played by three sisters with four and a half eyes between them."

Holly laughs delightedly. "Very true."

Dove strives for my November cake and I push her away with my elbow. "Annie's all right," I say. "Do you think she's pretty?"

"I do."

"I reckon she finds you agreeable, too," I say. I glance at him sideways with a sly smile. "Since she can't see any further than her arm, I wouldn't count on her baking you any of these cakes, though. There's a reason Palsson's is full of women. Thisby women are lazy."

"Lazy as you?"

"Just about."

"I think I could bear that." He glances up; Finn has just broached the door of Palsson's, bearing two bags, and he approaches us looking cheerful. Holly says to me, "I sure do wish you the best of luck, Miss Connolly. And I hope you won't wait for Sean Kendrick to realize that he's lonely."

I want to ask him, *Wait for what?* but Finn's come up then and it's not a question I want to ask in front of one of my brothers.

So we merely exchange pleasantries, and Holly goes on his way to watch the training on the beach, I go my way to get Dove to the cliff top, and Finn gets ready to go back to Dory Maud's to do odd jobs.

"Did you hear his accent?" Finn asks.

"I wasn't born deaf."

"If I were Gabe, I'd go to America instead of the mainland."

This statement ruins any good mood I had germinating in my soul. "If you were Gabe, I'd slap you."

Finn is unperturbed. He gives Dove's rump a friendly pat before starting away.

"*Hey.*" I stop him and remove another two cakes from the bag. "Now go."

He trots gleefully off, so easily pleased by the arrival of food. I balance my cakes in one hand and take Dove's reins with the other, leading her towards the cliffs. I think about George Holly's comment about food tasting better in memories. It strikes me as a strange, luxurious statement. It assumes you'll have not only that moment when you take the first bite but then enough moments in front of it for that mouthful to become a memory. My future's not that certain that I can afford to wonder what will become of the taste later. And in any case, the November cake tastes plenty sweet to me now.

FIFTY-ONE

Sean

I'm already waiting when Puck gets to the top of the cliffs. I'm not the only one; about two dozen race tourists have made perches out of rocks, watching Corr and me as closely as they dare. Puck glares at them all, searing enough that some of them flinch in surprise. I'm not certain what to expect from her after last night. I don't know how to address her. I don't know what she expects from me or what I expect from me.

What I get is a wordless hello and a November cake in my hand. We each silently eat one under the attentive audience of the tourists and then scrub our sticky palms on the grass.

Puck grimaces at the onlookers. "Dove is timid around the water horses."

"As she should be."

She turns her ferocious expression on me. "Well, it won't do for the race now, will it?"

I turn my attention to her dun mare. She's very aware of Corr's presence, but she doesn't look fearful.

"She doesn't have to love them," I say. "A little

respect will give her some speed. As long as you aren't afraid that she's afraid."

I can see Puck working it out, getting her mind in the right place. Her eyes are narrowed as she studies Corr, and I wonder if she's remembering our ride on the cliff tops.

"Myself I can trust," she says. She looks at me as if it's a question, but if it is, it's one only she can answer.

"Ready to work?" I ask her.

We work.

Corr's not at all tired from the gallop the night before, and Puck's horse is fresh and hot in the wind. We circle and tag, gallop and skirmish. I pull ahead until Corr is distracted and then Puck is suddenly beside us, her dun mare's ears pricked and clever. We match stride for stride, not racing, just running for the sake of it.

I forget that I am working, forget that the race is only days away, forget that she is on an island pony and I am on a *capall uisce*. There's just the air past my ears and the slender moon of her fleeting smile in my direction and the familiar weight of Corr in my hands.

Then it is an hour gone by without me noticing and I have to pull Corr up. I don't want to overwork him. Puck brings Dove to a halt, too. For a moment, I see that she's about to say something; her tongue presses against her teeth. But in the end, all she says is my own words back to me. "I'll see you on the cliffs tomorrow?"

· Puck ·

Sean's there the next day, and the next day, and the next. I think that I won't see him on Sunday, because I've never seen him in St Columba's and I don't know where he would go if he's not there. But after Mass I walk to the cliff top and there Sean is, his eyes already trained down on to the beach.

We watch the training below, exchanging only a few words, and the next day, we return on horseback. Sometimes we skirmish together, sometimes we ride dozens of lengths apart, just within sight of each other. I think every now and then about Sean's thumb pressed against my wrist and daydream about him touching me again. But mostly I think about the way he looks at me – with respect – and I think that's probably worth more than anything.

The only thing is, the more I see him and Corr together, the more I think of how unbearable it would be for Sean to lose him.

But we can't both win.

· Sean ·

For a week we ride together, until it's hard to remember my daily routine of going to the beach. I miss the lonely early mornings on the sand, but not enough to trade them for Puck's company. Some days we barely speak at all, so I'm not certain why it makes a difference to me. But then, Corr and I have never needed words, either.

So it's just hours of riding Corr slowly, building up what is already there, and hours of watching Puck invent new games for Dove to keep her interested in the work. Already Dove's hay belly has disappeared, either through regular schooling or through better feed. Puck's changing, too – she has a stillness about her when she rides now. More certainty and less self-conscious petulance. The transformation from the horse and rider I first saw in the surf weeks ago is startling. I no longer question why I'm training alongside her.

I'm not sure the exact moment when I realize that Corr is actually trying, not hard, but he is trying, and Dove keeps stride beside us. Even after an hour of schooling. Even beside a *capall uisce*.

I pull Corr up. He trips with purposeful clumsiness, showing off for the mare, and I wiggle his reins to remind him that I'm here. It takes Puck a moment to realize I've stopped. She doubles back. Dove's sides heave and her nostrils flare, but her ears are still pricked and game.

I say, "You might pull this off."

Puck's face is half frown, half smile. She didn't hear me. I repeat myself. I see the moment when she understands what I said, and her smile vanishes.

"I don't know if you're being serious," she says.

"I'm being serious. Tomorrow you should take her

down to the beach to make sure you can still handle her with all the others. To get used to it."

Now the frown really has taken over. "Two days isn't very long for her to get used to that."

"It's not for her. It's for you. And it's one day, not two," I remind her. Corr dances, and I still him with my legs. "Last day the beach's off-limits to horses. Tomorrow's the last day on the sand."

Dove scratches her belly with a back hoof, like a dog. She looks like less than a sure bet when she does this, and Puck must know it, because she looks annoyed and taps her boot into Dove's side to make her stop. "You aren't just saying that because I gave you a cake, are you?"

"No, it's been in the rules for as long as I've been racing."

She studies my expression to see if I'm serious and then makes a face. "I meant about us standing a chance."

Corr bends around my leg, restless and losing interest in the idea of standing still. It reminds me that I need to swap his stall with Edana's. Since she hasn't been worked on the beach, Edana has been getting more and more restless in her windowless stall in the back seven stalls of the stable. Corr's view isn't much, but it might keep her settled until after the races when I have time for her again.

"I wouldn't say it if I didn't mean it."

"I mean really have a chance." She looks away from me then, as if she thinks the idea we're both competing for first might offend me.

"There's a bit of money for second and third," I say. She fumbles her fingers through a knot in Dove's mane. "Would that be enough?"

Puck's voice is faint. "It would help." Then her tone changes abruptly. "You should come to dinner with us. It'll be beans or something else absolutely lovely."

I hesitate. My dinner is usually taken in my flat, standing up, the door hanging open, the stable waiting for me to go back out to the rest of my work. Not with my legs tucked under a table, trying to find words and answers to polite questions. Dinner with Puck and her brothers? It's mere days until the race. I have to clean my saddle and my boots. I need to wash my breeches and find my gloves in case it is rainy or the wind is brittle. I need to swap Corr and Edana and clean their stalls. I should go to the butcher's again to see if they have anything that would do Corr good.

"It's OK," Puck says. She has a quick way of hiding her disappointment. If you're not looking for it, she's put it away somewhere before you know it was there. "You're busy."

"No," I tell her. "No, I'll – think about it. I'm not sure if I can get away." I don't know what I'm thinking. I cannot find the time to get away. I'm not a good dinner companion. But it's hard to think of that. Instead

I'm wishing that I'd spoken sooner, before I'd seen her disappointment.

Puck rallies with the best of them. "If not, I'll see you on the beach tomorrow?"

This I'm certain of. On horseback, it's easy to be certain. "Yes."

FIFTY-TWO

Puck

Gabe brings home a chicken and Tommy Falk for dinner. Truth be told, I'm not unhappy to see any of them: Gabe, because it's been so long since we've had dinner with him; the chicken, because it's not beans; and Tommy Falk, because his presence makes Gabe cheerful and goofy. They toss the plucked chicken back and forth over my head until it loses its wrapping and I shout at them as I pick it up off the floor.

"If we all die of plague or whatever is on this floor, I want you to know it's not my fault," I say. There's a bit of silt stuck to the dimpled skin of the chicken's back.

"Just scrub it off. A little dirt never hurt anybody," Tommy Falk says. "Gabe says you make a mean chicken."

Finn, who is sitting by the fireplace making smoke, comments for the first time. "Well, she certainly doesn't make a nice one."

"You can shut up or make it yourself." It turns out that the dirt on the chicken is the least of my worries. My skin is filthy. It takes me quite a long time to make my hands clean, and even once they're mostly pale again, they still smell suspiciously like both Dove and Corr.

Gabe crouches over the radio, trying to get it to pick up one of the mainland music stations, which only works when the weather is just right and the appropriate slain sacrifices have been made. In the absence of radio entertainment, Tommy Falk sings a bit of a song that he caught on the radio before the storm. The house feels full for the first time in months.

"Bands, Gabe," Tommy says. He's settled next to Finn, helping him turn the smoke into fire. He stretches out to take my father's concertina where it had been abandoned near the armchair. He plays the same tune he just sang; it sounds more mournful on the concertina. "Can you imagine it? Concerts."

He's talking about the mainland, of course. Because it's not just the race that is days away.

"And the cars," adds Gabe. "And oranges every day."

"Also," says Tommy, "bands."

Finn studies the fire.

I study the chicken.

"Don't be down," Tommy says, leaping up when he sees my expression. "It's not like we won't come back. We'll send money, too. Haven't you seen Esther Quinn's clothing, Puck? Her brother's on the mainland selling something to somebody and he sends home money – that's why she looks like she was bought from a catalogue. When's a good visit, Gabe? Easter, maybe? Easter's a good time to come back. We'll throw more chickens."

Gabe takes the concertina from Tommy and slides out a tune; I'd forgotten how well he could play. Tommy grabs my waist and swings me around in a circle. I drag my feet because I am opposed to people touching me when I'm not expecting it. Also because it will take more than dancing to cheer me up. Tommy says, "Come now, you can move faster than that! Everyone says you were a spitfire on the cliffs this morning."

I let him spin me at that. "They do?"

"They're saying that you and Sean Kendrick were burning up the cliffs." Tommy spins me again and grins at me. "And when I say you and Sean Kendrick, I mean *you and Sean Kendrick*. And by burning, I mean *burning*."

I jerk to a stop and spin him instead. I pretend he's talking about racing. "You worried?"

"It's Gabe who should be worried," Tommy says. He takes my hands and swings me wide enough that I worry for the objects on the counter. "Because his baby sister's growing up so fine."

Mum said that I shouldn't be moved to do anything by someone with sweet words, but Tommy Falk doesn't seem to be trying to persuade me of anything, so I let his compliment slip down nice and easy. It's quite agreeable and I'd be happy enough with another.

Gabe stops playing mid-measure, his hands around the concertina spread as if he holds a book open. "Don't make me punch you in the mouth, Tommy. When's that chicken going to be done, Kate?"

Tommy mouths, *Oooooh, Kate* to me, but Gabe refuses to rise to the bait.

"Twenty minutes," I say. "Maybe thirty. Maybe ten." There's a tap on the door then. We all exchange looks, Tommy Falk's as uncertain as the rest of ours. No one moves, so I finally wipe my hands off on my trousers, go to the door, and open it a crack.

Sean stands on the other side, one hand in his trouser pocket, the other holding a loaf of bread.

I wasn't prepared for it to be Sean, and so my stomach does a neat little trick that feels like either hunger or escaping. There is something very shocking about seeing him standing dark and still on our doorstep.

I lean out the door a ways. The night's getting chilly. "You got away from the yard."

"Is it still all right?"

"It's all right. It's me and Gabe and Finn and Tommy Falk."

"I've brought this." He holds up the bread, which is clearly a Palsson's loaf, and it's still so fresh that I can smell the warmth of it. He must've come straight from there. "Is that what's done?"

"Well, you've done it, so it must be."

Gabe asks, "Puck, who is it?"

I open the door wide to reveal the answer. They all look at Sean standing there with his hand in his pocket and the other hand around a loaf of bread and it occurs to me all in a rush as they stare at him that Sean looks a little, just a little, like he's courting. I don't have time to explain the truth of it before Tommy laughs and jumps to his feet. "Sean Kendrick, the devil. How are you?"

We fold him into the house and Gabe shuts the door because I forget to in my sudden glee. Gabe tries to separate Sean from his jacket while Tommy says something about the weather, and it's quite loud for no reason at all, because it's only Gabe and Tommy and sometimes Finn speaking. Sean, as always, manages to get by on one word where everyone else needs five or six. In the middle of all this, as Sean slips out of his jacket, he looks over his shoulder at me and he smiles at me, just a glancing, faint thing before he turns back to Tommy.

I'm quite happy for the smile, because Dad told me once you should be grateful for the gifts that are the rarest.

After a few minutes, Tommy and Gabe begin to play cards in front of the fire because there's no one to tell them not to.

Finn just watches because he hasn't decided whether or not it's a sin. Sean joins me by the counter, standing close enough that I can smell hay and salt water and dust on him.

"Give me something to do," he says.

I put a knife in his hand. "Cut something. Your bread."

He begins to cut it with single-minded devotion. In a low voice, he says, "I saw Ian Privett after you'd gone. He took Penda out after the rest were gone and ran him hard. He was fast before and he's fast again. One to watch."

"I heard that he likes to come up fast from the outside at the end."

Sean glances at me, an eyebrow raised. "True enough. Privett lost him four years ago when he fell in the races. He beat me twice on him before that."

"He won't beat you this year," I say.

Sean doesn't say anything. He doesn't have to; I know he's thinking about losing Corr. I stir the chicken. It's done, but I don't want to have to sit at the table yet.

After a pause, he says, "I was thinking. No one will want the inside, since the sea will be bad on the first of the month."

"So I should hug the sea because Dove won't care."

Sean's done slicing the bread, too, but he rearranges the pieces as if he still works at it.

I say, "I was thinking, too, that I should hang back. Save Dove for the end."

"And maybe the pack will have thinned?" Sean considers. "I wouldn't wait too long or hang too far back. She's not strong enough to come up from too far back."

"I want to steer clear of the piebald, and she'll be at the front," I say. "I've seen the way Mutt rides her."

Sean narrows his eyes; I can tell he's pleased that I've noticed, and I'm pleased that he's pleased.

"Blackwell's the other one," Sean says. "He's the one whose stallion tried to take you down, but he got a replacement horse. This new one's a fast bitch." He says it without malice.

Of course, there's one horse that I know will be a contender. But I've never seen him in a real race and I've never seen his rider give me the slightest hint of how he likes to pace himself.

"Where will you and Corr be?" I ask.

Sean presses two fingers along the edge of the counter, sweeping crumbs into a pile. I notice that his fingers are permanently dirt-stained like mine. He says, "Right next to you and Dove."

I stare at him. "You can't risk not winning. Not because of me."

Sean doesn't lift his eyes from the counter. "We make our move when you make yours. You on the inside, me on the outside. Corr can come from the middle of the pack; he's done it before. It's one side you won't have to worry about."

I say, "I will not be your weakness, Sean Kendrick."

Now he looks at me. He says, very softly, "It's late for that, Puck."

He leaves me standing at the counter looking into

the sink, trying to remember what I was supposed to do next.

"Puck," snaps Gabe. "Your soup!"

The dumplings are boiling over and for a moment it appears that we may have flames for dinner, but I manage to snatch the pot and get the heat off.

The boys all hover around the table now that the presence of food seems imminent. Tommy says, "You're right, Gabe, she does make a mean chicken. Tried to bite her."

"Ah, but Puck bites back," Gabe says.

Finn begins to dole the dumplings out into bowls while I swipe up the spill. Tommy chatters on about how his *uisce* mare lets herself get pushed around by the other horses but perks up when she sees their asses. Gabe gives everyone a glass of water whether or not they asked for it. And all the while I try very hard to keep my eyes from darting to Sean because I'm quite certain that no one at the table will be able to miss how I look at him and how I find him looking back.

FIFTY-THREE

Sean

I wake to the sound of crying. I got back too late; it took sleep too long to come to me. For a moment, I just lie there. Exhaustion makes me unwilling to fully wake, and yet: the crying.

The sound resolves itself into an agonized keening, and I am awake. I am awake and I have my jacket and my boots and I am in the stairwell with my flashlight.

The stable is dark, but I hear the sounds of movement, not from the aisles, but from the stalls. The horses are awake. Either the sound has woken them, or someone has been here. I keep my flashlight switched off and make my way in the dark.

The moaning grows louder as I creep down to the main floor. It's coming from Corr's old stall, the one I just put Edana in.

I slide down the aisle as quickly as silence allows. The crying has gone silent but I'm certain now that it's Edana. In the darkness, I can barely see inside the stall. The night outside throws some dark blue light in, just enough for me to press myself against the bars and look in.

When she keens again, I start back. She's right by my face.

Her head lies against the bars, neck pressed against the wall, nose pointed towards the ceiling, jaw cracked open.

I whisper her name and she cries back to me softly. My eyes follow the line of her neck to her sloping withers and the slanting line her hips make low to the ground. I've never seen a horse stand like this. There's a sick knot inside me as I pull open the door and step into the stall. Now, her body silhouetted against the light of the window, I see that she leans against the wall with her head and neck, sunk down on to her haunches like a dog. Her back legs splay out as if the ground is slippery.

I touch her shoulder; it's trembling. I have a terrible feeling rising inside me. I run the flat of my hand from her withers down her spine, and then, crouching to keep searching, around the curve of her twitching haunches, and down towards her hamstring. Edana whimpers.

My hand comes away soaked. I lift it towards my eyes, but I don't need it any closer to smell the blood on it. I snatch my flashlight from my pocket and flick it on.

Both of her hamstrings have been sliced.

The top edge of the wound curves up like a ghastly smile, and blood pools around her hocks.

I go to her head and she struggles, trying to get her legs under her. I stroke her forelock and whisper in her ear. *Be still. Don't be afraid*. I wait for her breathing to become easier, for her to believe me.

She'll never walk again.

I can't understand it. I don't understand who would mutilate Edana, a horse that wasn't in the races, a horse that was no threat to anyone. And like this, this savage cruelty – I was meant to find her and be sickened. I can think of only one person who would want to hurt me like that.

I think I hear a rustle somewhere in the depths of the stable.

I flick off the flashlight.

In the dark, in his stall, Edana's bay coat looks very much like Corr's blood-red one. It would be very easy to mistake them if you were expecting Corr and were concentrating on getting into the stall without getting hurt.

There's movement again, further away in the stable.

I scramble out of the stall and into the aisle. I stand and wait, listening. My heart has already raced ahead of me. All I want is for the sound to be from anywhere but the back seven stalls. All I want is for Mutt Malvern to have guessed wrong when he went looking for Corr. There are five other stalls equipped for the *capaill uisce*. He could have gone looking in any of them after he discovered Edana was the wrong horse.

I hear the commotion again.

It's from the back seven stalls.

Now I run.

I strike the lights on as I round the corner by the door. If he knows I am here, surely he will abandon this.

"Mutt!" I shout. Now, under the light, I see blood on the floor, the edge of a shoe printing scarlet every step. I jog along, following, watchful. "You've gone too far! *Mutt!*"

My voice echoes in the high arches of the stable; there's no reply. Perhaps he's left.

Corr screams.

Now I run like I've never run. I can see Edana in my mind, her head stretched unnaturally towards the ceiling as she lies against the wall, ruined in her own skin and not yet knowing it.

If he has touched Corr, I will kill him.

I burst around the corner. The door to Corr's stall is open. Mutt Malvern stands with a wicked blade in one hand and, in the other, a three-pronged leister spear of the sort used to poach fish or birds. The iron heads of the spear press into Corr's shoulder, forcing him back against the wall. His skin shivers and ripples under the metal. Mutt Malvern has given some thought to this plan of his.

"Get away from him," I say. "Every drop of his blood will be ten of yours."

"Sean Kendrick," Mutt replies. "Pretty foul of you to swap stalls like that."

Corr makes a low roar in his throat, a sound that we feel in our feet instead of hear. But he's pinned by the leister spear, not only points of iron but three of them as well.

"If you knew a thing about the horses under this roof, you would've known the difference between them, even in the dark."

Mutt glances at me long enough to see that I've closed the distance between us. He jerks his chin towards the spear. "Stay out of this stall, knacker."

I slowly wipe my bloody hand across my jacket and draw my switchblade from my pocket. I show it to him.

Mutt regards it with contempt. "How is it you're thinking you'll stop me with that wee thing?"

The blade snaps out audibly. Mutt would not be the largest thing to die on the slender point of it.

"I don't think I'll stop you," I say. "I think that you will cut my horse and then when you come out of that stall, I will use this to cut your heart out and hand it to you."

I am sick to the ends of my fingers. I cannot look at Corr's eye or I won't be steady.

Mutt says, "Do you really think I believe that you can do anything to me while I have these in my hands?" But he does believe. I can see it in his eyes.

I say, "What's it you hope to prove in there? That you are the better horseman? That the horses love you better? Do you mean to carve your father's approval in the side of every *capall uisce* on this island?"

"No," says Mutt. "Just this one."

"Will that be enough?" I ask. "What will be next?"

"There is no next," Mutt says. "This beast's the only thing you care about."

He looks at my face, though, and he's not quite sure. Maybe because it wasn't meant to happen with me watching. I was meant to come down in the morning and find Corr as I just found Edana. Maybe because he is looking at me and dreaming of a better way to hurt me.

Surely I must know something that would satisfy Mutt more than crippling Corr. There must be something. I think of his contorted face at the auction and I say, "You really want to prove something to your father, you've got to win against us. Beat us on the sand."

His face shifts. That fiendish piebald has him well fascinated. Mutt glances at me again, then back at the points of the spear on Corr's shoulder.

I know what is going through his head, because it's going through mine as well. Benjamin Malvern telling George Holly that I am the rightful heir to the yard. The name *Skata* printed on the board at the butcher's. The breathless speed of the piebald.

It's a siren song, and it wins him over.

Mutt backs out of the stall. Corr charges up towards the space he leaves behind. His eyes are wild. I see the pricks of blood the spear has left in his shoulder, and when Mutt slides the door shut, I spring on to Mutt and press my little switchblade to his great bulging neck. I can see his skin sucking in with his pulse. My knife lies right next to it.

"I thought you said to beat you on the sand," Mutt says. Corr slams the wall of his stall with his hooves.

My voice hisses out through a cage of my teeth. "I also said ten drops of your blood for every drop of his." I want a pool of his blood around him like the one beneath Edana. I want him to lie against this wall and whimper like she does. I want him to know he'll never stand again. I want him to remember David Prince's death mask as he wears it for himself.

"Sean Kendrick."

The voice comes from behind me. I incline my head even as Mutt's eye catches mine.

"It is late for this sort of entertainment, isn't it?"

With great reluctance, I snap the blade away and step backwards from Mutt. Mutt's hands remain by his side with the spear and his wicked carving knife still dark with blood. We both face his father, who stands with Daly at the entrance to the aisle. He wears a buttoned undershirt that he must've been sleeping in, but he is no less powerful-looking in it. Daly, shamefaced, won't meet my eyes.

"Matthew, your bed is lonely." His voice is cordial although his posture is not. Malvern meets Mutt's gaze and for a moment, nothing happens. Then Malvern's expression hardens and Mutt strides past him without a word or glance towards me.

Malvern turns his eyes to me. I am shaking still, struck with what Mutt nearly did to Corr and with what I was ready to do to Mutt.

"Mr Daly," Malvern says without turning his head. "Thank you for your assistance. You may return to your bed."

Daly nods and vanishes.

Benjamin Malvern stands an arm's length from me, his eyes steady on me. He says, "Do you have anything to say?"

"I would not" – I close my eyes for a moment. I need to get my bearings. I need to find the stillness inside me. I cannot find it; I'm destroyed. I stand in the ocean, my hands cupped to the sky. I'm immovable in the current. I open my eyes – "have been sorry."

Malvern cocks his head. For a long moment he looks at me, at the switchblade in my hand, at my face. Then he folds his arms behind his back. "Mr Kendrick, go put that mare out of her misery."

He turns and walks from the stable.

FIFTY-FOUR

Sean

The next day is bitter and ruthless. The wind races around the horses' feet and makes them wild. Overhead, clouds like ragged breath flee in front of the cold. There's a grey ocean above and below us.

I meet Puck at the head of the cliff road. She frowns when she sees me; I know my face must be a wasteland of fatigue after last night. Her hair is held down by a lumpy knitted hat, but a few strands snap across her face. The vendors are struggling to keep their tents from flying away. The riders heading down the cliff path endeavour to keep their mounts from doing the same.

Puck tugs down the edge of her hat with one hand. Something nearby creaks and groans in the wind. Dove tosses her head. I see terror in her wide eyes.

"Take Dove home," I tell her. "This isn't a day to be on the beach."

"There isn't any more time," she replies. "I thought you said I should get used to the beach. There's no more time."

I have to shout to be heard over the wind. I spread my empty palms to the sky. "Do you see Corr in my hands? This isn't a beach you want to get used to." *Killing sands*, that was what my father called a day like today. Today the riders would die because they didn't know or because they were desperate or because they were foolishly brave.

Puck frowns at the cliff road. I see her uncertainty in the wrinkle between her eyebrows.

"If you trust me on anything, don't risk today. You're ready as you'll ever be," I say. "Everyone else is robbed the extra day, too."

She bites her lip in dark frustration, looks at the ground for a moment, and then, like that, she's done. "It is what it is, I reckon. Is Tommy Falk down there?"

I don't know. My interests don't lie with Tommy Falk.

"Hold Dove," she says, when I can't answer to her satisfaction. "I'm going to get him if he's down there."

I don't want her on the beach on a horse or off it. "I'll go look for him. Take her home."

"We'll both go," Puck says. "Wait a moment. I'll get Elizabeth to tie her behind the booth. Don't move."

I watch Puck make her way back to Fathom & Sons' booth and get into a spirited discussion with one of the sisters who tends it.

"That's a poor match, Sean Kendrick," says a voice at my elbow. It's the other sister from Fathom & Sons, and she follows my gaze to Puck. "Neither of you are a housewife."

I don't look away from Puck. "I think you assume too much, Dory Maud."

"You leave nothing to assumption," Dory Maud says. "You swallow her with your eyes. I'm surprised there's any of her left for the rest of us to see."

I shift my glance to her. Dory Maud is a hard-looking woman, clever and industrious, and even I know from my perch at the Malvern Yard that she could fight the strongest man on the island for the last penny in his pocket. "And what is she to you, then?"

Dory Maud's expression is canny. "What you are to Benjamin Malvern, only less salary and more affection."

We both look back to Puck, who has won the battle with Elizabeth and ties Dove behind the booth. This ill wind throws both the ends of her hair and Dove's mane to and fro. I remember the feel of Puck's ponytail in my hand, the heat of her skin when I tucked her hair into her collar.

"She doesn't know any better," Dory Maud says. "What a girl like her needs is a man with both his legs on the land. A man who will hold her down so that she doesn't fly away. She doesn't know yet that someone like you looks better on the shelf than in your hand."

I can hear in her voice that she means no cruelty by it. But I say, "Someone to hold her down just as you are held?"

"I hold myself down," snaps Dory Maud. "You and I both know what you love, and those races are a jealous lover."

And now I hear in her voice that she knows this firsthand. But she's pegged me wrong, because it's not the races I love.

Puck comes up to us just then, still wearing the vicious smile from winning the battle with Elizabeth. "Dory!"

"Watch yourself on that beach," Dory Maud says, and then she leaves us behind with a bit of a growl. Puck mutters something about bad tempers.

"Have you changed your mind?" I ask her.

"I never do," she says.

The beach is every bit as bad as I'd guessed. The sky is down near the sand and occasional rain hits our faces like sea spray. From our vantage on the cliff road, I can see the thrashing ocean, the *capaill uisce* blowing across the black wet sand, the quarrels between horses and the smears of red down the beach. A dark, dead *capall* lies out flat by the surf, every wave washing around its legs but not moving it. It's not only humans this is dangerous for.

Puck says, "Do you see Tommy?"

I do not, but only because there's much to see in this ceaselessly moving play. Rain hisses in my ears.

She pushes down the path and I have no choice but to follow her. At the base are a few huddled spectators and a race official. One of the Carrolls, I think, an uncle of Brian and Jonathan's. I stop to talk to him, my head ducked down into my collar.

"What's been happening down here?" My voice is thin in the wind; my eyes are on the dead water horse.

"Fighting. The horses are fighting. The sea's driving them mad."

"Is Tommy Falk down here?" I ask him.

"Falk?"

"Black mare!"

He says, "They're all black when they're wet."

"Tommy Falk?" echoes one of the spectators next to him, a mainlander by his navy suit coat and tie, even down here on the sand. "Good-looking boy?"

I have no idea if he is or not. "Maybe yes at that?"

He points towards the curve of the cliffs. The race official, as an afterthought, adds, "Someone was looking for you, Mr Kendrick." I wait for him to say who, but he doesn't, so I step away. In all this I've lost Puck. Everyone looks the same in this vile weather. If all of the *capaill uisce* are black when they're wet, so is every human. The beach is populated by dark, insensible beasts and the smaller dark creatures on their backs. There's no point calling for her; in a couple of metres all sound becomes the savage howl of the wind.

With my eyes, I finally find not Puck, not Tommy Falk, but his mare. She is blacker than a mirror and unmistakable with her fine bone. She stands about ten lengths away in the shelter of the cliffs, tied near another *capall uisce*, her head low to the ground. The mare's still in her tack, but there's no sign of Tommy Falk about her. I think perhaps that Puck has seen her as well, so I head towards the mare, across the loose stones of the high beach.

But before I get even halfway there, I find Puck. Tucked behind the curve of the cliff road, slightly protected from the weather, there are four bodies stretched out parallel to each other, dark outlines on the pale beach, casualties of the morning. Puck crouches beside one of them, not touching or even looking at it. Just hunched down against the wind, studying the ground between her feet.

I walk over to stand beside her and look down at the battered face of Tommy Falk.

FIFTY-FIVE

Puck

The next day is both the last day before the races and Tommy Falk's funeral. I am driven to distraction by the idea of the race tomorrow, which feels like a disservice to Tommy. But when I try to tell myself *Tommy Falk is dead*, all I can think about is him and Gabe tossing that chicken around our house.

When I leave with Dove, Gabe is still lying in his bed, his door cracked open so that I can see that he stares up at the ceiling. By the time I get home, he has moved the debris I've put in front of the fence section the *capall uisce* destroyed and is smashing nails into boards. I can't stay in the house because I keep thinking that tomorrow is the race and tomorrow is only one night's sleep away, so Finn and I go to Dory Maud's to help her get a new batch of catalogues ready to mail. When we get back, Gabe has transformed the yard – pulled up every weed and piled every bit of scrap into a heap behind the lean-to – but I can see that it hasn't made him forget that Tommy Falk is dead. When we walk into the yard, he looks at us for half a minute before his face changes into something like recognition. His hands are shaky, and I make him eat something. I don't think he's stopped working all day. As afternoon turns into evening, Beech Gratton arrives, and he and Gabe exchange a grim-lipped greeting. Then we're dressed and off to the western cliffs.

Gabe doesn't tell us much about Tommy's funeral, only that the Falks are "old Thisby" and that means that the funeral will involve neither St Columba nor Father Mooneyham, but will instead take place on the rocks by the sea. Finn looks nervous at this, as anything that involves his immortal soul tends to make him nervous, but Gabe tells him to be decent and that it's just as good a religion as any brand that our parents wore, that the Falks were the best sort of people you'd want to meet. He says it all in a very faraway sort of voice, like he is pulling the words from a storage cabinet for us. I sense that he's drowning but I don't have any idea of how to start to put my hand into the water to save him.

We have to pick our way across the long ragged cliffs to the western beach, which is rockier and more uncertain than the racing beach. The ocean is glazed gold in the evening light, and there is a fire burning just out of the reach of the water. We're met by a small funeral party; I recognize many of my father's fishermen friends among them.

"Thank you for coming, Gabe," says Tommy Falk's mother. I see now that she's the one who Tommy had got his lips from, but if the rest of her is beautiful, I can't tell, because her eyes are red and small from loss.

She takes Gabe's hands. Gabe says, so serious that I'm suddenly ferociously proud of him despite everything, "Tommy was my best friend on this island. I'd have done anything for him." She says something back, but I don't hear what it is, because I'm so surprised to see that Gabe is crying. He's still speaking to her quite plainly, but as he does, tears course down his cheeks with every blink. I find, weirdly, that I can't watch him do it, so I leave him and Finn with her and move towards the fire.

It only takes me a moment to realize that it's not just a bonfire, but a pyre. It smokes and crackles, the loudest thing on the beach. The flames are orange and white against the deep blue of the evening sky, and the wet, flat sand reflects them like a mirror. Each wave extinguishes the reflection and then returns it. It's been burning for a very long time, with a mound of glowing coals and ash beneath it, and I am stricken when I see a somehow unmolested scrap of Tommy Falk's jacket caught on the timbers.

I think: *He was just sitting at our table in that jacket.*

"Puck, isn't it?"

I look to my left and see a man standing there, his arms folded neatly in front of him, as if he stands in church. Of course I know that he's Norman Falk, now that I look at him, because I remember him standing in our kitchen the exact same way, talking to my mother.

I'd just always thought of his face and thought *fisherman*, not *Tommy Falk's father*. Beside him is a kid, possibly one of Tommy's siblings. Norman Falk doesn't look anything like Tommy. He smells like Gabe, which is to say, like fish.

"I'm sorry about this," I say, because that's what people said to me after our parents died.

Norman Falk's eyes are dry as he looks into the pyre. The boy leans against his leg, and Norman Falk puts a hand on his shoulder. "We would've lost him either way."

It seems a funny sort of comfort. I can't imagine thinking that about Gabe. There is Gabe being dead, which is for ever.

And there is Gabe being happy somewhere I might never see him again. It might feel the same to me, but I'm quite certain it wouldn't feel the same to Gabe.

"He was very brave," I offer, because it sounds polite in my head. My face is getting hot from the flames; I want to step back but I don't want to seem like I'm stepping away from the conversation.

"That he was. Everyone will remember him on that mare." There's naked pride in Norman Falk's voice. "We've asked Sean Kendrick to give her back to the sea, and he's said yes. We're doing it right for Tommy."

I ask, ever so polite, trying to pretend that Sean Kendrick's name hasn't interested me, "Give her back to the sea, sir?"

Norman Falk spits behind him, hard, so that he won't spit on the boy at his side, and then turns back to the pyre. "Yes, releasing her the proper way. Give the dead some respect, like we used to. Give the *capaill* some respect. It's not about the tourists coming in and lining pockets. It's about the *capaill uisce* and us, and anything less than that makes it a dirty sport." Then he seems to remember who he's talking to, because he says, "There's no place for you on the beach, now, Puck Connolly. You and your mare. Shouldn't be. I knew your father and I liked him, but I think what you're doing's wrong, if you'll hear me."

I feel shamed for no reason I can name, and then I feel bad that I've let myself be shamed. "I don't mean to be disrespectful."

Norman Falk's voice is kind enough. " 'Course you don't. You just don't have a mum and dad to set you right. That horse of yours is just a horse, is the problem. If the Scorpio Races are just horse races, then all this" – Norman Falk jerks his chin towards the flames – "was just a bloody shame and nothing else."

Two weeks ago, I would've thought he was crazy, that of course it was just about the race, the money, the thrill. And if I'd just been watching the training on the beach, I probably would've still said that. But now that I've spent time with Sean Kendrick, now that I've been on the back of Corr, I feel something inside me slipping. I'm still not sure it was worth Tommy dying for. But I can see the allure of having one foot on the land and one foot in the sea. I've never known Thisby so well as I have these last few weeks.

The boy says something to Norman Falk and he replies, "He's bringing her down now. Look there now."

We both turn our heads and there is Sean, halfway down one of the little paths to the beach. He holds Tommy's black mare, and in comparison to Corr, she looks fragile in his hands. Sean wears nothing ritual or unusual, just his same blue-black jacket with his collar turned up. I feel a strange, fierce squeeze in my heart when I see him, like pride, although there's nothing about Sean that I can take credit for. He leads the black mare across the sand towards us, pausing only when she half rears and squeals, soft as a bird cry.

The funeral party gathers by the pyre to watch as he walks her to the water's edge. It's only then that I notice that Sean's feet are bare. The surf rushes around his ankles, soaking the bottom few centimetres of his trousers. The mare lifts her hooves high as the water courses in around her pasterns and then she cries out to the sea. There is something not quite horselike about her eyes already. When she snaps at Sean, he simply ducks out of the way and twists his fingers in her forelock, pulling her head down. I see his mouth moving, but it's impossible to hear what he tells her.

Beside me, Tommy's father says, "From the sea, to the

sea," and I realize that the words match the movement of Sean's mouth.

I wonder then at how many times this moment's taken place. Not with Sean saying the words, but with anyone. It's like the moment at the bloody stone when I declared Dove as my mount. I feel the pull of my legs to Thisby, the invisible presences of a thousand rituals weights around my ankles.

Sean looks to the group and calls, "The ashes."

Another boy – another sibling, maybe, this one looks a little like Tommy – hurries across the sand towards Sean. The light is failing quickly, so I can't see what he's carrying the ashes in – they must have just been taken from the pyre. Sean holds a hand over the vessel as if testing the temperature, and then he cautiously reaches in. The mare tosses her head and calls out again, and Sean hurls the handful of ashes into the air above her. Sean's voice is a wind-torn, weightless thing across the sand, but Norman Falk says the words along with him: "May the ocean keep our brave."

With his back to us, Sean tugs the halter from the mare's head. She kicks out, but he steps out of the way as if it were nothing at all. With a shake of her mane, she leaps mightily into the water. For a moment she struggles over the waves, and then she is swimming. Just a wild black horse in a deep blue sea full of the ashes of other dead boys.

Then, so sudden and swift that I miss the moment

of her disappearing, she's gone, and there's only the swaying of the ocean surface.

Sean stands at the edge of the surf, looking out at the sea, and there is something curious and longing in his expression, like he, too, wishes to leap into the ocean and be gone. I think, just then, that this is why Norman Falk asked for Sean to be there. Not because he was the only one who could perform the ritual. But because Sean Kendrick, looking like that, *is* the races, even if no race was ever run. A reminder of what the horses mean to the island – a bridge between what we are and that thing about Thisby that we all want but can't seem to touch. When Sean stands there, his face turned out to the sea, he is no more civilized than any of the *capaill uisce*, and it unsettles me.

My heart feels full and empty with all of the beginnings and endings. Tomorrow is the races with all of their strategy and danger and hope and fear, and on the other side of it is Gabe getting into a boat and leaving us. I feel like Sean looking out over the ocean. I'm so full of an unnamed wanting that I can't bear it.

FIFTY-SIX

Sean

After I release Tommy Falk's mare, I am drawn into the funeral party. By the light of the fire, everyone's face is a secret until you are right upon them. I search one and then the other; I see Gabriel Connolly and Finn Connolly but not Puck.

I ask Finn with his scarecrow posture if Puck had come with them and he says, "Of course," but no more. I move through the group, touching elbows and asking after her, thinking all the while that to do so is to shout my feelings about her. No one has seen her.

The race is tomorrow and I've done my part for Tommy Falk and I should go back to the yard but I feel hollow, knowing that Puck's here somewhere and I haven't found her. I need to find her, and the needing disquiets me.

For a long moment I stand on the rocks, imagining where she would be, and then I climb back up the cliff path. The ground is dark but here, closer to the sky, the evening air is still dark and red. Elsewhere on Thisby it must be night, but here, we still have a whisper of the evening sun, far away across the western sea. I find her there at the top of the cliff, facing the horizon. Her knees are pulled up to her chin and her arms wrapped around them. She looks like she has grown from the rocks and dirt around her. Though she hears my footsteps, her eyes keep searching the sea.

I draw myself up next to her and look at her profile, making no effort to disguise my attention, here, where there is only Puck to see me. The evening sun loves her throat and her cheekbones. Her hair the colour of cliff grass rises and falls over her face in the breeze. Her expression is less ferocious than usual, less guarded.

I say, "Are you afraid?"

Her eyes are far away on the horizon line, out to the west where the sun has gone but the glow remains. Somewhere out there are my *capaill uisce*, George Holly's America, every gallon of water that every ship rides on.

Puck doesn't look away from the orange glow at the end of the world. "Tell me what it's like. The race."

What it's like is a battle. A mess of horses and men and blood. The fastest and strongest of what is left from two weeks of preparation on the sand. It's the surf in your face, the deadly magic of November on your skin, the Scorpio drums in the place of your heartbeat. It's speed, if you're lucky. It's life and it's death or it's both and there's nothing like it. Once upon a time, this moment – this last light of evening the day before the race — was the best moment of the year for me. The anticipation of the game to come. But that was when all I had to lose was my life.

"There's no one braver than you on that beach."

Her voice is dismissive. "That doesn't matter."

"It does. I meant what I said at the festival. This island cares nothing for love but it favours the brave."

Now she looks at me. She's fierce and red, indestructible and changeable, everything that makes Thisby what it is. She asks, "Do you feel brave?"

The mare goddess had told me to make another wish. It feels thin as a thread to me now, that gift of a wish. I remember the years when it felt like a promise. "I don't know what I feel, Puck."

Puck unfolds her arms just enough to keep her balance as she leans to me, and when we kiss, she closes her eyes.

She draws back and looks into my face. I have not moved, and she barely has, but the world feels strange beneath me.

"Tell me what to wish for," I say. "Tell me what to ask the sea for."

"To be happy. Happiness."

I close my eyes. My mind is full of Corr, of the ocean, of Puck Connolly's lips on mine. "I don't think such a thing is had on Thisby. And if it is, I don't know how you would keep it."

The breeze blows across my closed eyelids, scented

with brine and rain and winter. I can hear the ocean rocking against the island, a constant lullaby.

Puck's voice is in my ear; her breath warms my neck inside my jacket collar. "You whisper to it. What it needs to hear. Isn't that what you said?"

I tilt my head so that her mouth is on my skin. The kiss is cold where the wind blows across my cheek. Her forehead rests against my hair.

I open my eyes, and the sun has gone. I feel as if the ocean is inside me, wild and uncertain. "That's what I said. What do I need to hear?"

Puck whispers, "That tomorrow we'll rule the Scorpio Races as king and queen of Skarmouth and I'll save the house and you'll have your stallion. Dove will eat golden oats for the rest of her days and you will terrorize the races each year and people will come from every island in the world to find out how it is you get horses to listen to you. The piebald will carry Mutt Malvern into the sea and Gabriel will decide to stay on the island. I will have a farm and you will bring me bread for dinner."

I say, "That is what I needed to hear."

"Do you know what to wish for now?"

I swallow. I have no wishing-shell to throw into the sea when I say it, but I know that the ocean hears me nonetheless. "To get what I need."

FIFTY-SEVEN

It used to be that before Dad went on to the boat, the house would be alive with movement. Even if he left early in the morning or late at night to follow the shoals and the tides, Mum would be up baking things for him to take with him and Gabe would be sitting in his room making certain he packed his razor and Finn and I would be clutching his legs or climbing into his bag or getting into Mum's flour. The day that they both went out together, it was me baking for them and Gabe watching what Mum packed and Finn sulking, unhappy that they were leaving.

Now, the morning of the Scorpio Races, I feel like I'm the one going out on the boat. Finn's anxiously checking my pack and Gabe's polishing my boots and I'm tugging my hair into a ponytail and thinking, *Is this really it?* We can afford to be inefficient; the morning is dominated by the shorter, less serious races, and so I won't have to be out there with Dove until the early afternoon. At one point, I reach into the biscuit tin, meaning to get some money just in case I need to buy something for Dove. My fingers touch the cool, bare bottom of the jar. We've finally used it all.

As if I needed the reminder of why I was racing. Nerves creep along the back of my neck.

When I finally head out, Finn says that he will bring me lunch – not that I can imagine ever eating, as my guts are a bed of snakes, which makes for poor digestion – and Gabe follows me out of the house.

"Puck," he says. "Don't do this."

He leans over the fence and watches me toss Dove's girth over the back of her saddle. He looks a lot like Dad now, in this light, since he hasn't been sleeping and he's got the lines under his eyes. He's starting to look a little like one of the fishermen, with the crinkled corners of their eyes.

"I think it's a little late for that." I look over Dove's back at him. "Tell me how else I get to save the house, and I'll stay home."

"Would it be so bad, to leave this house?"

"*I* like it. It reminds me of Mum and Dad. And it's not even about the house. You know the first thing to go if we don't have it? Dove. I can't—" I stop and busy myself rubbing a smudge off the saddle.

"She's just a horse," Gabe says. "Don't look at me like that. I know you love her. But you can live without her. You can get jobs here and I'll send money back and it'll be OK."

I bury my fingers in Dove's mane. "No, it won't be

OK. I don't want to just get a job and work and be OK. I want Dove and I want to have space to breathe and I don't want Finn to work at the mill. I don't want to live in a closet in Skarmouth, with Finn in a separate little closet in Skarmouth, getting old."

"Then next year I'll have made enough that you can come to the mainland, too. There are better jobs there."

"I don't *want* to come to the mainland. I don't *want* a better job. Don't you get it? I'm happy here. Not everyone wants to leave, Gabe! This is where I want to be. If I could have Dove and my space and a sack of beans, I'd call that enough."

Gabriel looks at his feet and works his mouth, the way he used to when he and Dad would get into it and he didn't like the corners he was being pushed into. "And that's worth dying for?"

"Yeah. I think it is."

He works a loose splinter on the top of a board. "You didn't even think about it."

"I don't have to. How about this? I won't race, and you'll stay here." But as I say it, I know that he'll say no, and that I'd race anyway.

"Puck," Gabe says, "I can't."

"Well," I reply, pushing the gate open and leading Dove out past him, "there you go."

But I don't feel angry about it. There's the old sting, but no surprise. It feels like I've known all along, ever since I was little, that he was going to leave, and I'd just been ignoring it. I think Gabe knew, too, when he started this conversation, that there was no way that he'd keep me and Dove off the beach. It was just something we both had to say. As I pass by, Gabe snags my arm. Dove amiably stops as he pulls me into a hug. He doesn't say anything. It is like any number of hugs he'd given me growing up, when the six years of difference between us was a canyon, me a child on one side, him an adult.

"I'll miss you," I say into his sweater. For once it doesn't smell of fish; it smells of the hay that he moved for me the night before and the smoke from the funeral pyre.

"I'm sorry I made such a hash of things," he says. "I should've trusted you both more."

I wish that he'd said it before, before he was sad and scared. But I'll take it now.

Gabe lets me go. "I'll go find where they're handing out the race colours." He looks at me. "You look just like Mum right now."

FIFTY-EIGHT

Sean

It is the first day of November and so, today, someone will die.

I hear a tap on my cracked door and it pushes open.

"How is Skarmouth's prize hero on the morning of the races?"

I open my eyes and turn my head to where George Holly stands in my doorway. He glances around at the furnishings of my small flat; there's nothing but a bed and a sink and a tiny stove shoved under the slanted ceiling, everything turned lavender in the weak morning light.

I give a nod that's both a greeting and a gesture for him to enter.

"This is grim," he says. "You look grim as well." After a pause, he pulls a crate of tins out from next to the sink and sits on it, his legs folded up. He rests his red flat cap across his knees and strokes it like an animal.

"I cannot settle," I say. I close my eyes. "I can't go into his stall like this or Corr will feel this on me and I might as well not step foot on the beach at all."

"Is this about the races?" Holly asks. "Are you afraid of them?"

"I've never been afraid," I reply without opening my eyes.

Holly says, "Is this because you race for Corr this time? What is it you really want, Sean?"

I press my hand to my face, searching somewhere inside myself for the quiet that must be there. For the certainty I wear every year before every race. Every morning before I get on to any horse.

"Is it the freedom? Don't bother with the race. Come back to the States with me, and I'll make you partner in my stables. Not head groom. Not head trainer. Come and go as you please." When I still don't speak, Holly says, "Now, there, you see? So you were lying to me when you told me it was the freedom you wanted. We've discovered it's not about the freedom at all. I call that progress."

I turn my face away. Downstairs, I hear the commotion of the yard on race day, and me not among it.

"So it's about that red stallion, then, you say? You will lose the race and lose him in one swift stroke of Malvern justice? But you've won four years out of six, haven't you, and aren't those good odds? So I think it's not about that, either."

I open my eyes. Holly shifts his weight under my gaze; the crate creaks beneath him.

"Twice I've lost to Ian Privett on Penda. The third year he fell and lost Penda and this year he has him again. Blackwell has Margot—"

"—she's a fast bitch—" notes Holly, my words in his mouth.

"—and there is that piebald. I don't know her. I think we should all be afraid of her. I think I could lose it all."

Holly scratches his neck and looks at the shadows beneath my narrow bed. "This 'it all' seems to be the heart of it to me. When you say 'it all', do you by any chance mean Kate Connolly? Ah, I see that you do."

I say, "Myself I can be sure of."

"Hmm," he says.

"Don't say '*hmm*' to me, Mr Holly. You can't come in here with your red hat and those shoes and play the wise man."

"Yes, says the man wearing no shoes at all," says Holly. He stands and takes the step that brings him to my stove. "How do you live here, Sean? How do you make a cup of tea without burning your johnny? If you rolled over in your bed, you'd end up in the sink. Every morning is breakfast in bed because there's no floor to speak of."

"It's tolerable."

"Hmm," says Holly again. "Tolerable covers a wide range of situations. If you win, this is what you come back to?"

"My father's house is an hour's walk from here, on the north-western cliffs. If I was free to live anywhere, that's where I'd live." I can't quite remember living in my father's home, though I've ridden by it before. My memories of the space inside are fragmented: me in bed, me at a window, my mother in a chair. It's quite run-down now. It's still in my name, but it's too far to serve me well working for Malvern.

"That's where you would keep the broodmare I just bought until she had a lovely red colt by your stallion?"

I reach for my socks on the radiator and the boots beneath them. "I didn't say I would start a yard."

"You didn't have to. I'll come back next year and you'll have a nest of horses outside your window and Puck Connolly in your bed and I'll buy from you instead of Malvern. That's your future for you."

"The future sounds much kinder in your accent." I sigh and reach for my jacket.

"Where are you going? I'm not nearly done with my prognostication."

I shoulder on my jacket. "To the beach. You'll never get that colt of yours if I don't win Corr."

FIFTY-NINE

Puck

In the night, I've shrunk and everyone else on the island has grown. They're all nine feet tall and men and I'm four feet and a child. Dove, too, is a toy or possibly a dog as I lead her through the throngs of people. The cliff road is already seething; the early races began hours ago and fifths are running the short skirmishes down on the sand. I hear groans and laughs from the spectators on the cliff. The wind tears at us all.

I peer up at the clouds, but they're lacklustre clouds, the sort that stay for a moment, not a day. I'm relieved; I'd thought it might be as ill as the day that we'd found Tommy dead on the beach. It is cold, but it's November. I expected cold.

Everyone's watching me and I keep hearing my name, or keep thinking that I hear it, anyway. Someone spits at Dove's hooves, or maybe my feet. I hear exclamations in broad mainland accents and comments about my breeding in Thisby's clipped one. I feel, strangely, like I'm the stranger and the tourist, come to visit a friendless island. Everyone's touching Dove, and she's flighty and uncertain. At one point, she lifts her head and whinnies, though there's no one on this side of the island to answer her. Far down on the beach, a *capall uisce* screams back. Dove shivers and drags me at the end of the lead; it takes my heels several metres to find traction again.

I hear laughter and someone asks if I need help, not in a nice way. I snarl, "What I need is for your mother to have thought a little harder nine months before your birthday."

"She bites!" says someone.

I seal my mouth shut and push further on. Somewhere in this mess is Gabe, possibly, with my colours, and Finn, possibly, with my lunch.

"Kate Connolly, do you mean to change the establishment?"

I blink and step backwards. There's a man directly in front of me, dressed in a brown suit that looks like it cost more than our house, and he holds a notebook. Behind him stands a photographer with a massive flashbulb. There is an edge of people behind me and Dove. I feel cornered.

"I'm not trying to change anything but my own situation," I say.

"So you wouldn't say you were inspired by the women's suffrage movement?"

I crane my neck around, looking for my brothers or for Dory Maud or for anyone that I know. I've never seen so many bowler hats in my life. "I'm just a person with a horse, same as anyone else on this island. Do you mind? You're making my horse nervous."

The reporter asks, "What would you say to those on Thisby who say you don't belong in the Scorpio Races?"

"I don't have a clever answer for you," I say crossly.

"Just one more, Miss Connolly. Where do you think you'll end up? Do you think you stand a chance of finishing?" They trot to keep up with me as I turn Dove's shoulder towards them. I'm oddly undone by the reporter and the photographer, more than anything I've encountered so far. I hadn't considered eyes on me, much less eyes all the way from a mainland newspaper.

I scowl at him. "Go ask at Gratton's. They know everything."

I try to turn Dove again, to push them away from me.

"Puck!"

I turn in the direction of my name, my insides raw, and there is Sean. Unlike me, who had to push through this crowd, he cuts neatly through the people. They make room for him as if unaware that they do. He is in only white shirtsleeves and he's out of breath, which is to say that for a moment I cannot believe it's him.

He comes in close, turning his back to the reporter, and ducks his head to me. I'm very aware of all the eyes on us, but Sean seems oblivious. He asks, "Where are your colours?"

"Gabe went looking for them."

"They're down on the beach," he says. "You've got to pick them up down there."

"Have you got yours?"

"Yes. I can hold Dove while you go get yours."

Dove shudders as someone touches her rump. It's too loud and too much for her. I'm worried that she'll use up all of her spirit here on the cliffs, long before we ever get down to the beach. I remember Peg Gratton telling me not to let anyone else tighten my girth on race day. Sean, I decide, is not anyone else. "Can you make them leave her alone?"

He jerks a nod at me.

In a low voice, so he has to lean his head towards me, I say, "Thank you."

Sean reaches between us and slides a thin bracelet of red ribbons over my free hand. Lifting my arm, he presses his lips against the inside of my wrist. I'm utterly still; I feel my pulse tap several times against his lips, and then he releases my hand.

"For luck," he says. He takes Dove's lead from me.

"Sean," I say, and he turns. I take his chin and kiss his lips, hard. I'm reminded, all of a sudden, of that first day on the beach, when I pulled his head from the water.

"For luck," I say to his startled face.

A flashbulb goes off and there's appreciative hooting.

"OK," Sean says, as if we've just made a deal and it's

all right to him. He turns to the crowd and says, "If you want a race, you'll give this horse some room. Now."

As they scatter outward, I push my way through them towards the cliff path. Before I head down, I look over my shoulder to find Sean, and there he is with the wide berth around him and Dove, still watching me. I feel the island underneath me, and Sean's mouth on my lips, and I wonder if luck will be on our side today.

SIXTY

Puck

The beach is not as crowded as I had expected. It's between two of the smaller races, and only the *capaill uisce* who are entered in the next races are on the beach. All of the spectators who were down on the sand before are now huddled up on the cliffs, pressed as close as they dare to the edge. The sky above them has cleared to a deep, deep blue like you only get in November, and the ocean to my right is dark as night.

I can't think that I'll soon be racing beside it or I won't be able to move.

I quickly find the race officials' table in the shelter of the cliff; two men in bowler hats sit behind a table with tantalizingly varied racing colours folded in front of them. I hurry across the sand and duck close so that I won't have to shout.

"I need to pick up my colours," I say. I recognize the man on the right; he sits near us in St Columba's.

"None left for you," replies the other official. His crossed arms rest on a stack of them.

"I'm sorry?" I ask politely.

"None left. Goodbye." He turns to the official next to him and says, "What do you think of this weather? Warm, isn't it?"

"Sir," I say.

"I'm not complaining about the heat, that's for sure, but it'll bring out the midges," says the other official.

"You can't just pretend I'm not here," I say.

But they can. They make pointed small talk, ignoring my presence, until I swallow my anger and humiliation and give up. I tell them that they're bastards, because they won't say anything back to me anyway, and go back the way I've come. I meet Gabe on his way down the cliff road. The wind has made his hair a mess.

"Where are your colours?" he asks.

I don't really want to confess it to him, but I do. "They won't give them to me."

"Won't!"

I cross my arms over my chest. "It doesn't matter. I'll race without them." But it does matter, a little.

"I'm going to go talk to them," Gabe says. His righteous anger is a welcome thing to see, even if I don't think it will help. Sometimes it helps just to have it shared with another person. "This is stupid."

I watch him descend and cross the sand, but I can tell from their faces as they watch him approach that he won't get a different answer. I tell myself it doesn't matter. I don't need to look like one of them. I don't need to belong.

"Sod them," Gabe says when he returns. "Old Thisby biddies."

Beside us, someone shouts out that everyone but the entrants in this last match race need to clear the beach, because it's nearly time for the final race.

That means us.

SIXTY-ONE

Sean

By the afternoon, the sun is strong but cold on the beach. The wind tears the surface of the blue-black sea into a thousand whitecaps. Up on the cliffs, there is the silhouette of a crowd, watching the pale road of sand between them and the ocean.

Every so often, I can see the head of a *capall uisce* in the water, far out from shore, driven towards the sand by the November current. The ones we have caught struggle against us in bridles hung with bells and red ribbons, iron and holly leaves, daisies and prayers. The water horses are hungry and wicked, vicious and beautiful, hating us and loving us.

It is time for the Scorpio Races.

I am so, so alive.

Beneath me, Corr is powerful and restless. The sea sings to him in a way that it didn't yesterday, and when another *capall uisce* moves past us, he snaps at it. Before Puck, I'd never been so aware of how many of us there were on the beach for this race. *Capaill uisce* of every colour pressing against each other, crushing, biting, snorting, kicking. The north end of the beach has never seemed so distant.

In eighteen furlongs and five minutes, this will all be over.

I find Puck in the crowd. Unlike the others, she's not hanging last-minute baubles and trinkets on to her horse's mane. She's leaned over Dove's neck, her cheek pressed into Dove's mane.

"Sean Kendrick."

I recognize Mutt's voice before I turn my head. He sits nearby on the piebald mare. When she tosses her mane, the bells he's braided in the strands ring a discordant chord. I don't see how he means for her to be fast under all of the iron he has hanging off her breastplate and her crupper.

"Don't talk to me," I say.

"This race is going to be hell for you," Mutt replies.

Corr lays his ears flat back and the piebald mare responds in kind. I say, "You can't intimidate me on this beach."

Mutt Malvern backs the piebald away; she jangles and snorts. He follows my gaze back to Puck. "I know what you care about, Sean Kendrick."

· *Puck* ·

I'm trying, unsuccessfully, to pretend that this will be just another sprint. I'm trying not to look at how far we

451

have to go. I'm trying to remember that I not only have to survive but do well. I need to win. For a moment, I feel a pang of guilt, that if I get what I need, Sean doesn't, but maybe it doesn't have to be that way. If I win, surely there will be enough to both save the house and buy Corr?

"Puck. Climb off for a moment." I'm surprised to hear Peg Gratton's voice. She stands at Dove's shoulder, looking up at me. Her hair is frazzled in the wind and her face serious. I obediently slide off. She's holding her Scorpio bird costume in her arms, a fact that I can't understand. "How are you doing?"

"OK," I say.

"So, terrible," she says. "Gabe told me they wouldn't give you any colours."

I shake my head. I won't let my face show anything.

Peg says, "Right, then. Off with the saddle."

Mystified but trusting, I pull off the saddle and watch Peg carefully unfold the costume in her arms. I see now that the great, terrifying bird head is no longer attached; it's just the back of the feather-covered cape. Peg lays it down on Dove's back where the colours would have gone, and then she takes the saddle and looks to make certain that it won't chafe.

"Now you wear Thisby's colours," she says.

"Thank you."

"Don't thank me." Peg's already walking away. "Show them who you are."

I swallow. Who I am is crouched down inside this girl named Puck Connolly, praying that I'll make it through the next few minutes.

"Riders, line *up!*"

How can it be time to line up? We've only just got down here and I haven't seen Sean before the race. I swing on to Dove and stare over the *capaill uisce*, looking for him. If I can just see—

On the other side of the line, I see him lifting his chin and looking at me as well. Corr, wearing dark blue colours, is slicked with sweat already. Sean's still looking at my face so I lift up my wrist for him to see his ribbon on it.

"Riders, *line up!*"

I wish I were next to Sean and Corr, but there's no time. Three race officials are pressing us back into lines behind great wooden poles. The lines ring and shrill with hundreds of bells on dozens of hooves. The *capaill uisce* snap and snort, paw and shudder. I keep Dove as far from her neighbours as I can. Her ears are flattened back to her head. She's surrounded by predators.

Beside me, the *capall uisce* shakes its head and foam cascades down its neck and chest.

They're counting down.

The ocean says *shhhhhhhh, shhhhhhhh.*

They lift the poles.

SIXTY-TWO

Puck

We explode into action. There's no rhyme or reason; the only thing I can remember is to pull Dove to the inside. No one wants to be near that November sea unless they have to be. Dove's hooves touch the edge of the surf, and salt water mists my face. Somehow there is salt between my fingers and the reins, and the crystals burn and grate.

Something crushes my leg, hard, the buckle of my stirrup leather grinding into the bone, and I turn in time to see a great bay *capall uisce* pressed against me. I jerk Dove further into the surf just as the bay twists and snaps at her. Her ears flatten all the way back into her mane just as I see that it's Gerald Finney. His fists are white-knuckled around his reins and he doesn't glance at me. I can tell by the shiver working through the saddle that Dove recognizes his *capall*. I clamp my legs on either side of her. *Don't be afraid yet, Dove. We have a long way to go.*

I remember, too late, that I'm supposed to be conserving Dove's energy and I check her speed. Horses charge by us; the green of Ian Privett's colours, the light blue of Blackwell's, the gold of the piebald mare. No red stallion under dark blue, though. I have no idea if he is so far ahead that I can't see him or if he is behind me.

Sean

I look for Puck or Dove, but I can't see anything in this crush of bodies. Corr's strong in my hands; my exhausted shoulders already ache from the weight of him. My calves burn with the friction of the stirrup leathers. I'm not sure how long I should hold Corr back behind the pack to look for her. The back is the worst place to be; the *capaill* back here lag not because they're slow but because they're fighting with each other or fighting with the sea. The hooves in front of me kick sand into my face. My eyes sting, but I can't spare a hand to swipe at them.

To my left are a grey and a chestnut tearing at each other. They try to incorporate Corr into the skirmish. I hold him true and press him forward: not too far, because if Puck is back there, I don't want to leave her behind. My hands are buried in the sweaty mane at his withers, and I feel his muscles shaking at the touch of the November sea. I whisper at him to be steady.

I look under my arm to the right for Puck; there's nothing but the grey halfway into the surf. He's already mostly a creature of the sea. His eyes are slits in his lengthening head. The grey twists and scrabbles, more anxious for the rider on his back than the race before him. Seawater sprays from somewhere, the cold of it like claws on my cheek.

Another *capall* pushes on my left side; she snaps out and grazes my leg before her rider jerks her away. I can't stay back here. I'll get out in the open and find Puck. If she's not out of this rabble by now, she might already be dead.

I lean over Corr's neck to whisper to him, but for once, I can't think of what to whisper.

But it doesn't matter. Corr knows what I want without me having to speak, and he surges out of the bunched *capaill* in the rear.

There is a narrow corridor open right to the very front where the three front-runners are fighting it out. Last year I would've been through that hole with Corr and they would have been counting the lengths between the rest of the pack and Corr for the remainder of the race.

But I don't take that move.

· *Puck* ·

It only takes a minute for Dove to be bitten and another few seconds for me to be cut by some razor-sharp edge that I don't think can be horse teeth. I don't have time to look at the wound or guess what has cut me. We're trapped in a crush of bodies. Even over the rush of the wind in my ears, I hear their squeals and roars, the clucks and growls as they fight.

From the slice in my thigh, I feel the disconcerting heat of blood running down my leg but no pain, yet. Whatever cut me was sharp enough that the wound was clean.

Dove is beginning to panic. Movement to her right makes her jerk her head sharply enough that the rein rips open one of the searing blisters on my palm. I see white all the way around Dove's eyes.

I need to get out of here. Sand stings my cheeks and the corners of my eyes, but I can't spare a hand to swipe my skin. I don't see how we can move forward until the *capall uisce* to my right charges into the ocean, tripping over the waves, twisting in the air before throwing its rider.

It's Finney. I see his eyes meet mine for a bare second, his hands pedalling through the water, and then his bay *capall*'s dull teeth snap shut on his cheekbone.

Then I'm past them and they're gone and it's only seething water that sprays a dark pattern on Dove's shoulder. And I'm sick, sick, sick.

Suddenly, there is a narrow path where before there was a *capall uisce*. If I pull through the right, using some of Dove's precious strength, we might get clear.

It won't do any good to save her speed if we die in this fight. I press my calves into her hot sides and suddenly, it clicks. Dove finds her stride and we pull free of the little tempestuous pack that we were trapped in. And there, hanging behind the leaders, I see a red stallion under blue colours, and Sean Kendrick folded neatly on top of him.

I sweep blood off the bite on Dove's shoulder. It's not deep, but guilt pricks me anyway. I say *sorry* to her and she flicks a trembling ear back. I let out a barest length of rein. She's still terrified, but for a moment, I have her attention.

Focus. I think about riding on the cliffs, holding her steady, keeping her even. I remember the *uisce* mare leaping from the edge of the cliff. The secret is to remember the race while the others forget everything but the ocean.

I can be steady.

· Sean ·

There's a newcomer on our right, and Corr, mad at the touch of the sea, snakes his head to bite at them. I check him and the horse beside us jerks but holds steady. Black-tipped ears. Smaller than Corr. Smaller than any of the horses on this beach. Ordinary muscles pumping and moving beneath her skin.

It's Dove, matching us stride for stride, feathers fluttering on her saddle pad. I glance, once and then again, at Puck and then Dove. Dove's been bitten, but not deep. Puck's bleeding, too. But unlike Dove's untidy bite wound, Puck's is clean and long, the material of her breeches sliced. It was a knife that did that, not a horse. Someone angry that she was on the beach with us. To think too long on that is to be furious and to be furious is to lose focus, which I can't afford.

Because in front of us is chaos. The worst of it is the noise — the panting of winded *capaill*, the groaning as they fight, the continuous thunder of the hooves, the hissing of the sea. The squeals and the shouts and behind it all, the screams of the crowd. The noise would drive a horse mad even if the November ocean didn't.

A *capall* in front of us twists and wheels inward, its rider avoiding the ocean at all costs. Another two shove and squabble, slowing enough that we move past them. It's a wall of hocks and knees and hooves, blood coating bone, teeth against teeth. They make an attempt to bring us into it, but Corr blocks them, a trembling wall between them and Dove, who is a wall between him and the sea.

We are over halfway there. Halfway means we've made it a little over a mile. The first half weeds out those who weren't ready, those who weren't tame. It's a rite of passage. I look at Puck and she looks back me, expression fierce.

The sand blurs below us and the ocean becomes silent in comparison to the sounds of our lungs gasping for breath. We are the only two on the sand.

Blackwell's and Privett's mounts quarrel up at the front. They worry back and forth, teeth flashing, necks and shoulders rubbing. Just behind them, Mutt Malvern relentlessly beats Skata, the piebald. And still Puck moves up behind them, steady and even. I match Corr to Dove, stride for stride, and with each stride, we gain ground.

Corr has nothing but power left. There's a path ahead; I could cut ahead of Blackwell and then Privett. Mutt is nothing at all as he drops back from the lead and closer to us. I could be in the lead and taking this win as easily as I snatched it last year. In three minutes Corr could be mine.

Everything I've ever wanted. A roof over my head and reins in my hands and a horse beneath me. Corr.

I feel the mare goddess's breath in my face.

I told Puck I would stay until she made her move. Maybe she doesn't have the speed to overtake the leaders. Maybe I give everything away by waiting. I tell myself I have time, still. I have time for Corr to push forward.

Dove begins to make her move.

I realize then that Mutt Malvern has pulled Skata back intentionally.

He never meant to win.

· *Puck* ·

The piebald's attack takes me by surprise.

Between me and the sea, she rears back as if she

means to plunge forward, but then she drops on to Dove. Her teeth close down over Dove's poll, right behind her ears.

Dove staggers.

I turn my head and look right into Mutt Malvern's ghastly grin.

I hear Sean shout, his voice unstrung, "This is between you and me, Mutt!"

Trying to keep my stirrups, I lean far forward up Dove's sweaty neck to grab at the piebald's ear. Her skin feels slippery and unlike any horse I've ever touched. Dove's spine presses hard into my guts and my blistered hand aches, but I ignore all of that and twist the piebald's ear sharply. She squeals and drops off Dove.

I barely understand Sean's shout. "Get out of the way, Puck!"

Dove understands even if I don't; as Corr presses closer, she shoots from between him and the piebald. I barely have time to drop back down into the saddle, the leather slick with blood or water beneath me.

Skata twists and leaps beneath Mutt, but we are free of her. I glance behind me and only have time to see Corr's shoulder smashing up against the piebald mare's. Sean's gaze flicks towards me for a second. He's watching to make sure that I'm moving.

I want to wait for him. I know he's won this four times without me here, but I don't want to leave him.

I hear Sean Kendrick's voice: "*Go!*"

I let Dove's reins go.

· Sean ·

We can't get clear.

Corr could outstrip Skata if we could pull ahead, but Mutt Malvern has seized my rein. He drags Corr's face towards him, within reach of the piebald's teeth. It's Corr's blind side and he is wild with the fear of not knowing what he's up against. His eyes roll; his nose jerks into the air again and again. Skata snaps at him, her teeth grating against his cheek. As I fight Mutt for Corr's rein, my knee crashes into Mutt's, bone to bone, searing hot.

Skata and Corr gallop, shoulder to shoulder, every step taking us further into the surf. I taste salt water; my saddle is slimy with it. Every muscle in Corr's body shivers and shimmers. Glancing to Mutt, I see that he's having a hard time keeping his seat.

Too late I see his knife.

I lift my arm. I cannot protect myself or Corr.

But it's not me he stabs. He slides it along the piebald's neck, slicing a scarlet line. She is furious with pain.

"Manage this, Kendrick," Mutt says.

He lets go of the reins.

Skata slams into us.

· Puck ·

We catch up to Blackwell and Margot first. She's a big, lean bay, long as a train car, and she fights him hard. I see that her mouth is cracked open and grinning like the black *capall uisce* that found us in the lean-to. She was breathlessly fast before, but now he holds her tightly in check. When Blackwell tries to allow her some more rein, she darts towards the ocean.

But Dove cares nothing about the sea. I lean low over her mane – her neck is sweaty and my hands are sweaty and it's hard to keep my grip – and I ask her for more. She slides past Blackwell.

There is only Privett and Penda ahead of us now. He's keeping a good distance between him and the surf, and I could move up between them. But if I could push Penda closer to that November water, maybe I could distract him long enough to hold the lead. It would mean getting very close to a *capall uisce* without any escape plan, and Dove is already frightened to the breaking point.

It's not much further. Only three furlongs, maybe. I don't want to hope, but I can feel it pumping through me.

Only – Corr should be here now. I shouldn't be up here with Penda by myself.

When I glance behind me, I can't see him. I can see Margot gaining on us, fast. And the feathers of Dove's makeshift saddle colours flapping crazily in the wind.

I hear Sean's voice saying that this is possible. And Peg Gratton telling me to show them who we are. I know that it is not about Dove being brave, in the end. It's about me being brave for her. I lean over Dove's neck – Dove, my best friend – and I ask her for one last burst of speed.

· Sean ·

I am holding Corr, but I am holding nothing. Somewhere, there is a high, clear scream, and then I'm falling.

In the moment between Corr's back and the surf, I think first of the dozens of horses behind us and then of my father's death.

My only chance is if I can get clear. To hope that when I hit that ground, I hit it so that I can roll free of most of the hooves to come. If I stay conscious, I might survive.

For one moment, I see everything with perfect clarity: Corr, his face a mask of red, one of his nostrils torn; the horizon stretching away, far out of reach; the blue, blue November sky above us.

The piebald's knee lurches up to strike my head.

When I hit the sand, my vision breaks like a wave. I have the surf in my mouth and the sand beneath me rumbles with hoofbeats, and there is red, red, red above me.

SIXTY-THREE

Puck

The moment we pass Ian Privett and Penda, Ian meets my eyes, and I see that he doesn't believe it.

But then the race is over.

Even when I see that we have crossed the line first, even when it's another half second before Margot flashes by, and another second before Ake Palsson and Dr Halsal crash by nose to nose, I can't believe it.

I slow Dove, patting her neck, laughing and rubbing away tears with the back of my bloody hand. All of my pain's melted away; all that remains are ceaseless shivers. I stand shakily in my stirrups, steering her away from the other *capaill uisce* as they cross the finish. Greys and blacks and chestnuts and bays.

I don't see Sean.

My ears won't stop hissing. It takes me a long moment to realize that it's the audience roaring from up above.

They're shouting my name and Dove's. I think I hear Finn among them, but maybe I imagine it. And still there are the water horses at the end of the race, milling and rearing and twisting.

But I don't see Sean.

A race official comes towards me, his arm out towards Dove's bridle. My hands won't stop shaking; I have a terrible feeling inside me.

"Congratulations!" the official says.

I look at him, waiting for what he just said to make sense, and then I ask, "Where's Sean Kendrick?" When he doesn't answer me, I turn Dove back the way we came. The beach at this end is a mess of sweaty *capaill uisce* and tired riders. The beach looks nothing like what it looked like to me galloping the other direction. It is nothing but a stretch of sand when I'm trotting. The ocean is only wave after wave, not a hungry, dark thing. I direct Dove back the way we came, scanning the wet sand. There are smears of blood where fights went down and a dead chestnut *capall* lying very close to the water. They're putting a sheet over someone further inland, which makes my stomach squeeze, but it's too big to be Sean.

And then I see Corr, standing at the edge of the surf, reflected red in the wet sand beneath him. One of his hind legs is crooked under him, resting on the toe of the hoof. His head is curled low and as I get closer, I see that he's trembling. His saddle has been pulled around so that it hangs nearly upside down.

There's a dark, slender form beneath him, the reins all

tangled around it. Even filthy, I recognize the blue-black jacket. And the red I mistook for reflection is merely blood, slowly being washed away with each wave.

I think, suddenly, of how Gabe said that he *could not bear it* and I didn't believe him, because of course you could bear anything if you decided to.

But just then I understand him perfectly because I cannot bear it if Sean Kendrick is dead. Not after all this. Not after everyone else. It is bad enough to see Corr standing there with a leg I think is broken. But Sean cannot be dead.

I slide off Dove. There's another race official, and I press my reins into his hands. I scramble across the sand towards Corr. I slow for a moment as a gull swoops close to my face. They're already gathering around the carnage on the beach – why doesn't someone chase them away?

"*Sean.*"

As I get close, I startle backwards at a sudden movement. It's Sean – he reaches up an arm, fumbling. Finding the stirrup, he uses it to heave himself up. He's unsteady as a new colt.

I throw my arms around him. I can't tell which of us is shaking.

Sean's voice is hoarse. "Did you do it?"

I don't want to tell him, because it was only half of what was supposed to happen.

He pulls back and looks at my face. I'm not sure what he sees there, but he says, "Yes."

"Penda was second. Where were you? What happened?"

"Mutt," Sean says. He looks out to the ocean, his eyes narrowed. "Did you see him? No, I didn't think so. She took him. The piebald took him."

My wounds are starting to hurt, and my stomach feels tight. "He never meant to win. He just wanted you—"

"Corr stood here," Sean says wonderingly. "I would've died. He didn't have to stay." For a moment, I see that it doesn't matter that he didn't win. The fact of Corr's loyalty is a bigger thing than the ownership of him.

Then, I watch his eyes sweep over Corr, taking in his lowered head, the blood on his nostrils, the twist of the hind leg. From here, it looks terrible enough that my guts lurch. Sean steps forward and carefully touches Corr's hind leg, running his hand along it. I see the precise moment when Sean's hand stops and his shoulders slope and I know it is broken.

I remember what Sean wished for: to get what he needed.

And at that moment, I don't see how I can believe in any god or goddess or island at all, and if I do, how I could believe them to be anything but cruel.

Sean moves away and jerks up the girth so that the twisted saddle falls to the ground, leaving Corr bare and dark red, his hair curly and damp where the saddle

468

had been. Sean runs his hand over the sweat-curled hair.

Then he twists a handful of Corr's mane into his hand and presses his forehead against Corr's shoulder. I don't need him to tell me that Corr will never run again.

SIXTY-FOUR

Puck

The rest of the day passes in a rush. There are prize ceremonies and money, journalists and tourists. There are congratulations and handshaking and so many voices that I can't hear any of them. There's tending for my cut – *My, that's nasty, Puck Connolly, and how did a horse give you that? You're lucky it's not deep* – and pampering of Dove. It goes on for hours and hours and I can't get away from any of it to anything important.

After the sun has disappeared, I learn that Corr has been given a makeshift shelter in one of the coves on the beach because he cannot walk back to the Malvern Yard. I manage to escape from the mob and make it partway down the cliff path. There in the twilight I see Sean Kendrick sitting against the cliff, eyes closed, and I would have gone to him, but fair-haired George Holly is already shaking him awake and coaxing him away. Even from here, I see that Sean's expression is wrecked by everything that he's lost. Holly gives me a far-off nod to send me on, but it's not until Sean meets my eyes that I lead Dove back towards home.

Finn catches up to me on the way home, skipping a little until he falls into step with me. His hands are stuffed into the pockets of his jacket. For a few moments we walk in silence, the only sounds the pad of our feet on the dirt, and Dove's hooves occasionally chipping pebbles as she walks. Dusk makes everything seem smaller around us.

"You're frowning," he says finally.

I know he's right; I can feel the furrow between my eyebrows. "I'm counting, that's why." There's not much joy in it, though. The numbers always come up the same: enough for us to save the house, not enough for Sean to buy Corr, even if Malvern would let him.

Finn says, "You should be celebrating! Gabe says he's making a feast for us at home!" Even after this long day, he can't keep the spring out of his own step. He's like a colt on a windy day.

I do my best to keep the sting out of my words, because none of this is Finn's fault, but a crumb of bitterness creeps in. "I can't celebrate while Sean Kendrick's down there with a broken horse he can't afford because of me!"

"How do you know Sean Kendrick even wants him still?"

I don't have to be told. I know Sean still wants Corr. It's never been about the racing.

Finn glances over and gets my answer in my expression. "All right, then," he says. "Why can't he afford him?"

Saying it out loud makes it worse, though. I explain, "Sean had to win to get the rest of the money. He didn't have enough."

For a long moment, there's just the slap of our shoes again, the scrape of Dove's hooves, the wind gusting across our ears. I wonder if Holly's taken Sean away from the beach. I wonder if Sean will sleep down there. He's usually so pragmatic, but not where Corr's concerned.

"Why don't we give him some money?" asks Finn.

I swallow. "I didn't win enough for both the house and Corr."

Finn rummages in his pocket. "We can use this."

When I see the fat wad of bills in his hand, I stop so fast that Dove rams her head into my shoulder. I demand, "Finn—! Finn Connolly, where did you get that?"

I can see that Finn's having to try very hard not to show me a smile. The effort of it gives him the frog face like nobody's business. I can't stop looking at the roll of money in his hand, nearly as fat as the purse for the race.

He says, "Forty-five to one."

It takes me a long moment to puzzle out where I recognize the number from – the chalkboard at Gratton's. Suddenly, I understand where the rest of the money from the biscuit tin went.

"You gambled on—" I can't even finish the sentence.

Finn starts walking again, and now there's a bit of strut to it. He says, "Dory Maud said you were a good bet."

SIXTY-FIVE

Puck

My mother always told me that you should wear your best clothing when you are angry, because it would scare people. I'm not angry, but I'm in the mood to be terrifying, so I take great care in the morning after the races. I spend an hour before my mother's oval mirror in her room, turning my ginger hair around a brush and twisting the curls with my fingers. I keep an image of Peg Gratton's hair in my head as I sort it all out. There turned out to be much less of it when it was all going in the same direction, and when I pin it back, I see my mother's face in the mirror.

I go to her closet and look at her dresses, but none of them look like they would scare anyone. So instead I find a collared shirt and put on a pair of breeches and my boots after I polish all of the beach that was caked on them. I borrow her coral bracelet and her matching coral necklace. Then I step out into the hall.

"Kate," Gabe says, startled. He sits at the kitchen table and stares. I heard him packing last night. "Where are you going?"

"I am going to the Malvern Yard."

"Well, you sure do look nice."

I open the door. Outside, the morning is pastel and mild, scented with wood smoke, as soft as yesterday was hard. "I know."

I strap my school bag over my back and take the bicycle because Dove has earned a day off if she's earned anything, and I bike through the benevolent day to the Malvern Yard.

As before, when I get to the yard, it is bustling with activity. Grooms with horses going out to pasture, riders taking thoroughbreds out to the gallops for their run, stable boys sweeping down the cobbles.

"Kate Connolly," says one of the grooms. "Sean's not here."

I didn't think he would be, but I don't like to hear it anyway. Still, I say, "I'm looking for Benjamin Malvern, actually."

"He'll be up at the house — is he expecting you?"

"Yes," I say, because if he wasn't expecting me before, he'll be expecting me when I walk in.

"Well, then, let me," says the groom. He pulls open the gate for me and my bicycle.

I thank him and walk my bicycle up to the Malvern house. It sits behind the stable and is a big, grand old thing. Like Malvern himself, it's impressive and powerful-looking but not particularly handsome. I lean my bicycle against the wall and walk to the front door and knock.

For a long moment there is no answer, and then Benjamin Malvern opens the door.

"Good morning," I say, and I step past him into his centre hall. It is a naked thing, just wide-open ceiling and a little drawing-room table against the wall. I see a sitting room beyond it and a single cup sitting in the middle of a white tablecloth.

"I was just having tea," he says.

"Good timing, then," I reply. I don't wait for him to invite me and instead step into the sitting room. Like the centre hall, it's nearly empty. Just a round table in the middle of a high-ceilinged room with nothing but brass sconces on the walls. It seems rather lonely. I wonder if he was just sitting in here wondering if the sea would ever spit out the piebald or Mutt Malvern again. I sit in a chair opposite to the one already ajar.

Malvern's mouth works. "Milk and sugar?"

I fold my arms on the table and eye him. "I'll have what you're having."

He raises an eyebrow before making me a cup of his odd tea. He pushes it to me and settles down opposite, crossing his legs and leaning back.

"What brings you blowing into my house like a hurricane, Kate Connolly? It's quite rude."

"I expect it is. I've come for three things, really," I say. I tip the cup against my lips and he watches me. I close one eye. The tea is almost precisely like drinking a scone or licking the carpet. "Three things I'd like."

"That's quite a lot of things to like."

I reach into the school bag and place a small stack of notes on the tablecloth. "The first thing I'd like to do is pay everything owed on the house."

Malvern eyes the money but doesn't touch it. "And the second?"

I take another big drink of tea for emphasis. It requires quite a bit of heroics on my part but I manage. "I'd like you to give me a job."

He sets down his teacup. "And what is it you think you'll do in this job?"

"I think I'll probably muck stalls and ride horses and push wheelbarrows, to start, and I think I'll be good at it."

Malvern considers me. "Jobs are not the easiest thing to be had on this island, you know."

"So I've heard," I reply.

Benjamin Malvern rubs his fingers over his mouth and looks up at the empty ceiling high above us. There's a bit of a crack in the plaster and he frowns at it. "I think I could manage that. And what is your third thing you'd like?"

I set down my teacup and look at him, quite hard. If I am ever to look terrifying, this is the moment. "I would like you to sell Corr to Sean Kendrick even though Sean didn't win."

Malvern makes a face. "We had a bargain, he and I, and he knew it."

"That horse is useless to you, and both of you know it. What is it you think to do with him?"

He opens one of his hands skyward.

I say, "So you might as well sell him. Unless you just fancy tormenting Sean Kendrick." I consider adding *like your late son fancied* but figure that might be more foul than the situation requires.

"Did he ask you to ask me?"

I shake my head. "He doesn't know I'm here. And he might feel a little odd if he knew that I was."

Malvern looks into his tea. "You two are a strange pair. You are a pair, aren't you?"

"We're in training."

He shakes his head. "Fine. I'll sell him. But the price isn't changing just because the horse stands on three legs instead of four now. Is that all from you?"

"I said three things and that's what I gave you."

"Indeed it is. Well, then, leave me to my tea. Come back on Monday and we can talk about your wheelbarrow."

I stand up, leaving the notes sitting untouched on the table, and head out into the yard. The breeze runs long and low across the ground, sweeping up the sea and the island grass and the hay and the horses. I think it's the best smell in the world.

SIXTY-SIX

Sean

The November sea is a jewel in the evening, dark and glittering beyond the ruddy stones. Corr and I leave the white cliffs behind us as I lead him towards the water. As when I first pulled him from the sea, he wears just a rope halter. I have long since pulled the wrap from his hind leg; it won't heal him. Holly tells me that they have ways in California of setting the bone, but that he'd still never race again. He tells me that there's nothing more foolish than for me to buy Corr only to turn him back into the ocean.

But Corr could no sooner go to California than he could fly, and in any case, I'm uncertain what a life like that would hold for a *capall uisce*. He loves the sea and to run, and while I could give him one of those things, we were happy.

And so now I walk him slowly down to the surf. In the sea, his clumsiness will disappear, his weight cradled by the salt water, and he won't notice so much that his hind leg is not what it was.

I don't want to say goodbye.

Back by the cliffs, Puck Connolly and George Holly wait for me, both of them with their arms crossed over their chests, their postures identical. They give me this moment alone, and I'm grateful for it.

Despite his painful progress, Corr's ears prick to the sea. This November ocean sings sweetly to him, luring him and caressing him, quickening his blood. Together we step into the freezing water. In this light, he's red like the sun before night, a giant, a god. His ear flicks back as the ocean plays over his injured leg and then back out to the horizon. The sea out there is black and depthless, hiding more wonders, perhaps, than even the waters of Thisby.

It wasn't that long ago that Corr and I splashed in this surf, here at the base of these cliffs. Now he couldn't even take a step without thought.

I run my hands down his neck, over his withers, down his shoulder. It's something I'd taken for granted, just the presence of him. I rest my cheek against his shoulder, my eyes closed for just a second, and then I whisper to him. *Find happiness.*

Then I can't stand because my legs won't hold me here a moment longer. I blink to clear my vision and reach up. I pull off his halter.

I back out of the surf, watching him. His ears are still pricked on the horizon, not towards me. The ocean is his love and now, finally, he'll have it.

I flip up my collar and turn my back to him as I pick

my way back up towards the cliff base. I don't think I can watch him disappear into the water. It will break my heart.

Puck's scrubbing her eyes busily as if she has something in them. George Holly bites his lip. The cliffs tower above me and I try to console myself, *I will find another* capall uisce, *I will ride again, I will move to my father's home and be free.* But there's no comfort in my thoughts.

Behind me, the ocean says *shhhhhhhh, shhhhhhhhh.*

There's a thin, long wail. I keep walking, my bare feet slow on the uneven stones.

The wail comes again, low and keening. Puck and Holly are looking past me, so I turn around. Still at the shoreline, Corr has noticed my going, and he stands where I left him, looking back at me. He lifts his head again and keens to me.

The irresistible ocean sucks around his hooves. But still he looks over his withers at me and he wails, again and again. The hair on my arms stands with his call. I know he wants me to go to him, but I can't go with him where he needs to go.

Corr falls silent when I do not come to him. He looks back out to the endless horizon. I see him lift a hoof and put it back down. He tests his weight again.

Then Corr turns, stepping out of the ocean. His head jerks up when his injured leg touches the ground, but he takes another laboured step before keening to me again. Corr takes another step away from the November sea. And another.

He is slow, and the sea sings to us both, but he returns to me.

AUTHOR'S NOTE

As a teen, I was always intrigued when I read articles about authors mulling over story ideas for months or years before they knew how to write them. As a teen writer who scribbled down novel ideas as soon as they came to her, this seemed quaint and foreign. *How could you not know how to write your own story?* I thought, as I dashed out another terrible novel in a month.

Well, here I am, being one of those authors. I have wanted to write about water horses for a very long time. I've actually attempted it several times. First while in college, then again right after. I'd almost given up, but a few years ago – after I'd published three novels and really should've known what I was doing – I threw myself at the legend one more time. And failed again.

The only difference to this failure was that it was not a bang, as before, but a whimper.

The problem was that the myth was both complicated and plotless, with no inherent narrative to guide a daunted author. There were rather a lot of variations: a

Manx version called *glashtin*; Irish versions called *capall uisge*, *cabyll ushtey*, and *aughisky*; Scottish versions called *each uisge* and kelpies. Apart from being nearly universally impossible to pronounce (the name I went with, *capall uisce*, is pronounced CAPple ISHka), the main feature of each was a dangerous fairy horse from the water.

There were many magical elements that appealed to me: the horses were associated with November; they ate flesh; if you lured them away from the ocean, they made the finest mounts imaginable ... unless they touched salt water again.

But then there was also an eerie shape-shifting element to the myth. Some versions involved a water horse turning into a handsome young man with chestnut hair. The newly minted young man would wander by the waterside, luring maidens closer – because of course there is nothing more irresistible than a strange red-headed boy who smells vaguely of fish – and then drag the victims down into the water to devour them. Lungs and liver would wash up later.

It was this second half that slayed me. Every time I tried to work in the creature both man and horse, I realized I was telling a story I didn't want to tell. It wasn't until I wrote the *Shiver* trilogy with its rather corrupted version of the werewolf legend that I realized I didn't *have* to take the water horses at face value. I could be as choosy as I liked with my mythology.

I threw out absolutely everything that I didn't need

about the water horses, and ended up with *The Scorpio Races*, a story that isn't really about water horses or fairies at all, now that I think about it.

Now, if you'd like to find out more about the creepy red-headed water boys with kelp in their hair, I urge you to hunt down a copy of Katharine Briggs's *An Encyclopedia of Fairies: Hobgoblins, Brownies, Bogies, and Other Supernatural Creatures*, which is an excellent starting point for all things fairy.

I suppose it's still possible I might one day write the other half of the legend.

No, actually. No, it's not.

Aknowledgements

I could probably keep these acknowledgements pretty short by saying merely: I would like to thank everyone who enabled me to visit cliffs in the last year and a half.

But I suppose it would be lazy, and in any case, they deserve mention by name: my first publicist at Scholastic, Samantha Grefé, who moved my schedule around so that I could visit cliffs in California. My lovely foreign rights team, Rachel Horowitz, Janelle DeLuise, Maren Monitello, and Lisa Mattingly, who coordinated my overseas tours so that I had time to visit cliffs in Normandy. My Scholastic UK publicists, Alyx Price and Alex Sedgwick, who did their absolute best to make sure I got to cliffs in the south of England. And my very dear friends Erin and Richard Hill, who endured UK cliff hunting with me not once but twice, once facing south and once facing east.

I should thank those involved with the writing as well: my long-suffering editor, David Levithan, who didn't panic when I told him my next book was about killer horses. My passionate agent, Laura Rennert, for paving the slightly crooked way for this book. Tessa Gratton and Brenna Yovanoff, my critique partners, for playing Spot the Travesty! Carrie Ryan, Natalie "Good Point" Parker, Jackson Pearce, and Kate Hummel for plot commentary and stories about jockeys' locker rooms.

As always, I'm eternally grateful to my family for holding down the fort during deadlines – forts that have many movable parts, and deadlines that are often painted with holiday colours. I'm also grateful for my parents in particular, who protested, but only gently, when we rode our horses bareback.

And most of all, of course, I have to thank Ed, my husband, who always climbs cliffs with me.

ABOUT THE AUTHOR

Maggie Stiefvater's life decisions have revolved around her inability to be gainfully employed. Talking to yourself, staring into space, and coming to work in your pyjamas are frowned upon when you're a waitress, calligraphy instructor, or technical editor (all of which she's tried), but are highly prized traits in novelists and artists (she's made her living as one or the other since she was twenty-two). Maggie now lives a surprisingly

eccentric life in the middle of nowhere, Virginia, with her charmingly straight-laced husband, two kids, and multiple neurotic dogs.

Love Maggie

www.maggiestiefvater.com

Twitter: mstiefvater